MRS GASKELL

THE MANCHESTER MARRIAGE AND OTHER STORIES

ALAN SUTTON
1985

Alan Sutton Publishing Limited
30 Brunswick Road
Gloucester GL1 1JJ

British Library Cataloguing in Publication Data

Gaskell, Elizabeth
    The Manchester Marriage.
    I. Title
    823'.8[F]   PR4710

    ISBN 0-86299-247-8

Cover picture: detail from Manchester from the Cliff, Higher Broughton *by William Wyld.*
Manchester City Art Galleries.

Typesetting and origination by
Alan Sutton Publishing Limited.
Photoset Bembo 9/10
Printed in Great Britain
by The Guernsey Press Company Limited,
Guernsey, Channel Islands.

CONTENTS

BIOGRAPHICAL NOTE

MRS GASKELL (1810–65) was first and foremost a woman of her time, a lady of Victorian expansiveness. She was not a brilliant, nor a passionate novelist like George Eliot or Charlotte Brontë, but an intelligent, compassionate and enthusiastic woman, whose life centred around her family. At the same time she mixed in a variety of social circles, travelled widely in England and Europe, and wrote graphic, lively and rambling letters to her many acquaintances. Her greatest claim to fame today is perhaps her biography of Charlotte Brontë, but she also wrote several memorable novels, including *Mary Barton*, *Cranford*, *Ruth* and *Sylvia's Lovers*. The present volume provides an example of her many shorter stories, first published in serial form.

Elizabeth Cleghorn Stevenson was born on 29 September 1810, in Chelsea. She was the eighth child of William Stevenson, a Scot, and his English wife, Elizabeth Holland. Stevenson had been a Unitarian minister, an unsuccessful farmer, and finally Keeper of the Treasury Records. Mrs Stevenson, related to the Wedgwoods, the Darwins and the Turners, died thirteen months after the birth of Elizabeth, who was sent up to the Cheshire home of the Hollands to live with her Aunt, Hannah Lumb, at Knutsford. Her father remarried, but Elizabeth's home was in Cheshire, and she recalled later:

Long ago I lived in Chelsea occasionally with my father and step-mother, and *very, very* unhappy I used to be; and if it had not been for the beautiful, grand river, which was an inexplicable comfort to me, and a family by the name of Kennett, I think my child's heart would have broken. (From an undated letter to Mary Howitt.)

On the whole, however, her childhood was not unhappy,

iv

and she speaks enthusiastically of her school days in Stratford-on-Avon: 'I am unwilling to leave even in thought the haunts of such happy days as my schooldays were.' She attended Avonbank School, run by the Misses Byerley, probably from 1821–6, and received the traditional education in arts and the classics, decorum and propriety, suitable for young ladies of the day. Her aunts gave her the classics to read, and her father, himself a technical writer, with a keen interest in the literary world, encouraged her in her studies and personal writing. Her brother, John, provided an important early link with London publishers – he had hoped to become an author – and sent Elizabeth modern books to read, as well as vivid descriptions of life at sea, and in exotic countries when he travelled in India, where he tragically disappeared in 1828.

After she left school, at sixteen, Elizabeth appears to have spent time in London, with her Holland cousins, and her father, who died in 1829; in Newcastle, staying with the eminent Unitarian minister, William Turner, and in Edinburgh, where she was apparently sent during the cholera outbreak of 1831. It was at this time that her portrait was painted in miniature by the Edinburgh painter, Joseph Thomson, and a bust sculpted by David Dunbar, both works revealing a young woman of classical good looks. The attractiveness of both her appearance and her personality are borne out by a later description of her by Susanna Winkworth:

She was a noble-looking woman, with a queenly presence, and her high, broad, serene brow, and finely-cut mobile features, were lighted up by a constantly-varying play of expression as she poured forth her wonderful talk. It was like the ripple and rush of a clear deep stream in sunshine.

Later in 1831, Elizabeth, then staying with friends in Manchester, first met William Gaskell, a Unitarian minister, five years older than her. The following year they were married, and after a honeymoon in North Wales, always a favourite place, they established a home at 14 Dover Street, Manchester. There Elizabeth Gaskell became a conscientious minister's wife, and a mother. She had five children, four girls and a boy. Unfortunately the boy died at twelve months.

Literature was never totally excluded from Elizabeth's life. In 1836 she wrote of studying Crabbe, Dryden, Pope, Coleridge and Wordsworth. In 1837, she wrote *Sketches Among the Poor, No. 1* for *Blackwood's Magazine*, hoping to catch some of the 'poetry of the humble life'. But it was not until after the death of baby William, in 1845, that, with the encouragement of her husband, who, himself, taught English, she started writing seriously. Three short stories were published by William and Mary Howitt in *Howitt's Journal* in 1847–8, and *Mary Barton* was completed in 1847, and finally published on the recommendation of John Forster, friend of Dickens, by Chapman and Hall in 1849. It was a controversial novel showing a realistic picture of those experiencing first hand the effects of the industrial revolution, and it established Mrs Gaskell in the literary world. She must have possessed admirable energy and determination since from then until her death she was invariably involved in some literary work, in spite of the emotional and physical demands of a growing family and the social problems of industrial Manchester. Her output of short stories was prolific. She wrote for *The Ladies Companion*, including *Mr Harrison's Confession*, 1851; *Harper's Magazine*, including *The Doom of the Griffiths*, 1858; *The Cornhill Magazine* and other periodicals. Most of all she wrote for Dickens' magazines: *Household Words* and *All the Year Round*. She was his 'dear Scheherazade'. Stories which appeared for the first time in *Household Words* include *An Accursed Race*, *Half a Life Time Ago* and *The Poor Clare*, all in 1855, and also *Cranford*, told first in serial form between December 1851 and May 1853, and *North and South*, completed in 1855.

With her lively personality and enquiring mind, Mrs Gaskell could well have become a more active member of the literary world of her day. She visited London in 1849, meeting Dickens, Samuel Rogers, John Forster and Monckton Milnes among others. She was, however, essentially a home-loving family woman of high moral principals. Aware of her many-faceted personality, she wrote in 1850 of the effect of a new home in Plymouth Grove, to her sister-in-law:

And we've got a house. Yes! we *really* have. And if I had neither conscience nor prudence I should be delighted, for it certainly *is* a beauty. . . . You *must* come and see us in it . . . and try and make me see . . . that it is right to spend so much ourselves on *so* purely selfish a thing as a house is, while so many are wanting – that's the haunting thought to me; at least to one of my 'Mes', for I have a great number, and that's the plague. One of my mes is, I do believe, a true Christian – (only people call her socialist and communist), another of my mes is a wife and mother, and highly delighted at the delight of everyone in the house . . . Now that's my social self I suppose. Then again I've got another self with a full taste for beauty and convenience who is pleased on its own account. How am I to reconcile all these warring members? I try to drown myself (my *first* self) by saying it's Wm who is to decide on all these things, and his feeling it right ought to be my rule. And so it is – only that does not quite do.

And she concludes in another letter:

Well, I must try and make the house give as much pleasure to others as I can and make it as little a selfish thing as I can . . .

Plymouth Grove developed into a smallholding, with ducks, bantams, pigs and a cow, as well as an extensive garden, where Mrs Gaskell liked to work.

Running such a home and fulfilling her social commitments, educating her daughters and travelling abroad required a reasonable income, and Mrs Gaskell needed all the money her writing earned. In 1853 *Ruth* was published, another morally controversial work about a fallen woman, and at the end of the year, after a holiday in Normandy, she first visited Charlotte Brontë at Howarth. The biography of Charlotte appeared eighteen months after her death, in March, 1857. Mrs Gaskell and her daughters were on holiday in Italy, but they came home to a 'Hornet's nest' of bad feeling, because Mrs Gaskell had felt obliged to disclose certain 'painful truths'. The following years were difficult ones as the minister's wife supported her daughters through emotional and religious traumas. As she entered her fifties she was as

busy as at any other time in her life. She was writing regularly:
Sylvia's Lovers was published in 1863, and *Cousin Phyllis* and
Wives and Daughters appeared in *The Cornhill Magazine*,
1864–66. She maintained literary and social contacts,
corresponding with George Eliot, of whose *Adam Bede* she
wrote 'I have never read anything so complete and beautiful in
fiction, in my whole life before.' She met Rosetti, Holman
Hunt, Ruskin, Swinburne and the Nightingales, as she travelled around England. In 1862 the Lancashire Cotton Famine
was at its peak and Mrs Gaskell and her daughters were
involved in social work with the poor:

> Last autumn and winter, she wrote to the American,
> Charles Eliot Norton, whom she had met in Rome in 1857,
> was *such* hard work – we were often off at nine – not to
> come home till 7, or ½ past, too worn out to eat or do
> anything but go to bed.

But her family were always her most immediate concern. In
1865, no longer in the best of health, she was negotiating the
purchase of The Lawn, at Holybourne, near Alton,
Hampshire. Here she intended William, now sixty, should
retire. However, while she was still preparing the house, she
died, very suddenly and painlessly, of a heart attack, while she
was serving tea, on 12 November 1865. Four days later she
was buried at Brook Street Chapel, Knutsford.

SHEILA MICHELL

THE MANCHESTER MARRIAGE

Mr. and Mrs. Openshaw came from Manchester to settle in London. He had been what is called in Lancashire a salesman for a large manufacturing firm, who were extending their business, and opening a warehouse in the city, where Mr. Openshaw was now to superintend their affairs. He rather enjoyed the change; having a kind of curiosity about London, which he had never yet been able to gratify in his brief visits to the metropolis. At the same time, he had an odd, shrewd contempt for the inhabitants; whom he always pictured to himself as fine, lazy people; caring nothing but for fashion and aristocracy, and lounging away their days in Bond Street and such places; ruining good English, and ready in their turn to despise him as a provincial. The hours that the men of business kept in the city scandalised him, too, accustomed as he was to the early dinners of Manchester folk and the consequently far longer evenings. Still, he was pleased to go to London; though he would not for the world have confessed it, even to himself, and always spoke of the step to his friends as one demanded of him by the interests of his employers, and sweetened to him by a considerable increase of salary. This indeed, was so liberal that he might have been justified in taking a much larger house than the one he did, had he not thought himself bound to set an example to Londoners of how little a Manchester man of business cared for show. Inside, however, he furnished it with an unusual degree of comfort; and, in the winter-time, he insisted on keeping up as large fires as the grates would allow, in every room where the temperature was in the least chilly. Moreover, his northern sense of hospitality was such, that, if he were at home, he could hardly suffer a visitor to leave the house without forcing meat and drink upon him. Every servant in the house was well warmed, well fed, and kindly treated; for their master scorned all petty saving in aught that conduced to comfort; while he amused himself by following out all his accustomed habits and individual ways, in defiance of what any of his new neighbours might think.

His wife was a pretty, gentle woman, of suitable age and character. He was forty-two; she thirty-five. He was loud and decided; she soft and yielding. They had two children; or, rather, I should say, she had two; for the elder, a girl of eleven, was Mrs. Openshaw's child by Frank Wilson, her first husband. The younger was a little boy, Edwin, who could just prattle, and to whom his father delighted to speak in the broadest and most unintelligible Lancashire dialect, in order to keep up what he called the true Saxon accent.

Mrs. Openshaw's Christian name was Alice, and her first husband had been her own cousin. She was the orphan niece of a sea-captain in Liverpool, a quiet, grave little creature, of great personal attraction when she was fifteen or sixteen, with regular features and a blooming complexion. But she was very shy, and believed herself to be very stupid and awkward, and was frequently scolded by her aunt, her own uncle's second wife. So, when her cousin, Frank Wilson, came home from a long absence at sea, and first was kind and protective to her; secondly, attentive; and thirdly, desperately in love with her – she hardly knew how to be grateful enough to him. It is true, she would have preferred his remaining in the first or second stages of behaviour; for his violent love puzzled and frightened her. Her uncle neither helped nor hindered the love-affair though it was going on under his own eyes. Frank's stepmother had such a variable temper that there was no knowing whether what she liked one day she would like the next or not. At length she went to such extremes of crossness that Alice was only too glad to shut her eyes and rush blindly at the chance of escape from domestic tyranny offered her by a marriage with her cousin; and, liking him better than any one in the world, except her uncle (who was at this time at sea), she went off one morning and was married to him; her only bridesmaid being the housemaid at her aunt's. The consequence was, that Frank and his wife went into lodgings, and Mrs. Wilson refused to see them, and turned away Norah, the warm-hearted housemaid, whom they accordingly took into their service. When Captain Wilson returned from his voyage, he was very cordial with the young couple, and spent many an evening at their lodgings, smoking his pipe and sipping his grog; but he told them that, for quietness' sake, he could not ask them to his own house; for his wife was bitter against them. They were not, however, very unhappy about this.

The seed of future unhappiness lay rather in Frank's vehement, passionate disposition, which led him to resent his wife's shyness and want of demonstrativeness as failures in conjugal duty. He was already tormenting himself, and her too, in a slighter degree, by apprehensions and imaginations of what might befall her during his approaching absence at sea. At last, he went to his father and urged him to insist upon Alice's being once more received under his roof; more especially as there was now a prospect of her confinement while her husband was away on his voyage. Captain Wilson was, as he himself expressed it, 'breaking up', and unwilling to undergo the excitement of a scene; yet he felt that what his son said was true. So he went to his wife. And, before Frank set sail, he had the comfort of seeing his wife installed in her own little garret in his father's house. To have placed her in the one best spare room, was a step beyond Mrs. Wilson's powers of submission or generosity. The worst part about it, however, was that the faithful Norah had to be dismissed. Her place as housemaid had been filled up; and, even if it had not, she had forfeited Mrs. Wilson's good opinion for ever. She comforted her young master and mistress by pleasant prophecies of the time when they would have a household of their own; of which, whatever service she might be in meanwhile, she should be sure to form a part. Almost the last action of Frank, before his setting sail, was going with Alice to see Norah once more at her mother's house; and then he went away.

Alice's father-in-law grew more and more feeble as winter advanced. She was of great use to her step-mother in nursing and amusing him; and, although there was anxiety enough in the household, there was, perhaps more of peace than there had been for years; for Mrs. Wilson had not a bad heart, and was softened by the visible approach of death to one whom she loved, and touched by the lonely condition of the young creature, expecting her first confinement in her husband's absence. To this relenting mood Norah owed the permission to come and nurse Alice when her baby was born, and to remain and attend on Captain Wilson.

Before one letter had been received from Frank (who had sailed for the East Indies and China), his father died. Alice was always glad to remember that he had held the baby in his arms, and kissed and blessed it before his death. After that, and the consequent examination into the state of his affairs, it was found that he had left far less property than people had been led by his style of living to expect; and what money there was was all settled upon his wife, and at her disposal after her death. This did not signify much to Alice, as Frank was now first mate of his ship, and, in another voyage or two, would be captain. Meanwhile, he had left her rather more than two hundred pounds (all his savings) in the bank.

It became time for Alice to hear from her husband. One letter from the Cape she had already received. The next was to announce his arrival in India. As week after week passed over, and no intelligence of the ship having got there reached the office of the owners, and the captain's wife was in the same state of ignorant suspense as Alice herself, her fears grew most oppressive. At length the day came when, in reply to her inquiry at the Shipping Office, they told her that the owners had given up hope of ever hearing more of the *Betsy-Jane*, and had sent in their claim upon the under-writers. Now that he was gone for ever, she first felt a yearning, longing love for the kind cousin, the dear friend, the sympathising protector, whom she should never see again – first felt a passionate desire to show him his child, whom she had hitherto rather craved to have all to herself – her own sole possession. Her grief was, however, noiseless and quiet – rather to the scandal of Mrs. Wilson: who bewailed her step-son as if he and she had always lived together in perfect harmony, and who evidently thought it her duty to burst into fresh tears at every strange face she saw; dwelling on his poor young widow's desolate state, and the helplessness of the fatherless child, with an unction as if she liked the excitement of the sorrowful story.

So passed away the first days of Alice's widowhood. By-and-by things subsided into their natural and tranquil course. But, as if the young creature was always to be in some heavy trouble, her ewe-lamb began to be ailing, pining, and sickly. The child's mysterious illness turned out to be some affection of the spine, likely to affect health, but not to shorten life – at least, so the doctors said. But the long, dreary suffering of one whom a mother loves as Alice loved her only child is hard to look forward to. Only Norah guessed what Alice suffered; no one but God knew.

And so it fell out that, when Mrs. Wilson the elder came to her one day, in violent distress, occasioned by a very material diminution in the value of the property that her husband had left her – a diminution which made her income barely enough to support herself, much less Alice – the latter could hardly understand how anything which did not touch health or life could cause such grief; and she received the intelligence with irritating composure. But when, that afternoon, the little sick child was brought in, and the grandmother – who after all loved it well – began a fresh moan over her losses to its unconscious ears – saying how she had planned to consult this or that doctor, and to give it this or that comfort or luxury in after years, but that now all chance of this had passed away – Alice's heart was touched, and she drew near to Mrs. Wilson with unwonted caresses, and, in a spirit not unlike to that of Ruth, entreated that, come what would, they might remain together. After much discussion in succeeding days, it was arranged that Mrs. Wilson should take a house in Manchester, furnishing it partly with what furniture she had, and providing the rest with Alice's remaining two hundred pounds. Mrs. Wilson was herself a Manchester woman, and naturally longed to return to her native town; some connections of her own, too, at that time required lodgings, for which they were willing to pay pretty handsomely. Alice undertook the active superintendence and superior work of the household; Norah, willing, faithful, Norah, offered to cook, scour, do anything in short, so that she might but remain with them.

The plan succeeded. For some years their first lodgers remained with them, and all went smoothly – with the one sad exception of the little girl's increasing deformity. How that mother loved that child, it is not for words to tell!

Then came a break of misfortune. Their lodgers left, and no one succeeded to them. After some months, it became necessary to remove to a smaller house; and Alice's tender conscience was torn by the idea that she ought not to be a burden to her mother-in-law, but to go and seek her own maintenance. And leave her child! The thought came like a sweeping boom of a funeral bell over her heart.

By-and-by, Mr. Openshaw came to lodge with them. He had started in life as the errand-boy and sweeper-out of a warehouse; had struggled up through all the grades of employment in it, fighting his way through the hard striving Manchester life with strong, pushing energy of character. Every spare moment of time had been sternly given up to self-teaching. He was a capital accountant, a good French and German scholar, a keen, far-seeing tradesman – understanding markets, and the bearing of events, both near and distant, on trade: and yet, with such vivid attention to present details that I do not think he ever saw a group of flowers in the fields without thinking whether their colours would, or would not, form harmonious contrasts in the coming spring muslins and prints. He went to debating societies, and threw himself with all his heart and soul into politics; esteeming, it must be owned, every man a fool or a knave who differed from him, and overthrowing his opponents rather by the loud strength of his language than the calm strength of his logic. There was something of the Yankee in all this. Indeed, his theory ran parallel to the famous Yankee motto – 'England flogs creation, and Manchester flogs England.' Such a man, as may be fancied, had had no time for falling in love, or any such nonsense. At the age when most young men go through their courting and matrimony, he had not the means of keeping a wife, and was far too practical to think of having one. And now that he was in easy circumstances, a rising man, he considered women almost as incumbrances to the world, with whom a man had better have as little to do as possible. His first impression of Alice was indistinct. 'A pretty, yea-nay kind of woman,' would have been his description of her, if he had been pushed into a corner. He was rather afraid, in the beginning, that her quiet ways arose from a listlessness and laziness of character, which would have been exceedingly discordant to his active, energetic nature. But, when he found out the punctuality with which his wishes were attended to,

and her work was done; when he was called in the morning at
the very stroke of the clock, his shaving-water scolding hot, his
fire bright, his coffee made exactly as his peculiar fancy dictated
(for he was a man who had his theory about everything, based
upon what he knew of science and often perfectly original) –
then he began to think: not that Alice had any particular merit,
but that he had got into remarkably good lodgings; his restlessness wore away, and he began to consider himself as almost
settled for life in them.

Mr. Openshaw had been too busy, all his days, to be
introspective. He did not know that he had any tenderness in
his nature; and if he had become conscious of its abstract
existence he would have considered it as a manifestation of
disease in some part of him. But he was decoyed into pity
unawares; and pity led on to tenderness. That little helpless
child – always carried about by one of the three busy women of
the house, or else patiently threading coloured beads in the
chair from which, by no effort of its own, could it ever move –
the great, grave blue eyes, full of serious, not uncheerful,
expression, giving to the small delicate face a look beyond its
years – the soft plaintive voice dropping out but few words, so
unlike the continual prattle of a child – caught Mr. Openshaw's
attention in spite of himself. One day – he half scorned himself
for doing so – he cut short his dinner-hour to go in search of
some toy which should take the place of those eternal beads. I
forget what he bought; but, when he gave the present (which
he took care to do in a short, abrupt manner, and when no one
was by to see him), he was almost thrilled by the flash of
delight that came over that child's face, and he could not help,
all through that afternoon, going over and over again the
picture left on his memory by the bright effect of unexpected
joy on the little girl's face. When he returned home, he found
his slippers placed by his sitting-room fire; and even more
careful attention paid to his fancies than was habitual in those
model lodgings. When Alice had taken the last of his tea-things
away – she had been silent as usual till then – she stood for an
instant with the door in her hand. Mr. Openshaw looked as if
he were deep in his book – though in fact he did not see a line,
but was heartily wishing the woman would go, and not make
any palaver of gratitude. But she only said:

'I am very much obliged to you, sir. Thank you very much,' and was gone, even before he could send her away with a 'There, my good woman, that's enough!'

For some time longer he took no apparent notice of the child. He even hardened his heart into disregarding her sudden flush of colour and little timid smile of recognition when he saw her by chance. But, after all, this could not last for ever; and, on his having a second time given way to tenderness, there was no relapse. The insidious enemy having thus entered his heart, in the guise of compassion to the child, soon assumed the more dangerous form of interest in the mother. He was aware of this change of feeling – despised himself for it – struggled with it; nay, internally yielded to it and cherished it, long before he suffered the slightest expression of it, by word, action, or look to escape him. He watched Alice's docile, obedient ways to her step-mother; the love which she had inspired in the rough Norah (roughened by the wear and tear of sorrow and years); but, above all, he saw the wild, deep, passionate affection existing between her and her child. They spoke little to any one else, or when any one else was by; but, when alone together, they talked, and murmured, and cooed, and chatted so continually, that Mr. Openshaw first wondered what they could find to say to each other, and next became irritated because they were always so grave and silent with him. All this time he was perpetually devising small new pleasures for the child. His thoughts ran, in a pertinacious way, upon the desolate life before her; and often he came back from his day's work, loaded with the very thing Alice had been longing for, but had not been able to procure. One time it was a little chair for drawing the little sufferer along the streets; and many an evening that following summer, Mr. Openshaw drew her along himself, regardless of the remarks of his aquaintances. One day, in autumn, he put down his newspaper, as Alice came in with the breakfast, and said, in as different a voice as he could assume:

'Mrs. Frank, is there any reason why we two should not put up our horses together?'

Alice stood still in perplexed wonder. What did he mean? He had resumed the reading of his newspaper, as if he did not expect any answer; so she found silence her safest course, and went on quietly arranging his breakfast, without another word passing between them. Just as he was leaving the house, to go to the warehouse as usual, he turned back and put his head into the bright, neat, tidy kitchen, where all the women breakfasted in the morning:

'You'll think of what I said, Mrs. Frank' (this was her name with the lodgers), 'and let me have your opinion upon it tonight.'

Alice was thankful that her mother and Norah were too busy talking together to attend much to his speech. She determined not to think about it all through the day; and, of course, the effort not to think made her think all the more. At night she sent up Norah with his tea. But Mr. Openshaw almost knocked Norah down, as he was going out at the door, by pushing past her and calling out 'Mrs. Frank!' in an impatient voice, at the top of the stairs.

Alice went up, rather than seem to have affixed too much meaning to his words.

'Well, Mrs. Frank,' said he, 'what answer? Don't make it too long; for I have lots of office-work to get through tonight.'

'I hardly know what you meant, sir,' said truthful Alice.

'Well! I should have thought you might have guessed. You're not new at this sort of work, and I am. However, I'll make it plain this time. Will you have me to be thy wedded husband, and serve me, and love me, and honour me, and all that sort of thing? Because, if you will, I will do as much by you, and be a father to your child – and that's more than is put in the Prayer-Book. Now, I'm a man of my word; and what I say I feel; and what I promise, I'll do. Now, for an answer!'

Alice was silent. He began to make the tea, as if her reply was a matter of perfect indifference to him; but, as soon as that was done, he became impatient.

'Well?' said he.

'How long, sir, may I have to think over it?'

'Three minutes!' (looking at his watch) 'You've had two already – that makes five. Be a sensible woman, say "Yes", and sit down to tea with me, and we'll talk it over together; for after tea I shall be busy; say "No"' (he hesitated a moment to try and keep his voice in the same tone), 'and I shan't say another word about it, but pay up a year's rent for my rooms tomorrow, and be off. Time's up! Yes or no.'

'If you please, sir – you have been so good to little Ailsie —'

'There, sit down comfortably by me on the sofa, and let us have our tea together. I am glad to find you are as good and sensible as I took you for.'

And this was Alice Wilson's second wooing.

Mr. Openshaw's will was too strong, and his circumstances too good, for him not to carry all before him. He settled Mrs. Wilson in a comfortable house of her own, and made her quite independent of lodgers. The little that Alice said with regard to future plans was in Norah's behalf.

'No,' said Mr. Openshaw. 'Norah shall take care of the old lady as long a she lives; and after that she shall either come and live with us, or, if she likes it better, she shall have a provision for life – for your sake, missus. No one who has been good to you or the child shall go unrewarded. But even the little one will be better for some fresh stuff about her. Get her a bright, sensible girl as a nurse: one who won't go rubbing her with calf's-foot jelly, as Norah does – wasting good stuff outside that ought to go in – but will follow doctors' directions, which, as you must see pretty clearly by this time, Norah won't, because they give the poor little wench pain. Now, I'm not above being nesh for other folks myself. I can stand a good blow, and never change colour; but, set me in the operating-room of the Infimary, and I turn as sick as a girl. Yet, if need were, I would hold the little wench on my knees while she screeched with pain, if it were to do her poor back good. Nay, nay, wench! keep your white looks for the time when it comes – I don't say it ever will. But this I know, Norah will spare the child and cheat the doctor, if she can. Now, I say, give the bairn a year or two's chance; and then, when the pack of doctors have done their best – and, maybe the old lady has gone – we'll have Norah back or do better for her.'

The pack of doctors could do no good to little Ailsie. She was beyond their power. But her father (for so he insisted on being called, and also on Alice's no longer retaining the appellation of mamma, but becoming henceforth mother), by his healthy cheerfulness of manner, his clear decision of purpose, his odd turns and quirks of humour, added to his real strong love for the helpless little girl, infused a new element of brightness and confidence into her life; and, though her back remained the same, her general health was strengthened, and Alice – never going beyond a smile herself – had the pleasure of seeing her child taught to laugh.

As for Alice's own life. it was happier than it had ever been before. Mr. Openshaw required no demonstration, no expressions of affection from her. Indeed, these would rather have disgusted him. Alice could love deeply, but could not talk about it. The perpetual requirement of loving words, looks and caresses, and misconstruing their absence into absence of love, had been the great trial of her former married life. Now, all went on clear and straight under the guidance of her husband's strong sense, warm heart, and powerful will. Year by year their wordly prosperity increased. At Mrs. Wilson's death, Norah came back to them as nurse to the newly-born little Edwin, into which post she was not installed without a pretty strong oration on the part of the proud and happy father, who declared that if he found out that Norah ever tried to screen the boy by a falsehood, or to make him nesh either in body or mind, she should go that very day. Norah and Mr. Openshaw were not on the most thoroughly cordial terms, neither of them fully recognising or appreciating the other's best qualities.

This was the previous history of the Lancashire family, who had now removed to London.

They had been there about a year, when Mr. Openshaw suddenly informed his wife that he had determined to heal long-standing feuds, and had asked his uncle and aunt Chadwick to come and pay them a visit and see London. Mrs. Openshaw had never seen this uncle and aunt of her husband's. Years before she had married him, there had been a quarrel. All she knew was, that Mr. Chadwick was a small manuacturer in a country town in South Lancashire. She was extremely pleased that the breach was to be healed, and began making preparations to render their visit pleasant.

They arrived at last. Going to see London was such an event to them that Mrs. Chadwick had made all new linen fresh for the occasion, from night-caps downwards; and as for gowns, ribbons, and collars, she might have been going into the wilds of Canada where never a shop is, so large was her stock. A fortnight before the day of her departure for London, she had formally called to take leave of all her acquaintance, saying she should need every bit of the intermediate time for packing up. It was like a second wedding in her imagination; and, to complete the resemblance which an entirely new wardrobe made between the two events, her husband brought her back from Manchester, on the last market-day before they set off, a gorgeous pearl and amethyst brooch, saying, 'Lunnon should see that Lancashire folks knew a handsome thing when they saw it.'

For some time after Mr. and Mrs. Chadwick arrived at the Openshaws' there was no opportunity for wearing this brooch; but at length they obtained an order to see Buckingham Palace, and the spirit of loyalty demanded that Mrs. Chadwick should wear her best clothes in visiting the abode of her sovereign. On her return she hastily changed her dress; for Mr. Openshaw had planned that they should go to Richmond, drink tea, and return by moonlight. Accordingly, about five o'clock, Mr. and Mrs. Openshaw and Mr. and Mrs. Chadwick set off.

The housemaid and cook sat below, Norah hardly knew where. She was always engrossed in the nursery, in tending her two children, and in sitting by the restless, excitable Ailsie till she fell asleep. By-and-by the housemaid Bessy tapped gently at the door. Norah went to her, and they spoke in whispers.

'Nurse! there's someone downstairs wants you.'

'Wants me! who is it?'

'A gentleman —'

'A gentleman? Nonsense!'

'Well, a man, then; and he asks for you, and he rang at the front-door bell, and has walked into the dining-room.'

'You should never have let him in,' exclaimed Norah, 'master and missus out —'

'I did not want him to come in; but, when he heard you lived here, he walked past me, and sat down on the first chair, and said, "Tell her to come and speak to me." There is no gas lighted in the room, and supper is all set out.'

'He'll be off with the spoons!' exclaimed Norah, putting the housemaid's fears into words, and preparing to leave the room; first, however, giving a look to Ailsie, sleeping soundly and calmly.

Downstairs she went, uneasy fears stirring in her bosom. Before she entered the dining-room she provided herself with a candle, and, with it in her hand, she went in, looking around her in the darkness for her visitor.

He was standing up, holding by the table. Norah and he looked at each other; gradual recognition coming into their eyes.

'Norah?' at length he asked.

'Who are you?' asked Norah, with the sharp tones of alarm and incredulity. 'I don't know you!' trying by futile words of disbelief to do away with the terrible fact before her.

'Am I so changed?' he said pathetically. 'I dare say I am. But, Norah, tell me!' he breathed hard, 'where is my wife? Is she – is she alive?'

He came nearer to Norah, and would have taken her hand; but she backed away from him; looking at him all the time with staring eyes, as if he were some horrible object. Yet he was a handsome, bronzed, good-looking fellow, with beard and moustache, giving him a foreign-looking aspect; but his eyes! there was no mistaking those eager, beautiful eyes – the very same that Norah had watched not half-an-hour ago, till sleep stole softly over them.

'Tell me, Norah – I can bear it – I have feared it so often. Is she dead?' Norah still kept silent. 'She is dead!' He hung on Norah's words and looks, as if for confirmation or contradiction.

'What shall I do?' groaned Norah. 'O sir! why did you come? how did you find me out? where have you been? We thought you dead, we did indeed!' She poured out words and questions to gain time, as if time would help her.

'Norah! answer me this question straight, by "yes" or "no" – Is my wife dead?'

'No, she is not!' said Norah slowly and heavily.

'Oh, what a relief! Did she receive my letters? But perhaps you don't know. Why did you leave her? Where is she? O Norah, tell me all quickly!'

'Mr. Frank!' said Norah at last, almost driven to bay by her terror lest her mistress should return at any moment and find

him there – unable to consider what was best to be done or
said – rushing at something decisive, because she could not
endure her present state: 'Mr. Frank! we never heard a line
from you, and the ship-owners said you had gone down, you
and every one else. We thought you were dead, if ever man
was, and poor Miss Alice and her little sick, helpless child! O
sir, you must guess it,' cried the poor creature at last,
bursting out into a passionate fit of crying, 'for indeed I
cannot tell it. But it was no one's fault. God help us all this
night!'

Norah had sat down. She trembled too much to stand. He
took her hands in his. He squeezed them hard, as if, by
physical pressure, the truth could be wrung out.

'Norah!' This time his tone was calm, stagnant as despair.
'She has married again!'

Norah shook her head sadly. The grasp slowly relaxed. The
man had fainted.

There was brandy in the room. Norah forced some drops
into Mr. Frank's mouth, chafed his hands, and – when mere
animal life returned, before the mind poured in its flood of
memories and thoughts – she lifted him up, and rested his
head against her knees. Then she put a few crumbs of bread
taken from the supper-table, soaked in brandy, into his
mouth. Suddenly he sprang to his feet.

'Where is she? Tell me this instant'. He looked so wild, so
mad, so desperate, that Norah felt herself to be in bodily
danger; but her time of dread had gone by; she had been afraid
to tell him the truth, and then she had been a coward. Now
her wits were sharpened by the sense of his desperate state. He
must leave the house. She would pity him afterwards; but
now she must rather command and upbraid; for he must leave
the house before her mistress came home. That one necessity
stood clear before her.

'She is not here – that is good enough for you to know. Nor
can I say exactly where she is' (which was true to the letter if
not to the spirit). 'Go away, and tell me where to find you
tomorrow, and I will tell you all. My master and mistress may
come back at any minute, and then what would become of
me, with a strange man in the house?'

Such an argument was too petty to touch his excited mind.

'I don't care for your master and mistress. If your master is a man he must feel for me – poor shipwrecked sailor that I am – kept for years a prisoner amongst savages, always, always, always thinking of my wife, and my home – dreaming of her by night, talking to her, though she could not hear, by day. I loved her more than all heaven and earth put together. Tell me where she is, this instant, you wretched woman, who salved over her wickedness to her, as you do to me!

The clock struck ten. Desperate positions require desperate measures.

'If you will leave the house now, I will come to you tomorrow and tell you all. What is more, you shall see your child now. She lies sleeping upstairs. O sir, you have a child, you do not know that as yet – a little weakly girl – with just a heart and soul beyond her years. We have reared her up with such care! We watched her, for we thought for many a year she might die any day, and we tended her, and no hard thing has come near her, and no rough word has ever been said to her. And now you come and will take her life into your hands, and will crush it. Strangers to her have been kind to her; but her own father – Mr. Frank, I am her nurse, and I love her, and I tend her, and I would do anything for her that I could. Her mother's heart beats as her's beats; and if she suffers a pain, her mother trembles all over. If she is happy, it is her mother that smiles and is glad. If she is growing stronger, her mother is healthy – if she dwindles, her mother languishes. If she dies – well, I don't know: it is not every one can lie down and die when they wish it. Come upstairs, Mr. Frank, and see your child. Seeing her will do good to your poor heart. Then go away in God's name, just this one night; tomorrow, if need be, you can do anything – kill us all if you will, or show yourself a great, grand man, whom God will bless for ever and ever. Come, Mr. Frank, the look of a sleeping child is sure to give peace.

She led him upstairs; at first almost helping his steps, till they came near the nursery door. She had well-nigh forgotten the existence of little Edwin. It struck upon her with affright as the shaded light fell over the other cot; but she skilfully threw that corner of the room into darkness, and let the light fall on the sleeping Ailsie. The child had thrown down the coverings, and her deformity, as she lay with her back to them, was plainly visible through her slight night-gown. Her little face, deprived of the lustre of her eyes, looked wan and pinched, and had a pathetic expression in it, even as she slept. The poor father looked and looked with hungry, wistful eyes, into which the big tears came swelling up slowly and dropped wearily down, as he stood trembling and shaking all over. Norah was angry with herself for growing impatient at the length of time that long, lingering gaze lasted. She thought that she waited for full half-an-hour before Frank stirred. And then – instead of going away – he sank down on his knees by the bedside, and buried his face in the clothes. Little Ailsie stirred uneasily. Norah pulled him up in terror. She could afford no more time, even for prayer, in her extremity of fear; for surely the next moment would bring her mistress home. She took him forcibly by the arm, but, as he was going, his eye lighted on the other bed. He stopped. Intelligence came back into his face. His hands clenched.

'His child?' he asked.

'Her child,' replied Norah. 'God watches over him,' said she instinctively; for Frank's looks excited her fears, and she needed to remind herself of the Protector of the helpless.

'God has not watched over me,' he said in despair, his thoughts apparently recoiling on his own desolate, deserted state. But Norah had no time for pity. Tomorrow she would be as compassionate as her heart prompted. At length she guided him downstairs, and shut the outer door, and bolted it – as if by bolts to keep out facts.

Then she went back into the dining-room, and effaced all traces of his presence, as far as she could. She went upstairs to the nursery and sat there, her head on her hand, thinking what was to come of all this misery. It seemed to her very long before her master and mistress returned; yet it was hardly eleven o'clock. She heard the loud, hearty Lancashire voices on the stairs; and, for the first time, she understood the contrast of the desolation of the poor man who had so lately gone forth in lonely despair.

It almost put her out of patience to see Mrs. Openshaw come in, calmly smiling, handsomely dressed, happy, easy, to inquire after her children.

'Did Ailsie go to sleep comfortably?' she whispered to Norah.

'Yes.'

Her mother bent over her, looking at her slumbers with the soft eyes of love. How little she dreamed who had looked on her last! Then she went to Edwin, with perhaps less wistful anxiety in her countenance, but more of pride. She took off her things to go down to supper. Norah saw her no more that night.

Besides having a door into the passage, the sleeping-nursery opened out of Mr. and Mrs. Openshaw's room, in order that they might have the children more immediately under their own eyes. Early the next summer morning, Mrs. Openshaw was awakened by Ailsie's startled call of 'Mother! mother!' She sprang up, put on her dressing-gown, and went to her child. Ailsie was only half-awake, and in a not unusual state of terror.

'Who was he, mother? Tell me!'

'Who, my darling? No one is here. You have been dreaming, love. Waken up quite. See, it is broad daylight.'

'Yes,' said Ailsie, looking round her; then clinging to her mother, 'but a man was here in the night, mother.'

'Nonsense, little goose. No man has ever come near you.'

'Yes, he did. He stood there. Just by Norah. A man with hair and a beard. And he knelt down and said his prayers. Norah knows he was here, mother,' (half angrily, as Mrs. Openshaw shook her head in smiling incredulity).

'Well! we will ask Norah when she comes,' said Mrs. Openshaw soothingly. 'But we won't talk any more about him now. It is not five o'clock; it is too early for you to get up. Shall I fetch you a book and read to you?'

'Don't leave me, mother,' said the child, clinging to her. So Mrs. Openshaw sat on the bedside talking to Ailsie, and telling her of what they had done at Richmond the evening before, until the little girl's eyes slowly closed, and she once more fell asleep.

'What was the matter?' asked Mr. Openshaw, as his wife returned to bed.

'Ailsie wakened up in a fright, with some story of a man having been in her room to say his prayers – a dream, I suppose.' And no more was said at the time.

Mrs. Openshaw had almost forgotten the whole affair, when she got up about seven o'clock. But, by-and-by, she heard a sharp altercation going on in the nursery – Norah speaking angrily to Ailsie, a most unusual thing. Both Mr. and Mrs. Openshaw listened in astonishment.

'Hold your tongue, Ailsie! let me hear none of your dreams; never let me hear you tell that story again!'

Ailsie began to cry.

Mr. Openshaw opened the door of communication before his wife could say a word.

'Norah, come here!'

The nurse stood at the door, defiant. She perceived she had been heard, but she was desperate.

'Don't let me hear you speak in that manner to Ailsie again,' he said sternly, and shut the door.

Norah was infinitely relieved, for she had dreaded some questioning; and a little blame for sharp speaking was what she could well bear, if cross-examination was let alone.

Downstairs they went, Mr. Openshaw carrying Ailsie; the sturdy Edwin coming step by step, right foot foremost, always holding his mother's hand. Each child was placed in a chair by the breakfast-table, and then Mr. and Mrs. Openshaw stood together at the window, awaiting their visitors' appearance, and making plans for the day. There was a pause. Suddenly Mr. Openshaw turned to Ailsie, and said –

'What a little goosey somebody is with her dreams, wakening up poor, tired mother in the middle of the night, with a story of a man being in the room.'

'Father, I'm sure I saw him,' said Ailsie, half-crying. 'I don't want to make Norah angry; but I was not asleep, for all she says I was. I had been asleep, and I wakened up quite wide awake, though I was so frightened. I kept my eyes nearly shut, and I saw the man quite plain. A great brown man with a beard. He said his prayers. And then looked at Edwin. And then Norah took him by the arm and led him away, after they had whispered a bit together.'

'Now, my little woman must be reasonable,' said Mr. Openshaw, who was always patient with Ailsie. 'There was no man in the house last night at all. No man comes into the house, as you know, if you think; much less goes up into the nursery. But sometimes we dream something has happened, and the dream is so like reality, that you are not the first person, little woman, who has stood out that the thing has really happened.'

'But, indeed, it was not a dream!' said Ailsie, beginning to cry.

Just then Mr. and Mrs. Chadwick came down looking grave and discomposed. All during breakfast-time they were silent and uncomfortable. As soon as the breakfast things were taken away, and the children had been carried upstairs, Mr. Chadwick began, in an evidently preconcerted manner, to inquire if his nephew was certain that all his servants were honest; for that Mrs. Chadwick had that morning missed a very valuable brooch, which she had worn the day before. She remembered taking it off when she came home from Buckingham Palace. Mr. Openshaw's face contracted into hard lines; grew like what it was before he had known his wife and her child. He rang the bell, even before his uncle had done speaking. It was answered by the housemaid.

'Mary, was any one here last night, while we were away?'

'A man, sir, came to speak to Norah.'

'To speak to Norah! Who was he? How long did he stay?'

'I'm sure I can't tell, sir. He came – perhaps about nine. I went up to tell Norah in the nursery, and she came down to speak to him. She let him out, sir. She will know who he was and how long he stayed.'

She waited a moment to be asked any more questions; but she was not, so she went away.

A minute afterwards, Mr. Openshaw made as though he were going out of the room; but his wife laid her hand on his arm:

'Do not speak to her before the children,' she said in her low, quiet voice. 'I will go up and question her.'

'No; I must speak to her. You must know,' said he, turning to his uncle and aunt, 'my missus has an old servant, as faithful as ever woman was, I do believe, as far as love goes, but at the same time, who does not speak truth, as even the missus must allow. Now, my notion is, that this Norah of ours has been come over by some good-for-nothing chap (for she's at the time o' life when they say women pray for husbands – "any, good Lord, any"), and has let him into our house, and the chap has made off with your brooch, and m'appen many another thing beside. It's only saying that Norah is soft-hearted, and doesn't stick at a white lie – that's all, missus.'

It was curious to notice how his tone, his eyes, his whole face was changed, as he spoke to his wife; but he was the resolute man through all. She knew better than to oppose him; so she went upstairs, and told Norah her master wanted to speak to her, and that she would take care of the children in the meanwhile.

Norah rose to go, without a word. Her thoughts were these:

'If they tear me to pieces, they shall never know through me. He may come – and then, just Lord, have mercy upon us all! for some of us are dead folk to a certainty. But *he* shall do it; not me.'

You may fancy now her look of determination, as she faced her master alone in the dining-room; Mr. and Mrs. Chadwick having left the affair in their nephew's hands, seeing that he took it up with such vehemence.

'Norah! Who was that man that came to my house last night?'

'Man, sir!' As if infinitely surprised; but it was only to gain time.

'Yes; the man that Mary let in; that she went upstairs to the nursery to tell you about; that you came down to speak to; the same chap, I make no doubt, that you took into the nursery to have your talk out with; the one Ailsie saw, and afterwards dreamed about; thinking, poor wench! she saw him say his prayers, when nothing, I'll be bound, was further from his thoughts; the one that took Mrs. Chadwick's brooch, value ten pounds. Now, Norah! don't go off. I'm sure as my name's Thomas Openshaw, that you knew nothing of this robbery. But I do think you've been imposed on, and that's the truth. Some good-for-nothing chap has been making up to you, and you have been just like all other women, and have turned a soft place in your heart to him; and he came last night a-lovyering, and you had him up in the nursery, and he made use of his opportunities, and made off with a few things on his way down! Come, now, Norah; it's no blame to you, only you must not be such a fool again! Tell us,' he continued, 'what name he gave you, Norah. I'll be bound, it was not the right one; but it will be a clue for the police.'

Norah drew herself up. 'You may ask that question, and taunt me with my being single, and with my credulity, as you will, Master Openshaw. You'll get no answer from me. As for the brooch, and the story of theft and burglary; if any friend ever came to see me (which I defy you to prove, and deny), he'd be just as much above doing such a thing as you yourself, Mr. Openshaw – and more so, too; for I'm not at all sure as everything you have is rightly come by, or would be yours long, if every man had his own.' She meant, of course, his wife; but he understood her to refer to his property in goods and chattels.

'Now, my good woman,' said he, 'I'll just tell you truly, I never trusted you out and out; but my wife liked you, and I thought you had many a good point about you. If you once begin to sauce me, I'll have the police to you, and get out the truth in a court of justice, if you'll not tell it me quietly and civilly here. Now, the best thing you can do, is quietly to tell me who the fellow is. Look here! a man comes to my house; asks for you; you take him upstairs; a valuable brooch is missing next day; we know that you, and Mary, and cook, are honest; but you refuse to tell us who the man is. Indeed, you've told me one lie already about him, saying no one was here last night. Now, I just put it to you, what do you think a policeman would say to this, or a magistrate? A magistrate would soon make you tell the truth, my good woman.'

'There's never the creature born that should get it out of me,' said Norah. 'Not unless I choose to tell.'

'I've a great mind to see,' said Mr. Openshaw, growing angry at the defiance. Then, checking himself, he thought before he spoke again:

'Norah, for your missus' sake I don't want to go to extremities. Be a sensible woman, if you can. It's no great disgrace, after all, to have been taken in. I ask you once more – as a friend – who was this man that you let into my house last night?'

No answer. He repeated the question in an impatient tone. Still no answer. Norah's lips were set in determination not to speak.

'Then there is but one thing to be done; I shall send for a policeman.'

'You will not,' said Norah, starting forward. 'You shall not, sir! No policeman shall touch me. I know nothing of the brooch, but I know this; ever since I was four-and-twenty, I have thought more of your wife than of myself; ever since I saw her, a poor motherless girl, put upon in her uncle's house, I have thought more of serving her than of serving myself! I have cared for her and her child, as nobody ever cared for me. I don't cast blame on you, sir, but I say it's ill giving up one's life to any one; for, at the end, they will turn round upon you and forsake you.

'Why does not my missus come herself to suspect me? Maybe, she is gone for the police? But I don't stay here, either for police, or magistrate, or master. You're an unlucky lot. I believe there's a curse on you. I'll leave you this very day. Yes, I'll leave that poor Ailsie too. I will. No good will ever come to you!'

Mr. Openshaw was utterly astonished at this speech; most of which was completely unintelligible to him, as may easily be supposed. Before he could make up his mind what to say, or what to do, Norah had left the room. I do not think he had ever really intended to send for the police to this old servant of his wife's; for he had never for a moment doubted her perfect honesty. But he had intended to compel her to tell him whom the man was, and in this he was baffled. He was, consequently, much irritated. He returned to his uncle and aunt in a state of great annoyance and perplexity, and told them he could get nothing out of the woman; that some man had been in the house the night before; but that she refused to tell who he was. At this moment his wife came in, greatly agitated, and asked what had happened to Norah; for that she had put on her things in passionate haste, and left the house.

'This looks suspicious,' said Mr. Chadwick. 'It is not the way in which an honest person would have acted.'

Mr. Openshaw kept silence. He was sorely perplexed. But Mrs. Openshaw turned round on Mr. Chadwick, with a sudden fierceness no one ever saw in her before.

'You don't know Norah, uncle! She is gone because she is

deeply hurt at being suspected. Oh, I wish I had seen her – that I had spoken to her myself. She would have told me anything.' Alice rung her hands.

'I must confess,' continued Mr. Chadwick to his nephew, in a lower voice, 'I can't make you out. You used to be a word and a blow, and oftenest the blow first; and now, when there is every cause for suspicion, you just do nought. Your missus is a very good woman, I grant; but she may have been put upon as well as other folk, I suppose. If you don't send for the police, I shall.'

'Very well,' replied Mr. Openshaw surlily. 'I can't clear Norah. She won't clear herself, as I believe she might if she would. Only I wash my hands of it; for I am sure the woman herself is honest, and she's lived a long time with my wife, and I don't like her to come to shame.'

'But she will be forced to clear herself. That, at any rate, will be a good thing.'

'Very well, very well! I am heart-sick of the whole business. Come, Alice, come up to the babies; they'll be in a sore way. I tell you, uncle,' he said, turning round once more to Mr. Chadwick, suddenly and sharply, after his eye had fallen on Alice's wan, tearful, anxious face; 'I'll have no sending for the police after all. I'll buy my aunt twice as handsome a brooch this very day; but I'll not have Norah suspected, and my missus plagued. There's for you.'

He and his wife left the room. Mr. Chadwick quietly waited till he was out of hearing, and then said to his wife: 'For all Tom's heroics, I'm just quietly going for a detective, wench. Thou need'st know nought about it.'

He went to the police-station, and made a statement of the case. He was gratified by the impression which the evidence against Norah seemed to make. The men all agreed in his opinion, and steps were to be immediately taken to find out where she was. Most probably, as they suggested, she had gone at once to the man, who, to all appearance, was her lover. When Mr. Chadwick asked how they would find her out, they smiled, shook their heads, and spoke of mysterious but infallible ways and means. He returned to his nephew's house with a very comfortable opinion of his own sagacity. He was met by his wife with a penitent face:

'O master, I've found my brooch! It was just sticking by its pin in the flounce of my brown silk, that I wore yesterday. I took it off in a hurry, and it must have caught in it; and I hung up my gown in the closet. Just now, when I was going to fold it up, there was the brooch! I'm very vexed, but I never dreamt but what it was lost!'

Her husband, muttering something very like 'Confound thee and thy brooch, too! I wish I'd never given it to thee,' snatched up his hat, and rushed back to the station, hoping to be in time to stop the police from searching for Norah. But a detective was already gone off on the errand.

Where was Norah? Half mad with the strain of the fearful secret, she had hardly slept through the night for thinking what must be done. Upon this terrible state of mind had come Ailsie's questions, showing that she had seen the Man, as the unconscious child called her father. Lastly came the suspicion of her honesty. She was little less than crazy as she ran upstairs and dashed on her bonnet and shawl; leaving all else, even her purse, behind her. In that house she would not stay. That was all she knew or was clear about. She would not even see the children again, for fear it should weaken her. She dreaded above everything Mr. Frank's return to claim his wife. She could not tell what remedy there was for a sorrow so tremendous, for her to stay to witness it. The desire of escaping from the coming event was a stronger motive for her departure than her soreness about the suspicions directed against her; although this last had been the final goad to the course she took. She walked away almost at headlong speed; sobbing as she went, as she had not dared to do during the past night for fear of exciting wonder in those who might hear her. Then she stopped. An idea came into her mind that she would leave London altogether, and betake herself to her native town of Liverpool. She felt in her pocket for her purse, as she drew near the Euston Square station with this intention. She had left it at home. Her poor head aching, her eyes swollen with crying, she had to stand still, and think, as well as she could, where next she should bend her steps. Suddenly the thought flashed into her mind that she would go and find out poor Mr. Frank. She had been hardly kind to him the night before, though her heart had bled for him ever since. She remembered his telling her, when she inquired for his address, almost as she had pushed him out of the door, of some hotel in a street not far distant from Euston Square. Thither she went: with what intention she scarcely knew, but to assuage her conscience by telling him how much she pitied him. In her present state she felt herself unfit to counsel, or restrain, or assist, or do aught else but sympathise and weep. The people of the inn said that such a person had been there; had arrived only the day before; had gone out soon after his arrival, leaving his luggage in their care; but had never come back. Norah asked for leave to sit down, and await the gentleman's return. The landlady – pretty secure in the deposit of luggage against any probable injury – showed her into a room, and quietly locked the door on the outside. Norah was utterly worn out, and fell asleep – a shivering, starting, uneasy slumber, which lasted for hours.

The detective, meanwhile, had come up with her some time before she entered the hotel, into which he followed her. Asking the landlady to detain her for an hour or so, without giving any reason beyond showing his authority (which made the landlady applaud herself a good deal for having locked her in), he went back to the police-station to report his proceedings. He could have taken her directly; but his object was, if possible, to trace the man who was supposed to have committed the robbery. Then he heard of the discovery of the brooch; and consequently did not care to return.

Norah slept till even the summer evening began to close in. Then started up. Some one was at the door. It would be Mr. Frank; and she dizzily pushed back her ruffled grey hair, which had fallen over her eyes, and stood looking to see him. Instead, there came in Mr. Openshaw and a policeman.

'This is Norah Kennedy,' said Mr. Openshaw.

'O sir,' said Norah, 'I did not touch the brooch; indeed I did not. O sir, I cannot live to be thought so badly of;' and very sick and faint, she suddenly sank down on the ground. To·her surprise, Mr. Openshaw raised her up very tenderly. Even the policeman helped to lay her on the sofa; and, at Mr. Openshaw's desire, he went for some wine and sandwiches; for the poor gaunt woman lay there almost as if dead with weariness and exhaustion.

'Norah,' said Mr. Openshaw, in his kindest voice, 'the brooch is found. It was hanging to Mrs. Chadwick's gown. I beg your pardon. Most truly I beg your pardon, for having troubled you about it. My wife is almost broken-hearted. Eat, Norah – or, stay, first drink this glass of wine,' said he, lifting her head, and pouring a little down her throat.

As she drank, she remembered where she was, and who she was waiting for. She suddenly pushed Mr. Openshaw away, saying, 'O sir, you must go. You must not stop a minute. If he comes back he will kill you.'

'Alas, Norah! I do not know who "he" is. But some one is gone away who will never come back: someone who knew you, and whom I am afraid you cared for.'

'I don't understand you, sir,' said Norah, her master's kind and sorrowful manner bewildering her yet more than his words. The policeman had left the room at Mr. Openshaw's desire, and they two were alone.

'You know what I mean, when I say some one is gone who will never come back. I mean that he is dead!'

'Who?' said Norah, trembling all over.

'A poor man has been found in the Thames this morning – drowned.'

'Did he drown himself?' asked Norah solemnly.

'God only knows,' replied Mr. Openshaw, in the same tone. 'Your name and address at our house were found in his pocket; that, and his purse, were the only things that were found upon him. I am sorry to say it, my poor Norah; but you are required to go and identify him.'

'To what?' asked Norah.

'To say who it is. It is always done, in order that some reason may be discovered for the suicide – if suicide it was. I make no doubt, he was the man who came to see you at our house last night. It is very sad, I know.' He made pauses between each little clause, in order to try and bring back her senses, which he feared were wandering – so wild and sad was her look.

'Master Openshaw,' said she at last, 'I've a dreadful secret to tell you – only you must never breathe it to any one, and you and I must hide it away for ever. I thought to have done it all by myself, but I see I cannot. Yon poor man – yes! the dead, drowned creature is, I fear, Mr. Frank, my mistress's first husband!'

Mr. Openshaw sat down, as if shot. He did not speak; but after a while he signed to Norah to go on.

'He came to me the other night, when, God be thanked you were all away at Richmond. He asked me if his wife was dead or alive. I was a brute, and thought more of your all coming home than of his sore trial; I spoke out sharp, and said she was married again, and very content and happy; I all but turned him away; and now he lies dead and cold.'

'God forgive me!' said Mr. Openshaw.

'God forgive us all!' said Norah. 'Yon poor man needs forgiveness, perhaps, less than any one among us. He had been among the savages – shipwrecked – I know not what – and he had written letters which had never reached my poor missus.'

'He saw his child!'

'He saw her – yes! I took him up, to give his thoughts another start; for I believed he was going mad on my hands. I came to seek him here, as I more than half promised. My mind misgave me when I heard he never came in. O sir! it must be him!'

Mr. Openshaw rang the bell. Norah was almost too much stunned to wonder at what he did. He asked for writing materials, wrote a letter, and then said to Norah:

'I am writing to Alice to say I shall be unavoidably absent for a few days; that I have found you; that you are well, and send her your love, and will come home tomorrow. You must go with me to the police court; you must identify the body; I will pay high to keep names and details out of the papers.'

'But where are you going, sir?'

He did not answer her directly. Then he said:

'Norah, I must go with you, and look on the face of the man whom I have so injured – unwittingly, it is true; but it seems to me as if I had killed him. I will lay his head in the grave as if he were my only brother; and how he must have hated me! I cannot go home to my wife till all that I can do for him is done. Then I go with a dreadful secret on my mind. I shall never speak of it again, after these days are over. I know you will not, either.' He shook hands with her; and they never named the subject again, the one to the other.

Norah went home to Alice the next day. Not a word was said on the cause of her abrupt departure a day or two before. Alice had been charged by her husband, in his letter, not to allude to the supposed theft of the brooch; so she, implicitly obedient to those whom she loved both by nature and habit, was entirely silent on the subject, only treated Norah with the most tender respect, as if to make up for unjust suspicion.

Nor did Alice inquire into the reason why Mr. Openshaw had been absent during his uncle and aunt's visit, after he had once said that it was unavoidable. He came back grave and quiet; and from that time forth was curiously changed. More thoughtful, and perhaps less active; quite as decided in conduct, but with new and different rules for the guidance of that conduct. Towards Alice he could hardly be more kind than he had always been; but he now seemed to look upon her as some one sacred, and to be treated with reverence as well as tenderness. He throve in business, and made a large fortune, one half of which was settled upon her.

Long years after these events, a few months after her mother died, Ailsie and her 'father' (as she always called Mr. Openshaw) drove to a cemetery a little way out of town, and she was carried to a certain mound by her maid, who was then sent back to the carriage. There was a headstone with 'F.W.' and a date upon it. That was all. Sitting by the grave, Mr. Openshaw told her the story; and for the sad fate of that poor father whom she had never seen he shed the only tears she ever saw fall from his eyes.

AN ACCURSED RACE

AN ACCURSED RACE

We have our prejudices in England. Or, if that assertion offends any of my readers, I will modify it: we have had our prejudices in England. We have tortured Jews; we have burnt Catholics and Protestants, to say nothing of a few witches and wizards. We have satirised Puritans, and we have dressed up Guys. But, after all, I do not think we have been so bad as our Continental friends. To be sure, our insular poition has kept us free, to a certain degree, from the inroads of alien races: who, driven from one land of refuge, steal into another equally unwilling to receive them, and where, for long centuries, their presence is barely endured, and no pain is taken to conceal the repugnance which the natives of 'pure blood' experience towards them.

There yet remains a remnant of the miserable people called Cagots in the valleys of the Pyrenees; in the Landes near Bordeaux; and, stretching up on the west side of France, their numbers became larger in Lower Brittany. Even now, the origin of these families is a word of shame to them among their neighbours; although they are protected by the law, which confirmed them in the equal rights of citizens about the end of the last century. Before then they had lived, for hundreds of years, isolated from all those who boasted of pure blood, and they had been, all this time, oppressed by cruel local edicts. They were truly what they were popularly called, The Accursed Race.

All distinct traces of their origin are lost. Even at the close of that period which we call the Middle Ages, this was a problem which no one could solve; and as the traces, which even then were faint and uncertain, have vanished away one by one, it is a complete mystery at the present day. Why they were accursed in the first instance, why isolated from their kind, no one knows. From the earliest accounts of their state that are yet remaining to us, it seems that the names which they gave each other were ignored by the population they lived amongst, who spoke of them as Chrestiaa, or Cagots, just as we speak of animals by their generic names. Their houses or huts were always placed at some distance out of the villages of the country-folk, who unwillingly called in the services of the Cagots as carpenters, or tilers, or slaters – trades which seemed appropriated by this unfortunate race, who were forbidden to occupy land, or to bear arms, the usual occupations of those times. They had some small right of pasturage on the common lands, and in the forests; but the number of their cattle and livestock was strictly limited by the earliest laws relating to the Cagots. They were forbidden by one act to have more than twenty sheep, a pig, a ram, and six geese. The pig was to be fattened and killed for winter food; the fleece of the sheep was to clothe them; but if the said sheep had lambs, they were forbidden to eat them. Their only privilege arising from this increase was, that they might choose out the strongest and finest in preference to keeping the old sheep. At Martinmas the authorities of the commune came round, and counted over the stock of each Cagot. If he had more than his appointed number, they were forfeited; half went to the commune, and half to the *bailli*, or chief magistrate of the commune. The poor beasts were limited as to the amount of common land which they might stray over in search of grass. While the cattle of the inhabitants of the commune might wander hither and thither in search of the sweetest herbage, the deepest shade, or the coolest pool in which to stand on the hot days, and lazily switch their dappled sides, the Cagot sheep and pig had to learn imaginary bounds, beyond which if they strayed, any one might snap them up, and kill them, reserving a part of the flesh for his own use, but graciously restoring the inferior parts to their original owner. Any damage done by the sheep was, however, fairly appraised, and the Cagot paid no more for it than any other man would have done.

Did a Cagot leave his poor cabin, and venture into the towns, even to render services required of him in the way of his trade, he was bidden, by all the municipal laws, to stand by and remember his rude old state. In all the towns and villages in the large districts extending on both sides of the Pyrenees –

in all that part of Spain – they were forbidden to buy or sell anything eatable, to walk in the middle (esteemed the better) part of the streets, to come within the gates before sunrise, or to be found after sunset within the walls of the town. But still, as the Cagots were good-looking men, and (although they bore certain natural marks of their caste, of which I shall speak by-and-by) were not easily distinguished by casual passers-by from other men, they were compelled to wear some distinctive peculiarity which should arrest the eye; and, in the greater number of towns, it was decreed that the outward sign of a Cagot should be a piece of red cloth sewed conspicuously on the front of his dress. In other towns, the mark of Cagoterie was the foot of a duck or a goose hung over their left shoulder, so as to be seen by anyone meeting them. After a time, the more convenient badge of a piece of yellow cloth cut out in the shape of a duck's foot was adopted. If any Cagot was found in any town or village without his badge, he had to pay a fine of five sous, and to lose his dress. He was expected to shrink away from any passer-by, for fear that their clothes should touch each other; or else to stand still in some corner or by-place. If the Cagots were thirsty during the days which they passed in those towns where their presence was barely suffered, they had no means of quenching their thirst, for they were forbidden to enter into the little cabarets or taverns. Even the water gushing out of the common fountain was prohibited to them. Far away, in their own squalid village, there was the Cagot fountain, and they were not allowed to drink of any other water. A woman Cagot, having to make purchases in the town, was liable to be flogged out of it if she went to buy anything except on a Monday – a day on which all other people who could, kept their houses for fear of coming in contact with the accursed race.

In the Pays Basque, the prejudices – and for some time the laws – ran stronger against them than any which I have hitherto mentioned. The Basque Cagot was not allowed to possess sheep. He might keep a pig for provision, but his pig had no right of pasturage. He might cut and carry grass for the ass, which was the only other animal he was permitted to own; and this ass was permitted, because its existence was rather an advantage to the oppressor, who constantly availed himself of the Cagot's mechanical skill, and was glad to have him and his tools easily conveyed from one place to another.

The race was repulsed by the State. Under the small local governments they could hold no post whatsoever. And they were barely tolerated by the Church, although they were good Catholics, and zealous frequenters of the mass. They might only enter the churches by a small door set apart for them, through which no one of the pure race ever passed. This door was low, so as to compel them to make an obeisance. It was occasionally surrounded by sculpture, which invariably represented an oak-branch with a dove above it. When they were once in, they might not go to the holy water used by others. They had a *bénitier* of their own; nor where they allowed to share in the consecrated bread when that was handed round to the believers of the pure race. The Cagots stood afar off, near the door. There were certain bounderies – imaginary lines – in the nave and in the aisles which they might not pass. In one or two of the more tolerant of the Pyrenean villages, the blessed bread was offered to the Cagots, the priest standing on one side of the boundary, and giving the pieces of bread on a long wooden fork to each person successively.

When the Cagot died, he was interred apart, in a plot of burying-ground on the north side of the cemetery. Under such laws and prescriptions as I have described, it is no wonder that he was generally too poor to have much property for his children to inherit; but certain descriptions of it were forfeited to the commune. The only possession which all who were not of his own race refused to touch, was his furniture. That was tainted, infectious, unclean – fit for none but Cagots.

When such were, for at least three centuries, the prevalent usages and opinions with regard to this oppressed race, it is not surprising that we read of occasional outbursts of ferocious violence on their part. In the Basses-Pyrénées, for instance, it is only about a hundred years since that the Cagots of Rehouilhes rose up against the inhabitants of the neighbouring town of Lourdes, and got the better of them, by their magical powers, as it is said. The people of Lourdes were conquered and slain, and their ghastly, bloody heads served the triumphant Cagots for balls to play at ninepins with! The local parliaments had begun, by this time, to perceive how oppressive was the ban of public opinion under which the Cagots lay, and were not inclined to enforce too severe a punishment. Accordingly, the decree of the parliament of Toulouse condemned only the leading Cagots concerned in this affray to be put to death; but henceforward and for ever no Cagot was to be permitted to enter the town of Lourdes by any gate but that called Capdet-pourtet; they were only to be allowed to walk under the rain-gutters, and neither to sit, eat, nor drink in the town. If they failed in observing any of these rules, the parliament decreed, in the spirit of Shylock, that the disobedient Cagots should have two strips of flesh, weighing over more than two ounces apiece, cut out from each side of their spines.

In the fourteenth, fifteenth, and sixteenth centuries, it was considered no more a crime to kill a Cagot than to destroy obnoxious vermin. A 'nest of Cagots', as the old accounts phrase it, had assembled in a deserted castle of Mauvezin, about the year sixteen hundred; and, certainly, they made themselves not very agreeable neighbours, as they seemed to enjoy their reputation of magicians; and, by some acoustic secrets which were known to them, all sorts of moanings and groanings were heard in the neighbouring forests, very much to the alarm of the good people of the pure race: who could not cut off a withered branch for fire-wood, but some unearthly sound seemed to fill the air, nor drink water which was not poisoned, because the Cagots would persist in filling their pitchers at the same running stream. Added to these grievances, the various pilferings perpetually going on in the neighbourhood made the inhabitants of the adjacent towns and hamlets believe that they had a very sufficient cause for wishing to murder all the Cagots in the Château de Mauvezin. But it was surrounded by a moat, and only accessible by a drawbridge; besides which, the Cagots were fierce and vigilant. Some one, however, proposed to get into their confidence; and for this purpose he pretended to fall ill close to their path, so that on returning to their stronghold they perceived him, and took him in, restored him to health, and made a friend of him. One day, when they were all playing at ninepins in the woods, their treacherous friend left the party on pretence of being thirsty, and went back into the castle, drawing up the bridge after he had passed over it, and so cutting off their means of escape into safety. Then, going up to the highest part of the castle, he blew a horn; and the pure race, who were lying in wait on the watch for some such signal, fell upon the Cagots at their games, and slew them all. For this murder I find no punishment decreed in the Parliament of Toulouse or elsewhere.

As any intermarriage with the pure race was strictly forbidden, and as there were books kept in every commune in which the names and habitations of the reputed Cagots were written, these unfortunate people had no hope of ever becoming blended with the rest of the population. Did a Cagot marriage take place, the couple were serenaded with satirical songs. They also had minstrels, and many of their romances are still current in Brittany; but they did not attempt to make any reprisals of satire or abuse. Their disposition was amiable, and their intelligence great. Indeed, it required both these qualities, and their great love of mechanical labour, to make their lives tolerable.

At last, they began to petition that they might receive some protection from the laws; and, towards the end of the seventeenth century, the judicial power took their side. But they gained little by this. Law could not prevail against custom; and in the ten or twenty years just preceding the first French Revolution, the prejudice in France against the Cagots amounted to fierce and positive abhorrence.

At the beginning of the sixteenth century, the Cagots of Navarre complained to the Pope that they were excluded from the fellowship of men, and accursed by the Church, because their ancestors had given help to a certain Count Raymond of Toulouse in his revolt against the Holy See. They entreated his Holiness not to visit upon them the sins of their fathers. The Pope issued a bull – on the thirteenth of May, fifteen hundred and fifteen – ordering them to be well treated and to be admitted to the same privileges as other men. He charged Don Juan de Santa Maria of Pampeluna to see to the execution of this bull. But Don Juan was slow to help, and the poor Spanish Cagots grew impatient, and resolved to try the secular power. They accordingly applied to the Cortes of Navarre, and were opposed on a variety of grounds. First, it was stated that their ancestors had had 'nothing to do with Raymond Count of Toulouse, or with any such knightly personage; that they were in fact desendants of Gehazi, servant of Elisha (second book of Kings, fifth chapter, twenty-seventh verse), who had been accursed by his master for his fraud upon Naaman, and doomed, he and his descendants, to be lepers for evermore. Name, Cagots or Gahets; Gahets, Gehazites. What can be more clear? And if that is not enough, and you tell us that the Cagots are not lepers now, we reply that there are two kinds of leprosy, one perceptible and the other imperceptible, even to the person suffering from it. Besides, it is the country talk that, where the Cagot treads, the grass withers, proving the unnatural heat of his body. Many credible and trustworthy witnesses will also tell you that, if a Cagot holds a freshly-gathered apple in his hand, it will shrivel and wither up in an hour's time as much as if it had been kept for a whole winter in a dry room. They are born with tails; although the parents are cunning enough to pinch them off immediately. Do you doubt this? If it is not true, why do the children of the pure race delight in sewing on sheep's tails to the dress of any Cagot who is so absorbed in his work as not to perceive them? And their bodily smell is so horrible and detestable that it shows that they must be heretics of some vile and pernicious description; for do we not read of the incense of good workers, and the fragrance of holiness?'

Such were literally the arguments by which the Cagots were thrown back into a worse position than ever, as far as regarded their rights as citizens. The Pope insisted that they should receive all their ecclesiastical privileges. The Spanish priests said nothing; but tacitly refused to allow the Cagots to mingle with the rest of the faithful, either dead or alive. The Accursed Race obtained laws in their favour from the Emperor Charles the Fifth; which, however, there was no one to carry into effect. As a sort of revenge for their want of submission, and for their impertinence in daring to complain, their tools were all taken away from them by the local authorities: an old man and all his family died of starvation, being no longer allowed to fish.

They could not emigrate. Even to remove their poor mud habitations from one spot to another, excited anger and suspicion. To be sure, in sixteen hundred and ninety-five, the Spanish government ordered the alcaldes to search out all the Cagots, and to expel them before two months had expired under pain of having fifty ducats to pay for every Cagot remaining in Spain at the expiration of that time. The inhabitants of the villages rose up and flogged out any of the miserable race who might be in their neighbourhood; but the French were on their guard against this enforced irruption, and refused to permit them to enter France. Numbers were hunted up into the inhospitable Pyrenees, and there died of starvation, or became a prey to wild beasts. They were obliged to wear both gloves and shoes when they were thus put to flight; otherwise, the stones and herbage they trod upon and the balustrades of the bridges that they handled in crossing, would, according to popular belief, have become poisonous.

And all this time, there was nothing remarkable or disgusting in the outward appearance of this unfortunate people. There was nothing about them to countenance the idea of their being lepers – the most natural mode of accounting for the abhorrence in which they were held. They were repeatedly examined by learned doctors, whose experiments, although singular and rude, appear to have been made in a spirit of humanity. For instance, the surgeons of the king of Navarre, in sixteen hundred, bled twenty-two Cagots, in order to examine and analyse their blood. They were young and healthy people of both sexes: and the doctors seem to have expected that they would have been able to extract some new kind of salt from their blood which might account for the wonderful heat of their bodies. But their blood was just like that of other people. Some of these medical men have left us a description of the general appearance of this unfortunate race, at a time when they were more numerous and less intermixed than they are now. The families existing in the south and west of France, who are reputed to be of Cagot descent at this day, are, like their ancestors, tall, largely made, and powerful in frame; fair and ruddy in complexion, with grey-blue eyes, in which some observers see a pensive heaviness of look. Their lips are thick, but well-formed. Some of the reports name their sad expression of countenance with surprise and suspicion – 'They are not gay, like other folk.' The wonder would be if they were. Dr. Guyon, the medical man of the last century who has left the clearest report on the health of the Cagots, speaks of the vigorous old age they attain to. In one family alone, he found a man of seventy-four years of age; a woman as old, gathering cherries; and another woman, aged eighty-three, was lying on the grass, having her hair combed by her great-grandchildren. Dr. Guyon and other surgeons examined into the subject of the horribly infectious smell which the Cagots were said to leave behind them and upon everything they touched; but they could perceive nothing unusual on this head. They also examined their ears, which, according to common belief (a belief existing to this day), were differently shaped from those of other people; being round and gristly, without the lobe of flesh into which the earring is inserted. They decided that most of the Cagots whom they examined had the ears of this round shape; but they gravely added, that they saw no reason why this should exclude them from the good-will of men, and from the power of holding office in Church and State. They recorded the fact that the children of the towns ran baa-ing after any Cagot who had been compelled to come into the streets to make purchases, in allusion to this peculiarity of the shape of the ear, which bore some resemblance to the ears of the sheep as they are cut by the shepherds in this district. Dr. Guyon names the case of a beautiful Cagot girl, who sang most sweetly, and prayed to be allowed to sing canticles in the organ-loft. The organist, more musician than bigot, allowed her to come; but the indignant congregation, finding out whence proceeded that clear, fresh voice, rushed up to the organ-loft, and chased the girl out, bidding her 'remember her ears,' and not commit the sacrilege of singing praises to God along with the pure race.

But this medical report of Dr. Guyon's – bringing facts and arguments to confirm his opinion, that there was no physical reason why the Cagots should not be received on terms of social equality by the rest of the world – did no more for his clients than the legal decrees promulgated two centuries before had done. The French proved the truth of the saying in Hudibras:

'He that's convinced against his will
Is of the same opinion still.'

And, indeed, the being convinced by Dr. Guyon that they ought to receive Cagots as fellow-creatures only made them more rabid in declaring that they would not. One or two little occurrences which are recorded, show that the bitterness of the repugnance to the Cagots was in full force at the time just preceding the first French revolution. There was a M. d'Abedos, the curate of Lourdes, and brother to the seigneur of the neighbouring castle, who was living in seventeen hundred and eighty; he was well-educated for the time, a travelled man, and sensible and moderate in all respects but that of his abhorrence of the Cagots: he would insult them from the very altar, calling out to them, as they stood afar off, 'Oh! ye Cagots, damned for evermore!' One day, a half-blind Cagot stumbled and touched the censer borne before this Abbé de Lourdes. He was immediately turned out of the church, and forbidden ever to re-enter it. One does not know how to account for the fact, that the very brother of this bigoted abbé, the seigneur of the village, went and married a Cagot girl; but so it was, and the abbé brought a legal process against him, and had his estates taken from him, solely on account of his marriage, which reduced him to the condition of a Cagot, against whom the old law was still in force. The descendants of this Seigneur de Lourdes are simple peasants at this very day, working on the lands which belonged to their grandfather.

This prejudice against mixed marriages remained prevalent until very lately. The tradition of the Cagot descent lingered among the people, long after the laws againt the accursed race were abolished. A Breton girl, within the last few years, having two lovers, each of reputed Cagot descent, employed a notary to examine their pedigrees, and see which of the two had least Cagot in him; and to that one she gave her hand. In Brittany the prejudice seems to have been more virulent than anywhere else. M. Emile Souvestre records proofs of the hatred borne to them in Brittany so recently as in eighteen hundred and thirty-five. Just lately a baker at Hennebon, having married a girl of Cagot descent, lost all his custom.

The godfather and godmother of a Cagot child became Cagots themselves by the Breton laws, unless, indeed, the poor little baby died before attaining a certain number of days. They had to eat the butchers' meat condemned as unhealthy; but, for some unknown reason, they were considered to have a right to every cut loaf turned upside down, with its cut side towards the door, and might enter any house in which they saw a loaf in this position, and carry it away with them. About thirty years ago, there was a skeleton of a hand hanging up as an offering in a Breton church near Quimperlé; and the tradition was that it was the hand of a rich Cagot who had dared to take holy water out of the usual *bénetier*, some time at the beginning of the reign of Louis the Sixteenth; which an old soldier witnessing, he lay in wait; and, the next time the offender approached the *bénetier* he cut off his hand, and hung it up, dripping with blood, as an offering to the patron saint of the church. The poor Cagots in Brittany petitioned against their opprobrious name, and begged to be distinguished by the appellation of Malandrins. To English ears one is much the same as the other, as neither conveys any meaning; but, to this day, the descendants of the Cagots do not like to have this name applied to them, preferring that of Malandrin.

The French Cagots tried to destroy all the records of their pariah descent, in the commotions of seventeen hundred and eighty-nine; but, if writings have disappeared, the tradition yet remains, and points out such and such a family as Cagot, or Malandrin, or Oiselier, according to the old terms of abhorrence.

There are various ways in which learned men have attempted to account for the universal repugnance in which this well-made powerful race are held. Some say that the antipathy to them took its rise in the days when leprosy was a dreadfully prevalent disease; and that the Cagots are more liable than any other men to a kind of skin disease, not precisely leprosy, but resembling it in some of its symptoms: such as dead whiteness of complexion and swellings of the face and extremities. There was also some resemblance to the ancient Jewish custom in respect to lepers, in the habit of the people, who, on meeting a Cagot, called out, 'Cagote? Cagote?' to which they were bound to reply, 'Perlute!

perlute!' Leprosy is not properly an infectious complaint, in spite of the horror in which the Cagot furniture, and the cloth woven by them, are held in some places; the disorder is hereditary, and hence (say this body of wise men, who have troubled themselves to account for the origin of Cagoterie), the reasonableness and the justice of preventing any mixed marriages, by which this terrible tendency to leprous complaints might be spread far and wide. Another authority says that, though the Cagots are fine-looking men, hard-working, and good mechanics, yet they bear in their faces, and show in their actions, reasons for the detestation in which they are held: their glance, if you meet it, is the *jettatura*, or evil-eye, and they are spiteful and cruel, and deceitful above all other men. All these qualities they derive from their ancestor Gehazi, the servant of Elisha, together with their tendency to leprosy.

Again, it is said that they are descended from the Arian Goths who were permitted to live in certain places in Guienne and Languedoc, after their defeat by King Clovis, on condition that they abjured their heresy, and kept themselves separate from all other men for ever. The principal reason alleged in support of this supposition of their Gothic descent, is the specious one of derivation – *Chiens Gots, Cans Gots, Cagots,* equivalent to Dogs of Goths.

Again, they were thought to be Saracens, coming from Syria. In confirmation of this idea was the belief that all Cagots were possessed by a horrible smell. The Lombards, also, were an unfragrant race, or so reputed among the Italians; witness Pope Stephen's letter to Charlemagne, dissuading him from marrying Bertha, daughter of Didier, King of Lombardy. The Lombards boasted of Eastern descent, and were noisome. The Cagots were noisome, and therefore must be of Eastern descent. What could be clearer? In addition, there was the proof to be derived from the name Cagot, which those maintaining the opinion of their Saracen descent held to be *Chiens*, or *Chasseurs des Gots*, because the Saracens chased the Goths out of Spain. Moreover, the Saracens were originally Mahometans, and as such obliged to bathe seven times a day: whence the badge of the duck's foot. A duck was a water-bird: Mahometans bathed in the water. Proof upon proof!

In Brittany the common idea was, they were of Jewish
descent. Their unpleasant smell was again pressed into service.
The Jews, it was well known, had this physical infirmity,
which might be cured either by bathing in a certain fountain in
Egypt – which was a long way from Brittany – or by
annointing themselves with the blood of a Christian child.
Blood gushed out of the body of every Cagot on Good Friday.
No wonder, if they were of Jewish descent. It was the only way
of accounting for so portentous a fact. Again, the Cagots were
capital carpenters, which gave the Bretons every reason to
believe that their ancestors were the very Jews who made the
cross. When first the tide of emigration set from Brittany to
America, the oppressed Cagots crowded to the ports, seeking
to go to some new country, where their race might be
unknown. Here was another proof of their descent from
Abraham and his nomadic people; and the forty years' wandering in the wilderness, and the Wandering Jew himself, were
pressed into the service to prove that the Cagots derived their
restlessness and love of change from their ancestors, the Jews.
The Jews, also, practised arts-magic, and the Cagots sold bags
of wind to the Breton sailors, enchanted maidens to love them –
maidens who never would have cared for them, unless they had
been previously enchanted – made hollow rocks and trees give
out strange and unearthly noises, and sold the magical herb
called *bon-succès*. It is true enough that, in all the early acts of the
fourteenth century, the same laws apply to Jews as to Cagots,
and the appellations seem used indiscriminately; but their fair
complexions, their remarkable devotion to all the ceremonies
of the Catholic Church, and many other circumstances,
conspire to forbid our believing them to be of Hebrew descent.

Another very plausible idea is that they are the descendants of
unfortunate individuals afflicted with goîtres, which is, even to
this day, not an uncommon disorder in the gorges and valleys
of the Pyrenees. Some have even derived the word goître from
Got, or Goth; but their name, Chrestiaa, is not unlike Cretin,
and the same symptoms of idiotism were not unusual among
the Cagots; although sometimes, if old tradition is to be
credited, their malady of the brain took rather the form of
violent delirium, which attacked them at new and full moons.
Then the workmen laid down their tools, and rushed off from

their labour to play mad pranks up and down the the country. Perpetual motion was required to alleviate the agony of fury that seized upon the Cagots at such times. In this desire for rapid movement, the attack resembled the Neapolitan tarantella; while in the mad deeds they performed during such attacks, they were not unlike the northern Berserker. In Béarn especially, those suffering from this madness were dreaded by the pure race; the Béarnais, going to cut their wooden clogs in the great forests that lay around the base of the Pyrenees, feared above all things to go too near the periods when the Cagoutelle seized on the oppressed and accursed people; from whom it was then the oppressor's turn to fly. A man was living within the memory of some, who had married a Cagot wife; he used to beat her right soundly when he saw the first symptoms of the Cagoutelle, and, having reduced her to a wholesome state of exhaustion and insensibility, he locked her up until the moon had altered her shape in the heavens. If he had not taken such decided steps, say the oldest inhabitants, there is no knowing what might have happened.

From the thirteenth to the end of the eighteenth century, there are facts enough to prove the universal abhorrence in which this unfortunate race was held; whether called Cagots or Gahets in Pyrenean districts, Caqueaux in Brittany, or Vaqueros in Austria. The great French revolution brought some good out of its fermentation of the people: the more intelligent among them tried to overcome the prejudice against the Cagots.

In seventeen hundred and eighteen, there was a famous cause tried at Biarritz relating to Cagot rights and privileges. There was a wealthy miller, Etienne Arnauld by name, of the race of Gots, Quagotz, Bisigotz, Astragotz, or Gahetz, as his people are described in the legal document. He married an heiress, a Gotte (or Cagot) of Biarritz; and the newly married well-to-do couple saw no reason why they should stand near the door in the church, nor why he should not hold some civil office in the commune, of which he was the principal inhabitant. Accordingly, he petitioned the law that he and his wife might be allowed to sit in the gallery of the church, and that he might be relieved from his civil disabilities. This wealthy white miller, Etienne Arnauld, pursued his rights with some vigour against the *Bailli* of Labourd, the dignitary of the neighbourhood. Whereupon the inhabitants of Biarritz met in the open air, on the eighth of May, to the number of one hundred and fifty; approved of the conduct of the *Bailli* in rejecting Arnauld; made a subscription, and gave all power to their lawyers to defend the cause of the pure race against Etienne Arnauld – 'that stranger,' who, having married a girl of Cagot blood, ought also to be expelled from the holy places. This lawsuit was carried through all the local courts, and ended by an appeal to the highest court in Paris; where a decision was given against Basque superstitions; and Etienne Arnauld was thenceforward entitled to enter the gallery of the church.

Of course, the inhabitants of Biarritz were all the more ferocious for having been conquered; and, four years later, a carpenter, named Miguel Legaret, suspected of Cagot descent, having placed himself in the church among other people, was dragged out by the abbé and two of the jurets of the parish. Legaret defended himself with a sharp knife at the time, and went to law afterwards; the end of which was, that the abbé and his two accomplices were condemned to a public confession of penitence, to be uttered while on their knees at the church door, just after high mass. They appealed to the parliament of Bordeaux against this decision, but met with no better success than the opponents of the miller Arnauld. Legaret was confirmed in his right of standing where he would in the parish church. That a living Cagot had equal rights with other men in the town of Biarritz seemed now ceded to them; but a dead Cagot was a different thing. The inhabitants of pure blood struggled long and hard to be interred apart from the abhorred race. The Cagots were equally persistent in claiming to have a common burying-ground. Again the texts of the Old Testament were referred to, and the pure blood quoted triumphantly the precedent of Uzziah the leper (twenty-sixth chapter of the second book of Chronicles), who was buried in the field of the Sepulchres of the Kings, not in the sepulchres themselves. The Cagots pleaded that they were healthy and able-bodied, with no taint of leprosy near them. They were met by the strong argument so difficult to be refuted, which I quoted before. Leprosy was of two kinds, perceptible and imperceptible. If the Cagots were suffering from the latter kind, who could tell whether they were free from it or not? That decision must be left to the judgment of others.

One sturdy Cagot family alone, Belone by name, kept up a lawsuit, claiming the privilege of common sepulture, for forty-two years; while the curé of Biarritz had to pay one hundred livres for every Cagot not interred in the right place. The inhabitants indemnified the curate for all these fines.

M. de Romagne, Bishop of Tarbes, who died in seventeen hundred and sixty-eight, was the first to allow a Cagot to fill any office in the Church. To be sure, some were so spiritless as to reject office when it was offered to them, because, by so claiming their equality, they had to pay the same taxes as other men, instead of the Rancale or poll-tax levied on the Cagots; the collector of which had also a right to claim a piece of bread of a certain size for his dog at every Cagot dwelling.

Even in the present century, it has been necessary in some churches for the archdeacon of the district, followed by all his clergy, to pass out of the small door previously appropriated to the Cagots, in order to mitigate the superstition which, even so lately, made the people refuse to mingle with them in the house of God. A Cagot once played the congregation at Larroque a trick suggested by what I have just named. He slily locked the great parish-door of the church, while the greater part of the inhabitants were assisting at mass inside; put gravel into the lock itself, so as to prevent the use of any duplicate key – and had the pleasure of seeing the proud pure-blooded people file out with bended head, through the small low door used by the abhorred Cagots.

We are naturally shocked at discovering, from facts such as these, the causeless rancour with which innocent and industrious people were so recently persecuted. The moral of the history of the accursed race may, perhaps, be best conveyed in the words of an epitaph on Mrs. Mary Hand, who lies buried in the churchyard of Stratford-on-Avon:

> 'What faults you saw in me,
>   Pray strive to shun;
> And look at home; there's
>   Something to be done.'

THE DOOM OF THE GRIFFITHS

THE DOOM OF THE GRIFFITHS

CHAPTER I

I have always been much interested by the traditions which are scattered up and down North Wales relating to Owen Glendower (Owain Glendwr is the national spelling of the name), and I fully enter into the feeling which makes the Welsh peasant still look upon him as the hero of his country. There was great joy among many of the inhabitants of the principality, when the subject of the Welsh prize poem at Oxford, some fifteen or sixteen years ago, was announced to be 'Owain Glendwr.' It was the most proudly national subject that had been given for years.

Perhaps some may not be aware that this redoubted chieftain is, even in the present days of enlightenment, as famous among his illiterate countrymen for his magical powers as for his patriotism. He says himself – or Shakespeare says it for him, which is much the same thing:

> 'At my nativity
> The front of heaven was full of fiery shapes
> Of burning cressets . . .
> . . . I can call spirits from the vasty deep.'

And few among the lower orders in the principality would think of asking Hotspur's irreverent question in reply.

Among other traditions preserved relative to this part of the Welsh hero's character, is the old family prophecy which gives title to this tale. When Sir David Gam, 'as black a traitor as if he had been born in Bluith', sought to murder Owen at Machynlleth, there was one with him whose name Glendwr little dreamed of having associated with his enemies. Rhys ap Gryfydd, his 'old familiar friend,' his relation, his more than brother, had consented unto his blood. Sir David Gam might be forgiven, but one whom he had loved, and who had betrayed him, could never be forgiven. Glendwr was too deeply read in the human heart to kill him. No, he let him live on, the loathing and scorn of his compatriots, and the victim of bitter remorse. The mark of Cain was upon him.

But before he went forth – while he yet stood a prisoner, cowering beneath his conscience before Owain Glendwr – that chieftain passed a doom upon him and his race:

'I doom thee to live, because I know thou wilt pray for death. Thou shalt live on beyond the natural term of the life of man, the scorn of all good men. The very children shall point to thee with hissing tongue, and say, "There goes one who would have shed a brother's blood!" For I loved thee more than a brother, O Rhys ap Gryfydd! Thou shalt live on to see all of thy house, except the weakling in arms, perish by the sword. Thy race shall be accursed. Each generation shall see their lands melt away like snow; yea, their wealth shall vanish, though they may labour night and day to heap up gold. And when nine generations have passed from the face of the earth, thy blood shall no longer flow in the veins of any human being. In those days the last male of thy race shall avenge me. The son shall slay the father.'

Such was the traditionary account of Owain Glendwr's speech to his once-trusted friend. And it was declared that the doom had been fulfilled in all things; that, live in as miserly a manner as they would, the Griffiths never were wealthy and prosperous – indeed, that their worldly stock diminished without any visible cause.

But the lapse of many years had almost deadened the wonder-inspiring power of the whole curse. It was only brought forth from the hoards of Memory when some untoward event happened to the Griffiths family; and in the eighth generation the faith in the prophecy was nearly destroyed, by the marriage of the Griffiths of that day to a Miss Owen, who, unexpectedly, by the death of a brother, became an heiress – to no considerable amount, to be sure, but enough to make the prophecy appear reversed. The heiress and her husband removed from his small patrimonial estate in Merionethshire, to her heritage in Caernarvonshire, and for a time the prophecy lay dormant.

If you go from Tremadoc to Criccaeth, you pass by the parochial church of Ynysynhanarn, situated in a boggy valley running from the mountains, which shoulder up to the Rivals, down to Cardigan Bay. This tract of land has every appearance of having been redeemed at no distant period of time from the sea, and has all the desolate rankness often attendant upon such marshes. But the valley beyond, similar in character, had yet more of gloom at the time of which I write. In the higher part there were large plantations of firs, set too closely to attain any size, and remaining stunted in height and scrubby in appearance. Indeed, many of the smaller and more weakly had died, and the bark had fallen down on the brown soil neglected and unnoticed. These trees had a ghastly appearance, with their white trunks, seen by the dim light which struggled through the thick boughs above. Nearer to the sea, the valley assumed a more open, though hardly a more cheerful character; it looked dark and was overhung by sea-fog through the greater part of the year; and even a farmhouse, which usually imparts something of cheerfulness to a landscape, failed to do so here. This valley formed the greater part of the estate to which Owen Griffiths became entitled by right of his wife. In the higher part of the valley was situated the family mansion, or rather dwelling-house; for 'mansion' is too grand a word to apply to the clumsy, but substantially-built Bodowen. It was square and heavy-looking, with just that much pretension to ornament necessary to distinguish it from the mere farmhouse.

In this dwelling Mrs. Owen Griffiths bore her husband two sons – Llewellyn, the future Squire, and Robert, who was early destined for the Church. The only difference in their situation, up to the time when Robert was entered at Jesus College, was that the elder was invariably indulged by all around him, while Robert was thwarted and indulged by turns; that Llewellyn never learned anything from the poor Welsh parson, who was nominally his private tutor; while occasionally Squire Griffiths made a great point of enforcing Robert's diligence, telling him that, as he had his bread to earn, he must pay attention to his learning. There is no knowing how far the very irregular education he had received would have carried Robert through his college examinations; but, luckily for him in this respect, before such a trial of his learning came round, he heard of the death of his elder brother, after a short illness, brought on by a hard drinking-bout. Of course, Robert was summoned home; and it seemed quite as much of course, now that there was no necessity for him to 'earn his bread by his learning,' that he should not return to Oxford. So the half-educated, but not unintelligent, young man continued at home, during the short remainder of his parents' lifetime.

His was not an uncommon character. In general he was mild, indolent, and easily managed; but once thoroughly roused, his passions were vehement and fearful. He seemed, indeed, almost afraid of himself, and in common hardly dared to give way to justifiable anger – so much did he dread losing his self-control. Had he been judiciously educated, he would, probably, have distinguished himself in those branches of literature which call for taste and imagination, rather than for any exertion of reflection or judgment. As it was, his literary taste showed itself in making collections of Cambrian anti-quities of every description, till his stock of Welsh MSS. would have excited the envy of Dr. Pugh himself, had he been alive at the time of which I write.

There is one characteristic of Robert Griffiths whch I have omitted to note, and which was peculiar among his class. He was no hard drinker; whether it was that his head was easily affected, or that his partially-refined taste led him to dislike intoxication and its attendant circumstances, I cannot say; but at five-and-twenty Robert Griffiths was habitually sober – a thing so rare in Llyn, that he was almost shunned as a churlish, unsociable being, and passed much of his time in solitude.

About this time, he had to appear in some case that was tried at the Caernarvon assizes and, while there, was a guest at the house of his agent, a shrewd, sensible Welsh attorney, with one daughter, who had charms enough to captivate Robert Griffiths. Though he remained only a few days at her father's house, they were sufficient to decide his affections, and short was the period allowed to elapse before he brought home a mistress to Bodowen. The new Mrs. Griffiths was a gentle, yielding person, full of love toward her husband, of whom, nevertheless, she stood something in awe, partly arising from the difference in their ages, partly from his devoting much time to studies of which she could understand nothing.

She soon made him the father of a blooming little daughter, called Augharad after her mother. Then there came several uneventful years in the household of Bodowen: and, when the old women had one and all declared that the cradle would not rock again, Mrs. Griffiths bore the son and heir. His birth was soon followed by his mother's death: she had been ailing and low-spirited during her pregnancy, and she seemed to lack the buoyancy of body and mind requisite to bring her round after her time of trial. Her husband, who loved her all the more from having few other claims on his affections, was deeply grieved by her early death, and his only comforter was the sweet little boy whom she had left behind. That part of the squire's character, which was so tender, and almost feminine, seemed called forth by the helpless situation of the little infant, who stretched out his arms to his father with the same earnest cooing that happier children make use of to their mother alone. Augharad was almost neglected, while the little Owen was king of the house; still, next to his father, none tended him so lovingly as his sister. She was so accustomed to give way to him that it was no longer a hardship. By night and by day Owen was the constant companion of his father, and increasing years seemed only to confirm the custom. It was an unnatural life for the child, seeing no bright little faces peering into his own (for Augharad was, as I said before, five or six years older, and her face, poor motherless girl! was often anything but bright), hearing no din of clear ringing voices, but day after day sharing the otherwise solitary hours of his father, whether in the dim room surrounded by wizard-like antiquities, or pattering his little feet to keep up with his 'tada' in his mountain rambles or shooting excursions. When the pair came to some little foaming brook, where the stepping-stones were far and wide, the father carried his little boy across with the tenderest care; when the lad was weary, they rested, he cradled in his father's arms, or the Squire would lift him up and carry him to his home again. The boy was indulged (for his father felt flattered by the desire) in his wish of sharing his meals and keeping the same hours. All this indulgence did not render Owen unamiable, but it made him wilful, and not a happy child. He had a thoughtful look, not common to the face of a young boy. He knew no games, no merry sports; his information was of an imaginative and speculative character. His father delighted to interest him in his own studies, without considering how far they were healthy for so young a mind.

Of course Squire Griffiths was not unaware of the prophecy which was to be fulfilled in his generation. He would occasionally refer to it when among his friends, with sceptical levity; but in truth it lay nearer to his heart than he chose to acknowledge. His strong imagination rendered him peculiarly impressionable on such subjects; while his judgment, seldom exercised or fortified by severe thought, could not prevent his continually recurring to it. He used to gaze on the half-sad countenance of the child, who sat looking up into his face with his large dark eyes, so fondly yet so inquiringly, till the old legend swelled around his heart, and became too painful for him not to require sympathy. Besides, the overpowering love he bore to the child seemed to demand fuller vent than tender words; it made him like, yet dread, to upbraid its object for the fearful contrast foretold. Still Squire Griffiths told the legend, in a half-jesting manner, to his little son, when they were roaming over the wild heaths in the autumn days, 'the saddest of the year,' or while they sat in the oak-wainscoted room, surrounded by mysterious relics that gleamed strangely forth by the flickering fire-light. The legend was wrought into the boy's mind, and he would crave, yet tremble, to hear it told over and over again, while the words were intermingled with caresses and questions as to his love. Occasionally his loving words and actions were cut short by his father's light yet bitter speech – 'Get thee away, my lad; thou knowest not what is to come of all this love.'

When Augharad was seventeen, and Owen eleven or twelve, the rector of the parish in which Bodowen was situated endeavoured to prevail on Squire Griffiths to send the boy to school. Now, this rector had many tastes in common with his parishioner, and was his only intimate; and, by repeated arguments, he succeeded in convincing the Squire that the unnatural life Owen was leading was in every way injurious. Unwillingly was the father brought to part from his son; but he did at length send him to the Grammar School at Bangor, then under the management of an excellent classic. Here Owen showed that he had more talents than the rector had given him credit for, when he affirmed that the lad had been completely stupefied by the life he led at Bodowen. He bade fair to do credit to the school in the peculiar branch of learning for which it was famous. But he was not popular among his schoolfellows. He was wayward, though, to a certain degree, generous and unselfish; he was reserved but gentle, except when the tremendous bursts of passion (similar in character to those of his father) forced their way.

On his return from school one Christmas-time, when he had been a year or so at Bangor, he was stunned by hearing that the undervalued Augharad was about to be married to a gentleman of South Wales, residing near Aberystwith. Boys seldom appreciate their sisters; but Owen thought of the many slights with which he had requited the patient Augharad, and he gave way to bitter regrets, which, with a selfish want of control over his words, he kept expressing to his father, until the Squire was thoroughly hurt and chagrined at the repeated exclaimations of 'What shall we do when Augharad is gone?' 'How dull we shall be when Augharad is married!' Owen's holidays were prolonged a few weeks, in order that he might be present at the wedding; and when all the festivities were over, and the bride and bridegroom had left Bodowen, the boy and his father really felt how much they missed the quiet, loving Augharad. She had performed so many thoughtful, noiseless little offices, on which their daily comfort depended; and, now she was gone, the household seemed to miss the spirit that peacefully kept it in order; the servants roamed about in search of commands and directions; the rooms had no longer the unobtrusive ordering of taste to make them cheerful; the very fires burned dim, and were always sinking down into dull heaps of grey ashes. Altogether Owen did not regret his return to Bangor, and this also the mortified parent observed. Squire Griffiths was a selfish parent.

Letters in those days were a rare occurrence. Owen usually received one during his half-yearly absences from home, and occasionally his father paid him a visit. This half-year the boy had no visit, nor even a letter, till very near the time of his leaving school, and then he was astounded by the intelligence that his father was married again.

Then came one of his paroxysms of rage; the more disastrous in its effects upon his character because it could find no vent in action. Independently of slight to the memory of his first wife, which children are so apt to fancy such an action implies, Owen had hitherto considered himself (and with justice) the first object of his father's life. They had been so much to each other; and now a shapeless, but too real, something had come between him and his father for ever. He felt as if his permission should have been asked, as if he should have been consulted. Certainly he ought to have been told of the intended event. So the Squire felt, and hence his constrained letter, which had so much increased the bitterness of Owen's feelings.

With all this anger, when Owen saw his stepmother, he thought he had never seen so beautiful a woman for her age; for she was no longer in the bloom of youth, being a widow when his father married her. Her manners, to the Welsh lad, who had seen little of female grace among the families of the few antiquarians with whom his father visited, were so fascinating that he watched her with a sort of breathless admiration. Her measured grace, her faultless movements, her tones of voice, sweet, till the ear was sated with their sweetness, made Owen less angry at his father's marriage. Yet he felt, more than ever, that the cloud was between him and his father; that the hasty letter he had sent in answer to the announcement of his wedding was not forgotten, although no allusion was ever made to it. He was no longer his father's confidant – hardly ever his father's companion; for the newly-married wife was all in all to the Squire, and his son felt himself almost a cipher, where he had so long been everything. The lady herself had ever the softest consideration for her stepson; almost too obtrusive was the attention paid to his wishes; but still he fancied that the heart had no part in the winning advances. There was a watchful glance of the eye that Owen once or twice caught when she had imagined herself unobserved, and many other nameless little circumstances, that gave him a strong feeling of want of sincerity in his stepmother. Mrs. Owen brought with her into the family her little child by her first husband, a boy nearly three years old. He was one of those selfish, observant, mocking children, over whose feelings you seem to have no control; agile and mischievous, his little practical jokes, at first performed in ignorance of the pain he gave, but afterward proceeding to a malicious pleasure in suffering, really seemed to afford some ground to the superstitious notion of some of the common people that he was a fairy changeling.

Years passed on; and as Owen grew older he became more observant. He saw, even in his occasional visits at home (for from school he had passed on to college), that a great change had taken place in the outward manifestations of his father's character; and, by degrees, Owen traced this change to the influence of his stepmother; so slight, so imperceptible to the common observer, yet so resistless in its effects. Squire Griffiths caught up his wife's humbly advanced opinions, and, unawares to himself, adopted them as his own, defying all argument and opposition. It was the same with her wishes; they met their fulfilment, from the extreme and delicate art with which she insinuated them into her husband's mind as his own. She sacrificed the show of authority for the power. At last, when Owen perceived some oppressive act in his father's conduct towards his dependants, or some unaccountable thwarting of his own wishes, he fancied he saw his stepmother's secret influence thus displayed, however much she might regret the injustice of his father's actions in her conversations with him when they were alone. His father was fast losing his temperate habits, and frequent intoxication soon took its usual effect upon the temper. Yet even here was the spell of his wife upon him. Before her he placed a restraint upon his passion, yet she was perfectly aware of his irritable disposition, and directed it hither and thither with the same apparent ignorance of the tendency of her words.

Meanwhile Owen's situation became peculiarly mortifying to a youth whose early remembrances afforded such a contrast to his present state. As a child, he had been elevated to the consequence of a man before his years gave any mental check to the selfishness which such conduct was likely to engender; he could remember when his will was law to the servants and dependants, and his sympathy necessary to his father; now he was as a cipher in his father's house; and the Squire, estranged in the first instance by a feeling of the injury he had done his son in not sooner acquainting him with his purposed marriage, seemed rather to avoid than to seek him as a companion, and too frequently showed the most utter indifference to the feelings and wishes which a young man of a high and independant spirit might be supposed to indulge.

Perhaps Owen was not fully aware of the force of all these circumstances; for an actor in a family drama is seldom unimpassioned enough to be perfectly observant. But he became moody and soured; brooding over his unloved existence, and craving with a human heart after sympathy.

This feeling took more full possession of his mind when he had left college, and returned home to lead an idle and purposeless life. As the heir, there was no worldly necessity for exertion: his father was too much of a Welsh squire to dream of the moral necessity; and he himself had not sufficient strength of mind to decide at once upon abandoning a place and mode of life which abounded in daily mortifications. Yet to this course his judgment was slowly tending, when some circumstances occurred to detain him at Bodowen.

It was not to be expected that harmony would long be preserved, even in appearance, between an unguarded and soured young man, such as Owen, and his wary stepmother, when he had once left college, and come, not as a visitor, but as the heir, to his father's house. Some cause of difference occurred, where the woman subdued her hidden anger sufficiently to become convinced that Owen was not entirely the dupe she had believed him to be. Henceforward there was no peace between them. Not in vulgar altercations did this show itself; but in moody reserve on Owen's part, and in undisguised and contemptuous pursuance of her own plans by his stepmother. Bodowen was no longer a place where, if Owen was not loved or attended to, he could at least find peace and care for himself: he was thwarted at every step, and in every wish, by his father's desire, apparently, while the wife sat by with a smile of triumph on her beautiful lips.

So Owen went forth at the early day-dawn, sometimes roaming about on the shore or the upland, shooting or fishing, as the season might be, but oftener 'stretched in indolent repose' on the short, sweet grass, indulging in gloomy and morbid reveries. He would fancy that this mortified state of existence was a dream, a horrible dream, from which he should awake and find himself again the sole object and darling of his father. And then he would start up and strive to shake off the incubus. There was the molten sunset of his childish memory; the gorgeous crimson piles of glory in the west, fading away into the cold calm light of the rising moon, while here and there a cloud floated across the western heaven, like a seraph's wing, in its flaming beauty; the earth was the same as in his childhood's days, full of gentle evening sounds, and the harmonies of twilight – the breeze came sweeping low over the heather and bluebells by his side, and the turf was sending up its evening incense of perfume. But life, and heart, and hope were changed for ever since those bygone days!

Or he would seat himself in a favourite niche of the rocks on Moel Gêst, hidden by the stunted growth of the whitty, or mountain-ash, from general observation, with a rich-tinted cushion of stone-crop for his feet, and a straight precipice of rock rising just above. Here would he sit for hours, gazing idly at the bay below with its background of purple hills, and the little fishing-sail on its bosom, showing white in the sunbeam, and gliding on in such harmony with the quiet beauty of the glassy sea; or he would pull out an old school-volume, his companion for years, and in morbid accordance with the dark legend that still lurked in the recesses of his mind – a shape of gloom in those innermost haunts awaiting its time to come forth in distinct outline – would he turn to the old Greek dramas which treat of a family fore-doomed by an avenging Fate. The worn page opened of itself at the play of the Œdipus Tyrannus, and Owen dwelt with the craving disease upon the prophecy so nearly resembling that which concerned himself. With his consciousness of neglect, there was a sort of self-flattery in the consequence which the legend gave him. He almost wondered how they durst, with slights and insults, thus provoke the Avenger.

The days drifted onward. Often he would vehemently pursue some sylvan sport, till thought and feeling were lost in the violence of bodily exertion. Occasionally his evenings were spent at a small public-house, such as stood by the unfrequented wayside, where the welcome – hearty, though bought – seemed so strongly to contrast with the gloomy negligence of home – unsympathising home.

One evening (Owen might be four or five-and-twenty), wearied with a day's shooting on the Clenneny Moors, he passed by the open door of 'The Goat' at Penmorfa. The light and the cheeriness within tempted him, poor self-exhausted man! as it has done many a one more wretched in worldly circumstances, to step in, and take his evening meal where at least his presence was of some consequence. It was a busy day in that little hostel. A flock of sheep, amounting to some hundreds, had arrived at Penmorfa, on their road to England, and thronged the space before the house. Inside was the shrewd, kind-hearted hostess, butling to and fro, with merry greetings for every tired drover who was to pass the night in her house, while the sheep were penned in a field close by. Ever and anon, she kept attending to the second crowd of guests, who were celebrating a rural wedding in her house. It was busy work to Martha Thomas, yet her smile never flagged; and when Owen Griffiths had finished his evening meal she was there, ready with a hope that it had done him good, and was to his mind, and a word of intelligence that the wedding-folk were about to dance in the kitchen, and the harper was the famous Edward of Corwen.

Owen, partly from good-natured compliance with his hostess's implied wish, and partly from curiosity, lounged to the passage which led to the kitchen – not the every-day working, cooking kitchen, which was behind, but a good-sized room, where the mistress sat when her work was done, and the country people were commonly entertained at such merry-makings as the present. The lintels of the door formed a frame for the animated picture which Owen saw within, as he leaned against the wall in the dark passage. The red light of the fire, with every now and then a falling piece of turf sending forth a fresh blaze, shone full upon four young men who were dancing a measure something like a Scotch reel, keeping admirable time in their rapid movements to the capital tune the harper was playing. They had their hats on when Owen first took his stand, but as they grew more and more animated they flung them away, and presently their shoes were kicked off with like disregard to the spot where they might happen to alight. Shouts of applause followed any remarkable exertion of agility, in which each seemed to try to excel his companions. At length, wearied and exhausted, they sat down, and the harper gradually changed to one of those wild, inspiring national airs for which he was so famous. The thronged audience sat earnest and breathless, and you might have heard a pin drop, except when some maiden passed hurriedly, with flaring candle and busy look, through to the real kitchen beyond. When he had finished his beautiful theme of *The March of the Men of Harlech*, he changed the measure again to *Tri chant o' bunnan* (Three hundred pounds) and immediately a most unmusical-looking man began chanting 'Pennillion,' or a sort of recitative stanzas, which were soon taken up by another; and this amusement lasted so long that Owen grew weary, and was thinking of retreating from his post by the door, when some little bustle was occasioned, on the opposite side of the room, by the entrance of a middle-aged man, and a young girl, apparently his daughter. The man advanced to the bench occupied by the seniors of the party, who welcomed him with the usual pretty Welsh greeting, *'Pa sut mae dy galon?'* ('How is thy heart?') and drinking his health passed on to him the cup of excellent *cwrw*. The girl, evidently a village belle, was as warmly greeted by the young men, while the girls eyed her rather askance with a half-jealous look, which Owen set down to the score of her extreme prettiness. Like most Welsh women, she was of middle size as to height, but beautifully made, with the most perfect yet delicate roundness in every limb. Her little mob-cap was carefully adjusted to a face which was excessively pretty, though it never could be called handsome. It also was round, with the slightest tendency to the oval shape, richly coloured, though somewhat olive in complexion, with dimples in cheek and chin, and the most scarlet lips Owen had ever seen, that were too short to meet over the small pearly teeth. The nose was the most defective feature; but the eyes were splendid. They were so long, so lustrous, yet at times so very soft under their thick fringe of eyelash! The nut-brown hair was carefully braided beneath the border of delicate lace: it was evident the little village beauty knew how to make the most of all her attractions, for the gay colours which were displayed in her neckerchief were in complete harmony with the complexion.

Owen was much attracted, while yet he was amused, by the evident coquetry the girl displayed, collecting around her a whole bevy of young fellows, for each of whom she seemed to have some gay speech, some attractive look or action. In a few minutes young Griffiths of Bodowen was at her side, brought thither by a variety of idle motives, and as her undivided attention was given to the Welsh heir, her admirers, one by one, dropped off, to seat themselves by some less fascinating but more attentive fair one. The more Owen conversed with the girl, the more he was taken; she had more wit and talent than he had fancied possible; a self-abandon and thoughtfulness, to boot, that seemed full of charms; and then her voice was so clear and sweet, and her actions so full of grace, that Owen was fascinated before he was well aware, and kept looking into her bright, blushing face, till her uplifted flashing eye fell beneath his earnest gaze.

While it thus happened that they were silent – she from confusion at the unexpected warmth of his admiration, he from an unconsciousness of anything but the beautiful changes in her flexile countenance – the man whom Owen took for her father came up and addressed some observation to his daughter, from whence he glided into some commonplace though respectful remark to Owen; and at length, engaging him in some slight, local conversation, he led the way to the account of a spot on the peninsula of Penthryn, where teal abounded, and concluded with begging Owen to allow him to show him the exact place, saying that whenever the young Squire felt so inclined, if he would honour him by a call at his house, he would take him across in his boat. While Owen listened, his attention was not so much absorbed as to be unaware that the little beauty at his side was refusing one or two who endeavoured to draw her from her place by invitations to dance. Flattered by his own construction of her refusals, he again directed all his attention to her, till she was called away by her father, who was leaving the scene of festivity. Before he left he reminded Owen of his promise, and added:

'Perhaps, sir, you do not know me. My name is Ellis Pritchard, and I live at Ty Glas, on this side of Moel Gêst; any one can point it out to you.'

When the father and daughter had left, Owen slowly prepared for his ride home; but, encountering the hostess, he could not resist asking a few questions relative to Ellis Pritchard and his pretty daughter. She answered shortly but respectfully, and then said, rather hesitatingly:

'Master Griffiths, you know the triad, *Tri pheth tebyg y naill i'r llall, ysgnbwr heb yd, mail deg heb ddiawd, a merch deg heb ei geirda*' (Three things are alike: a fine barn without corn, a fine cup without drink, a fine woman without her reputation).' She hastily quitted him, and Owen rode slowly to his unhappy home.

Ellis Pritchard, half farmer and half fisherman, was shrewd, and keen, and worldly; yet he was good-natured, and sufficiently generous to have become rather a popular man among his equals. He had been struck with the young Squire's attention to his pretty daughter, and was not insensible to the advantages to be derived from it. Nest would not be the first peasant-girl, by any means, who had been transplanted to a Welsh manor-house, as its mistress; and, accordingly, her father had shrewdly given the admiring young man some pretext for further opportunities of seeing her.

As for Nest herself, she had somewhat of her father's worldliness, and was fully alive to the superior station of her new admirer, and quite prepared to slight all her old sweethearts on his account. But then she had something more of feeling in her reckoning; she had not been insensible to the earnest yet comparatively refined homage which Owen paid her; she had noticed his expressive and occasionally handsome countenance with admiration, and was flattered by his so immediately singling her out from her companions. As to the hint which Martha Thomas had thrown out, it is enough to say that Nest was very giddy, and that she was motherless. She had high spirits and a great love of admiration, or, to use a softer term, she loved to please; men, women, and children, all, she delighted to gladden with her smile and voice. She coquetted, and flirted, and went to the extreme lengths of Welsh courtship, till the seniors of the village shook their heads, and cautioned their daughters against her acquaintance. If not absolutely guilty, she had too frequently been on the verge of guilt.

Even at the time, Martha Thomas's hint made but little impression on Owen, for his senses were otherwise occupied; but in a few days the recollection thereof had wholly died away, and one warm glorious summer's day he bent his steps towards Ellis Pritchard's with a beating heart; for, except some very slight flirtations at Oxford, Owen had never been touched; his thoughts, his fancy, had been otherwise engaged.

Ty Glas was built against one of the lower rocks of Moel Gêst, which, indeed, formed a side to the low, lengthy house. The materials of the cottage were the shingly stones which had fallen from above, plastered rudely together, with deep recesses for the small oblong windows. Altogether, the exterior was much ruder than Owen had expected; but inside there seemed no lack of comforts. The house was divided into two apartments, one large, roomy and dark, into which Owen entered immediately; and before the blushing Nest came from the inner chamber (for she had seen the young Squire coming, and hastily gone to make some alteration in her dress), he had had time to look around him, and note the various little particulars of the room. Beneath the window (which commanded a magnificent view) was an oaken dresser, replete with drawers and cupboards, and brightly polished to a rich dark colour. In the farther part of the room Owen could at first distinguish little, entering as he did from the glaring sunlight; but he soon saw that there were two oaken beds, closed up after the manner of the Welsh: in fact, the dormitories of Ellis Pritchard and the man who served under him, both on sea and on land. There was the large wheel used for spinning wool, left standing on the middle of the floor, as if in use only a few minutes before; and around the ample chimney hung flitches of bacon, dried kids'-flesh, and fish, that was in process of smoking for winter's store.

Before Nest had shyly dared to enter, her father, who had been mending his nets down below, and seen Owen winding up to the house, came in and gave him a hearty yet respectful welcome; and then Nest, downcast and blushing, full of the consciousness which her father's advice and conversation had not failed to inspire, ventured to join them. To Owen's mind this reserve and shyness gave her new charms.

It was too bright, too hot, too anything to think of going to shoot teal till later in the day, and Owen was delighted to accept a hesitating invitation to share the noonday meal. Some ewe-milk cheese, very hard and dry, oat-cake, slips of the dried kid's-flesh broiled, after having been previously soaked in water for a few minutes, delicious butter and fresh butter-milk, with a liquor called *'diod griafol'* (made from the berries of the *Sorbus aucuparia*, infused in water and then fermented), composed the frugal repast; but there was something so clean and neat, and withal such a true welcome, that Owen had seldom enjoyed a meal so much. Indeed, at that time of day the Welsh squires differed from the farmers more in the plenty and rough abundance of their manner of living than in the refinement of style of their table.

At the present day, down in Llyn, the Welsh gentry are not a wit behind their Saxon equals in the expensive elegances of life; but then (when there was but one pewter-service in all Northumberland) there was nothing in Ellis Pritchard's mode of living that grated on the young Squire's sense of refinement.

Little was said by that young pair of wooers during the meal; the father had all the conversation to himself, apparently heedless of the ardent looks and inattentive mien of his guest. As Owen became more serious in his feelings, he grew more timid in their expression, and at night, when they returned from their shooting-excursion, the caress he gave Nest was almost as bashfully offered as received.

This was but the first of a series of days devoted to Nest in reality, though at first he thought some little disguise of his object was necessary. The past, the future, was all forgotten in those happy days of love.

And every worldly plan, every womanly wile was put in practice by Ellis Pritchard and his daughter, to render his visits agreeable and alluring. Indeed, the very circumstance of his being welcome was enough to attract the poor young man, to whom the feeling so produced was new and full of charms. He left a home where the certainty of being thwarted made him chary in expressing his wishes; where no tones of love ever fell

on his ear, save those addressed to others; where his presence
or absence was a matter of utter indifference; and when he
entered Ty Glas, all, down to the little cur which, with
clamorous barkings, claimed a part of his attention, seemed to
rejoice. His account of his day's employment found a willing
listener in Ellis; and when he passed on to Nest, busy at her
wheel or at her churn, the deepened colour, the conscious eye,
and the gradual yielding of herself up to his lover-like caress,
had worlds of charms. Ellis Pritchard was a tenant on the
Bodowen estate, and therefore had reasons in plenty for
wishing to keep the young Squire's visits secret; and Owen,
unwilling to disturb the sunny calm of these halcyon days by
any storm at home, was ready to use all the artifice which Ellis
suggested as to the mode of his calls at Ty Glas. Nor was he
unaware of the probable, nay, the hoped-for termination of
these repeated days of happiness. He was quite conscious that
the father wished for nothing better than the marriage of his
daughter to the heir of Bodowen; and when Nest had hidden
her face in his neck, which was encircled by her clasping arms,
and murmured into his ear her acknowledgment of love, he felt
only too desirous of finding some one to love him for ever.
Though not highly principled, he would not have tried to
obtain Nest on other terms save those of marriage: he did so
pine after enduring love, and fancied he should have bound
her heart for evermore to his, when they had taken the
solemn oaths of matrimony.

There was no great difficulty attending a secret marriage at
such a place and at such a time. One gusty autumn day, Ellis
ferried them round Penthryn to Llandutrwyn, and there saw
his little Nest become future Lady of Bodowen.

How often do we see giddy, coquetting, restless girls
become sobered by marriage? A great object in life is decided,
one on which their thoughts have been running in all their
vagaries; and they seem to verify the beautiful fable of
Undine. A new soul beams out in the gentleness and repose of
their future life. An undescribable softness and tenderness
takes the place of the wearying vanity of their former
endeavours to attract admiration. Something of this sort
happened to Nest Pritchard. If at first she had been anxious to
attract the young Squire of Bodowen, long before her

marriage this feeling had merged into a truer love than she had ever felt before; and now that he was her own, her husband, her whole soul was bent toward making him amends, as far as in her lay, for the misery which, with a woman's tact, she saw that he had to endure at his home. Her greetings were abounding in delicately-expressed love; her study of his tastes unwearying, in the arrangement of her dress, her time, her very thoughts.

No wonder that he looked back on his wedding-day with a thankfulness which is seldom the result of unequal marriages. No wonder that his heart beat aloud as formerly when he wound up the little path to Ty Glas, and saw – keen though the winter's wind might be – that Nest was standing out at the door to watch for his dimly-seen approach, while the candle flared in the little window as a beacon to guide him aright.

The angry words and unkind actions of home fell deadened on his heart; he thought of the love that was surely his, and of the new promise of love that a short time would bring forth; and he could almost have smiled at the impotent efforts to disturb his peace.

A few more months, and the young father was greeted by a feeble little cry, when he hastily entered Ty Glas, one morning early, in consequence of a summons conveyed mysteriously to Bodowen; and the pale mother, smiling, and feebly holding up her babe to its father's kiss, seemed to him even more lovely than the bright, gay Nest who had won his heart at the little inn of Penmorfa.

But the curse was at work! The fulfilment of the prophecy was nigh at hand!

CHAPTER II

It was the autumn after the birth of their boy; it had been a glorious summer, with bright, hot, sunny weather; and now the year was fading away as seasonably into mellow days, with mornings of silver mists and clear frosty nights. The blooming look of the time of flowers was past and gone; but instead there were even richer tints abroad in the sun-coloured leaves, the lichens, the golden-blossomed furze; if it was the time of fading, there was a glory in the decay.

Nest, in her loving anxiety to surround her dwelling with every charm for her husband's sake, had turned gardener, and the little corners of the rude court before the house were filled with many a delicate mountain-flower, transplanted more for its beauty than its rarity. The sweetbrier bush may even yet be seen, old and grey, which she and Owen planted, a green slipling, beneath the window of her little chamber. In those moments Owen forgot all besides the present; all the cares and griefs he had known in the past, and all that might await him of woe and death in the future. The boy, too, was as lovely a child as the fondest parent was ever blessed with, and crowed with delight, and clapped his little hands, as his mother held him in her arms at the cottage door to watch his father's ascent up the rough path that led to Ty Glas, one bright autumnal morning; and when the three entered the house together, it was difficult to say which was the happiest. Owen carried his boy, and tossed and played with him, while Nest sought out some little article of work, and seated herself on the dresser beneath the window, where, now busily plying the needle, and then again looking at her husband, she eagerly told him the little pieces of domestic intelligence, the winning ways of the child, the result of yesterday's fishing, and such of the gossip of Penmorfa as came to the ears of the now retired Nest. She noticed that, when she mentioned any little circumstance which bore the slightest reference to Bodowen, her husband appeared chafed and uneasy, and at last avoided anything that might in the least remind him of home. In truth, he had been suffering much of late from the irritability of his father, shown in trifles to be sure, but not the less galling on that account.

While they were thus talking, and caressing each other and the child, a shadow darkened the room, and before they could catch a glimpse of the object that had occasioned it, it vanished, and Squire Griffiths lifted the door-latch, and stood before them. He stood and looked – first on his son, so different, in his buoyant expression of content and enjoyment, with his noble child in his arms, like a proud and happy father, as he was, from the depressed, moody young man he too often appeared at Bodowen; then on Nest – poor, trembling, sickened Nest! – who dropped her work, but yet durst not stir from her seat on the dresser, while she looked to her husband as if for protection from his father.

The Squire was silent, as he glared from one to the other, his features white with restrained passion. When he spoke, his words came most distinct in their forced composure. It was to his son he addressed himself:

'That woman! who is she?'

Owen hesitated one moment, and then replied, in a steady, yet quiet, voice:

'Father, that woman is my wife.'

He would have added some apology for the long concealment of his marriage; have appealed to his father's forgiveness; but the foam flew from Squire Owen's lips as he burst forth with invective against Nest:

'You have married her! It is as they told me! Married Nest Pritchard, *yr buten!* And you stand there as if you had not disgraced yourself for ever and ever with your accursed wiving! And the fair harlot sits there, in her mocking modesty, practising the mimming airs that will become her state as future Lady of Bodowen. But I will move heaven and earth before that false woman darken the doors of my father's house as mistress!'

All this was said with such rapidity that Owen had no time for the words that thronged to his lips. 'Father!' (he burst forth at length) 'Father, whosoever told you that Nest Pritchard was a harlot told you a lie as false as hell! Ay! a lie as false as hell!' he added, in a voice of thunder, while he advanced a step or two nearer to the Squire. And then, in a lower tone, he said:

'She is as pure as your own wife; nay, God help me! as the dear, precious mother who brought me forth, and then left me – with no refuge in a mother's heart – to struggle on through life alone. I tell you Nest is as pure as that dear, dead mother!'

'Fool – poor fool!'

At this moment the child – the little Owen – who had kept gazing from one countenance to the other, and with earnest look, trying to understand what had brought the fierce glare into the face where till now he had read nothing but love, in some way attracted the Squire's attention, and increased his wrath.

'Yes,' he continued, 'poor, weak fool that you are, hugging the child of another as if it were your own offspring!' Owen involuntarily caressed the affrighted child, and half smiled at the implication of his father's words. This the Squire perceived, and raising his voice to a scream of rage, he went on:

'I bid you, if you call yourself my son, to cast away that miserable, shameless woman's offspring; cast it away this instant — this instant!'

In this ungovernable rage, seeing that Owen was far from complying with his command, he snatched the poor infant from the loving arms that held it, and throwing it to his mother, left the house inarticulate with fury.

Nest — who had been pale and still as marble during this terrible dialogue, looking on and listening as if fascinated by the words that smote her heart — opened her arms to receive and cherish her precious babe; but the boy was not destined to reach the white refuge of her breast. The furious action of the Squire had been almost without aim, and the infant fell against the sharp edge of the dresser down on to the stone floor.

Owen sprang up to take the child, but he lay so still, so motionless, that the awe of death came over the father, and he stooped down to gaze more closely. At that moment, the upturned, filmy eyes rolled convulsively — a spasm passed along the body — and the lips, yet warm with kissing, quivered into everlasting rest.

A word from her husband told Nest all. She slid down from her seat, and lay by her little son as corpse-like as he, unheeding all the agonising endearments and passionate adjurations of her husband. And that poor, desolate husband and father! Scarce one little quarter of an hour, and he had been so blessed in his consciousness of love! the bright promise of many years on his infant's face, and the new, fresh soul beaming forth in its awakened intelligence. And there it was: the little clay image, that would never more gladden up at the sight of him, nor stretch forth to meet his embrace; whose inarticulate, yet most eloquent cooings might haunt him in his dreams, but would never more be heard in waking life again! And by the dead babe, almost as utterly insensate, the poor mother had fallen in a merciful faint – the slandered, heart-pierced Nest! Owen struggled against the sickness that came over him, and busied himself in vain attempts at her restoration.

It was now near noon-day, and Ellis Pritchard came home, little dreaming of the sight that awaited him; but, though stunned, he was able to take more effectual measures for his poor daughter's recovery than Owen had done.

By-and-by she showed symptoms of returning sense, and was placed in her own little bed in a darkened room, where, without ever waking to complete consciousness, she fell asleep. Then it was that her husband, suffocated by pressure of miserable thought, gently drew his hand from her tightened clasp and, printing one long soft kiss on her white waxen forehead, hastily stole out of the room, and out of the house.

Near the base of Moel Gêst – it might be a quarter of a mile from Ty Glas – was a little neglected solitary copse, wild and tangled with the trailing branches of the dog-rose and the tendrils of the white bryony. Toward the middle of this thicket lay a deep crystal pool – a clear mirror for the blue heavens above – and round the margin floated the broad green leaves of the water-lily; and, when the regal sun shone down in his noon-day glory, the flowers arose from their cool depths to welcome and greet him. The copse was musical with many sounds; the warbling of birds rejoicing in its shades, the ceaseless hum of the distant waterfall, the occasional bleating of the sheep from the mountain-top, were all blended into the delicious harmony of nature.

It had been one of Owen's favourite resorts when he had been a lonely wanderer – a pilgrim in search of love in the years gone by. And thither he went, as if by instinct, when he left Ty Glas; quelling the uprising agony till he should reach that little solitary spot.

It was the time of day when a change in the aspect of the weather so frequently takes place, and the little pool was no longer the reflection of a blue and sunny sky; it sent back the dark and slaty clouds above; and, every now and then, a rough gust shook the painted autumn leaves from their branches, and all other music was lost in the sound of the wild winds piping down from the moorlands, which lay up and beyond the clefts in the mountain-side. Presently the rain came on and beat down in torrents.

But Owen heeded it not. He sat on the dank ground, his face buried in his hands, and his whole strength, physical and mental, employed in quelling the rush of blood which rose and boiled and gurgled in his brain, as if it would madden him.

The phantom of his dead child rose ever before him, and seemed to cry aloud for vengeance. And, when the poor young man thought upon the victim whom he required in his wild longing for revenge, he shuddered, for it was his father!

Again and again he tried not to think; but still the circle of thought came round, eddying through his brain. At length he mastered his passions, and they were calm; then he forced himself to arrange some plan for the future.

He had not, in the passionate hurry of the moment, seen that his father had left the cottage before he was aware of the fatal accident that befell the child. Owen thought he had seen all; and once he planned to go to the Squire and tell him of the anguish of heart he had wrought, and awe him, as it were, by the dignity of grief. But then again he durst not – he distrusted his self-control – the old prophecy rose up in its horror – he dreaded his doom.

At last he determined to leave his father for ever; to take Nest to some distant country where she might forget her first born, and where he himself might gain a livelihood by his own exertions.

But when he tried to descend to the various little arrangements which were involved in the execution of this plan, he remembered that all his money (and in this respect Squire Griffiths was no niggard) was locked up in his escritoire at Bodowen. In vain he tried to do away with this matter-of-fact difficulty; go to Bodowen he must; and his only hope – nay, his determination – was to avoid his father.

He rose and took a by-path to Bodowen. The house looked even more gloomy and desolate than usual in the heavy downpouring rain; yet Owen gazed on it with something of regret – for, sorrowful as his days in it had been, he was about to leave it for many, many years, if not for ever. He entered by a side door opening into a passage that led to his own room, where he kept his books, his guns, his fishing tackle, his writing materials, *et cetera*.

Here he hurriedly began to select the few articles he intended to take; for, besides the dread of interruption, he was feverishly anxious to travel far that very night, if only Nest was capable of performing the journey. As he was thus employed, he tried to conjecture what his father's feelings would be on finding that his once-loved son was gone away for ever. Would he then awaken to regret for the conduct which had driven him from home, and bitterly think on the loving and caressing boy who haunted his footsteps in former days? Or, alas! would he only feel that an obstacle to his daily happiness – to his contentment with his wife, and his strange, doting affection for the child – was taken away? Would they make merry over the heir's departure? Then he thought of Nest – the young childless mother, whose heart had not yet realised her fulness of desolation. Poor Nest! so loving as she was, so devoted to her child – how should he console her? He pictured her away in a strange land, pining for her native mountains, and refusing to be comforted because her child was not.

Even this thought of the home-sickness that might possibly beset Nest hardly made him hesitate in his determination; so strongly had the idea taken possession of him, that only by putting miles and leagues between him and his father could he avert the doom which seemed blending itself with the very purposes of his life, as long as he stayed in proximity with the slayer of his child.

He had now nearly completed his hasty work of preparation, and was full of tender thoughts of his wife, when the door opened, and the elfish Robert peered in, in search of some of his brother's possessions. On seeing Owen he hesitated, but then came boldly forward, and laid his hand on Owen's arm, saying:

'*Nesta yr buten!* How is Nest *yr buten?*'

He looked maliciously into Owen's face to mark the effect of his words, but was terrified at the expression he read there. He started off and ran to the door, while Owen tried to check himself, saying continually, 'He is but a child. He does not understand the meaning of what he says. He is but a child!'

Still Robert, now in fancied security, kept calling out his insulting words, and Owen's hand was on his gun, grasping it as if to restrain his rising fury.

But, when Robert passed on daringly to mocking words relating to the poor dead child, Owen could bear it no longer; and, before the boy was well aware, Owen was fiercely holding him in an iron clasp with one hand, while he struck him hard with the other.

In a minute he checked himself. He paused, relaxed his grasp, and, to his horror, he saw Robert sink to the ground; in fact, the lad was half-stunned, half-frightened, and thought it best to assume insensibility.

Owen – miserable Owen – seeing him lie there prostrate, was bitterly repentant, and would have dragged him to the carved settle, and done all he could to restore him to his senses; but at this instant the Squire came in.

Probably, when the household at Bodowen rose that morning, there was but one among them ignorant of the heir's relation to Nest Pritchard and her child; for, secret as he tried to make his visits to Ty Glas, they had been too frequent not to be noticed. and Nest's altered conduct – no longer frequenting dances and merry-makings – was a strongly corroborative circumstance. But Mrs. Griffiths' influence reigned paramount, if unacknowledged, at Bodowen; and, till she sanctioned the disclosure, none would dare to tell the Squire.

Now, however, the time drew near when it suited her to make her husband aware of the connection his son had formed; so, with many tears, and much seeming reluctance, she broke the intelligence to him – taking good care, at the same time, to inform him of the light character Nest had borne. Nor did she confine this evil reputation to her conduct before her marriage, but insinuated that even to this day she was a 'woman of the grove and brake' – for centuries the Welsh term of opprobrium for the loosest female characters.

Squire Griffiths easily tracked Owen to Ty Glas; and, without any aim but the gratification of his furious anger, followed him to upbraid him as we have seen. But he left the cottage even more enraged against his son than he had entered it, and returned home to hear the evil suggestions of the stepmother. He had heard a slight scuffle in which he caught the tones of Robert's voice, as he passed along the hall, and an instant afterwards he saw the apparently lifeless body of his little favourite dragged along by the culprit Owen – the marks of strong passion yet visible on his face, Not loud, but bitter and deep, were the evil words which the father bestowed on the son; and, as Owen stood proudly and sullenly silent, disdaining all exculpation of himself in the presence of one who had wrought him so much graver – so fatal an injury – Robert's mother entered the room. At sight of her natural emotion the wrath of the Squire was redoubled, and his wild suspicions that this violence of Owen's to Robert was a premeditated act appeared like the proven truth through the mists of rage. He summoned domestics, as if to guard his own and his wife's life from the attempts of his son; and the servants stood wondering around – now gazing at Mrs. Griffiths, alternately scolding and sobbing, while she tried to restore the lad from his really bruised and half-unconscious state; now at the fierce and angry Squire; and now at the sad and silent Owen. And he – he was hardly aware of their looks of wonder and terror; his father's words fell on a deadened ear; for before his eyes there rose a pale dead babe, and in that lady's violent sounds of grief he heard the wailing of a more sad, more hopeless mother. For by this time the lad Robert had opened his eyes, and though evidently suffering a good deal from the effects of Owen's blows, was fully conscious of all that was passing around him.

Had Owen been left to his own nature, his heart would have worked itself to love doubly the boy whom he had injured: but he was stubborn from injustice, and hardened by suffering. He refused to vindicate himself; he made no effort to resist the imprisonment the Squire had decreed, until a surgeon's opinion of the real extent of Robert's injuries was made known. It was not until the door was locked and barred, as if upon some wild and furious beast, that the recollection of poor Nest, without his comforting presence, came into his mind. Oh! thought he, how she would be wearying, pining for his tender sympathy; if, indeed, she had recovered from the shock of mind sufficiently to be sensible of consolation! What would she think of his absence? Could she imagine he

believed his father's words, and had left her in this her sore
trouble and bereavement? The thought maddened him, and he
looked around for some mode of escape.

He had been confined in a small unfurnished room on the
first floor, wainscoted, and carved all round, with a massy
door, calculated to resist the attempts of a dozen strong men,
even had he afterward been able to escape from the house
unseen, unheard. The window was placed; (as is common in
old Welsh houses) over the fireplace; with branching chimneys
on either hand, forming a sort of projection on the outside. By
this outlet his escape was easy, even had he been less
determined and desperate than he was. And when he had
descended, with a little care, a little winding, he might elude
all observation and pursue his original intention of going to
Ty Glas.

The storm had abated, and watery sunbeams were gilding
the bay, as Owen descended from the window, and, stealing
along in the broad afternoon shadows, made his way to the
little plateau of green turf in the garden at the top of a steep
precipitous rock, down the abrupt face of which he had often
dropped, by means of a well-secured rope, into the small
sailing-boat (his father's present, alas! in days gone by) which
lay moored in the deep sea-water below. He had always kept
his boat there, because it was the nearest available spot to the
house; but before he could reach the place – unless, indeed, he
crossed a broad sun-lighted piece of ground in full view of the
windows on that side of the house, and without the shadow of
a single sheltering tree or shrub – he had to skirt round a rude
semicircle of underwood, which would have been considered
as a shrubbery, had any one taken pains with it. Step by step
he stealthily moved along – hearing voices now; again seeing
his father and stepmother in no distant walk, the Squire
evidently caressing and consoling his wife, who seemed to be
urging some point with great vehemence; again forced to
crouch down to avoid being seen by the cook, returning from
the rude kitchen-garden with a handful of herbs. This was the
way the doomed heir of Bodowen left his ancestral house for
ever, and hoped to leave behind him his doom. At length he
reached the plateau – he breathed more freely. He stooped to
discover the hidden coil of rope, kept safe and dry in a hole

under a great round flat piece of rock; his head was bent down; he did not see his father approach, nor did he hear his footstep for the rush of blood to his head in the stooping effort of lifting the stone. The Squire had grappled with him before he rose up again, before he fully knew whose hands detained him, now, when his liberty of person and action seemed secure. He made a vigorous struggle to free himself; he wrestled with his father for a moment – he pushed him hard, and drove him on to the great displaced stone, all unsteady in its balance.

Down went the Squire, down into the deep waters below – down after him went Owen, half consciously, half unconsciously; partly compelled by the sudden cessation of any opposing body, partly from a vehement irrepressible impulse to rescue his father. But he had instinctively chosen a safer place in the deep sea-water pool than that into which his push had sent his father. The Squire had hit his head with much violence against the side of the boat, in his fall; it is, indeed, doubtful whether he was not killed before ever he sank into the sea. But Owen knew nothing save that the awful doom seemed even now present. He plunged down; he dived below the water in search of the body, which had none of the elasticity of life to buoy it up; he saw his father in those depths; he clutched at him; he brought him up and cast him, a dead weight, into the boat; and, exhausted by the effort, he had begun himself to sink again before he instinctively strove to rise and climb into the rocking boat. There lay his father, with a deep dent in the side of his head where his skull had been fractured by his fall; his face blackened by the arrested course of the blood. Owen felt his pulse, his heart – all was still. He called him by his name.

'Father, father!' he cried, 'come back! come back! You never know how I loved you! how I could love you still – if – Oh God!'

And the thought of his little child rose before him. 'Yes, father,' he cried afresh, 'you never knew how he fell – how he died! Oh, if I had but had patience to tell you! If you would but have borne with me and listened! And now it is over! Oh, father! father!'

Whether she had heard this wild wailing voice, or whether it was only that she missed her husband and wanted him for some little every-day question, or, as was perhaps more likely, she had discovered Owen's escape, and come to inform her husband of it, I do not know – but on the rock, right above his head, as it seemed, Owen heard his stepmother calling her husband.

He was silent, and softly pushed the boat right under the rock till the sides grated against the stones; and the over-hanging branches concealed him and it from all on a level with the water. Wet as he was, he lay down by his dead father, the better to conceal himself; and, somehow, the action recalled those early days of childhood – the first in the Squire's widowhood – when Owen had shared his father's bed, and used to waken him in the morning in order to hear one of the old Welsh legends. How long he lay thus – body chilled, and brain hard-working through the heavy pressure of a reality as terrible as a nightmare – he never knew; but at length he roused himself up to think of Nest.

Drawing out a great sail, he covered up the body of his father with it where he lay in the bottom of the boat. Then with his numbed hands he took the oars, and pulled out into the more open sea towards Criccaeth. He skirted along the coast till he found a shadowed cleft in the dark rocks; to that point he rowed, and anchored his boat close inland. Then he mounted, staggering, half longing to fall into the dark waters and be at rest – half instinctively finding out the surest foot-rests on that precipitous face of rock, till he was high up, safe landed on the turfy summit. He ran off, as if pursued, towards Penmorfa; he ran with maddened energy. Suddenly he paused, turned, ran again with the same speed, and threw himself prone on the summit, looking down into his boat with straining eyes to see if there had been any movement of life – any displacement of a fold of sail-cloth. It was all quiet deep down below, but as he gazed the shifting light gave the appearance of a slight movement. Owen ran to a lower part of the rock, stripped, plunged into the water, and swam to the boat. When there, all was still – awfully still! For a minute or two, he dared not lift up the cloth. Then, reflecting that the same terror might beset him again – of leaving his father unaided while yet a spark of life lingered – he removed the shrouding cover. The eyes looked into his with a dead stare! He closed the lids and bound up the jaw. Again he looked.

This time, he raised himself out of the water and kissed the brow.

'It was my doom, father! It would have been better if I had died at my birth!'

Daylight was fading away. Precious daylight! He swam back, dressed, and set off afresh for Penmorfa. When he opened the door of Ty Glas, Ellis Pritchard looked at him reproachfully from his seat in the darkly-shadowed chimney-corner.

'You're come at last,' said he. 'One of our kind' (*i.e.* station) 'would not have left his wife to mourn by herself over her dead child; nor would one of our kind have let his father kill his own true son. I've a good mind to take her from you for ever.'

'I did not tell him,' cried Nest, looking piteously at her husband; 'he made me tell him part, and guessed the rest.'

She was nursing her babe on her knee as if it was alive. Owen stood before Ellis Pritchard.

'Be silent,' said he quietly. 'Neither words nor deeds but what are decreed can come to pass. I was set to do my work, this hundred years and more. The time waited for me, and the man waited for me. I have done what was foretold of me for generations!'

Ellis Pritchard knew the old tale of the prophecy, and believed in it in a dull, dead kind of way, but somehow never thought it would come to pass in his time. Now, however, he understood it all in a moment, though he mistook Owen's nature so much as to believe that the deed was intentionally done, out of revenge for the death of his boy; and viewing it in this light, Ellis thought it little more than a just punishment for the cause of all the wild despairing sorrow he had seen his only child suffer during the hours of this long afternoon. But he knew the law would not so regard it. Even the lax Welsh law of those days could not fail to examine into the death of a man of Squire Griffiths' standing. So the acute Ellis thought how he could conceal the culprit for a time.

'Come,' said he; 'don't look so scared! It was your doom, not your fault;' and he laid a hand on Owen's shoulder.

'You're wet' said he suddenly. 'Where have you been? Nest, your husband is dripping, drookit wet. That's what makes him look so blue and wan.'

Nest softly laid her baby in its cradle; she was half stupefied with crying, and had not understood to what Owen alluded, when he spoke of his doom being fulfilled, if indeed she had heard the words.

Her touch thawed Owen's miserable heart.

'Oh, Nest!' said he, clasping her in his arms; 'do you love me still – can you love me, my own darling?'

'Why not?' asked she, her eyes filling with tears. 'I only love you more than ever, for you were my poor baby's father!'

'But Nest – Oh, tell her Ellis! *you* know.'

'No need, no need!' said Ellis. 'She's had enough to think on. Bustle, my girl, and get out my Sunday clothes.'

'I don't understand,' said Nest, putting her hand up to her head. 'What is to tell? and why are you so wet? God help me for a poor crazed thing; for I cannot guess at the meaning of your words and your strange looks! I only know my baby is dead!' and she burst into tears.

'Come, Nest! go and fetch him a change, quick!' and, as she meekly obeyed, too languid to strive further to understand, Ellis said rapidly to Owen, in a low, hurried voice:

'Are you meaning that the Squire is dead? Speak low, lest she hear? Well, well, no need to talk about how he died. It was sudden, I see; and we must all of us die; and he'll have to be buried. It's well the night is near. And I should not wonder now if you'd like to travel for a bit; it would do Nest a power of good; and then – there's many a one goes out of his own house and never comes back again; and – I trust he's not lying in his own house – and there's a stir for a bit, and a search, and a wonder – and, by-and-by, the heir just steps in, as quiet as can be. And that's what you'll do, and bring Nest to Bodowen after all. Nay, child, better stockings nor those; find the blue woollens I bought at Llanrwst fair. Only don't lose heart. It's done now and can't be helped. It was the piece of work set you to do from the days of the Tudors, they say. And he deserved it. Look in yon cradle. So tell us where he is, and I'll take heart of grace and see what can be done for him.'

But Owen sat wet and haggard, looking into the peat fire as if for visions of the past, and never heeding a word Ellis said. Nor did he move when Nest brought the armful of dry clothes.

'Come, rouse up, man!' said Ellis, growing impatient.

But he neither spoke nor moved.

'What is the matter, father?' asked Nest, bewildered.

Ellis kept on watching Owen for a minute or two, till on his daughter's repetition of the question, he said:

'Ask him yourself, Nest.'

'Oh, husband, what is it?' said she, kneeling down and bringing her face to a level with his.

'Don't you know?' said he heavily. 'You won't love me when you do know. And yet it was not my doing: it was my doom.'

'What does he mean, father?' asked Nest, looking up; but she caught a gesture from Ellis urging her to go on questioning her husband.

'I will love you, husband, whatever has happened. Only let me know the worst.'

A pause, during which Nest and Ellis hung breathless.

'My father is dead, Nest.'

Nest caught her breath with a sharp gasp.

'God forgive him!' said she, thinking on her babe.

'God forgive *me!*' said Owen.

'You did not' – Nest stopped.

'Yes, I did. Now you know it. It was my doom. How could I help it? The devil helped me – he placed the stone so that my father fell. I jumped into the water to save him. I did, indeed, Nest. I was nearly drowned myself. But he was dead – dead – killed by the fall!'

'Then he is safe at the bottom of the sea?' said Ellis, with hungry eagerness.

'No, he is not; he lies in my boat,' said Owen, shivering a little, more at the thought of his last glimpse at his father's face than from cold.

'Oh, husband, change your wet clothes!' pleaded Nest, to whom the death of the old man was simply a horror with which she had nothing to do, while her husband's discomfort was a present trouble.

While she helped him to take off the wet garments which he would never have had energy enough to remove of himself, Ellis was busy preparing food, and mixing a great tumbler of spirits and hot water. He stood over the unfortunate young man and compelled him to eat and drink, and made Nest, too, taste some mouthfuls – all the while planning in his own mind how best to conceal what had been done, and who had done it; not altogether without a certain feeling of vulgar triumph in the reflection that Nest, as she stood there, carelessly dressed, dishevelled in her grief, was in reality the mistress of Bodowen, than which Ellis Pritchard had never seen a grander house, though he believed such might exist.

By dint of a few dexterous questions he found out all he wanted to know from Owen, as he ate and drank. In fact, it was almost a relief to Owen to dilute the horror by talking about it. Before the meal was done, if meal it could be called, Ellis knew all he cared to know.

'Now, Nest, on with your cloak and haps. Pack up what needs to go with you, for both you and your husband must be half-way to Liverpool by tomorrow's morn, I'll take you past Rhyl Sands in my fishing boat, with yours in tow; and, once over the dangerous part, I'll return with my cargo of fish, and then learn how much stir there is at Bodowen. Once safe hidden in Liverpool, no one will know where you are, and you may stay quiet till your time comes for returning.'

'I will never come home again,' said Owen doggedly. 'The place is accursed!'

'Hoot! be guided by me, man. Why, it was but an accident, after all! And we'll land at the Holy Island, at the Point of Llyn; there is an old cousin of mine, the parson, there – for the Pritchards have known better days, Squire – and we'll bury him there. It was but an accident, man. Hold up your head! You and Nest will come home yet and fill Bodowen with children, and I'll live to see it.'

'Never!' said Owen. 'I am the last male of my race, and the son has murdered his father!'

Nest came in laden and cloaked. Ellis was for hurrying them off. The fire was extinguished, the door was locked.

'Here, Nest, my darling, let me take your bundle while I guide you down the steps.' But her husband bent his head, and spoke never a word. Nest gave her father the bundle (already loaded with such things as he himself had seen fit to take), but clasped another softly and tightly.

'No one shall help me with this,' said she, in a low voice. Her father did not understand her; her husband did, and placed his strong helping arm round her waist, and blessed her.

'We will all go together, Nest,' said he. 'But where?' and he looked up at the storm-tossed clouds coming up from windward.

'It is a dirty night,' said Ellis, turning his head round to speak to his companions at last. 'But never fear, we'll weather it.' And he made for the place where his vessel was moored. Then he stopped and thought a moment.

'Stay here!' said he, addressing his companions. 'I may meet folk, and I shall, maybe, have to hear and to speak. You wait here till I come back for you.' So they sat down close together in a corner of the path.

'Let me look at him, Nest!' said Owen.

She took her little dead son out from under her shawl; they looked at his waxen face long and tenderly; kissed it, and covered it up reverently and softly.

'Nest,' said Owen, at last, 'I feel as though my father's spirit had been near us, and as if it had bent over our poor little one. A strange, chilly air met me as I stooped over him. I could fancy the spirit of our pure, blameless child guiding my father's safe over the paths of the sky to the gates of heaven, and escaping those accursed dogs of hell that were darting up from the north in pursuit of souls not five minutes since.'

'Don't talk so, Owen,' said Nest, curling up to him in the darkness of the copse. 'Who knows what may be listening?'

The pair were silent, in a kind of nameless terror, till they heard Ellis Pritchard's loud whisper. 'Where are ye? Come along, soft and steady. There were folk about even now, and the Squire is missed, and madam in a fright.'

They went swiftly down to the little harbour, and embarked on board Ellis's boat. The sea heaved and rocked even there; the torn clouds went hurrying overhead in a wild tumultuous manner.

They put out into the bay; still in silence, except when some word of command was spoken by Ellis, who took the management of the vessel. They made for the rocky shore, where Owen's boat had been moored. It was not there. It had broken loose and disappeared.

Owen sat down and covered his face. This last event, so simple and natural in itself, struck on his excited and superstitious mind in an extraordinary manner. He had hoped for a certain reconciliation, so to say, by laying his father and his child both in one grave. But now it appeared to him as if there was to be no forgiveness; as if his father revolted even in death against any such peaceful union. Ellis took a practical view of the case. If the Squire's body was found drifting about in a boat known to belong to his son, it would create terrible suspicion as to the manner of his death. At one time in the evening, Ellis had thought of persuading Owen to let him bury the Squire in a sailor's grave; or, in other words, to sew him up in a spare sail, and weighing it well, sink it for ever. He had not broached the subject, from a certain fear of Owen's passionate repugnance to the plan; otherwise, if he had consented, they might have returned to Penmorfa, and passively awaited the course of events, secure of Owen's succession to Bodowen, sooner or later; or, if Owen was too much overwhelmed by what had happened, Ellis would have advised him to go away for a short time, and return when the buzz and the talk was over.

Now it was different. It was absolutely necessary that they should leave the country for a time. Through those stormy waters they must plough their way that very night. Ellis had no fear – would have had no fear, at any rate, with Owen as he had been a week, a day ago; but with Owen wild, despairing, helpless, fate-pursued, what could he do?

They sailed into the tossing darkness, and were never more seen of men.

The house of Bodowen has sunk into damp, dark ruins; and a Saxon stranger holds the lands of the Griffiths.

HALF A LIFETIME AGO

HALF A LIFETIME AGO

CHAPTER I

Half a lifetime ago, there lived in one of the Westmoreland
dales a single woman, of the name of Susan Dixon. She was
owner of the small farmhouse where she resided, and of some
thirty or forty acres of land by which it was surrounded. She
had also an hereditary right to a sheep-walk, extending to the
wild fells that overhang Blea Tarn. In the language of the
country she was a Stateswoman. Her house is yet to be seen on
the Oxenfell road, between Skelwith and Coniston. You go
along a moorland track, made by the carts that occasionally
come for turf from Oxenfell. A brook babbles and brattles by
the wayside, giving you a sense of companionship, which
relieves the deep solitude in which this way is usually traversed. Some miles on this side of Coniston, there is a
farmstead – a grey stone house, and a square of farm-buildings
surrounding a green space of rough turf, in the midst of which
stands a mighty, funereal umbrageous yew, making a solemn
shadow, as of death, in the very heart and centre of the light
and heat of the brightest summer day. On the side away from
the house, this yard slopes down to a dark-brown pool, which
is supplied with fresh water from the overflowings of a stone
cistern, into which some rivulet of the brook before-
mentioned continually and melodiously falls bubbling. The
cattle drink out of this cistern. The household bring their
pitchers and fill them with drinking-water by a dilatory, yet
pretty, process. The water-carrier brings with her a leaf of the
hound's-tongue fern, and, inserting it in the crevice of the
grey rock, makes a cool, green spout for the sparkling stream.

The house is no specimen, at the present day, of what it was
in the lifetime of Susan Dixon. Then, every small diamond
pane in the windows glittered with cleanliness. You might
have eaten off the floor; you could see yourself in the pewter

plates and the polished oaken awmry, or dresser, of the state kitchen into which you entered. Few strangers penetrated further than this room. Once or twice, wandering tourists, attracted by the lonely picturesqueness of the situation, and the exquisite cleanliness of the house itself, made their way into this house-place, and offered money enough (as they thought) to tempt the hostess to receive them as lodgers. They would give no trouble, they said; they would be out rambling or sketching all day long; would be perfectly content with a share of the food which she provided for herself; or would procure what they required from the Waterhead Inn at Coniston. But no liberal sum – no fair words – moved her from her stony manner, or her monotonous tone of indifferent refusal. No persuasion could induce her to show any more of the house than that first room; no appearance of fatigue procured for the weary an invitation to sit down and rest; and, if one more bold and less delicate did so without being asked, Susan stood by, cold and apparently deaf, or only replying by the briefest monosyllables, till the unwelcome visitor had departed. Yet those with whom she had dealings, in the way of selling her cattle or her farm produce, spoke of her as keen after a bargain – a hard one to have to do with; and she never spared herself exertion or fatigue, at market or in the field, to make the most of her produce. She led the hay-makers with her swift, steady rake, and her noiseless evenness of motion. She was about among the earliest in the market, examining samples of oats, pricing them, and then turning with grim satisfaction to her own cleaner corn.

She was served faithfully and long by those who were rather her fellow-labourers than her servants. She was even and just in her dealings with them. If she was peculiar and silent, they knew her, and knew that she might be relied on. Some of them had known her from her childhood; and deep in their hearts was an unspoken – almost unconscious – pity for her, for they knew her story, though they never spoke of it.

Yes; the time had been when that tall, gaunt, hard-featured, angular woman – who never smiled, and hardly ever spoke an unnecessary word – had been a fine-looking girl, bright-spirited and rosy; and when the hearth at the Yew Nook had been as bright as she, with family love and youthful hope and mirth. Fifty or fifty-one years ago, William Dixon and his wife Margaret were alive, and Susan, their daughter, was about eighteen years old – ten years older than the only other child, a boy named after his father. William and Margaret Dixon were rather superior people, of a character belonging – as far as I have seen – exclusively to the class of Westmoreland and Cumberland statesmen – just, independent, upright; not given to much speaking; kind-hearted, but not demonstrative; disliking change, and new ways, and new people; sensible and shrewd; each household self-contained, and its members having little curiosity as to their neighbours, with whom they rarely met for any social intercourse, save at the stated times of sheep-shearing and Christmas; having a certain kind of sober pleasure in amassing money, which occasionally made them miserable (as they call miserly people up in the north) in their old age; reading no light or ephemeral literature, but the grave, solid books brought round by the pedlars (such as *Paradise Lost* and *Regained, The Death of Abel, The Spiritual Quixote*, and *The Pilgrim's Progress*), which were to be found in nearly every house: the men occasionally going off laking, *i.e.* playing, drinking for days together, and having to be hunted up by anxious wives, who dared not leave their husbands to the chances of the wild precipitous roads, but walked miles and miles, lantern in hand, in the dead of night, to discover and guide the solemnly-drunken husband home; who had a dreadful headache the next day, and the day after that came forth as grave, and sober, and virtuous-looking as if there were no such thing as malt and spirituous liquors in the world and who were seldom reminded of their misdoings by their wives, to whom such occasional outbreaks were as things of course, when once the immediate anxiety produced by them was over. Such were – such are – the characteristics of a class now passing away from the face of the land, as their compeers, the yeoman, have done before them. Of such was William Dixon. He was a shrewd, clever farmer, in his day and generation, when shrewdness was rather shown in the breeding, and rearing of sheep and cattle than in the cultivation of land. Owing to this character of his, statesmen from a distance from beyond Kendal, or from Borrowdale, of greater wealth than he, would send their sons to be farm-servants for a year or two with him, in order to learn some of his methods before setting up on land of their own. When Susan, his daughter, was about seventeen, one Michael Hurst was farm-servant at Yew Nook. He worked with the master, and lived with the family, and was in all respects treated as an equal, except in the field. His father was a wealthy statesman at Wythburne, up beyond Grasmere; and through Michael's servitude the families had become acquainted, and the Dixons went over to the High Beck sheep-shearing, and the Hursts came down by Red Bank and Loughrig Tarn and across the Oxenfell when there was the Christmas-tide feasting at Yew Nook. The fathers strolled round the fields together, examined cattle and sheep, and looked knowing over each other's horses. The mothers inspected the dairies and household arrangements, each openly admiring the plans of the other, but secretly preferring their own. Both fathers and mothers cast a glance from time to time at Michael and Susan, who were thinking of nothing less than farm or dairy, but whose unspoken attachment was, in all ways, so suitable and natural a thing that each parent rejoiced over it, although with characteristic reserve it was never spoken about – not even between husband and wife.

Susan had been a strong, independent healthy girl; a clever help to her mother, and a spirited companion to her father; more of a man in her (as he often said) than her delicate little brother ever would have. He was his mother's darling, although she loved Susan well. There was no positive engagement between Michael and Susan – I doubt whether even plain words of love had been spoken; when, one winter-time, Margaret Dixon was seized with inflammation consequent upon a neglected cold. She had always been strong and notable, and had been too busy to attend to the early symptoms of illness. It would go off, she said to the woman who helped in the kitchen; or, if she did not feel better when they had got the hams and bacon out of hand, she would take some herb-tea and nurse up a bit. But Death could not wait till the hams and bacon were cured: he came on with rapid strides, and shooting arrows of portentous agony. Susan had never seen illness – never knew how much she loved her mother till now, when she felt a dreadful, instinctive certainty that she was losing her. Her mind was thronged with recollections of the many times she had slighted her mother's wishes; her heart was full of the echoes of careless and angry replies that she had spoken. What would she not now give to have opportunities of service and obedience, and trials of her patience and love, for that dear mother who lay gasping in torture! And yet Susan had been a good girl and an affectionate daughter.

The sharp pain went off, and delicious ease came on; yet still her mother sank. In the midst of this languid peace she was dying. She motioned Susan to her bedside, for she could only whisper; and, then, while the father was out of the room, she spoke as much to the eager, hungering eyes of her daughter by the motion of her lips, as by the slow, feeble sounds of her voice.

'Susan, lass, thou must not fret. It is God's will, and thou wilt have a deal to do. Keep father straight if thou canst; and, if he goes out Ulverstone ways, see that thou meet him before he gets to the Old Quarry. It's a dree bit for a man who has had a drop. As for lile Will' – here the poor woman's face began to work and her fingers to move nervously as they lay on the bed-quilt – 'lile Will will miss me most of all. Father's often vexed with him because he's not a quick, strong lad: he is not, my poor lile chap. And father thinks he's saucy, because he cannot always stomach oat-cake and porridge. There's better than three pound in th' old black tea-pot on the top shelf of the cupboard. Just keep a piece of loaf-bread by you, Susan dear, for Will to come to when he's not taken his breakfast. I have, maybe, spoilt him; but there'll be no one to spoil him now.'

She began to cry, a low, feeble cry, and covered up her face that Susan might not see her. That dear face! those precious moments, while yet the eyes could look out with love and intelligence! Susan laid her head down close by her mother's ear.

'Mother, I'll take tent of Will. Mother, do you hear? He shall not want aught I can give or get for him, least of all the kind words which you had ever ready for us both. Bless you! bless you! my own mother.'

'Thou'lt promise me that, Susan, wilt thou? I can die easy if thou'lt take charge of him. But he's hardly like other folk; he

tries father at times, though I think father'll be tender of him
when I'm gone, for my sake. And, Susan, there's one thing
more. I never spoke on it for fear of the bairn being called a
tell-tale, but I just comforted him up. He vexes Michael at
times, and Michael has struck him before now. I did not want
to make a stir; but he's not strong, and a word from thee,
Susan, will go a long way with Michael.'

Susan was as red now as she had been pale before; it was the
first time that her influence over Michael had been openly
acknowledged by a third person, and a flash of joy came
athwart the solemn sadness of the moment. Her mother had
spoken too much, and now came on the miserable faintness.
She never spoke again coherently; but when her children and
her husband stood by her bedside she took lile Will's hand and
put it into Susan's, and looked at her with imploring eyes.
Susan clasped her arms round Will, and leaned her head upon
his little curly one, and vowed within herself to be as a mother
to him.

Henceforward she was all in all to her brother. She was a
more spirited and amusing companion to him than his mother
had been, from her greater activity, and perhaps, also, from
her originality of character, which often prompted her to
perform her habitual actions in some new and racy manner.
She was tender to lile Will when she was prompt and sharp
with everybody else – with Michael most of all; for somehow
the girl felt that, unprotected by her mother, she must keep up
her own dignity, and not allow her lover to see how strong a
hold he had upon her heart. He called her hard and cruel, and
felt her so; and she smiled softly to herself, when his back was
turned, to think how little he guessed how deeply he was
loved. For Susan was merely comely and fine-looking;
Michael was strikingly handsome, admired by all the girls for
miles round, and quite enough of a country coxcomb to know
it and plume himself accordingly. He was the second son of
his father; the eldest would have High Beck farm, of course,
but there was a good penny in the Kendal bank in store for
Michael. When harvest was over, he went to Chapel Langdale
to learn to dance; and at night, in his merry moods, he would
do his steps on the flag floor of the Yew Nook kitchen, to the
secret admiration of Susan, who had never learned dancing,

but who flouted him perpetually, even while she admired, in accordance with the rule she seemed to have made for herself about keeping him at a distance so long as he lived under the same roof with her. One evening he sulked at some saucy remark of hers; he sitting in the chimney-corner with his arms on his knees, and his head bent forwards, lazily gazing into the wood-fire on the hearth, and luxuriating in rest after a hard day's labour; she sitting among the geraniums on the long, low window-seat, trying to catch the last slanting rays of the autumnal light to enable her to finish stitching a shirt-collar for Will, who lounged full length on the flags at the other side of the hearth to Michael, poking the burning wood from time to time with a long hazel-stick to bring out the leap of glittering sparks.

'And if you can dance a threesome reel, what good does it do ye?' asked Susan, looking askance at Michael, who had just been vaunting his proficiency. 'Does it help you plough, or reap, or even climb the rocks to take a raven's nest? If I were a man, I'd be ashamed to give in to such softness.'

'If you were a man, you'd be glad to do anything which made the pretty girls stand round and admire.'

'As they do to you, eh? Ho, Michael, that would not be my way o' being a man.'

'What would, then?' asked he, after a pause, during which he had expected in vain that she would go on with her sentence. No answer.

'I should not like you as a man, Susy; you'd be too hard and headstrong.'

'Am I hard and headstrong?' asked she, with as indifferent a tone as she could assume, but which yet had a touch of pique in it. His quick ear detected the inflection.

'No, Susy! You're wilful at times, and that's right enough. I don't like a girl without spirit. There's a mighty pretty girl comes to the dancing class; but she is all milk and water. Her eyes never flash like yours when you're put out; why, I can see them flame across the kitchen like a cat's in the dark. Now, if you were a man, I should feel queer before those looks of yours; as it is, I rather like them, because —'

'Because what?' asked she, looking up and perceiving that he had stolen close up to her.

'Because I can make all right in this way,' said he, kissing her suddenly.

'Can you?' said she, wrenching herself out of his grasp, and panting, half with rage. 'Take that, by way of proof that making right is none to easy.' And she boxed his ears pretty sharply. He went back to his seat discomfited and out of temper. She could no longer see to look, even if her face had not burnt and her eyes dazzled; but she did not choose to move her seat, so she still preserved her stooping attitude and pretended to go on sewing.

'Eleanor Hebthwaite may be milk-and-water,' muttered he, 'but – Confound thee, lad! what art thou doing?' exclaimed Michael, as a great piece of burning wood was cast into his face by an unlucky poke of Will's. 'Thou great lounging, clumsy chap, I'll teach thee better!' and with one or two good round kicks he sent the lad whimpering away into the back-kitchen. When he had a little recovered himself from his passion, he saw Susan standing before him, her face looking strange and almost ghastly by the reversed position of the shadows, arising from the firelight shining upwards right under it.

'I tell thee what, Michael,' said she, 'that lad's motherless, but not friendless.'

'His own father leathers him, and why should not I, when he's given me such a burn on my face?' said Michael, putting up his hand to his cheek as if in pain.

'His father's his father, and there is nought more to be said. But if he did burn thee, it was by accident, and not o' purpose, as thou kicked him; it's a mercy if his ribs are not broken.'

'He howls loud enough, I'm sure. I might ha' kicked many a lad twice as hard, and they'd ne'er ha' said ought but "damn ye;" but yon lad must needs cry out like a stuck pig if one touches him;' replied Michael sullenly.

Susan went back to the window-seat, and looked absently out of the window at the drifting clouds for a minute or two, while her eyes filled with tears. Then she got up and made for the outer door which led into the back-kitchen. Before she reached it, however, she heard a low voice, whose music made her thrill, say:

'Susan, Susan!'

Her heart melted within her, but it seemed like treachery to her poor boy, like faithlessness to her dead mother, to turn to her lover while the tears which he had caused to flow were yet unwiped on Will's cheeks. So she seemed to take no heed, but passed into the darkness, and, guided by the sobs, she found her way to where Willie sat crouched among the disused tubs and churns.

'Come out wi' me, lad;' and they went out into the orchard, where the fruit-trees were bare of leaves, but ghastly in their tattered covering of grey moss; and the soughing November wind came with long sweeps over the fells till it rattled among the crackling boughs, underneath which the brother and sister sat in the dark; he in her lap, and she hushing her head against her shoulder.

'Thou should'st na' play wi' fire. It's a naughty trick. Thou'lt suffer for it in worse ways nor this before thou'st done, I'm afeared. I should ha' hit thee twice as lungeous kicks as Mike, if I'd been in his place. He did na' hurt thee, I am sure,' she assumed, half as a question.

'Yes, but he did. He turned me quite sick.' And he let his head fall languidly down on his sister's breast.

'Come lad! come lad!' said she anxiously. 'Be a man. It was not much that I saw. Why, when first the red cow came she kicked me far harder for offering to milk her before her legs were tied. See thee! here's a peppermint-drop, and I'll make thee a pasty tonight; only don't give way so, for it hurts me sore to think that Michael has done thee any harm, my pretty.'

Willie roused himself up, and put back the wet and ruffled hair from his heated face; and he and Susan rose up, and hand-in-hand went towards the house, walking slowly and quietly except for a kind of sob which Willie could not repress. Susan took him to the pump and washed his tear-stained face, till she thought she had obliterated all traces of the recent disturbance, arranging his curls for him; and then she kissed him tenderly, and led him in, hoping to find Michael in the kitchen, and make all straight beween them. But the blaze had dropped down into darkness; the wood was a heap of grey ashes in which the sparks ran hither and thither; but even in the groping darkness Susan knew by the sinking at her heart that Michael was not there. She threw another brand on the hearth and lighted the candle, and sat down to her work in silence. Willie cowered on his stool by the side of the fire, eyeing his sister from time to time, and sorry and oppressed, he knew not why, by the sight of her grave, almost stern face. No one came. They two were in the house alone. The old woman who helped Susan with the household work had gone out for the night to some friend's dwelling. William Dixon, the father, was upon the fells seeing after the sheep. Susan had no heart to prepare the evening meal.

'Susy, darling, are you angry with me?' asked Willie, in his little piping, gentle voice. He had stolen up to his sister's side. 'I won't never play with the fire again; and I'll not cry if Michael does kick me. Only don't look so like dead mother – don't – don't – please don't!' he exclaimed hiding his face on her shoulder.

'I'm not angry, Willie,' said she. 'Don't be feared on me. You want your supper and you shall have it; and don't you be feared on Michael. He shall give reasons for every hair of your head that he touches – he shall.'

When William Dixon came home he found Susan and Willie sitting together, hand-in-hand, and apparently pretty cheerful. He bade them go to bed, for that he would sit up for Michael; and the next morning, when Susan came down, she found that Michael had started an hour before, with the cart for lime. It was a long day's work; Susan knew it would be late, perhaps later than on the preceding night, before he returned – at any rate, past her usual bed-time; and on no acccount would she stay up a minute beyond that hour in the kitchen, whatever she might do in her bedroom. Here she sat and watched till past midnight; and when she saw him coming up the brow of the hill with the carts, she knew full well, seen in that faint moonlight, that his gait was the gait of a man in liquor. But, though she was annoyed and mortified to find in what way he had chosen to forget her, the fact did not disgust her or shock her as it would have done many a girl even at that day, who had not been brought up as Susan had, among a class who considered it no crime, but rather a mark of spirit, in a man to get drunk occasionally. Nevertheless, she chose to hold herself very high all the next day, when Michael was, perforce, obliged to give up any attempt to do heavy work, and hung about the outbuildings and farm in a very disconsolate and sickly state. Willie had far more pity on him than Susan. Before evening, Willie and he were fast and, on his side, ostentatious friends. Willie rode the horses down to water; Willie helped him to chop wood. Susan sat gloomily at her work, hearing an indistinct but cheerful conversation going on in the shippon, while the cows were being milked. She almost felt irritated with her little brother, as if he were a traitor, and had gone over to the enemy in the very battle that she was fighting in his cause. She was alone with no one to speak to, while they prattled on regardless if she were glad or sorry.

Soon Willie burst in. 'Susan! Susan! come with me; I've something so pretty to show you. Round the corner of the barn – run! run!' (He was dragging her along, half-reluctant, half-desirous of some change in that weary day). Round the corner of the barn; and caught hold of by Michael, who stood there awaiting her.

'O Willie!' cried she, 'you naughty boy. There is nothing pretty – what have you brought me here for? Let me go; I won't be held.'

'Only one word. Nay, if you wish it so much, you may go,' said Michael, suddenly loosing his hold as she struggled. But now she was free, he only drew off a step or two, murmuring something about Willie.

'You are going, then?' said Michael, with seeming sadness. 'You won't hear me say a word of what is in my heart?'

'How can I tell whether it is what I should like to hear?' replied she, still drawing back.

'That is just what I want you to tell me; I want you to hear it, and then to tell me whether you like it or not.'

'Well, you may speak,' replied she, turning her back, and beginning to plait the hem of her apron.

He came close to her ear.

'I'm sorry I hurt Willie the other night. He has forgiven me. Can't you?'

'You hurt him very badly,' she replied. 'But you are right to be sorry. I forgive you.'

'Stop, stop!' said he, laying his hand upon her arm. 'There is something more I've got to say. I want you to be my – what is it they call it, Susan?'

'I don't know,' said she, half-laughing, but trying to get away with all her might now – and she was a strong girl; but she could not manage it.

'You do. My – what is it I want you to be?'

'I tell you I don't know, and you had best be quiet, and just let me go in; or I shall think you're as bad now as you were last night.'

'And how did you know what I was last night? It was past twelve when I came home. Were you watching? Ah, Susan! be my wife, and you shall never have to watch for a drunken husband. If I were your husband, I would come straight home, and count every minute an hour till I saw your bonny face. Now you know what I want you to be. I ask you to be my wife. Will you, my own dear Susan?'

She did not speak for some time. Then she only said 'Ask father'. And now she was really off like a lapwing, round the corner of the barn, and up in her own little room, crying with all her might, before the triumphant smile had left Michael's face where he stood.

The 'Ask father' was a mere form to be gone through. Old Daniel Hurst and William Dixon had talked over what they could respectively give their children before this, and that was the parental way of arranging such matters. When the probable amount of worldly gear that he could give his child had been named by each father, the young folk, as they said, might take their own time in coming to the point which the old men, with the prescience of experience, saw they were drifting to: no need to hurry them, for they were both young, and Michael, although active enough, was too thoughtless, old Daniel said, to be trusted with the entire management of a farm. Meanwhile, his father would look about him, and see after all the farms that were to be let.

Michael had a shrewd notion of this preliminary understanding between the fathers, and so felt less daunted than he might otherwise have done at making the application for Susan's hand. It was all right; there was not an obstacle, only a deal of good advice, which the lover thought might have as well been spared, and which it must be confessed he did not much attend to, although he assented to every part of it. Then Susan was called downstairs, and slowly came dropping into view down the steps which led from the two family apartments into the house-place. She tried to look composed and quiet, but it could not be done. She stood side by side with her lover, with her head drooping, her cheeks burning, not daring to look up or move, while her father made the newly-betrothed a somewhat formal address in which he gave his consent, and many a piece of worldly wisdom beside. Susan listened, as well as she could for the beating of her heart; but, when her father solemnly and sadly referred to his own lost wife, she could keep from sobbing no longer; but throwing her apron over her face, she sat down on the bench by the dresser, and fairly gave way to pent-up tears. Oh, how strangely sweet to be comforted as she was comforted, by tender caress, and many a low-whispered promise of love! Her father sat by the fire, thinking of the days that were gone; Willie was still out of doors: but Susan and Michael felt no one's presence or absence – they only knew they were together as betrothed husband and wife.

In a week or two, they were formally told of the arrangements to be made in their favour. A small farm in the neighbourhood happened to fall vacant; and Michael's father offered to take it for him, and be responsible for the rent for the first year, while William Dixon was to contribute a certain amount of stock, and both fathers were to help towards the furnishing of the house. Susan received all this information in a quiet, indifferent way; she did not care much for any of these preparations, which were to hurry her through the happy hours; she cared least of all for the money amount of dowry and of substance. It jarred on her to be made the confidante of occasional slight repinings of Michael's, as one by one his future father-in-law set aside a beast or a pig for Susan's portion, which were not always the best animals of their kind upon the farm. But he also complained of his own father's stinginess, which somewhat, though not much, alleviated Susan's dislike to being awakened out of her pure dream of love to the consideration of worldly wealth.

But, in the midst of all this bustle, Willie moped and pined. He had the same chord of delicacy running through his mind that made his body feeble and weak. He kept out of the way, and was apparently occupied in whittling and carving uncouth heads on hazel-sticks in an out-house. But he positively avoided Michael, and shrank away even from Susan. She was too much occupied to notice this at first. Michael pointed it out to her, saying, with a laugh:

'Look at Willie; he might be a cast-off lover and jealous of me, he looks so dark and downcast at me.' Michael spoke this jest out loud; and Willie burst into tears, and ran out of the house.

'Let me go. Let me go!' said Susan (for her lover's arm was round her waist.) 'I must go to him if he's fretting. I promised mother I would.' She pulled herself away, and went in search of the boy. She sought in byre and barn, through the orchard, where indeed in this leafless winter time there was no great concealment; up into the room where the wool was usually stored in the later summer, and at last she found him, sitting at bay, like some hunted creature, up behind the wood-stack.

'What are ye gone for, lad, and me seeking you everywhere?' asked she, breathless.

'I did not know you would seek me. I've been away many a time, and no one has cared to seek me,' said he, crying afresh.

'Nonsense,' replied Susan, 'don't be so foolish, ye little good-for-nought.' But she crept up to him in the hole he had made underneath the great, brown sheafs of wood, and squeezed herself down by him. 'What for should folk seek after you, when you get away from them whenever you can?' asked she.

'They don't want me to stay. Nobody wants me. If I go with father, he says I hinder more than I help. You used to like to have me with you. But now, you've taken up with Michael, and you'd rather I was away; and I can just bide away; but I cannot stand Michael jeering at me. He's got you to love him, and that might serve him.'

'But I love you too, dearly, lad!' said she, putting her arm round his neck.

'Which on us do you like best?' said he wistfully, after a little pause, putting her arm away, so that he might look in her face, and see if she spoke truth.

She went very red.

'You should not ask such questions. They are not fit for you to ask, nor for me to answer.'

'But mother bade you love me!' said he plaintively.

'And so I do. And so I ever will do. Lover nor husband shall come betwixt thee and me, lad – ne'er a one of them. That I promise thee (as I promised mother before), in the sight of God and with her hearkening now, if ever she can hearken to earthly word again. Only I cannot abide to have thee fretting, just because my heart is large enough for two.'

'And thou'lt love me always?'

'Always, and ever. And the more – the more thou'lt love Michael,' said she, dropping her voice.

'I'll try,' said the boy, sighing, for he remembered many a harsh word and blow of which his sister knew nothing. She would have risen up to go away, but he held her tight; for here and now she was all his own, and he did not know when such a time might come again. So the two sat crouched up and silent, till they heard the horn blowing at the field–gate, which was the summons home to any wanderers belonging to the farm, and, at this hour of the evening, signified that supper was ready. Then the two went in.

CHAPTER II

Susan and Michael were to be married in April. He had already gone to take possession of his new farm, three or four miles away from Yew Nook – but that is neighbouring, according to the acceptation of the word in that thinly-populated district, – when William Dixon fell ill. He came home one evening, complaining of headache and pains in his limbs, but seemed to loathe the posset which Susan prepared for him: the treacle-posset which was the homely country remedy against an incipient cold. He took to his bed with a sensation of exceeding weariness, and an odd, unusual looking-back to the days of his youth, when he was a lad living with his parents, in this very house.

The next morning he had forgotten all his life since then, and did not know his own children; crying, like a newly-weaned baby, for his mother to come and soothe away his terrible pain. The doctor from Coniston said it was the typhus fever, and warned Susan of its infectious character, and shook his head over his patient. There were no near friends to come and share her anxiety; only good, kind old Peggy, who was faithfulness itself, and one or two labourers' wives, who would fain have helped her, had not their hands been tied by the responsibility to their own families. But, somehow, Susan neither feared nor flagged. As for fear, indeed, she had no time to give way to it, for every energy of both body and mind was required. Besides, the young have had too little experience of the danger of infection to dread it much. She did indeed wish, from time to time, that Michael had been at home to have taken Willie over to his father's at High Beck; but then, again, the lad was docile and useful to her, and his fecklessness in many things might make him harshly treated by strangers; so, perhaps, it was as well that Michael was away at Appleby fair, or even beyond that – gone into Yorkshire after horses.

Her father grew worse; and the doctor insisted on sending over a nurse from Coniston. Not a professed nurse – Coniston could not have supported such a one; but a widow who was ready to go where the doctor sent her for the sake of the payment. When she came, Susan suddenly gave way; she was felled by the fever herself, and lay unconscious for long weeks. Her consciousness returned to her one spring afternoon: early spring; April – her wedding month. There was a little fire burning in the small corner grate, and the flickering of the blaze was enough for her to notice in her weak state. She felt that there was some one sitting on the window side of her bed, behind the curtain, but she did not care to know who it was; it was even too great a trouble for her languid mind to consider who it was likely to be. She would rather shut her eyes, and melt off again into the gentle luxury of sleep. The next time she wakened, the Coniston nurse perceived her movement, and made her a cup of tea, which she drank with eager relish; but still they did not speak, and once more Susan lay motionless – not asleep, but strangely, pleasantly conscious of all the small chamber and household sounds; the fall of a cinder on the hearth, the fitful singing of the half-empty kettle, the cattle tramping out to field again after they had been milked, the aged step on the creaking stair – old Peggy's, as she knew. It came to her door; it stopped; the person outside listened for a moment, and then lifted the wooden latch, and looked in. The watcher by the bedside arose, and went to her. Susan would have been glad to see Peggy's face once more, but was far too weak to turn, so she lay and listened.

'How is she?' whispered one trembling, aged voice.

'Better,' replied the other. 'She's been awake, and had a cup of tea. She'll do now.'

'Has she asked after him?'

'Hush! No; she has not spoken a word.'

'Poor lass! poor lass!'

The door was shut. A weak feeling of sorrow and self-pity came over Susan. What was wrong? Whom had she loved? And dawning, dawning, slowly rose the sun of her former life, and all particulars were made distinct to her. She felt that some sorrow was coming to her, and cried over it before she knew what it was, or had strength enough to ask. In the dead of night – and she had never slept again – she softly called to the watcher, and asked:

'Who?'

'Who what?' replied the woman, with a conscious affright, ill-veiled by a poor assumption of ease. 'Lie still, there's a darling, and go to sleep. Sleep's better for you than all the doctor's stuff.'

'Who?' repeated Susan. 'Something is wrong. Who?'

'Oh dear!' said the woman. 'There's nothing wrong. Willie has taken the turn, and is doing nicely.'

'Father?'

'Well! he's all right now,' she answered, looking another way, as if seeking for something.

'Then it's Michael! Oh me! oh me!' She set up a succession of weak, plaintive, hysterical cries before the nurse could pacify her by declaring that Michael had been at the house not three hours before to ask after her, and looked as well and as hearty as every man did.

'And you heard of no harm to him since?' inquired Susan.

'Bless the lass, no, for sure! I've ne'er heard his name named since I saw him go out of the yard as stout a man as ever trod shoe-leather.'

It was well, as the nurse said afterwards to Peggy, that Susan had been so easily pacified by the equivocating answer in respect of her father. If she had pressed the question home in his case as she did in Michael's she would have learnt that he was dead and buried more than a month before. It was well, too, that in her weak state of convalescence (which lasted long after this first day of consciousness) her perceptions were not sharp enough to observe the sad change that had taken place in Willie. His bodily strength returned; his appetite was something enormous – but his eyes wandered continually; his regard could not be arrested; his speech became slow, impeded, and incoherent. People began to say that the fever had taken away the little wit Willie Dixon had ever possessed, and that they feared that he would end in being a 'natural,' as they call an idiot in the Dales.

The habitual affection and obedience to Susan lasted longer than any other feeling that the boy had had previous to his illness; and, perhaps, this made her be the last to perceive what every one else had long anticipated. She felt the awakening rude when it did come. It was in this wise:

One June evening, she sat out of doors under the yew tree, knitting. She was pale still from her recent illness; and her languor, joined to the fact of her black dress, made her look more than usually interesting. She was no longer the buoyant self-sufficient Susan, equal to every occasion. The men were bringing in the cows to be milked, and Michael was about in the yard giving orders and directions with somewhat the air of a master, for the farm belonged of right to Willie, and Susan had succeeded to the guardianship of her brother. Michael and she were to be married as soon as she was strong enough – so perhaps, his authoritative manner was justified: but the labourers did not like it, although they said little. They remembered him a stripling on the farm, knowing far less than they did, and often glad to shelter his ignorance of all agricultural matters behind their superior knowledge. They would have taken orders from Susan with far more willingness: nay, Willie himself might have commanded them; and from the old hereditary feeling toward the owners of land, they would have obeyed him with far greater cordiality than they now showed to Michael. But Susan was tired with even three rounds of knitting, and seemed not to notice, or to care, how things went on around her; and Willie – poor Willie! – there he stood lounging against the door-sill, enormously grown and developed, to be sure, but with restless eyes and ever open mouth, and every now and then setting up a strange kind of howling cry, and then smiling vacantly to himself at the sound he had made. As the two labourers passed him, they looked at each other ominously, and shook their heads.

'Willie, darling,' said Susan, 'don't make that noise – it makes my head ache.'

She spoke feebly, and Willie did not seem to hear; at any rate, he continued his howl from time to time.

'Hold thy noise, wilt'a?' said Michael roughly, as he passed near him, and threatening him with his fist. Susan's back was turned to the pair. The expression of Willie's face turned from vacancy to fear, and he came shambling up to Susan, who put her arm round him; and, as if protected by that shelter, he began making faces at Michael. Susan saw what was going on, and, as if now first struck by the strangeness of her brother's manner, she looked anxiously at Michael for an explanation. Michael was irritated at Willie's defiance of him, and did not mince the matter.

'It's just that the fever has left him silly – he never was as wise as other folk, and now I doubt if he will ever get right.'

Susan did not speak, but she went very pale, and her lip quivered. She looked long and wistfully at Willie's face, as he watched the motion of the ducks in the great stable-pool. He laughed softly to himself every now and then.

'Willie likes to see the ducks go overhead,' said Susan, instinctively adopting the form of speech she would have used to a young child.

'Willie, boo! Willie, boo!' he replied, clapping his hands, and avoiding her eye.

'Speak properly, Willie,' said Susan, making a strong effort at self-control, and trying to arrest his attention.

'You know who I am – tell me my name!' She grasped his arm almost painfully tight to make him attend. Now he looked at her, and, for an instant, a gleam of recognition quivered over his face; but the exertion was evidently painful, and he began to cry at the vainness of the effort to recall her name. He hid his face upon her shoulder with the old affectionate trick of manner. She put him gently away, and went into the house into her own little bedroom. She locked the door, and did not reply at all to Michael's calls for her, hardly spoke to old Peggy, who tried to tempt her out to receive some homely sympathy; and through the open casement there still came the idiotic sound of 'Willie, boo! Willie, boo!'

CHAPTER III

After the stun of the blow came the realisation of the consequences. Susan would sit for hours trying patiently to recall and piece together fragments of recollection and consciousness in her brother's mind. She would let him go and pursue some senseless bit of play, and wait until she could catch his eye or his attention again, when she would resume her self-imposed task. Michael complained that she never had a word for him, or a minute of time to spend with him now; but she only said she must try, while there was yet a chance, to bring back her brother's lost wits. As for marriage in this state of uncertainty, she had no heart to think of it. Then Michael stormed, and absented himself for two or three days; but it was of no use. When he came back he saw that she had been crying till her eyes were all swollen up, and he gathered from Peggy's scolding (which she did not spare him) that Susan had eaten nothing since he went away. But she was as inflexible as ever.

'Not just yet. Only not just yet. And don't say again that I do not love you,' said she, suddenly hiding herself in his arms.

And so matters went on through August. The crop of oats was gathered in; the wheat-field was not ready as yet, when one fine day Michael drove up in a borrowed shandry, and offered to take Willie a ride. His manner, when Susan asked him where he was going to, was rather confused; but the answer was straight and clear enough.

He had business in Ambleside. He would never lose sight of the lad, and have him back safe and sound before dark. So Susan let him go.

Before night they were at home again: Willie in high delight at a little rattling paper windmill that Michael had bought for him in the street, and striving to imitate this new sound with perpetual buzzings. Michael, too, looked pleased. Susan knew the look, although afterwards she remembered that he had tried to veil it from her, and had assumed a grave appearance of sorrow whenever he caught her eye. He put up his horse; for, although he had three miles further to go, the moon was up – the bonny harvest moon – and he did not care how late he had to drive on such a road by such a light. After the supper which Susan had prepared for the travellers was over, Peggy went upstairs to see Willie safe in bed; for he had to have the same care taken of him that a little child of four years old requires.

Michael drew near to Susan.

'Susan,' said he, 'I took Will to see Dr. Preston, at Kendal. He is the first doctor in the county. I thought it were better for us – for you – to know at once what chance there were for him.'

'Well!' said Susan, looking eagerly up. She saw the same strange glance of satisfaction, the same instant change to apparent regret and pain. 'What did he say?' said she. 'Speak! can't you?'

'He said he would never get better of his weakness.'

'Never!'

'No; never. It's a long word, and hard to bear. And there's worse to come, dearest. The doctor thinks he will get badder from year to year. And he said, if he was us – you – he would send him off in time to Lancaster Asylum. They've ways there both of keeping such people in order and making them happy. I only tell you what he said,' continued he seeing the gathering storm in her face.

'There was no harm in his saying it,' she replied, with great self-constraint, forcing herself to speak coldly instead of angrily. 'Folk is welcome to their opinions.'

They sat silent for a minute or two, her breast heaving with suppressed feeling.

'He's counted a very clever man,' said Michael at length.

'He may be. He's none of my clever men, nor am I going to be guided by him, whatever he may think. And I don't thank them that went and took my poor lad to have such harsh notions formed about him. If I'd been there, I could have called out the sense that is in him.'

'Well! I'll not say more tonight, Susan. You're not taking it rightly, and I'd best be gone, and leave you to think it over. I'll not deny they are hard words to hear, but there's sense in them, as I take it; and I reckon you'll have to come to 'em. Anyhow, it's a bad way of thanking me for my pains; and I don't take it well in you, Susan,' said he, getting up, as if offended.

'Michael, I'm beside myself with sorrow. Don't blame me if I speak sharp. He and me is the only ones, you see. And mother did so charge me to have a care of him! And this is what he's come to, poor lile chap!' She began to cry, and Michael to comfort her with caresses.

'Don't,' said she. 'It's no use trying to make me forget poor Willie is a natural. I could hate myself for being happy with you, even for just a little minute. Go away, and leave me to face it out.'

'And you'll think it over, Susan, and remember what the doctor says?'

'I can't forget,' said she. She meant she could not forget what the doctor had said about the hopelessness of her brother's case; Michael had referred to the plan of sending Willie to an asylum, or madhouse, as they were called in that day and place. The idea had been gathering force in Michael's mind for some time; he had talked it over with his father, and secretly rejoiced over the possession of the farm and land which would then be his in fact, if not in law, by right of his wife. He had always considered the good penny her father could give her in his catalogue of Susan's charms and attractions. But of late he had grown to esteem her as the heiress of

Yew Nook. He, too, should have land like his brother – land to possess, to cultivate, to make profit from, to bequeath. For some time he had wondered that Susan had been so much absorbed in Willie's present, that she had never seemed to look forward to his future, state. Michael had long felt the boy to be a trouble; but of late he had absolutely loathed him. His gibbering, his uncouth gestures, his loose, shambling gait, all irritated Michael inexpressibly. He did not come near the Yew Nook for a couple of days. He thought that he would leave her time to become anxious to see him and reconciled to his plan. They were strange lonely days to Susan. They were the first she had spent face to face with the sorrows that had turned her from a girl into a woman; for hitherto Michael had never let twenty-four hours pass by without coming to see her since she had had the fever. Now that he was absent, it seemed as though some sort of irritation was removed from Will, who was much more gentle and tractable than he had been for many weeks. Susan thought that she observed him making efforts at her bidding; and there was something piteous in the way in which he crept up to her, and looked wistfully in her face, as if asking her to restore him the faculties that he felt to be wanting.

'I never will let thee go, lad. Never! There's no knowing where they would take thee to, or what they would do with thee. As it says in the Bible, "Nought but death shall part thee and me!"'

The country-side was full, in those days, of stories of the brutal treatment offered to the insane: stories that were, in fact, but too well founded, and the truth of one of which only would have been a sufficient reason for the strong prejudice existing against all such places. Each succeeding hour that Susan passed, alone, or with the poor affectionate lad for her sole companion, served to deepen her solemn resolution never to part with him. So, when Michael came, he was annoyed and surprised by the calm way in which she spoke, as if following Dr. Preston's advice was utterly and entirely out of the question. He had expected nothing less than a consent, reluctant it might be, but still a consent; and he was extremely irritated. He could have repressed his anger, but he chose rather to give way to it; thinking that he could thus best work upon Susan's affection, so as to gain his point. But, somehow, he over-reached himself; and now he was astonished in his turn at the passion of indignation that she burst into.

'Thou wilt not bide in the same house with him, say'st thou? There's no need for thy biding, as far as I can tell. There's solemn reason why I should bide with my own flesh and blood, and keep to the word I pledged my mother on her death-bed; but, as for thee, there's no tie that I know on to keep thee fro' going to America or Botany Bay this very night, if that were thy inclination. I will have no more of your threats to make me send my bairn away. If thou marry me, thou'lt help me to take charge of Willie. If thou doesn't choose to marry me on those terms – why, I can snap my fingers at thee, never fear. I'm not so far gone in love as that. But I will not have thee, if thou say'st in such a hectoring way that Willie must go out of the house – and the house his own too – before thou'lt set foot in it. Willie bides here, and I bide with him.'

'Thou hast may be spoken a word too much,' said Michael, pale with rage. 'If I am free, as thou say'st, to go to Canada, or Botany Bay, I reckon I'm free to live where I like; and that will not be with a natural who may turn into a madman some day, for aught I know. Choose between him and me, Susy, for I swear to thee, thou shan't have both.'

'I have chosen,' said Susan, now perfectly composed and still. 'Whatever comes of it, I bide with Willie.'

'Very well,' replied Michael, trying to assume an equal composure of manner. 'Then I'll wish you a very good night.' He went out of the house door, half-expecting to be called back again; but, instead, he heard a hasty step inside, and a bolt drawn.

'Whew!' said he to himself, 'I think I must leave my lady alone for a week or two, and give her time to come to her senses. She'll not find it so easy as she thinks to let me go.'

So he went past the kitchen window in nonchalant style, and was not seen again at Yew Nook for some weeks. How did he pass the time? For the first day or two, he was unusually cross with all things and people that came athwart him. Then wheat-harvest began, and he was busy, and exultant about his heavy crop. Then a man came from a distance to bid for the lease of his farm, which, by his father's advice, had been offered for sale, as he himself was so soon likely to remove to the Yew Nook. He had so little idea that Susan really would remain firm to her determination, that he at once began to haggle with the man who came after his farm, showed him the crop just got in, and managed skilfully enough to make a good bargain for himself. Of course, the bargain had to be sealed at the public house; and the companions he met with there soon became friends enough to tempt him into Langdale, where again he met with Eleanor Hebthwaite.

How did Susan pass the time? For the first day or so, she was too angry and offended to cry. She went about her household duties in a quick, sharp, jerking, yet absent way; shrinking one moment from Will, overwhelming him with remorseful caresses the next. The third day of Michael's absence, she had the relief of a good fit of crying; and, after that, she grew softer and more tender; she felt how harshly she had spoken to him, and remembered how angry she had been. She made excuses for him. 'It was no wonder,' she said to herself, 'that he had been vexed with her; and no wonder he would not give in, when she had never tried to speak gently or to reason with him. She was to blame, and she would tell him so, and tell him once again all that her mother had bade her to be to Willie, and all the horrible stories she had heard about madhouses; and he would be on her side at once.'

And so she watched for his coming, intending to apologise as soon as ever she saw him. She hurried over her household work, in order to sit quietly at her sewing, and hear the first distant sound of his well-known step or whistle. But even the sound of her flying needle seemed too loud – perhaps she was losing an exquisite instant of anticipation; so she stopped sewing, and looked longingly out through the geranium leaves, in order that her eye might catch the first stir of the branches in the wood-path by which he generally came. Now and then a bird might spring out of the covert; otherwise the leaves were heavily still in the sultry weather of early autumn. Then she would take up her sewing, and with a spasm of resolution, she would determine that a certain task should be fulfilled before she would again allow herself the poignant luxury of expectation. Sick at heart was she when the evening closed in, and the chances of that day diminished. Yet she stayed up longer than usual, thinking that if he were coming – if he were only passing along the distant road – the sight of a light in the window might encourage him to make his appearance even at that late hour, while seeing the house all darkened and shut up might quench any such intention.

Very sick and weary at heart, she went to bed; too desolate and despairing to cry, or make any moan. But in the morning hope came afresh. Another day – another chance! And so it went on for weeks. Peggy understood her young mistress's sorrow full well, and respected it by her silence on the subject. Willie seemed happier now that the irritation of Michael's presence was removed; for the poor idiot had a kind of antipathy to Michael, which was a kind of heart's echo to the repugnance in which the latter held him. Altogether, just at this time, Willie was the happiest of the three.

As Susan went into Coniston, to sell her butter, one Saturday, some inconsiderate person told her that she had seen Michael Hurst the night before. I said inconsiderate, but I might rather have said unobservant; for any one who had spent half-an-hour in Susan Dixon's company might have seen that she disliked having any reference made to the subjects nearest her heart, were they joyous or grievous. Now she went a little paler than usual (and she had never recovered her colour since she had had the fever), and tried to keep silence. But an irrepressible pang forced out the question:

'Where?'

'At Thomas Applethwaite's, in Langdale. They had a kind of harvest-home; and he were there among the young folk, and very thick wi' Nelly Hebthwaite, old Thomas's niece. Thou'lt have to look after him a bit, Susan!'

She neither smiled nor sighed. The neighbour who had been speaking to her was struck with the grey stillness of her face. Susan herself felt how well her self-command was obeyed by every little muscle, and said to herself in her Spartan manner, 'I can bear it without either wincing or blenching.' She went home early, at a tearing, passionate pace, trampling and breaking through all obstacles of briar or bush. Willie was moping in her absence – hanging listlessly on the farm-yard gate to watch for her. When he saw her, he set up one of his strange, inarticulate cries, of which she was now learning the meaning, and came towards her with his loose, galloping run, head and limbs all shaking and wagging with pleasant excitement. Suddenly she turned from him, and burst into tears. She sat down on a stone by the wayside, not a hundred yards from home, and buried her face in her hands, and gave way to a passion of pent-up sorrow; so terrible and full of agony were her low cries that the idiot stood by her, aghast and silent – all his joy gone for the time, but not, like her joy, turned into ashes. Some thought struck him. Yes! the sight of her woe made him think, great as the exertion was. He ran, and stumbled, and shambled home, buzzing with his lips all the time. She never missed him. He came back in a trice, bringing with him his cherished paper windmill, bought on that fatal day when Michael had taken him into Kendal to have his doom of perpetual idiotcy pronounced. He thrust it into Susan's face, her hands, her lap regardless of the injury his frail plaything thereby received. He leapt before her to think how he had cured all heart-sorrow, buzzing louder than ever. Susan looked up at him, and that glance of her sad eyes sobered him. He began to whimper, he knew not why; and she now, comforter in her turn, tried to soothe him by twirling his windmill. But it was broken; it made no noise; it would not go round. This seemed to afflict Susan more than him. She tried to make it right, although she saw the task was hopeless; and, while she did so, the tears rained down, unheeded, from her bent head on the paper toy.

'It won't do,' said she at last. 'It will never do again.' And, somehow, she took the accident and her words as omens of the love that was broken, and that she feared could never be pieced together more. She rose up and took Willie's hand, and the two went slowly into the house.

To her surprise, Michael Hurst sat in the house-place. House-place is a sort of better kitchen, where no cookery is done, but which is reserved for state occasions. Michael had gone in there because he was accompanied by his only sister, a woman older than himself, who was well married beyond Keswick, and who had come for the first time to make acquaintance with Susan. Michael had primed his sister with his wishes regarding Will, and the position in which he stood with Susan; and arriving at Yew Nook in the absence of the latter, he had not scrupled to conduct his sister into the guest-room, as he held Mrs. Gale's worldly position in respect and admiration, and therefore wished her to be favourably impressed with all the signs of property which he was beginning to consider as Susan's greatest charms. He had secretly said to himself that, if Eleanor Hebthwaite and Susan Dixon were equal in point of riches, he would sooner have Eleanor by far. He had begun to consider Susan as a termagant; and, when he thought of his intercourse with her, recollections of her somewhat warm and hasty temper came far more readily to his mind than any remembrance of her generous, loving nature.

And now she stood face to face with him; her eyes tear-swollen, her garments dusty, and here and there torn in consequence of her rapid progress through the bushy by-paths. She did not make a favourable impression on the well-clad Mrs. Gale, dressed in her best silk gown, and therefore unusually susceptible to the appearance of another. Nor were Susan's manners gracious or cordial. How could they be, when she remembered what had passed between Michael and herself the last time they met? For her penitence had faded away under the daily disappointment of these last weary weeks.

But she was hospitable in substance. She bade Peggy hurry on the kettle, and busied herself among the tea-cups; thankful that the presence of Mrs. Gale, as a stranger, would prevent the immediate recurrence to the one subject which she felt must be present in Michael's mind as well as in her own. But Mrs. Gale was withheld by no such feelings of delicacy. She had come ready-primed with the case, and had undertaken to bring the girl to reason. There was no time to be lost. It had been pre-arranged between the brother and sister that he was to stroll out into the farm-yard before his sister introduced the subject; but she was so confident in the success of her arguments that she must needs have the triumph of a victory as soon as possible; and, accordingly, she brought a hailstorm of good reasons to bear upon Susan. Susan did not reply for a long time; she was so indignant at this intermeddling of a stranger in the deep family sorrow and shame. Mrs. Gale thought she was gaining the day, and urged her arguments more pitilessly. Even Michael winced for Susan, and wondered at her silence. He shrunk out of sight, and into the shadow, hoping that his sister might prevail, but annoyed at the hard way in which she kept putting the case.

Suddenly Susan turned round from the occupation she had pretended to be engaged in, and said to him in a low voice, which yet not only vibrated itself, but made its hearers thrill through all their obtuseness:

'Michael Hurst! does your sister speak truth, think you?'

Both women looked at him for his answer; Mrs. Gale without anxiety, for had she not said the very words they had spoken together before? had she not used the very arguments that he himself had suggested? Susan, on the contrary, looked to his answer as settling her doom for life; and in the gloom of her eyes you might have read more despair than hope.

He shuffled his position. He shuffled in his words.

'What is it you ask? My sister has said many things.'

'I ask you,' said Susan, trying to give a crystal clearness both to her expressions and her pronunciation, 'if, knowing as you do how Will is afflicted, you will help me to take that charge of him which I promised my mother on her death-bed that I would do; and which means, that I shall keep him always with me, and do all in my power to make his life happy. If you will do this, I will be your wife; if not, I remain unwed.'

'But he may get dangerous; he can be but a trouble; his being here is a pain to you, Susan, not a pleasure.'

'I ask you for either yes or no.' said she, a little contempt at his evading her question mingling with her tone. He perceived it, and it nettled him.

'And I have told you. I answered your question the last time I was here. I said I would ne'er keep house with an idiot; no more I will. So now you've gotten your answer.'

'I have,' said Susan. And she sighed deeply.

'Come, now,' said Mrs. Gale, encouraged by the sigh; 'one would think you don't love Michael, Susan, to be so stubborn in yielding to what I'm sure would be best for the lad.'

'Oh! she does not care for me,' said Michael. 'I don't believe she ever did.'

'Don't I? Haven't I?' asked Susan, her eyes blazing out fire. She left the room directly, and sent Peggy in to make the tea; and, catching at Will, who was lounging about in the kitchen,

she went ustairs with him and bolted herself in, straining the
boy to her heart, and keeping almost breathless, lest any noise
she made might cause him to break out into the howls and
sounds which she could not bear that those below should
hear.

A knock on the door. It was Peggy.

'He wants for to see you, to wish you good-bye.'

'I cannot come. Oh, Peggy send them away.'

It was her only cry for sympathy; and the old servant
understood it. She sent them away, somehow; not politely, as
I have been given to understand.

'God go with them,' said Peggy, as she grimly watched
their retreating figures. 'We're rid of bad rubbish, anyhow.'
And she turned into the house, with the intention of making
ready some refreshment for Susan, after her hard day at the
market, and her harder evening. But in the kitchen, to which
she passed through the empty house-place, making a face of
contemptuous dislike, at the used tea-cups and fragments of a
meal yet standing there, she found Susan, with her sleeves
tucked up and her working apron on, busied in preparing to
make clap-bread, one of the hardest and hottest domestic
tasks of a Daleswoman. She looked up, and first met, and
then avoided, Peggy's eye; it was too full of sympathy. Her
own cheeks were flushed, and her own eyes were dry and
burning.

'Where's the board, Peggy? We need clap-bread; and, I
reckon, I've time to get through with it tonight.' Her voice
had a sharp, dry tone in it, and her motions a jerking
angularity about them.

Peggy said nothing, but fetched her all that she needed.
Susan beat her cakes thin with vehement force. As she
stooped over them, regardless even of the task in which she
seemed so much occupied, she was surprised by a touch on
her mouth of something – what she did not see at first. It was
a cup of tea, delicately sweetened and cooled, and held to her
lips, when exactly ready, by the faithful old woman. Susan
held it off a hand's breadth, and looked into Peggy's eyes,
while her own filled with the strange relief of tears.

'Lass!' said Peggy solemnly, 'Thou hast done well. It is not
long to bide, and then the end will come.'

'But you are very old, Peggy,' said Susan, quivering.

'It is but a day sin' I were young,' replied Peggy; but she stopped the conversation by again pushing the cup with gentle force to Susan's dry and thirsty lips. When she had drunken she fell again to her labour, Peggy heating the hearth and doing all that she knew would be required, but never speaking another word. Willie basked close to the fire, enjoying the animal luxury of warmth, for the autumn evenings were beginning to be chilly. It was one o'clock before they thought of going to bed on that memorable night.

CHAPTER IV

The vehemence with which Susan Dixon threw herself into occupation could not last for ever. Times of languor and remembrance would come – times when she recurred with a passionate yearning to bygone days, the recollection of which was so vivid and delicious that it seemed as though it were the reality, and the present bleak bareness the dream. She smiled anew at the magical sweetness of some touch or tone which in memory she felt or heard, and drank the delicious cup of poison, although at the very time she knew what the consequences of racking pain would be.

'This time, last year,' thought she, 'we went nutting together – this very day last year; just such a day as today. Purple and gold were the lights on the hills; the leaves were just turning brown; here and there on the sunny slopes the stubble-fields looked tawny; down in a cleft of yon purple slate-rock the beck fell like a silver glancing thread; all just as it is today. And he climbed the slender, swaying nut trees, and bent the branches for me to gather; or made a passage through the hazel copses, from time to time claiming a toll. Who could have thought he loved me so little? – who? – who?'

Or, as the evening closed in, she would allow herself to imagine that she heard his coming step, just that she might recall the feeling of exquisite delight which had passed by without the due and passionate relish at the time, Then she would wonder how she could have had strength, the cruel, self-piercing strength, to say what she had done; to stab herself with that stern resolution, of which the scar would remain till her dying day. It might have been right; but, as she sickened, she wished she had not instinctively chosen the right. How luxurious a life haunted by no stern sense of duty must be! And many led this kind of life; why could not she? Oh, for one hour again of his sweet company! If he came now, she would agree to whatever he proposed.

It was a fever of the mind. She passed through it, and came out healthy, if weak. She was capable once more of taking pleasure in following an unseen guide through briar and brake. She returned with tenfold affection to her protecting care of Willie. She acknowledged to herself that he was to be her all-in-all in life. She made him her constant companion. For his sake, as the real owner of Yew Nook, and as his steward and guardian, she began that course of careful saving, and that love of acquisition, which afterwards gained for her the reputation of being miserly. She still thought that he might regain a scanty portion of sense – enough to require some simple pleasures and excitement, which would cost money. And money should not be wanting. Peggy rather assisted her in the formation of her parsimonious habits than otherwise; economy was the order of the district, and a certain degree of respectable avarice the characteristic of her age. Only Willie was never stinted nor hindered of anything that the two women thought could give him pleasure, for want of money.

There was one gratification which Susan felt was needed for the restoration of her mind to its more healthy state, after she had passed through the whirling fever, when duty was as nothing, and anarchy reigned; a gratification that, somehow, was to be her last burst of unreasonableness; of which she knew and recognised pain as the sure consequence. She must see him once more – herself unseen.

The week before the Christmas of this memorable year, she went out in the dusk of the early winter evening, wrapped close in shawl and cloak. She wore her dark shawl under her cloak, putting it over her head in lieu of a bonnet; for she knew that she might have to wait long in concealment. Then she tramped over the wet fell-path, shut in by misty rain for miles and miles, till she came to the place where he was lodging: a farmhouse in Langdale, with a steep, stony lane leading up to it. This lane was entered by a gate out of the main road, and by the gate were a few bushes – thorns; but of them the leaves had fallen, and they offered no concealment; an old wreck of a yew tree grew among them, however; and underneath that Susan cowered down, shrouding her face, of which the colour might betray her, with a corner of her shawl. Long did she wait; cold and cramped she became, too damp and stiff to change her posture readily. And after all, he might never come! But, she would wait till daylight, if need were; and she pulled out a crust, with which she had providently supplied herself. The rain had ceased – a dull, still, brooding weather had succeeded; it was a night to hear distant sounds. She heard horses' hoofs striking and splashing in the stones, and in the pools of the road at her back. Two horses; not well-ridden, or evenly guided, as she could tell.

Michael Hurst and a companion drew near; not tipsy, but not sober. They stopped at the gate to bid each other a maudlin farewell. Michael stooped forward to catch the latch with the hook of the stick which he carried; he dropped the stick, and it fell with one end close to Susan – indeed, with the slightest change of posture she could have opened the gate for him. He swore a great oath, and struck his horse with his closed fist, as if that animal had been to blame; then he dismounted, opened the gate, and fumbled about for his stick. When he had found it (Susan had touched the other end) his first use of it was to flog his horse well, and she had much ado to avoid its kicks and plunges. Then, still swearing, he staggered up the lane, for it was evident he was not sober enough to remount.

By daylight Susan was back and at her daily labours at Yew Nook. When the spring came, Michael Hurst was married to Eleanor Hebthwaite. Others, too, were married, and christenings made their firesides merry and glad; or they travelled, and came back after long years with many wondrous tales. More rarely, perhaps, a Dalesman changed his dwelling. But to all households more change came than to Yew Nook. There the seasons came round with monotonous sameness; or, if they brought mutation, it was of a slow, and decaying, and depressing kind. Old Peggy died. Her silent sympathy, concealed under much roughness, was a loss to Susan Dixon. Susan was not yet thirty when this happened; but she looked a middle-aged, not to say an elderly woman. People affirmed that she had never recovered her complexion since that fever, a dozen years ago, which killed her father, and left Will Dixon an idiot. But besides her grey sallowness, the lines in her face were strong, and deep, and hard. The movements of her eyeballs were slow and heavy; the wrinkles at the corners of her mouth and eyes were planted firm and sure; not an ounce of unnecessary flesh was there on her bones – every muscle started strong and ready for use. She needed all this bodily strength, to a degree that no human creature, now Peggy was dead, knew of; for Willie had grown up large and strong in body, and, though in general, docile enough in mind, every now and then he became first moody, and then violent. These paroxysms lasted but a day or two; and it was Susan's anxious care to keep their very existence hidden and unknown. It is true, that occasional passers-by on that lonely road heard sounds at night of knocking about of furniture, blows, and cries, as of some tearing demon within the solitary farmhouse; but these fits of violence usually occurred in the night; and, whatever had been their consequence, Susan had tidied and redded up all signs of aught unusual before the morning. For, above all, she dreaded lest some one might find out in what danger and perils he occasionally was, and might assume a right to take away her brother from her care. The one idea of taking charge of him had deepened and deepened with years. It was graven into her mind as the object for which she lived. The sacrifice she had made for this object only made it more precious to her. Besides, she separated the idea of the docile, affectionate, loutish, indolent Will, and kept it distinct from the terror which the demon that occasionally possessed him inspired her with. The one was her flesh and blood – the child of her dead mother; the other was some fiend who came to torture and convulse the creature she so loved. She believed that she fought her brother's battle in holding down those tearing hands, in binding, whenever she could, those uplifted restless arms, prompt and prone to do mischief. All the time she subdued him with her cunning or her strength, she spoke to him in pitying murmurs, or abused the third person, the fiendish enemy, in no unmeasured tones. Towards morning the paroxysm was exhausted, and he would fall asleep, perhaps only to awaken with evil and renewed vigour. But when he was laid down, she would sally out to taste the fresh air, and to work off her wild sorrow in cries and mutterings to herself. The early labourers saw her gestures at a distance, and thought her as crazed as the idiot brother who made the neighbourhood a haunted place. But did any chance person call at Yew Nook later on in the day, he would find Susan Dixon, cold, calm, collected; her manner curt, her wits keen.

Once this fit of violence lasted longer than usual. Susan's strength both of mind and body was nearly worn out; she wrestled in prayer that somehow it might end before she, too, was driven mad; or worse, might be obliged to give up life's aim, and consign Willie to a madhouse. From that moment of prayer (as she afterwards superstitiously thought) Willie calmed – and then he drooped – and then he sank – and, last of all, he died in reality from physical exhaustion.

But he was so gentle and tender as he lay on his dying bed; such strange, childlike gleams of returning intelligence came over his face, long after the power to make his dull, inarticulate sounds had departed, that Susan was attracted to him by a stronger tie than she had ever felt before. It was something to have even an idiot loving her with dumb, wistful animal affection; something to have any creature looking at her with such beseeching eyes, imploring protection from the insidious enemy stealing on. And yet she knew that to him death was no enemy, but a true friend, restoring light and health to his poor clouded mind. It was to her that death was an enemy; to her, the survivor, when Willie died; there was no one to love her. Worse doom still, there was no one left on earth for her to love.

You now know why no wandering tourist could persuade her to receive him as a lodger; why no tired traveller could melt her heart to afford him rest and refreshment; why long habits of seclusion had given her a moroseness of manner, and how care for the interests of another had rendered her keen and miserly.

But there was a third act in the drama of her life.

CHAPTER V

In spite of Peggy's prophecy that Susan's life should not seem long, it did seem wearisome and endless, as the years slowly uncoiled their monotonous circles. To be sure, she might have made change for herself; but she did not care to do it. It was, indeed, more than 'not caring', which merely implies a certain degree of *vis interniæ* to be subdued before an object can be attained, and that the object itself does not seem to be of sufficient importance to call out the requisite energy. On the contrary, Susan exerted herself to avoid change and variety. She had a morbid dread of new faces, which originated in her desire to keep poor dead Willie's state a profound secret. She had a contempt for new customs; and, indeed, her old ways prospered so well under her active hand and vigilant eye, that it was difficult to know how they could be improved upon. She was regularly present in Coniston market with the best butter and the earliest chickens of the season. Those were the common farm produce that every farmer's wife about had to sell; but Susan, after she had disposed of the more feminine articles, turned to on the man's side. A better judge of a horse or cow there was not in all the country round. Yorkshire itself might have attempted to jockey her, and would have failed. Her corn was sound and clean; her potatoes well preserved to the latest spring. People began to talk of the hoards of money Susan Dixon must have laid up somewhere; and one young ne'er-do-weel of a farmer's son undertook to make love to the woman of forty, who looked fifty-five, if a day. He made up to her by opening a gate on the road-path home, as she was riding on a bare-backed horse, her purchase not an hour ago. She was off before him, refusing his civility; but the remounting was not so easy, and rather than fail she did not choose to attempt it. She walked, and he walked alongside, improving his opportunity, which, as he vainly thought, had been consciously granted to him. As they drew near Yew Nook, he ventured on some expression of a wish to keep company with her. His words were vague and clumsily arranged. Susan turned round and coolly asked him to explain himself. He took courage as he thought of her reputed wealth, and expressed his wishes this second time pretty plainly. To his surprise, the reply she made was in a series of smart strokes across his shoulders, administered through the medium of a supple hazel-switch.

'Take that!' said she, almost breathless, 'to teach thee how thou darest make a fool of an honest woman old enough to be thy mother. If thou com'st a step nearer the house, there's a good horse-pool, and there's two stout fellows who'll like no better fun than ducking thee. Be off wi' thee!'

And she strode into her own premises, never looking round to see whether he obeyed her injunction or not.

Sometimes three or four years would pass over without her hearing Michael's Hurst's name mentioned. She used to wonder at such times whether he were dead or alive. She would sit for hours by the dying embers of her fire on a winter's evening, trying to recall the scenes of her youth; trying to bring up living pictures of the faces she had then known – Michael's most especially. She thought it was possible, so long had been the lapse of years, that she might now pass by him in the street unknowing and unknown. His outward form she might not recognise, but himself she should feel in the thrill of her whole being. He could not pass her unawares.

What little she did hear about him, all testified a downward tendency. He drank – not at stated times when there was no other work to be done, but continually, whether it was seed-time or harvest. His children were all ill at the same time; then one died, while the others recovered, but were poor, sickly things. No one dared to give Susan any direct intelligence of her former lover; many avoided all mention of his name in her presence; but a few spoke out either in indifference to, or ignorance of, those bygone days. Susan heard every word, every whisper, every sound that related to him. But her eye never changed, nor did a muscle of her face move.

Late one November night she sat over her fire, not a human being besides herself in the house; none but she had ever slept there since Willie's death. The farm-labourers had foddered the cattle and gone home hours before. There were crickets chirping all round the warm hearth-stones; there was the clock ticking with the peculiar beat Susan had known from her childhood, and which then and ever since she had oddly associated with the idea of a mother and child talking together, one loud tick, and quick – a feeble, sharp one following.

The day had been keen, and piercingly cold. The whole lift of heaven seemed a dome of iron. Black and frost-bound was the earth under the cruel east wind. Now the wind had dropped; and, as the darkness had gathered in, the weather-wise old labourers prophesied snow. The sounds in the air arose again, as Susan sat still and silent. They were of a different character to what they had been during the prevalence of the east wind. Then they had been shrill and piping; now they were like low distant growling; not unmusical, but strangely threatening. Susan went to the window, and drew aside the little curtain. The whole world was white – the air was blinded with the swift and heavy fall of snow. At present it came down straight; but Susan knew those distant sounds in the hollows and gullies of the hills portended a driving wind and a more cruel storm. She thought of her sheep; were they all folded? the new-born calf, was it bedded well? Before the drifts were formed too deep for her to pass in and out – and by the morning she judged that they would be six or seven feet deep – she would go out and see after the comfort of her beasts. She took a lantern, and tied a shawl over her head, and went out into the open air. She had tenderly provided for all her animals, and was returning, when, borne on the blast as if some spirit-cry – for it seemed to come rather down from the skies than from any creature standing on earth's level – she heard a voice of agony; she could not distinguish words; it seemed rather as if some bird of prey was being caught in the whirl of an icy wind, and torn and tortured by its violence. Again! up high above! Susan put down her lantern, and shouted loud in return; it was an instinct, for, if the creature were not human, which she had doubted but a moment before, what good could her responding cry do? And her cry was seized on by the tyrannous wind, and borne farther away in the opposite direction to that from which the call of agony

had proceeded. Again she listened: no sound; then again it
rang through space, and this time she was sure it was human.
She turned into the house, and heaped turf and wood on the
fire, which, careless of her own sensations, she had allowed to
fade and almost die out. She put a new candle in her lantern;
she changed her shawl for a maud, and leaving the door on
latch, she sallied out. Just at the moment when her ear first
encountered the weird noises of the storm, on issuing forth
into the open air, she thought she heard the words, 'Oh, God!
Oh, help!' They were a guide to her – if words they were, for
they came straight from a rock not a quarter of a mile from
Yew Nook, but only to be reached, on account of its
precipitous character, by a round-about path. Thither she
steered, defying wind and snow; guided by here a thorn-tree,
there an old, doddered oak, which had not quite lost their
identity under the whelming mask of snow. Now and then
she stopped to listen; but never a word or sound heard she, till,
right from where the copse-wood grew thick and tangled at
the base of the rock, round which she was winding, she heard
a moan. Into the brake – all snow in appearance – almost a
plain of snow, looked on from the eminence where she stood –
she plunged, breaking down the bush, stumbling, bruising
herself, fighting her way, her lantern held between her teeth,
and she herself using head as well as hands to butt away a
passage, at whatever cost of bodily injury. As she climbed or
staggered, owing to the unevenness of the snow-covered
ground where the briars and weeds of years were tangled and
matted together, her foot felt something strangely soft and
yielding. She lowered her lantern; there lay a man, prone on
his face, early covered by the fast-falling flakes; he must have
fallen from the rock above, as, not knowing of the circuitous
path, he had tried to descend its steep, slippery face. Who
could tell? it was no time for thinking. Susan lifted him up
with her wiry strength; he gave no help – no sign of life; but
for all that he might be alive: he was still warm; she tied her
maud round him; she fastened the lantern to her apron-string;
she held him tight, half-carrying, half-dragging – what did a
few bruises signify to him, compared to dear life, to precious
life! She got him through the brake, and down the path.
There, for an instant, she stopped to take breath; but, as if

stung by the Furies, she pushed on again with almost super-human strength. Clasping him round the waist, and leaning his dead weight against the lintel of the door, she tried to undo the latch; but now, just at this moment, a trembling faintness came over her, and a fearful dread took possession of her – that here, on the very threshold of her home, she might be found dead, and buried under the snow, when the farm-servants came in the morning. This terror stirred her up to one more effort. Then she and her companion were in the warmth of the quiet haven of that kitchen; she laid him on the settle, and sank on the floor by his side. How long she remained in this swoon she could not tell – not very long, she judged by the fire, which was still red and sullenly glowing when she came to herself. She lighted the candle, and bent over her late burden to ascertain if indeed he were dead. She stood long gazing. The man lay dead. There could be no doubt about it. His filmy eyes glared at her, unshut. But Susan was not one to be affrighted by the stony aspect of death. It was not that; it was the bitter, woeful recognition of Michael Hurst.

She was convinced he was dead; but after a while she refused to believe in her conviction. She stripped off his wet outer-garments with trembling, hurried hands. She brought a blanket down from her own bed; she made up the fire. She swathed him in fresh, warm wrappings, and laid him on the flags before the fire, sitting herself at his head, and holding it in her lap, while she tenderly wiped his loose, wet hair, curly still, although its colour had changed from nut-brown to iron-grey since she had seen it last. From time to time she bent over the face afresh; sick, and fain to believe that the flicker of the fire-light was some slight convulsive motion. But the dim, staring eyes struck chill to her heart. At last she ceased her delicate, busy caress; but she still held the head softly, as if caressing it. She thought over all the possibilities and chances in the mingled yarn of their lives that might, by so slight a turn, have ended far otherwise. If her mother's cold had been early tended, so that the responsibility as to her brother's weal or woe had not fallen upon her; if the fever had not taken such rough, cruel hold on Will; nay, if Mrs. Gale, that hard, worldly sister, had not accompanied him on his last visit to Yew Nook – his very last before this fatal, stormy night; if she had heard his cry, – cry uttered by those pale, dead lips with such wild, despairing agony, not yet three hours ago! – Oh! if she had but heard it sooner, he might have been saved before that blind, false step had precipitated him down the rock! In going over this weary chain of unrealised possibilities, Susan learnt the force of Peggy's words. Life was short, looking back upon it. It seemed but yesterday since all the love of her being had been poured out, and run to waste. The intervening years – the long, monotonous years that had turned her into an old woman before her time – were but a dream.

The labourers coming in the dawn of the winter's day were surprised to see the fire-light through the low kitchen window. They knocked; and, hearing a moaning answer, they entered, fearing that something had befallen their mistress. For all explanation they got these words:

'It is Michael Hurst. He was belated, and fell down the Raven's Crag. Where does Eleanor, his wife, live?'

How Michael Hurst got to Yew Nook no one but Susan ever knew. They thought he had dragged himself there, with some sore internal bruise sapping away his minuted life. They could not have believed the superhuman exertion which had first sought him out, and then draggd him hither. Only Susan knew of that.

She gave him into the charge of her servants, and went out and saddled her horse. Where the wind had drifted the snow on one side, and the road was clear and bare, she rode, and rode fast; where the soft, deceitful heaps were massed up, she dismounted and led her steed, plunging in deep, with fierce energy, the pain at her heart urging her onwards with a sharp, digging spur.

The grey, solemn, winter's noon was more night-like than the depth of summer's night; dim-purple brooded the low skies over the white earth, as Susan rode up to what had been Michael Hurst's abode while living. It was a small farmhouse – carelessly kept outside, slatternly tended within. The pretty Nelly Hebthwaite was pretty still; her delicate face had never suffered from any long-enduring feeling. If anything, its expression was that of plaintive sorrow; but the soft, light hair had scarcely a tinge of grey; the wood-rose tint of complexion yet remained, if not so brilliant as in youth; the straight nose, the small mouth were untouched by time. Susan felt the contrast even at that moment. She knew that her own skin was weather-beaten, furrowed, brown – that her teeth were gone, and her hair grey and ragged. And yet she was not two years older than Nelly – she had not been, in youth, when she took account of these things. Nelly stood wondering at the strange-enough horsewoman, who stopped and panted at the door, holding her horse's bridle, and refusing to enter.

'Where is Michael Hurst?' asked Susan at last.

'Well, I can't rightly say. He should have been at home last night; but he was off, seeing after a public-house to be let at Ulverstone, for our farm does not answer, and we were thinking —'

'He did not come home last night?' said Susan, cutting short the story, and half-affirming, half-questioning, by way of letting in a ray of the awful light before she let it full in, in its consuming wrath.

'No! he'll be stopping somewhere out Ulverstone ways. I'm sure we've need of him at home, for I've no one but lile Tommy to help me tend the beasts. Things have not gone well with us, and we don't keep a servant now. But you're trembling all over, ma'am. You'd better come in, and take something warm, while your horse rests. That's the stable-door, to your left.'

Susan took her horse there; loosened his girths, and rubbed him down with a wisp of straw. Then she looked about her for hay; but the place was bare of food, and smelt damp and unused. She went to the house, thankful for the respite, and got some clap-bread, which she mashed up in a pailful of luke-warm water. Every moment was a respite, and yet every moment made her dread the more the task that lay before her. It would be longer than she thought at first. She took the saddle off, and hung about her horse, which seemed, somehow, more like a friend than anything else in the world. She laid her cheek against its neck, and rested there, before returning to the house for the last time.

Eleanor had brought down one of her own gowns, which hung on a chair against the fire, and had made her unknown visitor a cup of hot tea. Susan could hardly bear all these little attentions: they choked her, and yet she was so wet, so weak with fatigue and excitement, that she could neither resist by voice nor by action. Two children stood awkwardly about, puzzled at the scene, and even Eleanor began to wish for some explanation of who her strange visitor was.

'You've, may be, heard him speaking of me? I'm called Susan Dixon.'

Nelly coloured, and avoided meeting Susan's eye.

'I've heard other folk speak of you. He never named your name.'

This respect of silence came like balm to Susan: balm not felt or heeded at the time it was applied, but very grateful in its effects for all that.

'He is at my house,' continued Susan, determined not to stop or quaver in the operation – the pain which must be inflicted.

'At your house? Yew Nook?' questioned Eleanor, surprised. 'How came he there?' – half jealously. 'Did he take shelter from the coming storm? Tell me, – there is something – tell me, woman.'

'He took no shelter. Would to God he had!'

'Oh! would to God! would to God!' shrieked out Eleanor, learning all from the woeful import of those dreary eyes. Her cries thrilled through the house; the children's piping wailings and passionate cries on 'Daddy! Daddy!' pierced into Susan's very marrow. But she remained as still and tearless as the great round face upon the clock.

At last in a lull of crying, she said – not exactly questioning, but as if partly to herself:

'You loved him, then?'

'Loved him! he was my husband! He was the father of three bonny bairns that lie dead in Grasmere churchyard. I wish you'd go, Susan Dixon, and let me weep without your watching me! I wish you'd never come near the place.'

'Alas! alas! it would not have brought him to life. I would have laid down my own to save his. My life has been so very sad! No one would have cared if I had died. Alas! alas!'

The tone in which she said this was so utterly mournful and despairing that it awed Nelly into quiet for a time. But by-and-by she said, 'I would not turn a dog out to do it harm; but the night is clear, and Tommy shall guide you to the Red

Cow. But, oh, I want to be alone! If you'll come back tomorrow, I'll be better, and I'll hear all, and thank you for every kindness you have shown him – and I do believe you've showed him kindness – though I don't know why.'

Susan moved heavily and strangely.

She said something – her words came thick and unintelligible. She had had a paralytic stroke since she had last spoken. She could not go, even if she would. Nor did Eleanor, when she became aware of the state of the case, wish her to leave. She had her laid on her own bed; and, weeping silently all the while for her lost husband, she nursed Susan like a sister. She did not know what her guest's worldly position might be; and she might never be repaid. But she sold many a little trifle to purchase such small comforts as Susan needed. Susan, lying still and motionless, learnt much. It was not a severe stroke; it might be the forerunner of others yet to come, but at some distance of time. But for the present she recovered, and regained much of her former health. On her sick-bed, she matured her plans. When she returned to Yew Nook, she took Michael Hurst's widow and children with her to live there, and fill up the haunted hearth with living forms, that should banish the ghosts.

And so it fell out that the latter days of Susan Dixon's life were better than the former.

THE POOR CLARE

THE POOR CLARE

CHAPTER I

December 12th, 1747 – My life has been strangely bound up with extraordinary incidents, some of which occurred before I had any connection with the principal actors in them, or, indeed, before I even knew of their existence. I suppose, most old men are, like me, more given to looking back upon their own career with a kind of fond interest and affectionate remembrance than to watching the events – though these may have far more interest for the multitude – immediately passing before their eyes. If this should be the case with the generality of old people, how much more so with me! . . . If I am to enter upon that strange story connected with poor Lucy, I must begin a long way back. I myself only came to the knowledge of her family history after I knew her; but, to make the tale clear to any one else, I must arrange events in the order in which they occurred – not that in which I became acquainted with them.

There is a great old hall in the north-east of Lancashire, in a part they called the Trough of Bolland, adjoining that other district named Craven. Starkey Manor-house is rather like a number of rooms clustered round a grey, massive, old keep than a regularly-built hall. Indeed, I suppose that the house only consisted of a great tower in the centre, in the days when the Scots made their raids terrible as far south as this; and that after the Stuarts came in, and there was a little more security of property in those parts, the Starkeys of that time added the lower building, which runs, two storeys high, all round the base of the keep. There has been a grand garden laid out in my days, on the southern slope near the house; but when I first knew the place, the kitchen garden at the farm was the only piece of cultivated ground belonging to it. The deer used to come within sight of the drawing-room windows, and might have browsed quite close up to the house if they had not been too wild and shy. Starkey Manor-house itself stood on a projection or peninsula of high land, jutting out from the abrupt hills that form the sides of the Trough of Bolland. These hills were rocky and bleak enough towards their summit; lower down they were clothed with tangled copsewood and green depths of fern, out of which a grey giant of an ancient forest-tree would tower here and there, throwing up its ghastly white branches, as if in imprecation, to the sky. These trees, they told me, were the remnants of that forest which existed in the days of the Heptarchy, and were even then noted as landmarks. No wonder that their upper and more exposed branches were leafless, and that the dead bark had peeled away, from sapless old age.

Not far from the house there were a few cottages, apparently of the same date as the keep; probably built for some retainers of the family, who sought shelter – they and their families and their small flocks and herds – at the hands of their feudal lord. Some of them had pretty much fallen to decay. They were built in a strange fashion. Strong beams had been sunk firm in the ground at the requisite distance, and their other ends had been fastened together, two and two, so as to form the shape of one of those rounded waggon-headed gipsy-tents, only very much larger. The spaces between were filled with mud, stones, osiers, rubbish, mortar – anything to keep out the weather. The fires were made in the centre of these rude dwellings, a hole in the roof forming the only chimney. No Highland hut or Irish cabin could be of rougher construction.

The owner of this property at the beginning of the present century, was a Mr. Patrick Byrne Starkey. His family had kept to the old faith, and were staunch Roman Catholics, esteeming it even a sin to marry any one of Protestant descent, however willing he or she might have been to embrace the Romish religion. Mr. Patrick Starkey's father had been a follower of James the Second; and during the disastrous campaign of that monarch he had fallen in love with an Irish beauty, a Miss Byrne, as zealous for her religion and for the Stuarts as himself. He had returned to Ireland after his escape to France, and married her, bearing her back to the court at St. Germains. But some license, on the part of the disorderly

gentlemen who surrounded King James in his exile, had
insulted his beautiful wife, and disgusted him; so he removed
from St. Germains to Antwerp, whence, in a few years' time,
he quietly returned to Starkey Manor-house – some of his
Lancashire neighbours having lent their good offices to reconcile him to the powers that were. He was as firm a Catholic as
ever, and as staunch an advocate for the Stuarts and the divine
rights of kings; but his religion almost amounted to asceticism,
and the conduct of those with whom he had been brought in
such close contact at St. Germains would little bear the
inspection of a stern moralist. So he gave his allegiance where
he could not give his esteem and learned to respect sincerely the
upright and moral character of one whom he yet regarded as an
usurper. King William's government had little need to fear
such a one. So he returned, as I have said, with a sobered heart
and impoverished fortunes, to his ancestral house, which had
fallen sadly to ruin while the owner had been a courtier, a
soldier, and an exile. The roads into the Trough of Bolland
were little more than cart-ruts; indeed, the way up to the house
lay along a ploughed field before you came to the deer-park.
Madam, as the country-folk used to call Mrs. Starkey, rode on
a pillion behind her husband, holding on to him with a light
hand by his leather riding-belt. Little master (he that was
afterwards Squire Patrick Byrne Starkey) was held on to his
pony by a serving-man. A woman past middle age walked,
with a firm and strong step, by the cart that held much of the
baggage; and, high up on the mails and boxes, sat a girl of
dazzling beauty, perched lightly on the topmost trunk, and
swaying herself fearlessly to and fro, as the cart rocked and
shook in the heavy roads of late autumn. The girl wore the
Antwerp *faille,* or black Spanish mantle, over her head; and
altogether her appearance was such that the old cottager, who
described the procession to me many years after, said that all
the country-folk took her for a foreigner. Some dogs, and the
boy who held them in charge, made up the company. They
rode silently along, looking with grave, serious eyes at the
people, who came out of the scattered cottages to bow or
curtsey to the real Squire, 'come back at last,' and gazed after
the little procession with gaping wonder, not deadened by the
sound of the foreign language in which the few necessary

words that passed among them were spoken. One lad, called
from his staring by the Squire to come and help about the cart,
accompanied them to the Manor-house. He said that when the
lady had descended from her pillion, the middle-aged woman
whom I have described as walking while the others rode,
stepped quickly forward; and, taking Madame Starkey (who
was of a slight and delicate figure) in her arms, she lifted her
over the threshold, and set her down in her husband's house, at
the same time uttering a passionate and outlandish blessing.
The Squire stood by, smiling gravely at first; but when the
words of blessing were pronounced, he took off his fine feath-
ered hat and bent his head. The girl with the black mantle
stepped onward into the shadow of the dark hall, and kissed the
lady's hand; and that was all the lad could tell to the group that
gathered round him on his return, eager to hear everything, and
to know how much the Squire had given him for his services.

From all I could gather, the Manor-house, at the time of
the Squire's return, was in the most dilapidated state. The
stout grey walls remained firm and entire; but the inner
chambers had been used for all kinds of purposes. The great
withdrawing-room had been a barn; the state tapestry-
chamber had held wool, and so on. But, by-and-by, they were
cleared out; and, if the Squire had no money to spend on new
furniture, he and his wife had the knack of making the best
of the old. He was no despicable joiner; she had a kind of grace
in whatever she did, and imparted an air of elegant picturesqueness to whatever she touched. Besides, they had
brought many rare things from the Continent; perhaps I
should rather say, things that were rare in that part of England
– carvings, and crosses, and beautiful pictures. And then,
again, wood was plentiful in the Trough of Bolland, and great
log-fires danced and glittered in all the dark, old rooms, and
gave a look of home and comfort to everything.

Why do I tell you all this? I have little to do with the Squire
and Madame Starkey; and yet I dwell upon them, as if I were
unwilling to come to the real people with whom my life was
so strangely mixed up. Madam had been nursed in Ireland by
the very woman who lifted her in her arms, and welcomed her
to her husband's home in Lancashire. Excepting for the short
period of her own married life, Bridget Fitzgerald had never

left her nursling. Her marriage – to one above her in rank – had been unhappy. Her husband had died, and left her in even greater poverty than that in which she was when he had first met with her. She had one child, the beautiful daughter who came riding on the waggon-load of furniture that was brought to the Manor-house. Madame Starkey had taken her again into her service when she became a widow. She and her daughter had followed 'the mistress' in all her fortunes; they had lived at St. Germains and at Antwerp, and were now come to her home in Lancashire. As soon as Bridget had arrived there, the Squire gave her a cottage of her own, and took more pains in furnishing it for her than he did in anything else out of his own house. It was only nominally her residence. She was constantly up at the great house; indeed, it was but a short cut across the woods from her own home to the home of her nursling. Her daughter Mary, in like manner, moved from one house to the other at her own will. Madam loved both mother and child dearly. They had great influence over her and, through her, over her husband. Whatever Bridget or Mary willed was sure to come to pass. They were not disliked; for though wild and passionate, they were also generous by nature. But the other servants were afraid of them, as being in secret the ruling spirits of the household. The Squire had lost his interest in all secular things; Madam was gentle, affectionate, and yielding. Both husband and wife were tenderly attached to each other and to their boy; but they grew more and more to shun the trouble of decision on any point; and hence it was that Bridget could exert such despotic power. But, if every one else yielded to her 'magic of a superior mind,' her daughter not unfrequently rebelled. She and her mother were too much alike to agree. There were wild quarrels between them, and wilder reconciliations. There were times when, in the heat of passion, they could have stabbed each other. At all other times they both – Bridget especially – would have willingly laid down their lives for one another. Bridget's love for her child lay very deep – deeper than that daughter ever knew; or, I should think, she would never have wearied of home as she did, and prayed her mistress to obtain for her some situation – as waiting-maid – beyond the seas, in that more cheerful continental life, among the scenes of which so many of her happiest years had been spent. She thought, as youth thinks, that life would last for ever, and that two or three years were but a small portion of it to pass away from her mother, whose only child she was. Bridget thought differently, but was too proud ever to show what she felt. If her child wished to leave her, why – she should go. But people said Bridget became ten years older in the course of two months at this time. She took it that Mary wanted to leave her. The truth was that Mary wanted for a time to leave the place, and to seek some change, and would thankfully have taken her mother with her.

Indeed, when Madame Starkey had gotten her a situation with some grand lady abroad, and the time drew near for her to go, it was Mary who clung to her mother with passionate embrace, and, with floods of tears, declared that she would never leave her; and it was Bridget who at last loosened her arms, and, grave and tearless herself, bade her keep her word, and go forth into the wide world. Sobbing aloud, and looking back continuously, Mary went away. Bridget was still as death, scarcely drawing her breath, or closing her stony eyes; till at last she turned back into her cottage, and heaved a ponderous old settle against the door. There she sat, motionless, over the grey ashes of her extinguished fire, deaf to Madam's sweet voice, as she begged leave to enter and comfort her nurse. Deaf, stony, and motionless, she sat for more than twenty hours; till, for the third time, Madam came across the snowy path from the great house carrying with her a young spaniel, which had been Mary's pet up at the hall, and which had not ceased all night long to seek for its absent mistress, and to whine and moan after her. With tears Madam told this story, through the closed door – tears excited by the terrible look of anguish, so steady, so immovable, so the same today as it was yesterday – on her nurse's face. The little creature in her arms began to utter its piteous cry, as it shivered with the cold. Bridget stirred; she moved – she listened. Again that long whine; she thought it was for her daughter; and what she had denied to her nursling and mistress she granted to the dumb creature that Mary had cherished. She opened the door, and took the dog from Madam's arms. Then Madam came in, and kissed and comforted the old woman, who took but little notice of her or anything.

And, sending up Master Patrick to the hall for fire and food, the sweet young lady never left her nurse all that night. Next day the Squire himself came down, carrying a beautiful foreign picture – Our Lady of the Holy Heart, the Papists call it. It is a picture of the Virgin, her heart pierced with arrows, each arrow representing one of her great woes. That picture hung in Bridget's cottage when I first saw her; I have that picture now.

Years went on. Mary was still abroad. Bridget was still and stern, instead of active and passionate. The little dog, Mignon, was indeed her darling. I have heard that she talked to it continually; although, to most people, she was so silent. The Squire and Madam treated her with the greatest consideration, and well they might; for to them she was as devoted and faithful as ever. Mary wrote pretty often, and seemed satisfied with her life. But at length the letters ceased – I hardly know whether before or after a great and terrible sorrow came upon the house of the Starkeys. The Squire sickened of a putrid fever; and Madam caught it in nursing him, and died. You may be sure, Bridget let no other woman tend her but herself; and in the very arms that had received her at birth, that sweet young woman laid her head down, and gave up her breath. The Squire recovered, in a fashion. He was never strong – he had never the heart to smile again. He fasted and prayed more than ever; and people did say that he tried to cut off the entail, and leave all the property away to found a monastery abroad, of which he prayed that some day little Squire Patrick might be the reverend father. But he could not do this, for the strictness of the entail and the laws against the Papists. So he could only appoint gentlemen of his own faith as guardians to his son, with many charges about the lad's soul, and a few about the land, and the way it was to be held while he was a minor. Of course, Bridget was not forgotten. He sent for her as he lay on his death-bed, and asked her if she would rather have a sum down, or have a small annuity settled upon her. She said at once she would have a sum down; for she thought of her daughter, and how she could bequeath the money to her, whereas an annuity would have died with her. So the Squire left her her cottage for life, and a fair sum of money. And then he died, with as ready and willing a heart as, I suppose, any gentleman took out of this world with him. The young Squire was carried off by his guardians, and Bridget was left alone.

I have said that she had not heard from Mary for some time. In her last letter, she had told of travelling about with her mistress, who was the English wife of some great foreign officer, and had spoken of her chances of making a good marriage, without naming the gentleman's name, keeping it rather back as a pleasant surprise to her mother; his station and fortune being, as I had afterwards reason to know, far superior to anything she had a right to expect. Then came a long silence; and Madam was dead, and the Squire was dead; and Bridget's heart was gnawed by anxiety, and she knew not whom to ask for news of her child. She could not write, and the Squire had managed her communication with her daughter. She walked off to Hurst; and got a good priest there – one whom she had known at Antwerp – to write for her. But no answer came. It was like crying into the awful stillness of night.

One day, Bridget was missed by those neighbours who had been accustomed to mark her goings-out and comings-in. She had never been sociable with any of them; but the sight of her had become a part of their daily lives, and slow wonder arose in their minds, as morning after morning came, and her house-door remained closed, her window dead from any glitter, or light of fire within. At length, some one tried the door; it was locked. Two or three laid their heads together, before daring to look in through the blank unshuttered window. But, at last, they summoned up courage, and then saw that Bridget's absence from their little world was not the result of accident or death, but of premeditation. Such small articles of furniture as could be secured from the effects of time and damp by being packed up, were stowed away in boxes. The picture of the Madonna was taken down, and gone. In a word, Bridget had stolen away from her home, and left no trace whither she had departed. I knew afterwards, that she and her little dog had wandered off on a long search for her lost daughter. She was too illiterate to have faith in letters, even had she had the means of writing and sending many. But she had faith in her own strong love, and believed that her passionate instinct would guide her to her child. Besides, foreign travel was no new thing to her, and she could speak enough of French to explain the object of her journey, and had, moreover, the advantage of being, from her faith, a welcome object of charitable hospitality at many a distant convent. But the country people round Starkey Manor-house knew nothing of all this. They wondered what had become of her, in a torpid, lazy fashion, and then left off thinking of her altogether. Several years passed. Both Manor-house and the cottage were deserted. The young Squire lived far away under the direction of his guardians. There were inroads of wool and corn into the sitting-rooms of the Hall; and there was some low talk, from time to time, among the hinds and country people, whether it would not be as well to break into old Bridget's cottage, and save such of her goods as were left from the moth and rust which must be making sad havoc. But this idea was always quenched by the recollection of her strong character and passionate anger; and tales of her masterful spirit, and vehement force of will, were whispered about, till the very thought of offending her, by touching any article of hers, became invested with a kind of horror: and it was believed that, dead or alive, she would not fail to avenge it.

Suddenly she came home; with as little noise or note of preparation as she had departed. One day some one noticed a thin, blue curl of smoke ascending from her chimney. Her door stood open to the noon-day sun; and, ere many hours had elapsed, some one had seen an old travel-and-sorrow-stained woman, dipping her pitcher in the well, and said, that the dark, solemn eyes that looked up at him were more like Bridget Fitzgerald's than any one else's in this world; and yet, if it were she, she looked as if she had been scorched in the flames of hell, so brown, and scared, and fierce a creature did she seem. By-and-by many saw her; and those who met her eye once cared not to be caught looking at her again. She had got into the habit of perpetually talking to herself; nay, more, answering herself, and varying her tones according to the side she took at the moment. It was no wonder that those who dared to listen outside her door at night believed that she held converse with some spirit; in short, she was unconsciously earning for herself the dreadful reputation of a witch.

Her little dog, which had wandered half over the Continent with her, was her only companion; a dumb remembrancer of happier days. Once he was ill; and she carried him more than three miles to ask about his management from one who had been groom to the last Squire, and had then been noted for his skill in all diseases of animals. Whatever this man did, the dog recovered; and they who heard her thanks, intermingled with blessings (that were rather promises of good fortune than prayers), looked grave at his good luck when, next year, his ewes twinned, and his meadow-grass was heavy and thick.

Now it so happened that, about the year seventeen hundred and eleven, one of the guardians of the young squire, a certain Sir Philip Tempest, bethought him of the good shooting there must be on his ward's property; and in consequence he brought down four or five gentlemen, of his friends, to stay for a week or two at the hall. From all accounts, they roystered and spent pretty freely. I never heard any of their names but one, and that was Squire Gisborne's. He was hardly a middle-aged man then; he had been abroad; and there, I believe, he had known Sir Philip Tempest, and done him some service. He was a daring and dissolute fellow in those days: careless and fearless, and one who would rather be in a quarrel than out of it. He had his fits of ill-temper besides, when he would spare neither man nor beast. Otherwise, those who knew him well, used to say he had a good heart, when he was neither drunk, nor angry, nor in any way vexed. He had altered much when I came to know him.

One day, the gentlemen had all been out shooting, and with but little success, I believe; anyhow, Mr. Gisborne had none, and was in a black humour accordingly. He was coming home, having his gun loaded, sportsman-like, when little Mignon crossed his path, just as he turned out of the wood by Bridget's cottage. Partly for wantonness, partly to vent his spleen upon some living creature, Mr. Gisborne took his gun, and fired – he had better have never fired gun again, than aimed that unlucky shot: he hit Mignon, and at the creature's sudden cry, Bridget came out, and saw at a glance what had been done. She took Mignon up in her arms, and looked hard at the wound; the poor dog looked at her with his glazing eyes, and tried to wag his tail and lick her hand, all covered with blood. Mr. Gisborne spoke in a kind of sullen penitence:

'You should have kept the dog out of my way – a little poaching varmint.'

At this very moment, Mignon stretched out his legs, and stiffened in her arms – her lost Mary's dog, who had wandered and sorrowed with her for years. She walked right into Mr. Gisborne's path, and fixed his unwilling, sullen look, with her dark and terrible eye.

'Those never throve that did me harm,' said she. 'I'm alone in the world, and helpless: the more do the saints in the heaven hear my prayers. Hear me, ye blessed ones! hear me, while I ask for sorrow on this bad, cruel man. He has killed the only creature that loved me – the dumb beast that I loved. Bring down heavy sorrow on his head for it, O ye saints! He thought that I was helpless, because he saw me lonely and poor; but are not the armies of heaven for the like of me?'

'Come, come,' said he, half remorseful, but not one whit afraid. 'Here's a crown to buy thee another dog. Take it, and leave off cursing! I care none for thy threats.'

'Don't you?' said she, coming a step closer, and changing her imprecatory cry for a whisper which made the gamekeeper's lad, following Mr. Gisborne, creep all over. 'You shall live to see the creature you love best, and who alone loves you – ay, a human creature, but as innocent and fond as my poor, dead darling – you shall see this creature, for whom death would be too happy, become a terror and a loathing to all, for this blood's sake. Hear me, O holy saints, who never fail them that have no other help!'

She threw up her right hand, filled with poor Mignon's life-drops; they spirted, one or two of them, on his shooting dress – an ominous sight to the follower. But the master only laughed a little, forced, scornful laugh, and went on to the Hall. Before he got there, however, he took out a gold piece, and bade the boy carry it to the old woman on his return to the village. The lad was 'afeared', as he told me in after years; he came to the cottage, and hovered about, not daring to enter. He peeped through the window at last; and by the flickering wood-flame, he saw Bridget kneeling before the picture of Our Lady of the Holy Heart, with dead Mignon lying between her and the Madonna. She was praying wildly, as her outstretched arms betokened. The lad shrank away in redoubled terror; and contented himself with slipping the gold-piece under the ill-fitting door. The next day it was thrown out upon the midden; and there it lay, no one daring to touch it.

Meanwhile Mr. Gisborne, half curious, half uneasy, thought to lessen his uncomfortable feelings by asking Sir Philip who Bridget was? He could only describe her – he did not know her name. Sir Philip was equally at a loss. But an old servant of the Starkeys, who had resumed his livery at the Hall on this occasion – a scoundrel whom Bridget had saved from dismissal more than once during her palmy days – said:

'It will be the old witch, that his worship means. She needs a ducking, if ever a woman did, does that Bridget Fitzgerald.'

'Fitzgerald!' said both the gentlemen at once. But Sir Philip was the first to continue:

'I must have no talk of ducking her, Dickon. Why, she must be the very woman poor Starkey bade me have a care of; but when I came here last she was gone, no one knew where. I'll go and see her tomorrow. But mind you, sirrah, if any harm comes to her, or any more talk of her being a witch – I've a pack of hounds at home, who can follow the scent of a lying knave as well as ever they followed a dog-fox; so take care how you talk about ducking a faithful old servant of your dead master's.'

'Had she ever a daughter?' asked Mr. Gisborne, after a while.

'I don't know – yes! I've a notion she had: a kind of waiting-woman to Madame Starkey.'

'Please your worship,' said humbled Dickon. 'Mistress Bridget had a daughter – one Mistress Mary – who went abroad, and has never been heard of since; and folks do say that has crazed her mother.'

Mr. Gisborne shaded his eyes with his hand.

'I could wish she had not cursed me,' he muttered. 'She may have power – no one else could.' After a while, he said aloud, no one understanding rightly what he meant; 'Tush! it is impossible!'– and called for claret; and he and the other gentlemen set-to to a drinking bout.

CHAPTER II

I now come to the time in which I myself was mixed up with the people that I have been writing about. And to make you understand how I became connected with them, I must give you some little account of myself. My father was the younger son of a Devonshire gentleman of moderate property; my eldest uncle succeeded to the estate of his forefathers, my second became an eminent attorney in London, and my father took orders. Like most poor clergymen, he had a large family; and I have no doubt was glad enough when my London uncle, who was a bachelor, offered to take charge of me, and bring me up to be his successor in business.

In this way I came to live in London, in my uncle's house, not far from Gray's Inn, and to be treated and esteemed as his son, and to labour with him in his office. I was very fond of the old gentleman. He was the confidential agent of many country squires, and had attained to his present position, as much by knowledge of human nature as by knowledge of law; though he was learned enough in the latter. He used to say his business was law, his pleasure heraldry. From his intimate acquaintance with family history, and all the tragic courses of life therein involved, to hear him talk, at leisure times, about any coat of arms that came across his path was as good as a play or a romance. Many cases of disputed property, dependent on a love of genealogy, were brought to him, as to a great authority on such points. If the lawyer who came to consult him was young, he would take no fee, only give him a long lecture on the importance of attending to heraldry; if the lawyer was of mature age and good standing, he would mulct him pretty well, and abuse him to me afterwards as negligent of one great branch of the profession. His house was in a stately new street called Ormond Street, and in it he had a handsome library; but all the books treated of things that were past; none of them planned or looked forward into the future.

I worked away – partly for the sake of my family at home, partly because my uncle had really taught me to enjoy the kind of practice in which he himself took such delight. I suspect I worked too hard; at any rate, in seventeen hundred and eighteen I was far from well, and my good uncle was disturbed by my ill looks.

One day, he rang the bell twice into the clerk's room at the dingy office in Gray's Inn Lane. It was the summons for me, and I went into his private room just as a gentleman – whom I knew well enough by sight as an Irish lawyer of more reputation than he deserved – was leaving.

My uncle was slowly rubbing his hands together and considering. I was there two or three minutes before he spoke. Then he told me that I must pack up my portmanteau that very afternoon, and start that night by post-horse for West Chester. I should get there, if all went well, at the end of five days' time, and must then wait for a packet to cross over to Dublin; from thence I must proceed to a certain town named Kildoon; and in that neighbourhood I was to remain, making certain inquiries as to the existence of any descendants of the younger branch of a family to whom some valuable estates had descended in the female line. The Irish lawyer whom I had seen was weary of the case, and would willingly have given up the property, without further ado, to a man who appeared to claim them; but on laying his tables and trees before my uncle, the latter had foreseen so many possible prior claimants, that the lawyer had begged him to undertake the management of the whole business. In his youth, my uncle would have liked nothing better than going over to Ireland himself, and ferreting out every scrap of paper or parchment, and every word of tradition respecting the family. As it was, old and gouty, he deputed me.

Accordingly, I went to Kildoon. I suspect I had something of my uncle's delight in following up a genealogical scent, for I very soon found out, when on the spot, that Mr. Rooney, the Irish lawyer, would have got both himself and the first claimant into a terrible scrape, if he had pronounced his opinion that the estates ought to be given up to him. There were three poor Irish fellows, each nearer of kin to the last possessor; but, a generation before, there was a still nearer relation, who had never been accounted for, nor his existence ever discovered by the lawyers, I venture to think, till I routed him out from the memory of some of the old dependants of the family. What had become of him? I travelled backwards and forwards; I crossed over to France, and came back again with a slight clue, which ended in my discovering that, wild and dissipated himself, he had left one child, a son, of yet worse character than his father; that this same Hugh Fitzgerald had married a very beautiful serving-woman of the Byrnes – a person below him in hereditary rank, but above him in character; that he had died soon after his marriage, leaving one child, whether a boy or girl I could not learn, and that the mother had returned to live in the family of the Byrnes. Now, the chief of this latter family was serving in the Duke of Berwick's regiment, and it was long before I could hear from him; it was more than a year before I got a short, haughty letter – I fancy he had a soldier's contempt for a civilian, an Irishman's hatred for an Englishman, an exiled Jacobite's jealousy of one who prospered and lived tranquilly under the government he looked upon as an usurpation. 'Bridget Fitzgerald,' he said, 'had been faithful to the fortunes of his sister – had followed her abroad, and to England when Mrs. Starkey had thought fit to return. Both his sister and her husband were dead; he knew nothing of Bridget Fitzgerald at the present time: perhaps Sir Philip Tempest, his nephew's guardian, might be able to give me some information.' I have not given the little contemptuous terms; the way in which faithful service was meant to imply more than it said – all that has nothing to do with my story. Sir Philip, when applied to, told me that he paid an annuity regularly to an old woman named Fitzgerald, living at Coldholme (the village near Starkey Manor-house). Whether she had any descendants he could not say.

One bleak March evening, I came in sight of the places described at the beginning of my story. I could hardly understand the rude dialect in which the direction to old Bridget's house was given.

'Yo' see yon furleets,' all run together, gave me no idea that I was to guide myself by the distant lights that shone in the windows of the Hall, occupied for a time by a farmer who held the post of steward, while the Squire, now four or five and twenty, was making the grand tour. However, at last, I reached Bridget's cottage – a low, moss-grown place; the palings that had once surrounded it were broken and gone; and the underwood of the forest came up to the walls, and must have darkened the windows. It was about seven o'clock – not late to my London's notions – but, after knocking for some time at the door and receiving no reply, I was driven to conjecture that the occupant of the house was gone to bed. So I betook myself to the nearest church I had seen, three miles back on the road I had come, sure that close to that I should find an inn of some kind; and early the next morning I set off back to Coldholme, by a field-path which my host assured me I should find a shorter cut than the road I had taken the night before. It was a cold, sharp morning; my feet left prints in the sprinkling of hoar-frost that covered the ground; nevertheless, I saw an old woman, whom I instinctively suspected to be the object of my search, in a sheltered covert on one side of my path. I lingered and watched her. She must have been considerably above the middle size in her prime; for, when she raised herelf from the stooping position in which I first saw her, there was something fine and commanding in the erectness of her figure. She drooped again in a minute or two, and seemed looking for something on the ground, as, with bent head, she turned off from the spot where I gazed upon her, and was lost to my sight. I fancy I missed my way, and made a round in spite of the landlord's directions; for by the time I had reached Bridget's cotage she was there, with no semblance of hurried walk or discomposure of any kind. The door was slightly ajar. I knocked, and the majestic figure stood before me silently awaiting the explanation of my errand. Her teeth were all gone, so the nose and chin were brought near together; the grey eyebrows were straight, and almost hung over her deep, cavernous eyes, and the thick white hair lay in silvery masses over the low, wide, wrinkled forehead. For a moment, I stood uncertain how to shape my answer to the solemn questioning of her silence.

'Your name is Bridget Fitzgerald, I believe?'

She bowed her head in assent.

'I have something to say to you. May I come in? I am unwilling to keep you standing.'

'You cannot tire me,' she said; and at first she seemed inclined to deny me the shelter of her roof. But the next moment – she had searched the very soul in me with her eyes during that instant – she led me in, and dropped the shadowing hood of her grey, draping cloak, which had previously hid part of the character of her countenance. The cottage was rude and bare enough. But before the picture of the Virgin, of which I have made mention, there stood a little cup filled with fresh primroses. While she paid her reverence to the Madonna, I understood why she had been out seeking through the clumps of green in the sheltered copse. Then she turned round, and bade me be seated. The expression of her face, which all this time I was studying, was not bad, as the stories of my last night's landlord had led me to expect; it was a wild, stern, fierce, indomitable countenance, seamed and scarred by agonies of solitary weeping; but it was neither cunning nor malignant.

'My name is Bridget Fitzgerald.' said she, by way of opening our conversation.

'And your husband was Hugh Fitzgerald, of Knock-Mahon, near Kildoon, in Ireland?'

A faint light came into the dark gloom of her eyes.

'He was.'

'May I ask if you had any children by him?'

The light in her eyes grew quick and red. She tried to speak, I could see; but something rose in her throat, and choked her, and until she could speak calmly, she would fain not speak at all before a stranger. In a minute or so she said:

'I had a daughter – one Mary Fitzgerald' – then her strong nature mastered her strong will, and she cried out, with a trembling wailing cry: 'Oh, man! what of her? – what of her?'

She rose from her seat, and came and clutched at my arm and looked in my eyes. There she read, as I suppose, my utter ignorance of what had become of her child; for she went blindly back to her chair, and sat rocking herself and softly moaning, as if I were not there; I not daring to speak to the lone and awful woman. After a little pause, she knelt down before the picture of Our Lady of the Holy Heart, and spoke to her by all the fanciful and poetic names of the Litany.

'O Rose of Sharon! O Tower of David! O Star of the Sea!
have ye no comfort for my sore heart? Am I for ever to hope?
Grant me at least despair!' – and so on she went, heedless of
my presence. Her prayers grew wilder and wilder, till they
seemed to touch on the borders of madness and blasphemy.
Almost involuntarily, I spoke as if to stop her.

'Have you any reason to think that your daughter is dead?'
She rose from her knees, and came and stood before me.

'Mary Fitzgerald is dead,' said she. 'I shall never see her
again in the flesh. No tongue ever told me; but I know she is
dead. I have yearned so to see her, and my heart's will is
fearful and strong: it would have drawn her to me before now,
if she had been a wanderer on the other side of the world. I
wonder often it has not drawn her out of the grave to come
and stand before me, and hear me tell her how I loved her.
For, sir, we parted unfriends.'

I knew nothing but the dry particulars needed for my
lawyer's quest, but I could not help feeling for the desolate
woman; and she must have read the unusual sympathy with
her wistful eyes.

'Yes, sir, we did. She never knew how I loved her; and we
parted unfriends; and I fear me that I wished her voyage might
not turn out well, only meaning – Oh, blessed Virgin! you
know I only meant that she should come home to her
mother's arms as to the happiest place on earth; but my wishes
are terrible – their power goes beyond my thought – and there
is no hope for me, if my words brought Mary harm.'

'But,' I said, 'you do not know that she is dead. Even now,
you hoped she might be alive. Listen to me;' and I told her the
tale I have already told you, giving it all in the driest manner,
for I wanted to recall the clear sense that I felt almost sure she
had possessed in her younger days, and by keeping up her
attention to details, restrain the vague wildness of her grief.

She listened with deep attention, putting from time to time
such questions as convinced me I had to do with no common
intelligence, however dimmed and shorn by solitude and
mysterious sorrow. Then she took up her tale, and in few brief
words, told me of her wanderings abroad in vain search after
her daughter: sometimes in the wake of armies, sometimes in
camp, sometimes in city. The lady, whose waiting-woman

Mary had gone to be, had died soon after the date of her last letter home; her husband, the foreign officer, had been serving in Hungary, whither Bridget had followed him, but too late to find him. Vague rumours reached her that Mary had made a great marriage; and this sting of doubt was added – whether the mother might not be close to her child under her new name, and even hearing of her every day, and never recognising the lost one under the appellation she then bore. At length the thought took possession of her, that it was possible that all this time Mary might be at home at Coldholme, in the Trough of Bolland, in Lancashire, in England; and home came Bridget, in that vain hope, to her desolate hearth and empty cottage. Here she had thought it safest to remain; if Mary was in life, it was here she would seek for her mother.

I noted down one or two particulars out of Bridget's narrative that I thought might be of use to me; for I was stimulated to further search in a strange and extraordinary manner. It seemed as if it were impressed upon me, that I must take up the quest where Bridget had laid it down: and this for no reason that had previously influenced me (such as my uncle's anxiety on the subject, my own reputation as a lawyer, and so on), but from some strange power which had taken possession of my will only that very morning, and which forced it in the direction it chose.

'I will go,' said I. 'I will spare nothing in the search. Trust to me. I will learn all that can be learnt. You shall know all that money, or pains, or wit can discover. It is true she may be long dead: but she may have left a child.'

'A child!' she cried, as if for the first time this idea had struck her mind. 'Hear him, Blessed Virgin! he says she may have left a child. And you have never told me, though I have prayed so for a sign, waking or sleeping!'

'Nay,' said I, 'I know nothing but what you tell me. You say you heard of her marriage.'

But she caught nothing of what I said. She was praying to the Virgin in a kind of ecstasy, which seemed to render her unconscious of my very presence.

From Coldholme I went to Sir Philip Tempest's. The wife of the foreign officer had been a cousin of his father's; and from him I thought I might gain some particulars as to the existence of the Count de la Tour d'Auvergne, and where I could find him; for I knew questions *de vive voix* aid the flagging recollection, and was determined to lose no chance for want of trouble. But Sir Philip had gone abroad, and it would be some time before I could receive an answer. So I followed my uncle's advice, to whom I had mentioned how wearied I felt, both in body and mind, by my will-o'-the-wisp search. He immediately told me to go to Harrogate, there to await Sir Philip's reply. I should be near to one of the places connected with my search, Coldholme; not far from Sir Philip Tempest, in case he returned, and I wished to ask him any further questions; and, in conclusion, my uncle bade me try to forget all about my business for a time.

This was far easier said than done. I have seen a child on a common blown along by a high wind, without power of standing still and resisting the tempestuous force. I was somewhat in the same predicament as regarded my mental state. Something resistless seemed to urge my thoughts on, through every possible course by which there was a chance of attaining to my object. I did not see the sweeping moors when I walked out: when I held a book in my hand, and read the words, their sense did not penetrate to my brain. If I slept, I went on with the same ideas, always flowing in the same direction. This could not last long without having a bad effect on the body. I had an illness, which, although I was racked with pain, was a positive relief to me, as it compelled me to live in the present suffering, and not in the visionary researches I had been continually making before. My kind uncle came to nurse me; and, after the immediate danger was over, my life seemed to slip away in delicious languor for two or three months. I did not ask – so much did I dread falling into the old channel of thought – whether any reply had been received to my letter to Sir Philip. I turned my whole imagination right away from all that subject. My uncle remained with me until nigh mid-summer, and then returned to his business in London, leaving me perfectly well, although not completely strong. I was to follow him in a fortnight; when, as he said, 'we would look over letters, and talk about several things.' I knew what this little speech alluded to, and shrank from the train of thought it suggested, which was so intimately connected with my first feelings of illness. However, I had a fortnight more for roaming on those invigorating Yorkshire moors.

In those days, there was one large, rambling inn, at Harrogate, close to the Medicinal Spring; but it was already becoming too small for the accommodation of the influx of visitors, and many lodged round about, in the farmhouses of the district. It was so early in the season, that I had the inn pretty much to myself, and, indeed, felt rather like a visitor in a private house, so intimate had the landlord and landlady become with me during my long illness. She would chide me for being out so late on the moors, or for having been too long without food, quite in a motherly way; while he consulted me about vintages and wines, and taught me many a Yorkshire wrinkle about horses. In my walks I met other strangers from time to time. Even before my uncle left me, I had noticed, with half-torpid curiosity, a young lady of very striking appearance, who went about always accompanied by an elderly companion – hardly a gentlewoman, but with something in her look that prepossessed me in her favour. The younger lady always put her veil down when any one approached; so it had been only once or twice, when I had come upon her at a sudden turn in the path, that I had even had a glimpse at her face. I am not sure if it was beautiful, though in after-life I grew to think it so. But it was at this time overshadowed by a sadness that never varied: a pale, quiet, resigned look of intense suffering that irresistibly attracted me, not with love, but with a sense of infinite compassion for one so young yet so hopelessly unhappy. The companion wore something of the same look: quite melancholy, hopeless, yet resigned. I asked my landlord who they were. He said they were called Clarke, and wished to be considered as mother and daughter; but that, for his part, he did not believe that to be their right name, or that there was any such relationship between them. They had been in the neighbourhood of Harrogate for some time, lodging in a remote farmhouse. The people there would tell nothing about them; saying that they paid handsomely, and never did any harm; so why should they be speaking of any strange things that might happen? That, as the landlord shrewdly observed, showed there was something out of the common way: he had heard that the elderly woman was a cousin of the farmer's where they lodged, and so the regard existing between relations might help to keep them quiet.

'What did he think, then, was the reason of their extreme seclusion?' asked I.

'Nay, he could not tell – not he. He had heard that the young lady, for all as quiet as she seemed, played strange pranks at times.' He shook his head when I asked him for more particulars, and refused to give them, which made me doubt if he knew any, for he was in general a talkative and communicative man. In default of other interests, after my uncle left, I set myself to watch these two people. I hovered about their walks, drawn towards them with a strange fascination, which was not diminished by their evident annoyance at so frequently meeting me. One day, I had the sudden good fortune to be at hand when they were alarmed by the attack of a bull, which, in those unenclosed grazing districts, was a particularly dangerous occurrence. I have other and more imporant things to relate than to tell of the accident which gave me an opportunity of rescuing them; it is enough to say, that this event was the beginning of an acquaintance, reluctantly acquiesced in by them, but eagerly prosecuted by me. I can hardly tell when intense curiosity became merged in love, but in less than ten days after my uncle's departure I was passionately enamoured of Mistress Lucy, as her attendant called her: carefully – for this I noted well – avoiding any address which appeared as if there was an equality of station between them. I noticed also that Mrs. Clarke, the elderly woman, after her first reluctance to allow me to pay them any attentions had been overcome, was cheered by my evident attachment to the young girl; it seemed to lighten her heavy burden of care, and she evidently favoured my visits to the farmhouse where they lodged. It was not so with Lucy. A more attractive person I never saw, in spite of her depression of manner, and shrinking avoidance of me. I felt sure at once, that whatever was the source of her grief, it rose from no fault of her own. It was difficult to draw her into conversation; but when at times, for a moment or two, I beguiled her into talk, I could see a rare intelligence in her face, and a grave, trusting look in the soft, grey eyes that were raised for a minute to mine. I made every excuse I possibly could for going there. I sought wild flowers for Lucy's sake; I planned walks for Lucy's sake; I watched the heavens by night, in hopes that some unusual beauty of sky would justify me in tempting Mrs. Clarke and Lucy forth upon the moors, to gaze at the great purple dome above.

It seemed to me that Lucy was aware of my love; but that, for some motive which I could not guess, she would fain have repelled me; but then again I saw, or fancied I saw, that her heart spoke in my favour, and that there was a struggle going on in her mind, which at times (I loved so dearly) I could have begged her to spare herself, even though the happiness of my whole life should have been the sacrifice; for her complexion grew paler, her aspect of sorrow more hopeless, her delicate frame yet slighter. During this period I had written, I should say, to my uncle, to beg to be allowed to prolong my stay at Harrogate, not giving any reason; but such was his tenderness towards me that in a few days I heard from him, giving me a willing permission, and only charging me to take care of myself, and not use too much exertion during the hot weather.

One sultry evening I drew near the farm. The windows of their parlour were open, and I heard voices when I turned the corner of the house, as I passed the first window (there were two windows in their little ground floor room). I saw Lucy distinctly; but when I had knocked on their door – the house-door always ajar – she was gone, and I saw only Mrs. Clarke, turning over the work-things lying on the table, in a nervous and purposeless manner. I felt by instinct that a conversation of some importance was coming on, in which I should be expected to say what was my object in paying these frequent visits. I was glad of the opportunity. My uncle had several times alluded to the pleasant possibility of my bringing home a young wife, to cheer and adorn the old house in Ormond Street. He was rich, and I was to succeed him, and had, as I knew, a fair reputation for so young a lawyer. So on my side I saw no obstacle. It was true that Lucy was shrouded in mystery; her name (I was convinced it was not Clarke), birth, parentage and previous life were unknown to me. But I was sure of her goodness and sweet innocence, and although I knew that there must be something painful to be told, to account for her mournful sadness, yet I was willing to bear my share in her grief, whatever it might be.

Mrs. Clarke began, as if it was a relief to her to plunge into the subject.

'We have thought, sir – at least I have thought – that you knew very little of us, or we of you, indeed; not enough to warrant the intimate acquaintance we have fallen into. I beg you pardon, sir,' she went on nervously; 'I am but a plain kind of woman, and I mean to use no rudeness; but I must say straight out that I – we – think it would be better for you not to come so often to see us. She is very unprotected, and —'

'Why should I not come to see you, dear madam?' asked I eagerly, glad of the opportunity of explaining myself. 'I come, I own, because I have learnt to love Mistress Lucy, and wish to teach her to love me.'

Mistress Clarke shook her head, and sighed.

'Don't sir – neither love her, nor, for the sake of all you hold sacred, teach her to love you! If I am too late, and you love her already, forget her – forget these last few weeks. Oh! I should never have allowed you to come!' she went on passionately; 'but what am I to do? We are forsaken by all, except the great God, and even He permits a strange and evil power to afflict us – what am I to do? Where is it to end?' She wrung her hands in her distress; then she turned to me: 'Go away, sir! go away, before you learn to care any more for her. I ask it for your own sake – I implore! You have been good and kind to us, and we shall always recollect you with gratitude; but go away now, and never come back to cross our fatal path!'

'Indeed, madam,' said I, 'I shall do no such thing. You urge it for my own sake. I have no fear, so urged, nor wish, except to hear more – all. I cannot have seen Mistress Lucy in all the intimacy of this last fortnight, without acknowledging her goodness and innocence; and without seeing – pardon me, madam – that for some reason you are two very lonely women, in some mysterious sorrow and distress. Now, though I am not powerful myself, yet I have friends who are so wise and kind that they may be said to possess power. Tell me some particulars. Why are you in grief – what is your secret – why are you here? I declare solemnly that nothing you have said has daunted me in my wish to become Lucy's husband; nor will I shrink from any difficulty that, as such an aspirant, I may have to encounter. You say you are friendless – why cast away an honest friend? I will tell you of people to whom you may write, and who will answer any questions as to my character and prospects. I do not shun enquiry.'

She shook her head again. 'You had better go away, sir. You know nothing about us.'

'I know your names,' said I, 'and I have heard you allude to the part of the country from which you came, which I happen to know as a wild and lonely place. There are so few people living in it that, if I chose to go there, I could easily ascertain all about you; but I would rather hear it from yourself.' You see I wanted to pique her into telling me something definite.

'You do not know our true names, sir,' said she hastily.

'Well, I may have conjectured as much. But tell me, then, I conjure you. Give me your reasons for distrusting my willingness to stand by what I have said with regard to Mistress Lucy.'

Oh, what can I do?' exclaimed she. 'If I am turning away a true friend, as he says? – Stay!' coming to a sudden decision – 'I will tell you something – I cannot tell you all – you would not believe it. But perhaps, I can tell you enough to prevent your going on in your hopeless attachment. I am not Lucy's mother.'

'So I conjectured,' I said. 'Go on.'

'I do not even know whether she is the legitimate or illegitimate child of her father. But he is cruelly turned against her; and her mother is long dead; and, for a terrible reason, she has no other creature to keep constant to her but me. She – only two years ago – such a darling and such a pride in her father's house! Why, sir, there is a mystery that might happen in connection with her any moment; and then you would go away like all the rest; and, when you next heard her name, you would loathe her. Others, who have loved her longer, have done so before now. My poor child! whom neither God nor man has mercy upon – or, surely, she would die!'

The good woman was stopped by her crying. I confess, I was a little stunned by her last words; but only for a moment.

At any rate, till I knew definitely what was this mysterious stain upon one so simple and pure, as Lucy seemed, I would not desert her, and so I said; and she made me answer:

'If you are daring in your heart to think harm of my child, sir, after knowing her as you have done, you are no good man yourself; but I am so foolish and helpless in my great sorrow, that I would fain hope to find a friend in you. I cannot help trusting that, although you may no longer feel toward her as a lover, you will have pity upon us, and perhaps, by your learning, you can tell us where to go for aid.'

'I implore you to tell me what this mystery is,' I cried, almost maddened by this suspense.

'I cannot,' said she solemnly. 'I am under a deep vow of secrecy. If you are to be told it must be by her.' She left the room, and I remained to ponder over this strange interview. I mechanically turned over the few books, and with eyes that saw nothing at the time, examined the tokens of Lucy's frequent presence in that room.

When I got home at night, I remembered how all these trifles spoke of a pure and tender heart and innocent life. Mistress Clarke returned; she had been crying sadly.

'Yes,' said she, 'it is as I feared: she loves you so much that she is willing to run the fearful risk of telling you all herself – she acknowledges it is but a poor chance; but your sympathy will be a balm, if you give it. Tomorrow, come here at ten in the morning; and, as you hope for pity in your hour of agony, repress all show of fear or repugnance you may feel towards one so grievously afflicted.'

I half smiled. 'Have no fear,' said I. It seemed too absurd to imagine my feeling dislike to Lucy.

'Her father loved her well.' said she gravely; 'yet he drove her out like some monstrous thing.'

Just at this moment came a peal of ringing laughter from the garden. It was Lucy's voice; it sounded as if she were standing just on one side of the open casement – and as though she were suddenly stirred to merriment – merriment verging on bois-terousness, by the doings or sayings of some other person. I can scarcely say why, but the sound jarred on me inexpressibly. She knew the subject of our conversation, and must have been at least aware of the state of agitation her friend was in; she herself usually so gentle and quiet. I half rose to go to the window, and satisfy my instinctive curiosity as to what had provoked this burst of ill-timed laugher; but Mrs. Clarke threw her whole weight and power upon the hand with which she pressed and kept me down

'For God's sake!' she said, white and trembling all over, 'sit still; be quiet. Oh! be patient. Tomorrow you will know all. Leave us, for we are all sorely afflicted. Do not seek to know more about us.'

Again that laugh – so musical in sound, yet so discordant to my heart. She held me tight – tighter; without positive violence I could not have risen. I was sitting with my back to the window, but I felt a shadow pass between the sun's warmth and me, and a strange shudder ran through my frame. In a minute or two she released me.

'Go,' repeated she. 'Be warned, I ask you once more. I do not think you can stand this knowledge that you seek. If I had had my own way, Lucy should never have yielded, and promised to tell you all. Who knows what may come of it?'

'I am firm in my wish to know all. I return at ten tomorrow morning, and then expect to see Mistress Lucy herself.'

I turned away; having my own suspicions, I confess, as to Mistress Clark's sanity.

Conjectures as to the meaning of her hints, and uncomfortable thoughts connected with that strange laughter, filled my mind. I could hardly sleep. I rose early; and long before the hour I had appointed, I was on the path over the common that led to the old farmhouse where they lodged. I suppose that Lucy had passed no better a night than I; for there she was also, slowly pacing with her even step, her eyes bent down, her whole look most saintly and pure. She started when I came close to her, and grew paler as I reminded her of my appointment, and spoke with something of the impatience of obstacles that seeing her once more had called up afresh in my mind. All strange and terrible hints, and giddy merriment were forgotten. My heart gave forth words of fire, and my tongue uttered them. Her colour went and came, as she listened; but, when I had ended my passionate speeches, she lifted her soft eyes to me, and said:

'But you know that you have something to learn about me yet. I only want to say this: I shall not think less of you – less well of you, I mean – if you, too, fall away from me when you know all. Stop!' said she, as if fearing another burst of mad words. 'Listen to me. My father is a man of great wealth. I never knew my mother; she must have died when I was very young. When first I remember anything, I was living in a great, lonely house, with my dear and faithful Mistress Clarke. My father, even, was not there; he was – he is – a soldier, and his duties lie abroad. But he came from time to time, and every time I think he loved me more and more. He brought me rarities from foreign lands, which prove to me now how much he must have thought of me during his absences. I can sit down and measure the depth of his lost love now, by such standards as these. I never thought whether he loved me or not, then; it was so natural that it was like the air I breathed. Yet he was an angry man at times, even then; but never with me. He was very reckless, too; and, once or twice, I heard a whisper among the servants that a doom was over him, and that he knew it, and tried to drown his knowledge in wild activity, and even sometimes, sir, in wine. So I grew up in this grand mansion, in that lonely place. Everything around me seemed at my disposal, and I think every one loved me; I am sure I loved them. Till about two years ago – I remember it well – my father had come to England, to us; and he seemed so proud and so pleased with me and all I had done. And one day his tongue seemed loosened with wine, and he told me much that I had not known till then – how dearly he had loved my mother, yet how his wilful usage had caused her death; and then he went on to say how he loved me better than any creature on earth, and how, some day, he hoped to take me to foreign places, for that he could hardly bear these long absences from his only child. Then he seemed to change suddenly, and said, in a strange, wild way, that I was not to believe what he said; that there was many a thing he loved better – his horse – his dog – I know not what.

'And 'twas only the next morning that, when I came into his room to ask his blessing as was my wont, he received me with fierce and angry words, "Why had I," so he asked, "been delighting myself in such wanton mischief – dancing over the tender plants in the flower-beds, all set with the famous Dutch bulbs he had brought from Holland?" I had never been out of doors that morning, sir, and I could not conceive what he meant, and so I said; and then he swore at me for a liar, and said I was of no true blood, for he had seen me doing all that mischief himself – with his own eyes. What could I say? He would not listen to me, and even my tears seemed only to irritate him. That day was the beginning of my great sorrows. Not long after, he reproached me for my undue familiarity – all unbecoming a gentlewoman – with his grooms. I had been in the stableyard, laughing and talking, he said. Now, sir, I am something of a coward by nature, and I had always dreaded horses; besides that, my father's servants – those whom he brought with him from foreign parts – were wild fellows, whom I had always avoided, and to whom I had never spoken, except as a lady must needs from time to time speak to her father's people. Yet my father called me by names of which I hardly know the meaning, but my heart told me they were such as shame any modest woman; and from that day he turned quite against me; – nay, sir, not many weeks after that, he came in with a riding-whip in his hand; and, accusing me harshly of evil doings, of which I knew no more than you, sir, he was about to strike me, and I, all in bewildering tears, was ready to take his stripes as great kindness compared to his harder words, when suddenly he stopped his arm midway, gasped and staggered, crying out, "The curse – the curse!" I looked up in terror. In the great mirror opposite I saw myself, so like me that my soul seemed to quiver within me, as though not knowing to which similitude of body it belonged. My father saw my Double at the same moment, either in its dreadful reality, whatever that might be, or in the scarcely less terrible reflection in the mirror; but what came of it at that moment I cannot say, for I suddenly swooned away; and when I came to myself I was lying in my bed, and my faithful Clarke sitting by me. I was in my bed for days; and even while I lay there my Double was seen by all, flitting about the house and gardens, always about some mischievous or detestable work. What wonder that everyone shrank from me in dread – that my father drove me forth at length, when the disgrace of which I was the cause was past his patience to bear. Mistress

Clarke came with me; and here we try to live such a life of piety and prayer as may in time set me free from the curse.'

All the time she had been speaking, I had been weighing her story in my mind. I had hitherto put cases of witchcraft on one side, as mere superstitions; and my uncle and I had had many an argument, he supporting himelf by the opinion of his good friend Sir Matthew Hale. Yet this sounded like the tale of one bewitched; or was it merely the effect of a life of extreme seclusion telling on the nerves of a sensitive girl? My scepticism inclined me to the latter belief, and when she paused I said:

'I fancy that some physician could have disabused your father of his belief in visions —'

Just at that moment, standing as I was opposite to her in the full and perfect morning light, I saw behind her another figure – a ghastly resemblance, complete in likeness, so far as form and feature and minutest touch of dress could go, but with a loathsome demon soul looking out of the grey eyes, that were in turns mocking and voluptuous. My heart stood still within me; every hair rose up erect; my flesh crept with horror. I could not see the grave and tender Lucy – my eyes were fascinated by the creature beyond. I know not why, but I put out my hand to clutch it; I grasped nothing but empty air, and my whole blood curdled to ice. For a moment I could not see; then my sight came back, and I saw Lucy standing before me, alone, deathly pale, and, I could have fancied, almost shrunk in size.

'IT has been near me?' she said, as if asking a question.

The sound seemed taken out of her voice; it was husky as the notes on an old harpsichord when the strings have ceased to vibrate. She read her answer in my face, I suppose, for I could not speak. Her look was one of intense fear, but that died away into an aspect of most humble patience. At length she seemed to force herself to face behind and around her: she saw the purple moors, the blue distant hills, quivering in the sunlight, but nothing else.

'Will you take me home?' she said meekly.

I took her by the hand, and led her silently through the budding heather –we dared not speak; for we could not tell but that the dread creature was listening, although unseen – but

that IT might appear and push us asunder. I never loved her
more fondly than now when – and that was the unspeakable
misery – the idea of her was becoming so inextricably blended
with the shuddering thought of IT. She seemed to understand
what I must be feeling. She let go my hand, which she had
kept clasped until then, when we reached the garden gate, and
went forwards to meet her anxious friend, who was standing
by the window looking for her. I could not enter the house: I
needed silence, society, leisure, change – I knew not what – to
shake off the sensation of that creature's presence. Yet I
lingered about the garden – I hardly know why; partly, I
suppose, because I feared to encounter the resemblance again
on the solitary common, where it had vanished, and partly
from a feeling of inexpressible compassion for Lucy. In a few
minutes Mistress Clarke came forth and joined me. We
walked some paces in silence.

'You know all, now,' said she solemnly.

'I saw IT,' said I, below my breath.

'And you shrink from us, now,' she said, with a hopelessness which stirred up all that was brave or good in me.

'Not a whit,' said I. 'Human flesh shrinks from encounter
with the powers of darkness; and, for some reason unknown
to me, the pure and holy Lucy is their victim.'

'The sins of the fathers shall be visited upon the children,'
she said.

'Who is her father?' asked I. 'Knowing as much as I do, I
may surely know more – know all. Tell me, I entreat you,
madam, all that you can conjecture respecting this demoniac
persecution of one so good.'

'I will; but not now. I must go to Lucy now. Come this
afternoon, I will see you alone; and oh, sir, I will trust that you
may yet find some way to help us in our sore trouble!'

I was miserably exhausted by the swooning affright which
had taken possession of me. When I reached the inn, I
staggered in like one overcome by wine. I went to my own
private room. It was some time before I saw that the weekly
post had come in, and brought me my letters. There was one
from my uncle, one from my home in Devonshire, and one,
re-directed over the first address, sealed with a great coat of
arms. It was from Sir Philip Tempest: my letter of inquiry

respecting Mary Fitzgerald had reached him at Liége, where it
so happened that the Count de la Tour d'Auvergne was
quartered at the very time. He remembered his wife's beautiful attendant; she had had high words with the deceased
countess, respecting her intercourse with an English gentleman of good standing, who was also in the foreign service.
The countess augured evil of his intentions; while Mary,
proud and vehement, asserted that he would soon marry her,
and resented her mistress's warning as an insult. The consequence was, that she had left Madame de la Tour
d'Auvergne's service, and, as the Count believed, had gone to
live with the Englishman; whether he had married her, or not,
he could not say. 'But,' added Sir Philip Tempest, 'you may
easily hear what particulars you wish to know respecting
Mary Fitzgerald from the Englishman himself, if, as I suspect,
he is no other than my neighbour and former acquaintance,
Mr. Gisborne, of Skipford Hall, in the West Riding. I am led
to the belief that he is no other, by several small particulars,
none of which are in themselves conclusive, but which, taken
together, furnish a mass of presumptive evidence. As far as I
could make out from the Count's foreign pronunciation,
Gisborne was the name of the Englishman; I know that
Gisborne of Skipford was abroad and in the foreign service at
that time – he was a likely fellow enough for such an exploit,
and, above all, certain expressions recur to my mind which he
used in reference to old Bridget Fitzgerald, of Coldholme,
whom he once encountered while staying with me at Starkey
Manor-house. I remember that the meeting seemed to have
produced some extraordinary effect upon his mind, as though
he had suddenly discovered some connection which she might
have had with his previous life. I beg you to let me know if I
can be of any further service to you. Your uncle once rendered
me a good turn, and I will gladly repay it, so far as in me lies,
to his nephew.'

I was now apparently close on the discovery which I had
striven so many months to attain. But success had lost its zest.
I put my letters down, and seemed to forget them all in
thinking of the morning I had passed that very day. Nothing
was real but the unreal presence, which had come like an evil
blast across my bodily eyes, and burnt itself down upon my

brain. Dinner came, and went away untouched. Early in the afternoon I walked to the farmhouse. I found Mistress Clarke alone, and I was glad and relieved. She was evidently prepared to tell me all I might wish to hear.

'You asked me for Mistress Lucy's true name; it is Gisborne,' she began.

'Not Gisborne of Skipford?' I exclaimed, breathless with anticipation.

'The same,' said she quietly, not regarding my manner. 'Her father is a man of note; although, being a Roman Catholic, he cannot take that rank in this country to which his station entitles him. The consequence is that he lives much abroad – has been a soldier, I am told.'

'And Lucy's mother? I asked.

She shook her head. 'I never knew her,' said she. 'Lucy was about three years old when I was engaged to take charge of her. Her mother was dead.'

'But you know her name? – you can tell if it was Mary Fitzgerald?'

She looked astonished. 'That was her name. But, sir, how came you to be so well acquainted with it? It was a mystery to the whole household at Skipford Court. She was some beautiful young woman whom he lured away from her protectors while he was abroad. I have heard that he practised some terrible deceit upon her, and when she came to know it, she was neither to have nor to hold, but rushed off from his very arms, and threw herself into a rapid stream and was drowned. It stung him deep with remorse, but I used to think the remembrance of the mother's cruel death made him love the child yet dearer.'

I told her, as briefly as might be, of my researches after the descendant and heir of the Fitzgeralds of Kildoon, and added – something of my old lawyer spirit returning into me for the moment – that I had no doubt but that we should prove Lucy to be by right possessed of large estates in Ireland.

No flush came over her grey face; no light into her eyes. 'And what is all the wealth in the whole world to that poor girl?' she said. 'It will not free her from the ghastly bewitchment which persecutes her. As for money, what a pitiful thing it is! it cannot touch her.'

'No more can the Evil Creature harm her,' I said. 'Her holy nature dwells apart, and cannot be defiled or stained by all the devilish arts in the whole world.'

'True! but it is a cruel fate to know that all shrink from her, sooner or later, as from one possessed – accursed.'

'How came it to pass?' I asked.

'Nay, I know not. Old rumours there are, that were bruited through the household at Skipford.'

'Tell me,' I demanded.

'They came from servants, who would fain account for everything. They say that, many years ago, Mr. Gisborne killed a dog belonging to an old witch at Coldholme; that she cursed, with a dreadful and mysterious curse, the creature, whatever it might be, that he should love best; and that it struck so deeply into his heart that for years he kept himself aloof from any temptation to love aught. But who could help loving Lucy?'

'You never heard the old witch's name?' I gasped.

'Yes – they called her Bridget; they said he would never go near the spot again for terror of her. Yet he was a brave man!'

'Listen,' said I, taking hold of her arm, the better to arrest her full attention; 'if what I suspect holds true, that man stole Bridget's only child – the very Mary Fitzgerald who was Lucy's mother; if so, Bridget cursed him in ignorance of the deeper wrong he had done her. To this hour she yearns after her lost child, and questions the saints whether she be living or not. The roots of that curse lie deeper than she knows: she unwittingly banned him for a deeper guilt than that of killing a dumb beast. The sins of the fathers are indeed visited upon the children.'

'But,' said Mistress Clarke eagerly, 'she would never let evil rest on her own grandchild? Surely, sir, if what you say be true, there are hopes for Lucy. Let us go – go at once, and tell this fearful woman all that you suspect, and beseech her to take off the spell she has put upon her innocent grandchild.'

It seemed to me, indeed, that something like this was the best course we could pursue. But first it was necessary to ascertain more than what mere rumour or careless hearsay could tell. My thoughts turned to my uncle – he could advise me wisely – he ought to know all. I resolved to go to him without delay; but I did not choose to tell Mistress Clarke of all the visionary plans that flitted through my mind. I simply declared my intention of proceeding straight to London on Lucy's affairs. I bade her believe that my interest on the young lady's behalf was greater than ever, and that my whole time should be given up to her cause. I saw that Mistress Clarke distrusted me, because my mind was too full of thoughts for my words to flow freely. She sighed and shook her head, and said, 'Well, it is all right!' in such a tone that it was an implied reproach. But I was firm and constant in my heart, and I took confidence from that.

I rode to London. I rode long days drawn out into the lovely summer nights: I could not rest. I reached London. I told my uncle all, though in the stir of the great city the horror had faded away, and I could hardly imagine that he would believe the account I gave him of the fearful double of Lucy which I had seen on the lonely moor-side. But my uncle had lived many years and learnt many things; and, in the deep secrets of family history that had been confided to him, he had heard of cases of innocent people bewitched and taken possession of by evil spirits yet more fearful than Lucy's. For, as he said, to judge from all I told him, that resemblance had no power over her – she was too pure and good to be tainted by its evil, haunting presence. It had, in all probability, so my uncle conceived, tried to suggest wicked thoughts and to tempt to wicked actions; but she, in her saintly maidenhood, had passed on undefiled by evil thought or deed. It could not touch her soul; but true, it set her apart from all sweet love or common human intercourse. My uncle threw himself with an energy more like six-and-twenty than sixty into the consideration of the whole case. He undertook the proving Lucy's descent, and volunteered to go and find out Mr. Gisborne, and obtain, firstly, the legal proofs of her descent from the Fitzgeralds of Kildoon, and, secondly, to try and hear all that he could respecting the working of the curse, and whether any and what means had been taken to exorcise that terrible appearance. For he told me of instances where, by prayers and long fasting, the evil possessor had been driven forth with howling and many cries from the body which it had come to inhabit; he spoke of those strange New England cases which

had happened not so long before; of Mr. Defoe, who had
written a book, wherein he had named many modes of
subduing apparitions and sending them back whence they
came; and, lastly, he spoke low of dreadful ways of compelling
witches to undo their witchcraft. But I could not endure to hear
of those tortures and burnings. I said that Bridget was rather a
wild and savage woman than a malignant witch; and, above all,
that Lucy was of her kith and kin; and that, in putting her to the
trial, by water or by fire, we should be torturing – it might be
to the death – the ancestress of her we sought to redeem.

My uncle thought awhile, and then said, that in this last
matter I was right – at any rate, it should not be tried, with his
consent, till all other modes of remedy had failed; and he
assented to my proposal that I should go myself and see
Bridget, and tell her all.

In accordance with this, I went down once more to the
wayside inn near Coldholme. It was late at night when I arrived
there; and, while I supped, I inquired of the landlord more
particulars as to Bridget's ways. Solitary and savage had been
her life for many years. Wild and despotic were her words and
manner to those few people who came across her path. The
country-folk did her imperious bidding, because they feared to
disobey. If they pleased her, they prospered; if, on the
contrary, they neglected or traversed her behests, misfortune,
small or great, fell on them and theirs. It was not detestation so
much as an indefinable terror that she excited.

In the morning I went to see her. She was standing on the
green outside her cottage, and received me with the sullen
grandeur of a throneless queen. I read in her face that she
recognized me, and that I was not unwelcome; but she stood
silent till I had opened my errand.

'I have news of your daughter,' said I, resolved to speak
straight to all that I knew she felt of love, and not to spare her.
'She is dead!'

The stern figure scarcely trembled, but her hand sought the
support of the door-post.

'I knew that she was dead,' said she, deep and low, and then
was silent for an instant. 'My tears that should have flowed
for her were burnt up long years ago. Young man, tell me
about her.'

'Not yet,' said I, having a strange power given me of confronting one whom, nevertheless, in my secret soul I dreaded.

'You had once a little dog,' I continued. The words called out in her more show of emotion than the intelligence of her daughter's death. She broke in upon my speech:

'I had! It was hers – the last thing I had of hers – and it was shot for wantonness! It died in my arms. The man who killed that dog rues it to this day. For that dumb beast's blood, his best-beloved stands accursed.'

Her eyes distended, as if she were in a trance and saw the working of her curse. Again I spoke:

'O woman!' I said, 'that best-beloved, standing accursed before men, is your dead daughter's child.'

The life, the energy, the passion, came back to the eyes with which she pierced through me, to see if I spoke truth; then, without another question or word, she threw herself on the ground with fearful vehemence, and clutched at the innocent daisies with convulsed hands.

'Bone of my bone! flesh of my flesh! I cursed thee – and art thou accursed?'

So she moaned, as she lay prostrate in her great agony. I stood aghast at my own work. She did not hear my broken sentences; she asked no more, but the dumb confirmation which my sad looks had given that one fact, that her curse rested on her own daughter's child. The fear grew on me lest she should die in her strife of body and soul; and then might not Lucy remain under the spell as long as she lived?

Even at this moment, I saw Lucy coming through the woodland path that led to Bridget's cottage; Mistress Clarke was with her; I felt at my heart that it was she, by the balmy peace which the look of her sent over me, as she slowly advanced, a glad surprise shining out of her soft quiet eyes. That was as her gaze met mine. As her looks fell on the woman lying stiff, convulsed on the earth, they became full of tender pity; and she came forward to try and lift her up. Seating herself on the turf, she took Bridget's head ino her lap; and, with gentle touches, she arranged the dishevelled grey hair streaming thick and wild from beneath her mutch.

'God help her!' murmured Lucy. 'How she suffers!'

At her desire we sought for water; but when we returned, Bridget had recovered her wandering senses, and was kneeling with clasped hands before Lucy, gazing at that sweet sad face as though her troubled nature drank in health and peace from every moment's contemplation. A faint tinge on Lucy's pale cheeks showed me that she was aware of our return; otherwise it appeared as if she was conscious of her influence for good over the passionate and troubled woman kneeling before her, and would not willingly avert her grave and loving eyes from that wrinkled and careworn countenance.

Suddenly – in the twinkling of an eye – the creature appeared, there, behind Lucy; fearfully the same as to outward semblance, but kneeling exactly as Bridget knelt, and clasping her hands in jesting mimicry as Bridget clasped hers in her ecstasy that was deepening into a prayer. Mistress Clarke cried out – Bridget arose slowly, her gaze fixed on the creature beyond; drawing her breath with a hissing sound, never moving her terrible eyes, that were steady as stone, she made a dart at the phantom, and caught, as I had done, a mere handful of empty air. We saw no more of the creature – it vanished as suddenly as it came, but Bridget looked slowly on, as if watching some receding form. Lucy sat still, white, trembling, drooping – I think she would have swooned if I had not been there to uphold her. While I was attending to her, Bridget passed us, without a word to any one, and, entering her cottage, she barred herself in, and left us without.

All our endeavours were now directed to get Lucy back to the house where she had tarried the night before. Mistress Clarke told me that, not hearing from me (some letter must have miscarried), she had grown impatient and despairing, and had urged Lucy to the enterprise of coming to seek her grandmother; not telling her, indeed, of the dread reputation she possessed, or how we suspected her of having so fearfully blighted that innocent girl; but, at the same time, hoping much from the mysterious stirring of blood, which Mistress Clarke trusted in for the removal of the curse. They had come, by a different route from that which I had taken, to a village inn not far from Coldholme, only the night before.

This was the first interview between ancestress and descendant.

All through the sultry noon I wandered along the tangled
brushwood of the old neglected forest, thinking where to turn
for remedy in a matter so complicated and mysterious.
Meeting a countryman, I asked my way to the nearest
clergyman, and went, hoping to obtain some counsel from
him. But he proved to be a coarse and common-minded man,
giving no time or attention to the intricacies of a case, but
dashing out a strong opinion involving immediate action. For
instance, as soon as I named Bridget Fitzgerald, he exclaimed:

'The Coldholme witch! the Irish Papist! I'd have had her
ducked long since but for that other Papist, Sir Philip
Tempest. He has had to threaten honest folk about here over
and over again, or they'd have had her up before the justices
for her black doings. And it's the law of the land that witches
should be burnt! Ay, and of Scripture, too, sir! Yet you see a
Papist, if he's a rich squire, can overrule both law and
Scripture. I'd carry a faggot myself to rid the country of her!'

Such a one could give me no help. I rather drew back what I
had already said, and tried to make the parson forget it, by
treating him to several pots of beer in the village inn, to which
we had adjourned for our conference at his suggestion. I left
him as soon as I could, and returned to Coldholme, shaping
my way past deserted Starkey Manor-house and coming upon
it by the back. At that side were the oblong remains of the old
moat, the waters of which lay placid and motionless under the
crimson rays of the setting sun; with the forest-trees lying
straight along each side, and their deep-green foliage mirrored
to blackness in the burnished surface of the moat below – and
the broken sundial at the end nearest the hall – and the heron,
standing on one leg at the water's edge, lazily looking down
for fish – the lonely and desolate house scarce needed the
broken windows, the weeds on the door-sill, the broken
shutter softly flapping to and fro in the twilight breeze, to fill
up the picture of desertion and decay. I lingered about the
place until the growing darkness warned me on. And then I
passed along the path, cut by the orders of the last lady of
Starkey Manor-house, that led me to Bridget's cottage. I
resolved at once to see her; and, in spite of closed doors – it

might be of resolved will – she should see me. So I knocked at her door, gently, loudly, fiercely. I shook it so vehemently that at length the old hinges gave way, and with a crash it fell inwards, leaving me suddenly face to face with Bridget – I, red, heated, agitated with my so long baffled efforts – she, stiff as any stone, standing right facing me, her eyes dilated with terror, her ashen lips trembling, but her body motionless. In her hands she held her crucifix, as if by that holy symbol she sought to oppose my entrance. At sight of me, her whole frame relaxed, and she sank back into a chair. Some mighty tension had given way. Still her eyes looked fearfully into the gloom of the outer air, made more opaque by the glimmer of the lamp inside, which she had placed before the picture of the Virgin.

'Is she there?' asked Bridget hoarsely.

'No! Who! I am alone. You remember me.'

'Yes,' replied she, still terror-stricken. 'But she – that creature – has been looking in upon me through the window all day long. I closed it up with my shawl; and then I saw her feet below the door, as long as it was light, and I knew she heard my very breathing – nay, worse, my very prayers; and I could not pray, for her listening choked the words ere they rose to my lips. Tell me, who is she? – what means that double girl I saw this morning? One had the look of my dead Mary; but the other curdled my blood, and yet it was the same!'

She had taken hold of my arm, as if to secure herself some human companionship. She shook all over with the slight, never-ceasing tremor of intense terror. I told her my tale as I have told it you, sparing none of the details.

How Mistress Clarke had informed me that the resemblance had driven Lucy forth from her father's house – how I had disbelieved, until, with mine own eyes, I had seen another Lucy standing behind my Lucy, the same in form and feature, but with the demon-soul looking out of the eyes. I told her all, I say, believing that she – whose curse was working so upon the life of her innocent grandchild – was the only person who could find the remedy and the redemption. When I had done, she sat silent for many minutes.

'You love Mary's child?' she asked.

'I do, in spite of the fearful working of the curse – I love her. Yet I shrink from her ever since that day on the moor-side. And men must shrink from one so accompanied; friends and lovers must stand afar off. Oh, Bridget Fitzgerald! loosen the curse! Set her free!'

'Where is she?'

I eagerly caught at the idea that her presence was needed, in order that, by some strange power or exorcism, the spell might be reversed.

'I will go and bring her to you!' I exclaimed. But Bridget tightened her hold upon my arm.

'Not so,' said she, in a low, hoarse voice. 'It would kill me to see her again as I saw her this morning. And I must live till I have worked my work. Leave me!' said she suddenly, and again taking up the cross. 'I defy the demon I have called up. Leave me to wrestle with it!'

She stood up, as if in an ecstasy of inspiration, from which all fear was banished. I lingered – why I can hardly tell – until once more she bade me begone. As I went along the forest way, I looked back and saw her planting the cross in the empty threshold, where the door had been.

The next morning Lucy and I went to seek her, to bid her join her prayers with ours. The cottage stood open and wide to our gaze. No human being was there; the cross remained on the threshold, but Bridget was gone.

CHAPTER III

What was to be done next? was the question that I asked myself. As for Lucy, she would fain have submitted to the doom that lay upon her. Her gentleness and piety, under the pressure of so horrible a life, seemed over-passive to me. She never complained. Mrs. Clarke complained more than ever. As for me, I was more in love with the real Lucy than ever; but I shrank from the false similitude with an intensity proportioned to my love. I found out by instinct that Mrs. Clarke had occasional temptations to leave Lucy. The good lady's nerves were shaken; and, from what she said, I could almost have concluded that the object of the Double was to drive away from Lucy this last, and almost earliest friend. At times, I could scarcely bear to own it, but I myself felt inclined to turn recreant; and I would accuse Lucy of being too patient – too resigned. One after another, she won the little children of Coldholme. (Mrs. Clarke and she had resolved to stay there, for was it not as good a place as any other, to such as they? and did not all our faint hopes rest on Bridget – never seen or heard of now, but still, we trusted, to come back, or give some token?) So, as I say, one after another, the little children came about my Lucy, won by her soft tones, and her gentle smiles, and kind actions. Alas! one after another they fell away, and shrunk from her path with blanching terror; and we too surely guessed the reason why. It was the last drop. I could bear it no longer. I resolved no more to linger around the spot, but to go back to my uncle, and among the learned divines of the city of London, seek for some power whereby to annul the curse.

My uncle, meanwhile, had obtained all the requisite testimonials relating to Lucy's descent and birth, from the Irish lawyers, and from Mr. Gisborne. The latter gentleman had written from abroad (he was again serving in the Austrian army) a letter alternately passionately self-reproachful and stoically repellant. It was evident that, when he thought of Mary – her short life – how he had wronged her, and of her violent death, he could hardly find words severe enough for his own conduct; and from this point of view, the curse that Bridget had laid upon him and his, was regarded by him as a prophetic doom, to the utterance of which she was moved by a Higher Power, working for the fulfilment of a deeper vengeance than for the death of the poor dog. But then, again, when he came to speak of his daughter, the repugnance which the conduct of the demoniac creature had produced in his mind, was but ill disguised under a show of profound indifference as to Lucy's fate. One almost felt as if he would have been as content to put her out of existence, as he would have been to destroy some disgusting reptile that had invaded his chamber or his couch.

The great Fitzgerald property was Lucy's; and that was all – was nothing.

My uncle and I sat in the gloom of a London November evening, in our house in Ormond Street. I was out of health, and felt as if I were in an inextricable coil of misery. Lucy and I wrote to each other, but that was little; and we dare not see each other for dread of the fearful Third, who had more than once taken her place at our meetings. My uncle had, on the day I speak of, bidden prayers to be put up on the ensuing Sabbath in many a church and meeting-house in London, for one grievously tormented by an evil spirit. He had faith in prayers – I had none; I was fast losing faith in all things. So we sat, he trying to interest me in the old talk of other days, I oppressed by one thought – when our old servant, Anthony, opened the door, and, without speaking, showed in a very gentlemanly and prepossessing man, who had something remarkable about his dress, betraying his profession to be that of the Roman Catholic priesthood. He glanced at my uncle first, then at me. It was to me he bowed.

'I did not give my name,' said he, 'because you would hardly have recognised it; unless, sir, when, in the north, you heard of Father Bernard, the chaplain at Stonyhurst?'

I remembered afterwards that I had heard of him, but at the time I had utterly forgotten it; so I professed myself a complete stranger to him; while my ever-hospitable uncle, although hating a Papist as much as it was in his nature to hate anything, placed a chair for the visitor, and bade Anthony bring glasses, and a fresh jug of claret.

Father Bernard received this courtesy with the graceful ease and pleasant acknowledgement which belonged to a man of the world. Then he turned to scan me with his keen glance. After some slight conversation, entered into on his part, I am certain, with an intention of discovering on what terms of confidence I stood with my uncle, he paused, and said gravely:

'I am sent here with a message to you, sir, from a woman to whom you have shown kindness, and who is one of my penitents in Antwerp – one Bridget Fitzgerald.'

'Bridget Fitzgerald!' exclaimed I. 'In Antwerp? Tell me sir, all that you can about her.'

'There is much to be said,' he replied. 'But may I inquire if this gentleman – if your uncle is acquainted with the particulars of which you and I stand informed?'

'All that I know, he knows,' said I, eagerly laying my hand on my uncle's arm, as he made a motion as if to quit the room.

'Then I have to speak before two gentleman who, however they may differ from me in faith, are yet fully impressed with the fact that there are evil powers going about continually to take cognisance of our evil thoughts; and, if their Master gives them power, to bring them into overt action. Such is my theory of the nature of that sin which I dare not disbelieve – as some sceptics would have us do – the sin of witchcraft. Of this deadly sin, you and I are aware, Bridget Fitzgerald has been guilty. Since you saw her last, many prayers have been offered in our churches, many masses sung, many penances undergone, in order that if God and the Holy Saints so willed it, her sin might be blotted out. But it has not been so willed.'

'Explain to me,' said I, 'who you are, and how you come connected with Bridget. Why is she at Antwerp? I pray you, sir, tell me more. If I am impatient, excuse me; I am ill and feverish, and in consequence bewildered.'

There was something to me inexpressibly soothing in the tone of voice with which he began to narrate, as it were from the beginning, his acquaintance with Bridget.

'I had known Mr. and Mrs. Starkey during their residence abroad, and so it fell out naturally that, when I came as chaplain to the Sherburnes at Stonyhurst, our acquaintance was renewed; and thus I became the confessor of the whole family, isolated as they were from the offices of the church, Sherburne being their nearest neighbour who professed the true faith. Of course, you are aware that facts revealed in confession are sealed as in the grave; but I learnt enough of Bridget's character to be convinced that I had to do with no common woman; one powerful for good as for evil. I believe that I was able to give her spiritual assistance from time to time, and that she looked upon me as a servant of that Holy Church which has such wonderful power of moving men's hearts, and relieving them of the burden of their sins. I have known her cross the moors on the wildest nights of storm, to confess and be absolved; and then she would return, calmed and subdued, to her daily work about her mistress, no one witting where she had been during the hours that most passed in sleep upon their beds. After her daughter's departure – after

Mary's mysterious disappearance – I had to impose many a long penance, in order to wash away the sin of impatient repining that was fast leading her into the deeper guilt of blasphemy. She set out on that long journey of which you have possibly heard – the fruitless journey in search of Mary – and, during her absence, my superiors ordered my return to my former duties at Antwerp; and for many years I heard no more of Bridget.

'Not many months ago, as I was passing homewards in the evening, along one of the streets near St. Jacques, leading into the Meer Straet, I saw a woman sitting crouched up under the shrine of the Holy Mother of Sorrows. Her hood was drawn over her head, so that the shadow caused by the light of the lamp above fell deep over her face; her hands were clasped round her knees. It was evident that she was some one in hopeless trouble, and as such it was my duty to stop and speak. I naturally addressed her first in Flemish, believing her to be one of the lower class of inhabitants. She shook her head, but did not look up. Then I tried French, and she replied in that language, but speaking it so indifferently that I was sure she was either English or Irish, and consequently spoke to her in my own native tongue. She recognised my voice; and, starting up, caught at my robes, dragging me before the blessed shrine, and throwing herself down, and forcing me, as much by her evident desire as by her actions, to kneel beside her, she exclaimed:

'"O Holy Virgin! you will never hearken to me again, but hear him; for you know him of old, that he does your bidding, and strives to heal broken hearts. Hear him!"

'She turned to me.

'"She will hear you, if you will only pray. She never hears me: she and all the saints in heaven cannot hear my prayers, for the Evil One carries them off as he carried that first away. Oh, Father Bernard, pray for me!"

'I prayed for one in sore distress, of what nature I could not say; but the Holy Virgin would know. Bridget held me fast, gasping with eagerness at the sound of my words. When I had ended, I rose, and, making the sign of the Cross over her, I was going to bless her in the name of the Holy Church, when she shrank away like some terrified creature, and said:

'"I am guilty of deadly sin, and am not shriven."

'"Arise, my daughter," said I, "and come with me." And I led the way into one of the confessionals of St. Jacques.

'She knelt; I listened. No words came. The evil powers had stricken her dumb, as I heard afterwards they had many a time before, when she approached confession.

'She was too poor to pay for the necessary forms of exorcism; and hithereto those priests to whom she had addressed herself were either so ignorant of the meaning of her broken French, or her Irish-English, or else esteemed her to be one so crazed – as, indeed, her wild and excited manner might easily have led anyone to think – that they had neglected the sole means of loosening her tongue, so that she might confess her deadly sin, and, after due penance, obtain absolution. But I knew Bridget of old, and felt that she was a penitent sent to me. I went through those holy offices appointed by our Church for the relief of such a case. I was the more bound to do this, as I found that she had come to Antwerp for the sole purpose of discovering me, and making confession to me. Of the nature of that fearful confession I am forbidden to speak. Much of it you know; possibly all.

'It now remains for her to free herself from mortal guilt and to set others free from the consequences thereof. No prayers, no masses, will ever do it, although they may strengthen her with that strength by which alone acts of deepest love and purest self-devotion may be performed. Her words of passion, and cries for revenge – her unholy prayers could never reach the ears of the holy saints! Other powers intercepted them, and wrought so that the curses thrown up to heaven have fallen on her own flesh and blood, and so, through her very strength of love, have bruised and crushed her heart. Henceforward her former self must be buried, – yea, buried quick, if need be, – but never more to make sign, or utter cry on earth! She has become a Poor Clare, in order that, by perpetual penance and constant service to others, she may at length so act as to obtain final absolution and rest for her soul. Until then, the innocent must suffer. It is to plead for the innocent that I come to you; not in the name of the witch, Bridget Fitzgerald, but of the penitent and servant of all men, the Poor Clare, Sister Magdalen.'

'Sir,' said I, 'I listen to your request with respect; only I may tell you it is not needed to urge me to do all that I can on behalf of one, love for whom is part of my very life. If for a time I have absented myself from her, it is to think and work for her redemption. I, a member of the English Church – my uncle, a Puritan – pray morning and night for her by name: the congregations of London, on the next Sabbath, will pray for one unknown, that she may be set free from the Powers of Darkness. Moreover, I must tell you, sir, that those evil ones touch not the great calm of her soul. She lives her own pure and loving life, unharmed and untainted, though all men fall off from her. I would I could have her faith!'

My uncle now spoke

'Nephew,' said he, 'it seems to me that this gentleman, although professing what I consider an erroneous creed, has touched upon the right point in exhorting Bridget to acts of love and mercy, whereby to wipe out her sin of hate and vengeance. Let us strive after our fashion, by almsgiving and visiting of the needy and fatherless, to make our prayers acceptable. Meanwhile, I myself will go down into the north, and take charge of the maiden. I am too old to be daunted by man or demon. I will bring her to this house as to a home; and let the Double come if it will! A company of godly divines shall give it the meeting, and we will try issue.'

The kindly, brave old man! But Father Bernard sat on musing.

'All hate,' said he, 'cannot be quenched in her heart; all Christian forgiveness cannot have entered into her soul, or the demon would have lost its power. You said, I think, that her grandchild was still tormented?'

'Still tormented!' I replied sadly, thinking of Mistress Clarke's last letter.

He rose to go. We afterwards heard that the occasion of his coming to London was a secret political mission on behalf of the Jacobites. Nevertheless, he was a good and a wise man.

Months and months passed away without any change. Lucy entreated my uncle to leave her where she was – dreading, as I learnt, lest if she came, with her fearful companion, to dwell in the same house with me, that my love could not stand the repeated shocks to which I should be doomed. And this she thought from no distrust of the strength of my affection, but from a kind of pitying sympathy for the terror to the nerves which she clearly observed that the demoniac visitation caused in all.

I was restless and miserable. I devoted myself to good works; but I performed them from no spirit of love, but solely from the hope of reward and payment, and so the reward was never granted. At length, I asked my uncle 's leave to travel; and I went forth, a wanderer, with no distincter end than that of many another wanderer – to get away from myself. A strange impulse led me to Antwerp, in spite of the wars and commotions then raging in the Low Countries – or rather, perhaps, the very craving to become interested in something external, led me into the thick of the struggle then going on with the Austrians. The cities of Flanders were all full at that time of civil disturbances and rebellions, only kept down by force and the presence of an Austrian garrison in every place.

I arrived in Antwerp, and made inquiry for Father Bernard. He was away in the country for a day or two. Then I asked my way to the Convent of Poor Clares; but, being healthy and prosperous, I could only see the dim, pent-up, grey walls, shut closely in by narrow streets, in the lowest part of the town. My landlord told me that, had I been stricken by some loathsome disease, or in desperate case of any kind, the Poor Clares would have taken me, and tended me. He spoke of them as an order of mercy of the strictest kind; dressed scantily in the coarsest materials; going barefoot; living on what the inhabitants of Antwerp chose to bestow, and sharing even those fragments and crumbs with the poor and helpless that swarmed all around; receiving no letters or communication with the outer world; utterly dead to everything but the alleviation of suffering. He smiled at my inquiring whether I could get speech of one of them, and told me that they were even forbidden to speak for the purposes of begging their daily food; while yet they lived, and fed others upon what was given in charity.

'But,' exclaimed I, 'supposing all men forgot them? Would they quietly lie down and die, without making sign of their extremity?'

'If such were the rule, the Poor Clares would willingly do it; but their founder appointed a remedy for such extreme cases as you suggest. They have a bell – 'tis but a small one, as I have heard, and has yet never been rung in the memory of man: when the Poor Clares have been without food for twenty-four hours, they may ring the bell, and then trust to our good people of Antwerp for rushing to the rescue of the Poor Clares, who have taken such blessed care of us in all our straits.'

It seemed to me that such rescue would be late in the day; but I did not say what I thought. I rather turned the conversation, by asking my landlord if he knew, or had ever heard, anything of a certain Sister Magdalen.

'Yes,' said he, rather under his breath, 'news will creep out, even from a convent of Poor Clares. Sister Magdalen is either a great sinner or a great saint. She does more, as I have heard, than all the other nuns put together; yet, when last month they would fain have made her mother superior, she begged rather that they would place her below all the rest, and make her the meanest servant of all.'

'You never saw her?' asked I.

'Never,' he replied.

I was weary of waiting for Father Bernard, and yet I lingered in Antwerp. The political state of things became worse than ever, increased to its height by the scarcity of food consequent on many deficient harvests. I saw groups of fierce, squalid men at every corner of the street, glaring out with wolfish eyes at my sleek skin and handsome clothes.

At last Father Bernard returned. We had a long conversation, in which he told me that, curiously enough, Mr. Gisborne, Lucy's father, was serving in one of the Antwerp regiments, then in garrison at Antwerp. I asked Father Bernard if he would make us acquainted; which he consented to do. But a day or two afterwards, he told me that, on hearing my name, Mr. Gisborne had declined responding to any advances on my part, saying he had abjured his country, and hated his countrymen.

Probably he recollected my name in connection with that of his daughter Lucy. Anyhow, it was clear enough that I had no chance of making his acquaintance. Father Bernard confirmed me in my suspicions of the hidden fermentation, for some coming evil, working among the 'blouses' of Antwerp, and he

would fain have had me depart out of the city; but I rather
craved the excitement of danger, and stubbornly refused to
leave.

One day, when I was walking with him in the Place Verte,
he bowed to an Austrian officer, who was crossing towards
the cathedral.

'That is Mr. Gisborne,' said he, as soon as the gentleman
was past.

I turned to look at the tall, slight figure of the officer. He
carried himself in a stately manner, although he was past
middle age, and from his years might have had some excuse
for a slight stoop. As I looked at the man, he turned round, his
eyes met mine, and I saw his face. Deeply lined, sallow, and
scathed was that countenance; scarred by passion as well as by
the fortunes of war. 'Twas but a moment our eyes met. We
each turned round, and went on our separate way.

But his whole appearance was not one to be easily forgotten; the thorough appointment of the dress, and evident
thought bestowed on it, made an incongruous whole with the
dark, gloomy expression of his countenance. Because he was
Lucy's father, I sought instinctively to meet him everywhere.
At last he must have become aware of my pertinacity, for he
gave me a haughty scowl whenever I passed him. In one of
these encounters, however, I chanced to be of some service to
him. He was turning the corner of a street, and came suddenly
on one of the groups of discontented Flemings of whom I
have spoken. Some words were exchanged, when my gentleman out with his sword, and with a slight but skilful cut
drew blood from one of those who had insulted him, as he
fancied, though I was too far off to hear the words. They
would all have fallen upon him had I not rushed forwards and
raised the cry, then well known in Antwerp, of rally, to the
Austrian soldiers who were perpetually patrolling the streets,
and who came in numbers to the rescue. I think that neither
Mr. Gisborne nor the mutinous group of plebeians owed me
much gratitude for my interference. He had planted himself
against a wall, in a skilful attitude of fence, ready with his
bright glancing rapier to do battle with all the heavy, fierce,
unarmed men, some six or seven in number. But when his
own soldiers came up, he sheathed his sword; and, giving

some careless word of command, sent them away again, and
continued his saunter all alone down the street, the workmen
snarling in his rear, and more than half-inclined to fall on me
for my cry for rescue. I cared not if they did, my life seemed so
dreary a burden just then; and, perhaps, it was this daring
loitering among them that prevented their attacking me.
Instead, they suffered me to fall into conversation with them;
and I heard some of their grievances. Sore and heavy to be
borne were they, and no wonder the sufferers were savage and
desperate.

The man whom Gisborne had wounded across his face
would fain have got out of me the name of his aggressor; but I
refused to tell it. Another of the group heard his inquiry, and
made answer:

'I know the man. He is one Gisborne, aide-de-camp to the
General-Commandant. I know him well.'

He began to tell some story in connection with Gisborne in
a low and muttering voice; and while he was relating a tale,
which I saw excited their evil blood, and which they evidently
wished me not to hear, I sauntered away back to my lodgings.

That night Antwerp was in open revolt. The inhabitants
rose in rebellion against their Austrian masters. The Austrians,
holding the gates of the city, remained at first pretty quiet in
the citadel; only, from time to time, the boom of the great
cannon swept sullenly over the town. But if they expected the
disturbance to die away, and spend itself in a few hours' fury,
they were mistaken. In a day or two, the rioters held
possession of the principal municipal buildings. Then the
Austrians poured forth in bright, flaming array, calm and
smiling, as they marched to the posts assigned, as if the fierce
mob were no more to them than the swarms of buzzing
summer flies. Their practised manœuvres, their well-aimed
shot, told with terrible effect; but in the place of one slain
rioter three sprang up of his blood to avenge his loss. But a
deadly foe, a ghastly ally of the Austrians, was at work. Food,
scarce and dear for months, was now hardly to be obtained at
any price. Desperate efforts were being made to bring
provisions into the city, for the rioters had friends without.
Close to the city port, nearest to the Scheldt, a great struggle
took place. I was there, helping the rioters, whose cause I had

adopted. We had a savage encounter with the Austrians. Numbers fell on both sides; I saw them lie bleeding for a moment; then a volley of smoke obscured them; and, when it cleared away, they were dead – trampled upon or smothered, pressed down and hidden by the freshly-wounded whom those last guns had brought low. And then a grey-robed and grey-veiled figure came right across the flashing guns and stooped over someone, whose life-blood was ebbing away; sometimes it was to give him drink from cans which they carried slung at their sides; sometimes I saw the cross held above a dying man, and rapid prayers were being uttered, unheard by men in that hellish din and clangour, but listened to by One above. I saw all this as in a dream: the reality of that stern time was battle and carnage. But I knew that these grey figures, their bare feet all wet with blood, and their faces hidden by their veils, were the Poor Clares – sent forth now because dire agony was abroad and imminent danger at hand. Therefore, they left their cloistered shelter, and came into that thick and evil mêlée.

Close to me – driven past me by the struggle of many fighters – came the Antwerp burgess with the scarce-healed scar upon his face; and, in an instant more, he was thrown by the press upon the Austrian officer Gisborne, and ere either had recovered the shock, the burgess had recognised his opponent.

'Ha! the Englishman Gisborne!' he cried, and threw himself upon him with redoubled fury. He had struck him hard – the Englishman was down: when out of the smoke came a dark-grey figure, and threw herself right under the uplifted flashing sword. The burgess's arm stood arrested. Neither Austrians nor Anversois willingly harmed the Poor Clares.

'Leave him to me!' said a low, stern voice. 'He is mine enemy – mine for many years.'

Those words were the last I heard. I myself was struck down by a bullet. I remember nothing more for days. When I came to myself, I was at the extremity of weakness, and was craving for food to recruit my strength. My landlord sat watching me. He, too, looked pinched and shrunken; he had heard of my wounded state, and sought me out. Yes! the struggle still continued, but the famine was sore: and some, he had heard, had died for lack of food. The tears stood in his eyes as he spoke. But soon he shook off his weakness, and his natural cheerfulness returned. Father Bernard had been to see me – no one else. (Who should, indeed?) Father Bernard would come back that afternoon – he had promised. But Father Bernard never came, although I was up and dressed, and looking eagerly for him.

My landlord brought me a meal which he had cooked himself; of what it was composed he would not say, but it was most excellent, and with every mouthful I seemed to gain strength. The good man sat looking at my evident enjoyment with a happy smile of sympathy; but, as my appetite became satisfied, I began to detect a certain wistfulness in his eyes, as if craving for the food I had so nearly devoured – for, indeed, at that time I was hardly aware of the extent of the famine. Suddenly, there was a sound of many rushing feet past our window. My landlord opened one of the sides of it, the better to learn what was going on. Then we heard a faint, cracked, tinkling bell, coming shrill upon the air, clear and distinct from all other sounds. 'Holy Mother!' exclaimed my landlord, 'the Poor Clares!'

He snatched up the fragments of my meal, and crammed them into my hands, bidding me follow. Downstairs he ran, clutching at more food, as the women of the house eagerly held it out to him; and in a moment we were in the street, moving along with the great current, all tending towards the Convent of the Poor Clares. And still, as if piercing our ears with its inarticulate cry, came the shrill tinkle of the bell. In that strange crowd were old men trembling and sobbing, as they carried their little pittance of food; women with tears running down their cheeks, who had snatched up what provisions they had in the vessels in which they stood, so that the burden of these was in many cases much greater than that which they contained; children with flushed faces, grasping tight the morsel of bitten cake or bread, in their eagerness to carry it safe to the help of the Poor Clares; strong men – yea, both Anversois and Austrians – pressing onward with set teeth, and no word spoken; and over all, and through all, came that sharp tinkle – that cry for help in extremity.

We met the first torrent of people returning with blanched and piteous faces; they were issuing out of the convent to make way for the offerings of others. 'Haste, haste!' said they. 'A Poor Clare is dying! A Poor Clare is dead for hunger! God forgive us and our city!'

We pressed on. The stream bore us along where it would. We were carried through refectories, bare and crumbless; into cells over whose doors the conventual name of the occupant was written. Thus it was that I, with others, was forced into Sister Magdalen's cell. On her couch lay Gisborne, pale unto death, but not dead. By his side was a cup of water, and a small morsel of mouldy bread, which he had pushed out of his reach and could not move to obtain. Over against his bed were these words, copied in the English version: 'Therefore, if thine enemy hunger, feed him; if he thirst, give him drink.'

Some of us gave him of our food, and left him eating greedily, like some famished wild animal. For now it was no longer the sharp tinkle, but that one solemn toll, which in all Christian countries tells of the passing of the spirit out of earthly life into eternity; and again a murmur gathered and grew, as of many people speaking with awed breath, 'A Poor Clare is dying! A Poor Clare is dead!'

Borne along once more by the motion of the crowd, we were carried into the chapel belonging to the Poor Clares. On a bier before the high altar, lay a woman – lay Sister Magdalen – lay Bridget Fitzgerald. By her side stood Father Bernard, in his robes of office, and holding the crucifix on high while he pronounced the solemn absolution of the Church, as on one who had newly confessed herself of deadly sin. I pushed on with passionate force, till I stood close to the dying woman, as she received extreme unction amid the breathless and awed hush of the multitude around. Her eyes were glazing, her limbs were stiffening; but, when the rite was over and finished, she raised her gaunt figure slowly up, and her eyes brightened to a strange intensity of joy, as with the gesture of her finger and the trance-like gleam of her eye, she seemed like one who watched the disappearance of some loathed and fearful creature.

'She is freed from the curse!' said she, as she fell back dead.

THE HALF-BROTHERS

THE HALF-BROTHERS

My mother was twice married. She never spoke of her first husband, and it is only from other people that I have learnt what little I know about him. I believe she was scarcely seventeen when she was married to him: and he was barely one-and-twenty. He rented a small farm up in Cumberland, somewhere towards the sea-coast; but he was perhaps too young and inexperienced to have the charge of land and cattle: anyhow, his affairs did not prosper, and he fell into ill health, and died of consumption before they had been three years man and wife, leaving my mother a young widow of twenty, with a little child only just able to walk, and the farm on her hands for four years more by the lease, with half the stock on it dead or sold off one by one to pay the more pressing debts, and with no money to purchase more, or even to buy the provisions needed for the small consumption of every day. There was another child coming, too; and sad and sorry, I believe, she was to think of it. A dreary winter she must have had in her lonesome dwelling, with never another near it for miles around; her sister came to bear her company, and they two planned and plotted how to make every penny they could raise go as far as possible. I can't tell you how it happened that my little sister, whom I never saw, came to sicken and die; but, as if my poor mother's cup was not full enough, only a fortnight before Gregory was born the little child took ill of scarlet fever, and in a week she lay dead. My mother was, I believe, just stunned with this last blow. My aunt has told me that she did not cry; aunt Fanny would have been thankful if she had; but she sat holding the poor wee lassie's hand, and looking in her pretty pale, dead face, without so much as shedding a tear. And it was all the same, when they had to take her away to be buried. She just kissed the child, and sat her down in the window-seat to watch the little black train of people (neighbours – my aunt, and one far-off cousin, who were all the friends they could muster) go winding away amongst the snow, which had fallen thinly over the country the night before. When my aunt came back from the funeral, she found my mother in the same place, and as dry-eyed as ever. So she continued until after Gregory was born: and, somehow, his coming seemed to loosen the tears, and she cried day and night, till my aunt and the other watcher looked at each other in dismay, and would fain have stopped her if they had but known how. But she bade them let her alone, and not be over-anxious, for every drop she shed eased her brain, which had been in a terrible state before for want of the power to cry. She seemed after that to think of nothing but her new little baby; she had hardly appeared to remember either her husband or her little daughter that lay dead in Brigham churchyard – at least so aunt Fanny said; but she was a great talker, and my mother was very silent by nature, and I think aunt Fanny may have been mistaken in believing that my mother never thought of her husband and child just because she never spoke about them. Aunt Fanny was older than my mother, and had a way of treating her like a child; but, for all that, she was a kind, warm-hearted creature, who thought more of her sister's welfare than she did of her own; and it was on her bit of money that they principally lived, and on what the two could earn by working for the great Glasgow sewing-merchants. But by-and-by my mother's eyesight began to fail. It was not that she was exactly blind, for she could see well enough to guide herself about the house, and to do a good deal of domestic work; but she could no longer do fine sewing and earn money. It must have been with the heavy crying she had had in her day, for she was but a young creature at this time, and as pretty a young woman, I have heard people say, as any on the country side. She took it sadly to heart that she could no longer gain anything towards the keep of herself and her child. My aunt Fanny would fain have persuaded her that she had enough to do in manging their cottage and minding Gregory; but my mother knew that they were pinched, and that aunt Fanny herself had not as much to eat, even of the commonest kind of food, as she could have done with; and as for Gregory, he was not a strong lad, and needed, not more food – for he always had enough, whoever went short – but better nourishment, and more flesh-meat. One day – it was aunt Fanny who told me all this about my poor mother, long after her death – as the sisters were sitting together, aunt Fanny working, and my mother hushing Gregory to sleep. William Preston, who was afterwards my father, came in. He was reckoned an old bachelor; I suppose he was long past forty, and he was one of the wealthiest farmers thereabouts, and had known my grandfather well, and my mother and my aunt in their more prosperous days. He sat down, and began to twirl his hat by way of being agreeable; my aunt Fanny talked, and he listened and looked at my mother. But he said very little, either on that visit, or on many another that he paid before he spoke out what had been the real purpose of his calling so often all along, and from the very first time he came to their house. One Sunday, however, my aunt Fanny stayed away from church and took care of the child, and my mother went alone. When she came back, she ran straight upstairs, without going into the kitchen to look at Gregory or speak any word to her sister, and aunt Fanny heard her cry as if her heart was breaking; so she went up and scolded her right well through the bolted door, till at last she got her to open it. And then she threw herself on my aunt's neck, and told her that William Preston had asked her to marry him, and had promised to take good charge of her boy, and to let him want for nothing, neither in the way of keep nor of education, and that she had consented. Aunt Fanny was a good deal shocked at this; for, as I have said, she had often thought that my mother had forgotten her first husband very quickly, and now here was proof positive of it, if she could so soon think of marrying again. Besides, as aunt Fanny used to say, she herself would have been a far more suitable match for a man of William Preston's age than Helen, who, though she was a widow, had not seen her four-and-twentieth summer. However, as aunt Fanny said, they had not asked her advice; and there was much to be said on the other side of the question. Helen's eye sight would never be good for much again, and as William Preston's wife she would never need to do anything, if she chose to sit with her hands before her; and a boy was a great charge to a widowed mother; and now there would be a decent, steady man to see after him. So, by-and-by, aunt Fanny seemed to take a brighter view of the marriage than did my mother herself, who hardly ever looked up, and never smiled after the day when she promised William Preston to be his wife. But much as she had loved Gregory before, she seemed to love him more now. She was continually talking to him when they were alone, though he was far too young to understand her moaning words, or give her any comfort, except by his caresses.

At last William Peston and she were wed; and she went to be mistress of a well-stocked house, not above half-an-hour's walk from where aunt Fanny lived. I believe she did all that she could to please my father; and a more dutiful wife, I have heard him himself say, could never have been. But she did not love him, and he soon found it out. She loved Gregory, and she did not love him. Perhaps, love would have come in time, if he had been patient enough to wait; but it turned him sour to see how her eye brightened and her colour came at the sight of that little child while for him who had given her so much she had only gentle words as cold as ice. He got to taunt her with the difference in her manner, as if that would bring love: and he took a positive dislike to Gregory – he was so jealous of the ready love that always gushed out like a spring of fresh water when he came near. He wanted her to love him more, and perhaps that was all well and good; but he wanted her to love her child less, and that was an evil wish. One day, he gave way to his temper, and cursed and swore at Gregory, who had got into some mischief, as children will; my mother made some excuse for him; my father said it was hard enough to have to keep another man's child, without having it perpetually held up in its naughtiness by his wife, who ought to be always in the same mind that he was; and so from little they got to more; and the end of it was, that my mother took to her bed before her time, and I was born that very day. My father was glad, and proud, and sorry, all in a breath; glad and proud that a son was born to him; and sorry for his poor wife's state, and to think how his angry words had brought it on. But he was a man who liked better to be angry than sorry: so he soon found out that it was all Gregory's fault, and owed him an additional grudge for having hastened my birth. He had another grudge against him before long. My mother began to sink the day after I was born. My father sent to Carlisle for doctors, and would have coined his heart's blood into gold to save her, if that could have been; but it could not. My aunt Fanny used to say sometimes that she thought that Helen did not wish to live, and so just let herself die away without trying to take hold on life; but, when I questioned her, she owned that my mother did all the doctors bade her do, with the same sort of uncomplaining patience with which she had acted through life. One of her last requests was to have little Gregory laid in her bed by my side, and then she made him take hold of my little hand. Her husband came in while she was looking at us so; and, when he bent tenderly over her to ask her how she felt now; and seemed to gaze on us two little half-brothers, with a grave sort of kindliness, she looked up in his face and smiled, almost her first smile at him; and such a sweet smile! as more besides aunt Fanny have said. In an hour she was dead. Aunt Fanny came to live with us. It was the best thing that could be done. My father would have been glad to return to his old mode of bachelor life, but what could he do with two little children? He needed a woman to take care of him, and who so fitting as his wife's elder sister? So she had the charge of me from my birth; and for a time I was weakly, as was but natural, and she was always beside me, night and day watching over me, and my father nearly as anxious as she. For his land had come down from father to son for more than three hundred years, and he would have cared for me merely as his flesh and blood that was to inherit the land after him. But he needed something to love, for all that, to most people, he was a stern, hard man; and he took to me as, I fancy, he had taken to no human being before – as he might have taken to my mother, if she had had no former life for him to be jealous of. I loved him back again right heartily. I loved all around me, I believe, for everybody was kind to me. After a time, I overcame my original weakliness of constitution, and was just a bonny, strong-looking lad, whom every passer-by noticed when my father took me with him to the nearest town.

At home I was the darling of my aunt, the tenderly-beloved of my father, the pet and plaything of the old domestics, the 'young master' of the farm-labourers, before whom I played many a lordly antic, assuming a sort of authority which sat oddly enough, I doubt not, on such a baby as I was.

Gregory was three years older than I. Aunt Fanny was always kind to him in deed and in action, but she did not often think about him, she had fallen so completely into the habit of being engrossed by me, from the fact of my having come into her charge as a delicate baby. My father never got over his grudging dislike to his stepson, who had so innocently wrestled with him for the possession of my mother's heart. I mistrust me, too, that my father always considered him as the cause of my mother's death, and my early delicacy; and, utterly unreasonable as this may seem, I believe my father rather cherished his feeling of alienation to my brother as a duty than strove to repress it. Yet not for the world would my father have grudged him anything that money could purchase. That was, as it were, in the bond when he had wedded my mother. Gregory was lumpish and loutish, awkward and ungainly, marring whatever he meddled in; and many a hard word and sharp scolding did he get from the people about the farm, who hardly waited till my father's back was turned before they rated the stepson. I am ashamed – my heart is sore to think how I fell into the fashion of the family, and slighted my poor orphan stepbrother. I don't think I ever scouted him, or was wilfully ill-natured to him; but the habit of being considered in all things, and being treated as something uncommon and superior, made me insolent in my prosperity, and I exacted more than Gregory was always willing to grant; and then, irritated, I sometimes repeated the disparaging words I had heard others use with regard to him, without fully understanding their meaning. Whether he did or not I cannot tell. I am afraid he did. He used to turn silent and quiet – sullen and sulky, my father thought it: stupid, aunt Fanny used to call it. But every one said he was stupid and dull, and this stupidity and dullness grew upon him. He would sit without speaking a word, sometimes, for hours; then my father would bid him rise and do some piece of work, may be, about the farm. And he would take three or four tellings before he would go. When we were sent to school, it was all the same. He could never be made to remember his lessons; the schoolmaster grew weary of scolding and flogging, and at last advised my father just to take him away, and set him to some farm-work that might not be above his comprehension. I think he was more gloomy and stupid than ever after this; yet he was not a cross lad; he was patient and good-natured, and would try to do a kind turn for any one, even if they had been scolding or cuffing him not a minute before. But very often his attempts at kindness ended in some mischief to the very people he was trying to serve, owing to his awkward, ungainly ways. I suppose I was a clever lad; at any rate, I always got plenty of praise, and was, as we called it, the cock of the school. The schoolmaster said I could learn anything I chose; but my father, who had no great learning himself, saw little use in much for me, and took me away betimes, and kept he with him about the farm. Gregory was made into a kind of shepherd, receiving his training under old Adam, who was nearly past his work. I think old Adam was almost the first person who had a good opinion of Gregory. He stood to it that my brother had good parts, though he did not rightly know how to bring them out; and, for knowing the bearings of the Fells, he said he had never seen a lad like him. My father would try to bring Adam round to speak of Gregory's faults and shortcomings; but, instead of that, he would praise him twice as much, as soon as he found out what was my father's object.

One winter-time, when I was about sixteen, and Gregory nineteen, I was sent by my father on an errand to a place about seven miles distant by the road, but only about four by the Fells. He bade me return by the road, whichever way I took in going, for the evenings closed in early, and were often thick and misty; besides which, old Adam, now paralytic and bedridden, foretold a downfall of snow before long. I soon got to my journey's end, and soon had done my business; earlier by an hour, I thought, than my father had expected, so I took the decision of the way by which I would return into my own hands, and set off back again over the Fells, just as the first shades of evening began to fall. It looked dark and gloomy enough; but everything was so still that I thought I should have plenty of time to get home before the snow came down. Off I set at a pretty quick pace. But night came on quicker. The right path was clear enough in the daytime, although at several points two or three exactly similar diverged from the same place; but when there was a good light, the traveller was guided by the sight of distant objects – a piece of rock – a fall in the ground – which were quite invisible to me now. I plucked up a brave heart, however, and took what seemed to me the right road. It was wrong, nevertheless, and led me whither I knew not, but to some wild boggy moor where the solitude seemed painful, intense, as if never footfall of man had come thither to break the silence. I tried to shout – with the dimmest possible hope of being heard – rather to reassure myself by the sound of my own voice; but my voice came husky and short, and yet it dismayed me; it seemed so weird and strange, in that noiseless expanse of black darkness. Suddenly the air was filled with dusky flakes, my face and hands were wet with snow. It cut me off from the slightest knowledge of where I was, for I lost every idea of the direction from which I had come, so that I could not even retrace my steps; it hemmed me in, thicker, thicker, with a darkness that might be felt. The boggy soil on which I stood quaked under me if I remained long in one place, and yet I dared not move far. All my youthful hardiness seemed to leave me at once. I was on the point of crying, and only very shame seemed to keep it down. To save myself from shedding tears, I shouted – terrible, wild shouts for bare life they were. I turned sick as I paused to listen; no answering sound came but the unfeeling echoes. Only the noiseless, pitiless snow kept falling thicker, thicker – faster, faster! I was growing numb and sleepy. I tried to move about, but I dared not go far, for fear of the precipices which, I knew, abounded in certain places on the Fells. Now and then, I stood still and shouted again; but my voice was getting choked with tears, as I thought of the desolate, helpless death I was to die, and how little they at home, sitting round the warm, red, bright fire, wotted what was become of me – and how my poor father would grieve for me – it would surely kill him – it would break his heart, poor old man! Aunt Fanny too – was this to be the end of all her cares for me? I began to review my life in a strange kind of vivid dream, in which the various scenes of my few boyish years passed before me like visions. In a pang of agony, caused by such remembrance of my short life, I gathered up my strength, and called out once more – a long despairing, wailing cry, to which I had no hope of obtaining any answer, save from the echoes around, dulled as the sound might be by the thickened air. To my surprise I heard a cry – almost as long, as wild as mine – so wild, that it seemed unearthly, and I almost thought it must be the voice of some of the mocking spirits of the Fells, about whom I had heard so many tales. My heart suddenly began to beat fast and loud. I could not reply for a minute of two. I nearly fancied I had lost the power of utterance. Just at this moment a dog barked. Was it Lassie's bark – my brother's collie? – an ugly enough brute, with a white, ill-looking face, that my father always kicked whenever he saw it, partly for its own demerits, partly because it belonged to my brother. On such occasions, Gregory would whistle Lassie away, and go and sit with her in some outhouse. My father had once or twice been ashamed of himself, when the poor collie had yowled out with the suddenness of the pain, and had relieved himself of his self-approach by blaming my brother, who, he said, had no notion of training a dog, and was enough to ruin any collie in Christendom with his stupid way of allowing them to lie by the kitchen fire. To all which Gregory would answer nothing, nor even seem to hear, but go on looking absent and moody.

Yes! there again! it was Lassie's bark! Now or never! I lifted up my voice and shouted 'Lassie! Lassie! for God's sake, Lassie!' Another moment, and the great white-faced Lassie was curving and gambolling with delight round my feet and legs, looking, however, up in my face with her intelligent, apprehensive eyes, as if fearing lest I might greet her with a blow, as I had done oftentimes before. But I cried with gladness, as I stooped down and patted her. My mind was sharing in my body's weakness, and I could not reason, but I knew that help was at hand. A grey figure came more and more distinctly out of the thick, close-pressing darkness. It was Gregory wrapped in his maud.

'Oh, Gregory!' said I, and I fell upon his neck, unable to speak another word. He never spoke much, and made me no answer for some little time. Then he told me we must move, we must walk for the dear life – we must find our road home, if possible; but we must move, or we should be frozen to death.

'Don't you know the way home?' asked I.

'I thought I did when I set out, but I am doubtful now. The snow blinds me, and I am feared that, in moving about just now, I have lost the right gait homewards.'

He had his shepherd's staff with him, and by dint of plunging it before us at every step we took – clinging close to each other, we went on safely enough, as far as not falling down any of the steep rocks; but it was slow, dreary work. My brother, I saw, was more guided by Lassie and the way she took than anything else, trusting to her instinct. It was too dark to see far before us; but he called her back continually, and noted from what quarter she returned, and shaped our slow steps accordingly. But the tedious motion scarcely kept my very blood from freezing. Every bone, every fibre in my body seemed first to ache, and then to swell, and then to turn numb with intense cold. My brother bore it better than I, from having been more out upon the hills. He did not speak, except to call Lassie. I strove to be brave, and not complain; but now I felt the deadly fatal sleep stealing over me.

'I can go no farther,' I said, in a drowsy tone. I remember I suddenly became dogged and resolved. Sleep I would, were it only for five minutes. If death were to be the consequence, sleep I would. Gregory stood still. I suppose, he recognised the peculiar phase of suffering to which I had been brought by the cold.

'It is of no use,' said he, as if to himself. 'We are no nearer home than we were when we started, as far as I can tell. Our only chance is in Lassie. Here! roll thee in my maud, lad, and lay thee down on this sheltered side of this bit of rock. Creep close under it, lad, and I'll lie by thee, and strive to keep the warmth in us. Stay! hast gotten aught about thee they'll know at home?'

I felt him unkind thus to keep me from slumber, but, on his repeating the question, I pulled out my pocket-handkerchief, of some showy pattern, which aunt Fanny had hemmed for me. Gregory took it, and tied it round Lassie's neck.

'Hie thee, Lassie, hie thee home!' And the white-faced ill-favoured brute was off like a shot in the darkness. Now I might lie down – now I might sleep. In my drowsy stupor I felt that I was being tenderly covered up by my brother; but what with I neither knew nor cared – I was too dull, too selfish, too numb to think and reason, or I might have known that in that bleak bare place there was naught to wrap me in, save what was taken off another. I was glad enough when he ceased his caress and lay down by me. I took his hand.

'Thou canst not remember, lad, how we lay together thus by our dying mother. She put thy small, wee hand in mine – I reckon she sees us now; and belike we shall soon be with her. Anyhow, God's will be done.'

'Dear Gregory,' I muttered, and crept nearer to him for warmth. He was talking still, and again about our mother, when I fell asleep. In an instant – or so it seemed – there were many voices about me – many faces hovering round me – the sweet luxury of warmth was stealing into every part of me. I was in my own little bed at home. I am thankful to say, my first word was 'Gregory?'

A look passed from one to another – my father's stern old face strove in vain to keep its sternness; his mouth quivered, his eyes filled slowly with unwonted tears.

'I would have given him half my land – I would have blessed him as my son – Oh, God! I would have knelt at his feet, and asked him to forgive my hardness of heart.'

I heard no more. A whirl came through my brain, catching me back to death.

I came slowly to my consciousness, weeks afterwards. My father's hair was white when I recovered, and his hands shook as he looked into my face.

We spoke no more of Gregory. We could not speak of him; but he was strangely in our thoughts. Lassie came and went with never a word of blame; nay, my father would try to stroke her, but she shrank away; and he, as if reproved by the poor dumb beast, would sigh, and be silent and abstracted for a time.

Aunt Fanny – always a talker – told me all. How, on that fatal night, my father, irritated by my prolonged absence, and probably more anxious than he cared to show, had been fierce and imperious, even beyond his wont, to Gregory; had upbraided him with his father's poverty, his own stupidity which made his services good for nothing – for so, in spite of the old shepherd, my father always chose to consider them. At last, Gregory had risen up, and whistled Lassie out with him – poor Lassie, crouching underneath his chair for fear of a kick or a blow. Some time before, there had been some talk between my father and my aunt respecting my return; and, when aunt Fanny told me all this, she said she fancied that

Gregory might have noticed the coming storm, and gone out silently to meet me. Three hours afterwards, when all were running about in wild alarm, not knowing whither to go in search of me – not even missing Gregory, or heeding his absence, poor fellow – poor, poor fellow! – Lassie come home, with my handkerchief tied round her neck. They knew and understood, and the whole strength of the farm was turned out to follow her, with wraps, and blankets, and brandy, and everything that could be thought of. I lay in chilly sleep, but still alive, beneath the rock that Lassie guided them to. I was covered over with my brother's plaid, and his thick shepherd's coat was carefully wrapped round my feet. He was in his shirt-sleeves – his arm thrown over me – a quiet smile (he had hardly ever smiled in life) upon his still, cold face.

My father's last words were, 'God forgive me my hardness of heart towards the fatherless child!'

And what marked the depth of his feeling of repentance, perhaps more than all, considering the passionate love he bore my mother, was this: we found a paper of directions after his death, in which he desired that he might lie at the foot of the grave, in which, by his desire, poor Gregory had been laid with OUR MOTHER.

MR. HARRISON'S CONFESSIONS

MR. HARRISON'S CONFESSIONS

CHAPTER I

The fire was burning gaily. My wife had just gone upstairs to
put baby to bed. Charles sat opposite to me, looking very
brown and handsome. It was pleasant enough that we should
feel sure of spending some weeks under the same roof, a thing
which we had never done since we were mere boys. I felt too
lazy to talk, so I ate walnuts and looked into the fire. But
Charles grew restless.

'Now that your wife is gone upstairs, Will, you must tell
me what I've wanted to ask you ever since I saw her this
morning. Tell me all about the wooing and winning. I want to
have the receipt for getting such a charming little wife of my
own. Your letters gave the barest details. So set to, man, and
tell me every particular.'

'If I tell you all, it will be a long story.'

'Never fear. If I get tired, I can go to sleep, and dream that I
am back again, a lonely bachelor, in Ceylon; and I can waken
up when you have done, to know that I am under your roof.
Dash away, man! "Once upon a time, a gallant young
bachelor" – There's a beginning for you!'

'Well, then: "Once upon a time, a gallant young bachelor"
was sorely puzzled where to settle, when he had completed
his education as a surgeon – I must speak in the first person; I
cannot go on as a gallant young bachelor. I had just finished
walking the hospitals when you went to Ceylon, and, if you
remember, I wanted to go abroad like you, and thought of
offering myself as a ship-surgeon; but I found I should rather
lose caste in my profession; so I hesitated, and, while I was
hesitating, I received a letter from my father's cousin, Mr.
Morgan – that old gentleman who used to write such long
letters of advice to my mother, and who tipped me a
five-pound note when I agreed to be bound apprentice to Mr.

Howard, instead of going to sea. Well, it seems the old
gentleman had all along thought of taking me as his partner, if
I turned out pretty well; and, as he heard a good account of me
from an old friend of his, who was a surgeon at Guy's, he
wrote to propose this arrangement: I was to have a third of the
profits for five years, after that, half; and eventually I was to
succeed to the whole. It was no bad offer for a penniless man
like me, as Mr. Morgan had a capital country practice, and,
though I did not know him personally, I had formed a pretty
good idea of him, as an honourable, kind-hearted, fidgety,
meddlesome old bachelor; and a very correct notion it was, as
I found out in the very first half-hour of seeing him. I had had
some idea that I was to live in his house, as he was a bachelor
and a kind of family friend, and I think he was afraid that I
should expect this arrangement; for, when I walked up to his
door, with the porter carrying my portmanteau, he met me on
the steps, and while he held my hand and shook it, he said to
the porter, "Jerry, if you'll wait a moment, Mr. Harrison will
be ready to go with you to his lodgings, at Jocelyn's, you
know;" and then, turning to me, he addressed his first words
of welcome. I was a little inclined to think him inhospitable,
but I got to understand him better afterwards. "Jocelyn's" said
he, "is the best place I have been able to hit upon in a hurry,
and there is a good deal of fever about, which made me
desirous that you should come this month – a low kind of
typhoid, in the oldest part of the town. I think you'll be
comfortable there for a week or two. I have taken the liberty
of desiring my housekeeer to send down one or two things
which give the place a little more of a home aspect – an
easy-chair, a beautiful case of preparations, and one or two
little matters in the way of eatables; but, if you'll take my
advice, I've a plan in my head which we will talk about
tomorrow morning. At present, I don't like to keep you
standing out on the steps here; so I'll not detain you from your
lodgings, where I rather think my housekeeper is gone to get
tea ready for you."

'I thought I understood the old gentleman's anxiety for his
own health, which he put upon care for mine; for he had on a
kind of loose grey coat, and no hat on his head. But I
wondered that he did not ask me indoors, instead of keeping

me on the steps. I believe, after all, I made a mistake in supposing he was afraid of taking cold; he was only afraid of being seen in dishabille. And for his apparent inhospitality, I had not been long in Duncombe before I understood the comfort of having one's house considered as a castle into which no one might intrude, and saw good reason for the practice Mr. Morgan had established of coming to his door to speak to every one. It was only the effect of habit that made him receive me so. Before long, I had the free run of his house.

'There was every sign of kind attention and forethought on the part of someone, whom I could not doubt to be Mr. Morgan, in my lodgings. I was too lazy to do much that evening, and sat in the little bow-window which projected over Jocelyn's shop, looking up and down the street. Duncombe calls itself a town, but I should call it a village. Really, looking from Jocelyn's, it is a very picturesque place. The houses are anything but regular; they may be mean in their details; but altogether they look well; they have not that flat unrelieved front, which many towns of far more pretensions present. Here and there a bow-window – every now and then a gable, cutting up against the sky – occasionally a projecting upper storey – throws good effect of light and shadow along the street; and they have a queer fashion of their own of colouring the whitewash of some of the houses with a sort of pink blotting-paper tinge, more like the stone of which Mayence is built than anything else. It may be very bad taste, but to my mind it gives a rich warmth to the colouring. Then, here and there a dwelling-house had a court in front, with a grass-plot on each side of the flagged walk, and a large tree or two – limes or horse-chestnut – which sent their great projecting upper branches over into the street, making round dry places of shelter on the pavement in the times of summer showers.

'While I was sitting in the bow-window, thinking of the contrast between this place and the lodgings in the heart of London, which I had left only twelve hours before – the window open here, and, although in the centre of the town, admitting only scents from the mignonette boxes on the sill, instead of the dust and smoke of — Street – the only sound heard in this, the principal street, being the voices of mothers calling their playing children home to bed, and the eight o'clock bell of the old parish church bimbomming in remembrance of the curfew: while I was sitting thus idly, the door opened, and the little maid-servant, dropping a courtesy, said:

'"Please, sir, Mrs. Munton's compliments, and she would be glad to know how you are after your journey."

'There! was not that hearty and kind? Would even the dearest chum I had at Guy's have thought of doing such a thing? while Mrs Munton, whose name I had never heard of before, was doubtless suffering anxiety till I could relieve her mind by sending back word that I was pretty well.

'"My compliments to Mrs. Munton, and I am pretty well: much obliged to her." It was as well to say only "pretty well", for "very well" would have destroyed the interest Mrs. Munton evidently felt in me. Good Mrs. Munton! Kind Mrs. Munton! Perhaps, also, young – handsome – rich – widowed Mrs. Munton! I rubbed my hands with delight and amusement, and, resuming my post of observation, began to wonder at which house Mrs. Munton lived.

'Again the little tap, and the little maid-servant:

'"Please, sir, the Miss Tomkinsons' compliments, and they would be glad to know how you feel yourself after your journey."

'I don't know why, but the Miss Tomkinsons' name had not such a halo about it as Mrs. Munton's. Still it was very pretty in the Miss Tomkinsons to send and inquire. I only wished I did not feel so perfectly robust. I was almost ashamed that I could not send word I was quite exhausted by fatigue, and had fainted twice since my arrival. If I had but had a headache, at least! I heaved a deep breath: my chest was in perfect order; I had caught no cold: so I answered again:

'"Much obliged to the Miss Tomkinsons; I am not much fatigued; tolerably well: my compliments."

'Little Sally could hardly have got downstairs, before she returned, bright and breathless:

'"Mr. and Mrs. Bullock's compliments, sir, and they hope you are pretty well after your journey."

'Who would have expected such kindness from such an unpromising name? Mr. and Mrs. Bullock were less interesting, it is true, than their predecessors; but I graciously replied:

'"My compliments; a night's rest will perfectly recruit me."

'The same message was presently brought up from one or two more unknown kind hearts. I really wished I were not so ruddy-looking. I was afraid I should disappoint the tender-hearted town when they saw what a hale young fellow I was. And I was almost ashamed of confessing to a great appetite when Sally came up to inquire what I would have. Beefsteaks were so tempting; but perhaps I ought rather to have water-gruel, and go to bed. The beefsteak carried the day, however. I need not have felt such a gentle elation of spirits, as this mark of the town's attention is paid to every one when they arrive after a journey. Many of the same people have sent to inquire after you – great, hulking, brown fellow as you are – only Sally spared you the infliction of devising interesting answers.

CHAPTER II

'The next morning Mr. Morgan came before I had finished breakfast. He was the most dapper little man I ever met. I see the affection with which people cling to the style of dress that was in vogue when they were beaux and belles, and received the most admiration. They are unwilling to believe that their youth and beauty are gone, and think that the prevailing mode is unbecoming. Mr. Morgan will inveigh by the hour together against frock-coats, for instance, and whiskers. He keeps his chin close shaven, wears a black dress-coat, and dark-grey pantaloons; and in his morning round to his town patients, he invariably wears the brightest and blackest of Hessian boots, with dangling silk tassels on each side. When he goes home, about ten o'clock, to prepare for his ride to see his country patients, he puts on the most dandy top-boots I ever saw, which he gets from some wonderful bootmaker a hundred miles off. His appearance is what one calls "jemmy"; there is no other word that will do for it. He was evidently a little discomfited when he saw me in my breakfast costume, with the habits which I brought with me from the fellows at Guy's; my feet against the fireplace, my chair balanced on its hind legs (a habit of sitting which I afterwards discovered he particularly abhorred); slippers on my feet (which, also, he considered a most ungentlemanly piece of untidiness "out of a bedroom"); in short, from what I afterwards learned, every prejudice he had was outraged by my appearance on this first visit of his. I put my book down, and sprang up to receive him. He stood, hat and cane in hand.

'" I came to inquire if it would be convenient for you to accompany me on my morning's round, and to be introduced to a few of our friends." I quite detected the little tone of coldness, induced by his disappointment at my appearance, though he never imagined that it was in any way perceptible. "I will be ready directly, sir," said I; and bolted into my bedroom, only too happy to escape his scrutinising eye.

'When I returned, I was made aware, by sundry indescribable little coughs and hesitating noises, that my dress did not satisfy him. I stood ready, hat and gloves in hand; but still he did not offer to set off on our round. I grew very red and hot. At length he said:

'"Excuse me, my dear young friend, but may I ask if you have no other coat besides that – 'cut-away,' I believe you call them? We are rather sticklers for propriety, I believe, in Duncombe; and much depends on a first impression. Let it be professional, my dear sir. Black is the garb of our profession. Forgive my speaking so plainly; but I consider myself *in loco parentis*."

'He was so kind, so bland, and, in truth, so friendly, that I felt it would be most childish to take offence; but I had a little resentment in my heart at this way of being treated. However, I murmured, "Oh, certainly, sir, if you wish it;" and returned once more to change my coat – my poor cut-away.

'"Those coats, sir, give a man rather too much of a sporting appearance, not quite befitting the learned professions; more as if you came down here to hunt than to be the Galen or

Hippocrates of the neighbourhood." He smiled graciously, so I smothered a sigh; for, to tell you the truth, I had rather anticipated – and, in fact, had boasted at Guy's of – the runs I hoped to have with the hounds; for Duncombe was in a famous hunting district. But all these ideas were quite dispersed when Mr. Morgan led me to the inn-yard, where there was a horse-dealer on his way to a neighbouring fair, and "strongly advised me" – which in our relative circumstances was equivalent to an injunction – to purchase a little, useful, fast-trotting, brown cob, instead of a fine showy horse, "who would take any fence I put him to," as the horse-dealer assured me. Mr. Morgan was evidently pleased when I bowed to his decision, and gave up all hopes of an occasional hunt.

'He opened out a great deal more after this purchase. He told me his plan of establishing me in a house of my own, which looked more respectable, not to say professional, than being in lodgings; and then he went on to say that he had lately lost a friend, a brother surgeon in a neighouring town, who had left a widow with a small income, who would be very glad to live with me, and act as mistress to my establishment; thus lessening the expense.

'"She is a lady-like woman," said Mr. Morgan, "to judge from the little I have seen of her; about forty-five or so; and may really be of some help to you in the little etiquettes of our profession – the slight delicate attentions which every man has to learn, if he wishes to get on in life. This is Mrs. Munton's, sir" said he, stopping short at a very unromantic-looking green door, with a brass knocker.

'I had no time to say, "Who is Mrs. Munton?" before we had heard Mrs. Munton was at home, and were following the tidy elderly servant up the narrow carpeted stairs into the drawing-room. Mrs. Munton was the widow of a former vicar, upwards of sixty, rather deaf; but, like all the deaf people I have ever seen, very fond of talking; perhaps because she then knew the subject, which passed out of her grasp when another began to speak. She was ill of a chronic complaint, which often incapacitated her from going out; and the kind people of the town were in the habit of coming to see her and sit with her, and of bringing her the newest, freshest, tit-bits of news; so that her room was the centre of the gossip of Duncombe – not of scandal, mind; for I make a distinction between gossip and scandal. Now you can fancy the discrepancy between the ideal and the real Mrs. Munton. Instead of any foolish notion of a beautiful blooming widow, tenderly anxious about the health of the stranger, I saw a homely, talkative, elderly person, with a keen observant eye, and marks of suffering on her face; plain in manner and dress, but still unmistakably a lady. She talked to Mr. Morgan, but she looked at me; and I saw that nothing I did escaped her notice. Mr. Morgan annoyed me by his anxiety to show me off; but he was kindly anxious to bring out every circumstance to my credit in Mrs. Munton's hearing, knowing well that the town-crier had not more opportunities to publish all about me than she had.

"'What was that remark you repeated to me of Sir Astley Cooper's?" asked he. It had been the most trivial speech in the world that I had named as we walked along, and I felt ashamed of having to repeat it: but it answered Mr. Morgan's purpose, and before night all the town had heard that I was a favourite pupil of Sir Astley's (I had never seen him but twice in my life); and Mr. Morgan was afraid that as soon as he knew my full value I should be retained by Sir Astley to assist him in his duties as surgeon to the Royal Family. Every little circumstance was pressed into the conversation which could add to my importance.

"'As I once heard Sir Robert Peel remark to Mr. Harrison, the father of our young friend here – The moons in August are remarkably full and bright.'' If you remember, Charles, my father was always proud of having sold a pair of gloves to Sir Robert, when he was staying at the Grange, near Biddicombe, and I suppose good Mr. Morgan had paid his only visit to my father at the time; but Mrs. Munton evidently looked at me with double respect after this incidental remark, which I was amused to meet with, a few months afterwards, disguised in the statement that my father was an intimate friend of the Premier's, and had, in fact, been the adviser of most of the measures taken by him in public life. I sat by, half indignant and half amused. Mr. Morgan looked so complacently pleased at the whole effect of the conversation, that I did not care to mar it by explanations; and, indeed, I had little idea at the time how small sayings were the seeds of great events in the town of Duncombe. When we left Mrs. Munton's, he was in a blandly communicative mood.

'"You will find it a curious statistical fact, but five-sixths of our householders of a certain rank in Duncombe are women. We have widows and old maids in rich abundance. In fact, my dear sir, I believe that you and I are almost the only gentlemen in the place – Mr. Bullock, of course, excepted. By gentlemen, I mean professional men. It behoves us to remember, sir, that so many of the female sex rely upon us for the kindness and protection which every man who is worthy of the name is always so happy to render."

'Miss Tomkinson, on whom we next called, did not strike me as remarkably requiring protection from any man. She was a tall, gaunt, masculine-looking woman, with an air of defiance about her, naturally; this, however, she softened and mitigated, as far as she was able, in favour of Mr. Morgan. He, it seemed to me, stood a little in awe of the lady, who was very *brusque* and plain spoken, and evidently piqued herself on her decision of character and sincerity of speech.

'"So this is the Mr. Harrison we have heard so much of from you, Mr. Morgan? I must say, from what I had heard, that I had expected something a little more – hum – hum! But he's young yet; he's young. We have been all anticipating an Apollo, Mr. Harrison, from Mr. Morgan's description, and an Æsculapius combined in one; or, perhaps I might confine myself to saying Apollo, as he, I believe, was the god of medicine!"

'How could Mr. Morgan have described me without seeing me? I asked myself.

'Miss Tomkinson put on her spectacles, and adjusted them on her Roman nose. Suddenly relaxing from her severity of inspection, she said to Mr. Morgan – "But you must see Caroline. I had nearly forgotton it; she is busy with the girls, but I will send for her. She had a bad headache yesterday, and looked very pale; it made me very uncomfortable."

'She rang the bell, and desired the servant to fetch Miss Caroline.

'Miss Caroline was the younger sister – younger by twenty years; and so considered as a child by Miss Tomkinson, who was fifty-five, at the very least. If she was considered as a child, she was also petted and caressed, and cared for as a child; for she had been left as a baby to the charge of her elder sister; and when the father died, and they had to set up a school, Miss Tomkinson took upon herself every difficult arrangement, and denied herself every pleasure, and made every sacrifice in order that "Carry" might not feel the change in their circumstances. My wife tells me she once knew the sisters purchase a piece of silk, enough, with management, to have made two gowns; but Carry wished for flounces, or some such fal-lals; and without a word, Miss Tomkinson gave up her gown to have the whole made up as Carry wished, into one handsome one; and wore an old shabby affair herself as cheerfully as if it were Genoa velvet. That tells the sort of relationship between the sisters as well as anything, and I consider myself very good to name it thus early; for it was long before I found out Miss Tomkinson's real goodness, and we had a great quarrel first. Miss Caroline looked very delicate and die-away when she came in; she was as soft and sentimental as Miss Tomkinson was hard and masculine; and had a way of saying, "Oh, sister, how can you?" at Miss Tomkinson's startling speeches, which I never liked – especially as it was accompanied by a sort of protesting look at the company present, as if she wished to have it understood that she was shocked at her sister's *outré* manners. Now, that was not faithful between sisters. A remonstrance in private might have done good – though, for my own part, I have grown to like Miss Tomkinson's speeches and ways; but I don't like the way some people have of separating themselves from what may be unpopular in their relations. I know I spoke rather shortly to Miss Caroline when she asked me whether I could bear the change from "the great metropolis" to a little country village. In the first place, why could not she call it "London," or "town," and have done with it? And, in the next place, why should she not love the place that was her home well enough to fancy that every one would like it when they came to know it as well as she did?

'I was conscious I was rather abrupt in my conversation with her, and I saw that Mr. Morgan was watching me, though he pretended to be listening to Miss Tomkinson's whispered account of her sister's symptoms. But when we were once more in the street, he began, "My dear young friend —"

'I winced; for all the morning I had noticed that when he was going to give a litle unpalatable advice, he always began with "My dear young friend." He had done so about the horse.

'"My dear young friend, there are one or two hints I should like to give you about your manner. The great Sir Everard Home used to say, "A general practitioner should either have a very good manner, or a very bad one." Now, in the latter case, he must be possessed of talents and acquirements sufficient to ensure his being sought after, whatever his manner might be. But the rudeness will give notoriety to these qualifications. Abernethy is a case in point. I rather, myself, question the taste of bad manners. I, therefore, have studied to acquire an attentive, anxious politeness, which combines ease and grace with a tender regard and interest. I am not aware whether I have succeeded (few men do) in coming up to my ideal; but I recommend you to strive after this manner, peculiarly befitting our profession. Identify yourself with your patients, my dear sir. You have sympathy in your good heart, I am sure, to really feel pain when listening to their account of their sufferings, and it soothes them to see the expression of this feeling in your manner. It is, in fact, sir, manners that make the man in our profession. I don't set myself up as an example – far from it; but – This is Mr. Hutton's, our vicar; one of the servants is indisposed, and I shall be glad of the opportunity of introducing you. We can resume our conversation at another time."

'I had not been aware that we had been holding a conversation, in which, I believe, the assistance of two persons is required. Why had not Mr. Hutton sent to ask after my health the evening before, according to the custom of the place? I felt rather offended.

CHAPTER III

'The vicarage was on the north side of the street, at the end opening towards the hills. It was a long low house, receding behind its neighbours; a court was between the door and the street, with a flag-walk and an old stone cistern on the right-hand side of the door; Solomon's seal growing under the windows. Some one was watching from behind the window-curtain; for the door opened, as if by magic, as soon as we reached it; and we entered a low room, which served as hall, and was matted all over, with deep old-fashioned window-seats, and Dutch tiles in the fire-place; altogether it was very cool and refreshing, after the hot sun in the white and red street.

'"Bessie is not so well, Mr. Morgan," said the sweet little girl of eleven or so, who had opened the door. "Sophy wanted to send for you; but papa said he was sure you would come soon this morning, and we were to remember that there were other sick people wanting you."

'"Here's Mr. Morgan, Sophy," said she, opening the door into an inner room, to which we descended by a step, as I remember well; for I was nearly falling down it, I was so caught by the picture within. It was like a picture – at least, seen through the door-frame. A sort of mixture of crimson and sea-green in the room, and a sunny garden beyond; a very low casement window, open to the amber air; clusters of white roses peeping in; and Sophy sitting on a cushion on the ground, the light coming from above on her head, and a little sturdy round-eyed brother kneeling by her, to whom she was teaching the alphabet. It was a mighty relief to him when we came in, as I could see; and I am much mistaken if he was easily caught again to say his lesson, when he was once sent off to find papa. Sophy rose quietly; and of course we were just introduced, and that was all, before she took Mr. Morgan upstairs to see her sick servant. I was left to myself in the

216

room. It looked so like a home that it at once made me know the full charm of the word. There were books and work about, and tokens of employment; there was a child's plaything on the floor, and against the sea-green walls there hung a likeness or two, done in water-colours; one, I am sure, was that of Sophy's mother. The chairs and sofa were covered with chintz, the same as the curtains – a little pretty red rose on a white ground. I don't know where the crimson came from, but I am sure there was crimson somewhere; perhaps in the carpet. There was a glass door besides the window, and you went up a step into the garden. This was, first, a grass plot, just under the windows, and, beyond that, straight gravel walks, with box-borders and narrow flower-beds on each side, most brilliant and gay at the end of August, as it was then; and behind the flower-borders were fruit-trees trained over woodwork, so as to shut out the beds of kitchen-garden within.

'While I was looking round, a gentleman came in, who, I was sure, was the Vicar. It was rather awkward, for I had to account for my presence there.

'"I came with Mr. Morgan; my name is Harrison," said I, bowing. I could see he was not much enlightened by this explanation, but we sat down and talked about the time of year, or some such matter, till Sophy and Mr. Morgan came back. Then I saw Mr. Morgan to advantage. With a man whom he respected, as he did the Vicar, he lost the prim, artificial manner he had in general, and was calm and dignified; but not so dignified as the Vicar. I never saw any one like him. He was very quiet and reserved, almost absent at times; his personal appearance was not striking; but he was altogether a man you would talk to with your hat off whenever you met him. It was his character that produced this effect – character that he never thought about, but that appeared in every word, and look, and motion.

'"Sophy," said he, "Mr. Morgan looks very warm; could you not gather a few jargonelle pears off the south wall? I fancy there are some ripe there. Our jargonelle pears are remarkably early this year."

'Sophy went into the sunny garden, and I saw her take a rake and tilt at the pears, which were above her reach, apparently. The parlour had become chilly (I found out afterwards it had a flag floor, which accounts for its coldness), and I thought I should like to go into the warm sun. I said I would go and help the young lady; and, without waiting for an answer, I went into the warm scented garden, where the bees were rifling the flowers, and making a continual busy sound. I think Sophy had begun to despair of getting the fruit, and was glad of my assistance. I thought I was very senseless to have knocked them down so soon, when I found we were to go in as soon as they were gathered. I should have liked to have walked round the garden, but Sophy walked straight off with the pears, and I could do nothing but follow her. She took up her needlework while we ate them: they were very soon finished, and, when the Vicar had ended his conversation with Mr. Morgan about some poor people, we rose up to come away. I was thankful that Mr. Morgan had said so little about me. I could not have endured that he should have introduced Sir Astley Cooper or Sir Robert Peel at the vicarage; nor yet could I have brooked much mention of my "great opportunities for acquiring a thorough knowledge of my profession," which I had heard him describe to Miss Tomkinson, while her sister was talking to me. Luckily, however, he spared me all this at the Vicar's. When we left, it was time to mount our horses and go the country rounds, and I was glad of it.

CHAPTER IV

'By-and-by the inhabitants of Duncombe began to have parties in my honour. Mr. Morgan told me it was on my account, or I don't think I should have found it out. But he was pleased at every fresh invitation, and rubbed his hands, and chuckled, as if it was a compliment to himself, as in truth it was.

'Meanwhile, the arrangement with Mrs. Rose had been brought to a conclusion. She was to bring her furniture and place it in a house, of which I was to pay the rent. She was to be the mistress, and, in return, she was not to pay anything for her board. Mr. Morgan took the house and delighted in advising and settling all my affairs. I was partly indolent, and partly amused, and was altogether passive. The house he took for me was near his own: it had two sitting-rooms downstairs, opening into each other by folding-doors, which were, however, kept shut in general. The back room was my consulting-room ("the library," he advised me to call it), and he gave me a skull to put on the top of my bookcase, in which the medical books were all ranged on the conspicuous shelves; while Miss Austen, Dickens and Thackeray were, by Mr. Morgan himself, skilfully placed in a careless way, upside down or with their backs turned to the wall. The front parlour was to be the dining-room, and the room above was furnished with Mrs. Rose's drawing-room chairs and table, though I found she preferred sitting downstairs in the dining room close to the window, where, between every stitch, she could look up and see what was going on in the street. I felt rather queer to be the master of this house, filled with another person's furniture, before I had even seen the lady whose property it was.

Presently she arrived. Mr. Morgan met her at the inn where the coach stopped, and accompanied her to my house. I could see them out of the drawing-room window, the little gentleman stepping daintily along, flourishing his cane, and evidently talking away. She was a little taller than he was, and in deep widow's mourning; such veils and falls, and capes and cloaks, that she looked like a black crape haycock. When we were introduced, she put up her thick veil and looked around and sighed.

'"Your appearance and circumstances, Mr. Harrison, remind me forcibly of the time when I was married to my dear husband, now at rest. He was then, like you, commencing practice as a surgeon. For twenty years I sympathised with him, and assisted him by every means in my power, even to making up pills when the young man was out. May we live together in like harmony for an equal length of time! May the regard between us be equally sincere, although, instead of being conjugal, it is to be maternal and filial!"

'I am sure she had been concocting this speech in the coach, for she afterwards told me she was the only passenger. When she had ended, I felt as if I ought to have had a glass of wine in my hand to drink, after the manner of toasts. And yet I doubt if I should have done it heartily, for I did not hope to live with her for twenty years; it had rather a dreary sound. However, I only bowed and kept my thoughts to myself. I asked Mr. Morgan, while Mrs. Rose was upstairs taking off her things, to stay to tea; to which he agreed, and kept rubbing his hands with satisfaction, saying:

'"Very fine woman, sir; very fine woman! And what a manner! How she will receive patients, who may wish to leave a message during your absence. Such a flow of words to be sure!"

'Mr. Morgan could not stay long after tea, as there were one or two cases to be seen. I would willingly have gone, and had my hat on, indeed, for the purpose, when he said it would not be respectful, "not the thing," to leave Mrs. Rose the first evening of her arrival.

'"Tender deference to the sex – to a widow in the first months of her loneliness – requires a little consideration, my dear sir. I will leave that case at Miss Tomkinson's for you; you will perhaps call early tomorrow morning. Miss Tomkinson is rather particular, and is apt to speak plainly if she does not think herself properly attended to."

'I had often noticed that he shuffled off the visits to Miss Tomkinson's on me, and I suspect he was a little afraid of the lady.

'It was rather a long evening with Mrs. Rose. She had nothing to do, thinking it civil, I suppose, to stop in the parlour, and not go upstairs and unpack. I begged I might be no restraint upon her if she wished to do so; but (rather to my disappointment) she smiled in a measured, subdued way, and said it would be a pleasure to her to become better acquainted with me. She went upstairs once, and my heart misgave me when I saw her come down with a clean folded pocket-handkerchief. Oh, my prophetic soul! – she was no sooner seated, than she began to give me an account of her late husband's illness, and symptoms, and death. It was a very common case, but she evidently seemed to think it had been peculiar. She had just a smattering of medical knowledge and used the technical terms so very *mal-àpropos* that I could hardly keep from smiling; but I would not have done it for the world, she was evidently in such deep and sincere distress. At last she said:

"'I have the 'dognoses' of my dear husband's complaint in my desk, Mr. Harrison, if you would like to draw up the case for the *Lancet*. I think he would have felt gratified, poor fellow, if he had been told such a compliment would be paid to his remains, and that his case should appear in those distinguished columns."

'It was rather awkward; for the case was of the very commonest, as I said before. However, I had not been even this short time in practice without having learnt a few of those noises which do not compromise one, and yet may bear a very significant construction if the listener chooses to exert a little imagination.

'Before the end of the evening, we were such friends that she brought me down the late Mr. Rose's picture to look at. She told me she could not bear herself to gaze upon the beloved features; but that, if I would look upon the miniature, she would avert her face. I offered to take it into my own hands, but she seemed wounded at the proposal, and said she never, never could trust such a treasure out of her own possession; so she turned her head very much over her left shoulder, while I examined the likeness held by her extended right arm.

'The late Mr. Rose must have been rather a good-looking jolly man; and the artist had given him such a broad smile, and such a twinkle about the eyes, that it really was hard to help smiling back at him. However, I restrained myself.

'At first Mrs. Rose objected to accepting any of the invitations which were sent her to accompany me to the tea-parties in the town. She was so good and simple that I was sure she had no other reason than the one which she alleged – the short time that had elapsed sine her husband's death; or else, now that I had had some experience of the entertainments which she declined so pertinaciously, I might have suspected that she was glad of the excuse. I used sometimes to wish that I was a widow. I came home tired from a hard day's riding, and, if I had but felt sure that Mr. Morgan would not come in, I should certainly have put on my slippers and my loose morning coat, and have indulged in a cigar in the garden. It seemed a cruel sacrifice to society to dress myself in tight boots, and a stiff coat, and go to a five-o'clock tea. But Mr. Morgan read me such lectures upon the necessity of cultivating the goodwill of the people among whom I was settled, and seemed so sorry, and almost hurt, when I once complained of the dulness of these parties, that I felt I could not be so selfish as to decline more than one out of three. Mr. Morgan, if he found that I had an invitation for the evening, would often take the longer round, and the more distant visits. I suspected him at first of the design, which I confess I often entertained, of shirking the parties; but I soon found out he was really making a sacrifice of his inclinations for what he considered to be my advantage.

CHAPTER V

'There was one invitation which seemed to promise a good deal of pleasure. Mr. Bullock (who is the attorney of Duncombe) was married a second time to a lady from a large provincial town; she wished to lead the fashion – a thing very easy to do, for every one was willing to follow her. So, instead of giving a tea-party in my honour, she proposed a picnic to some old hall in the neighbourhood; and really the arrangement sounded tempting enough. Every patient we had seemed full of the subject – both those who were invited and those who were not. There was a moat round the house, with a boat on it; and there was a gallery in the hall, from which music sounded delightfully. The family to whom the place belonged were abroad, and lived at a newer and grander mansion when they were at home; there were only a farmer and his wife in the old hall, and they were to have the charge of the preparations. The little kind-hearted town was delighted when the sun shone bright on the October morning of our picnic; the shopkeepers and cottagers all looked pleased as they saw the cavalcade gathering at Mr. Bullock's door. We were somewhere about twenty in number; a "silent few," she called us; but I thought we were quite enough. There were the Miss Tomkinsons, and two of their young ladies – one of them belonged to a "county family," Mrs. Bullock told me in a whisper; then came Mr. and Mrs. and Miss Bullock, and a tribe of little children, the offspring of the present wife. Miss Bullock was only a step-daughter. Mrs. Munton had accepted the invitation to join our party, which was rather unexpected by the host and hostess, I imagine, from little remarks that I overheard; but they made her very welcome. Miss Horsman (a maiden lady who had been on a visit from home till last week) was another. And last, there were the Vicar and his children. These, with Mr. Morgan and myself, made up the party. I was very much pleased to see something more of the Vicar's family. He had come in occasionally to the evening parties, it is true; and spoken kindly to us all; but it was not his habit to stay very long at them. And his daughter was, he said, too young to visit. She had had the charge of her little sisters and brother since her mother's death, which took up a good deal of her time, and she was glad of the evenings to pursue her own studies. But today the case was different; and Sophy, and Helen, and Lizzie, and even little Walter, were all there, standing at Mrs. Bullock's door; for we none of us could be patient enough to sit still in the parlour with Mrs. Munton and the elder ones, quietly waiting for the two chaises and the spring-cart, which were to have been there by two o'clock, and now it was nearly a quarter past. "Shameful! the brightness of the day would be gone." The sympathetic shopkeepers, standing at their respective doors with their hands in their pockets, had, one and all, their heads turned in the direction from which the carriages (as Mrs. Bullock called them) were to come. There was a rumble along the paved street; and the shopkeepers turned and smiled, and bowed their heads congratulatingly to us; all the mothers and all the little children of the place stood clustering round the door to see us set off. I had my horse waiting; and, meanwhile, I assisted people into their vehicles. One sees good deal of management on such occasions. Mrs. Munton was handed first into one of the chaises; then there was a little hanging back, for most of the young people wished to go in the cart – I don't know why. Miss Horsman, however, came forward, and as she was known to be the intimate friend of Mrs. Munton, so far it was satisfactory. But who was to be third – bodkin with two old ladies, who liked the windows shut? I saw Sophy speaking to Helen; and then she came forward and offered to be the third. The two old ladies looked pleased and glad (as every one did near Sophy); so that chaise-full was arranged. Just as it was going off, however, the servant from the vicarage came running with a note for her master. When he had read it, he went to the chaise door, and I suppose told Sophy, what I afterwards heard him say to Mrs. Bullock, that the clergyman of a neighbouring parish was ill, and unable to read the funeral service for one of his parishioners, who was to be buried that afternoon. The Vicar was, of course, obliged to go, and said he should not return home that night. It seemed a relief to some, I perceived, to be without the little restraint of his dignified presence. Mr. Morgan came up just at the moment, having ridden hard all the morning to be in time to join our party; so we were resigned, on the whole, to the Vicar's absence. His own family regretted him the most, I noticed, and I liked them all the better for it. I believe that I came next in being sorry for his departure; but I respected and admired him, and felt always the better for having been in his company. Miss Tomkinson, Mrs. Bullock, and the 'county' young lady, were in the next chaise. I think the last would rather have been in the cart with the younger and merrier set, but I imagine that was considered *infra dig*. The remainder of the party were to ride and tie; and a most riotous laughing set they were. Mr. Morgan and I were on horseback; at least I led my horse, with little Walter riding on him; his fat, sturdy legs standing stiff out on each side of my cob's broad back. He was a little darling, and chattered all the way, his sister Sophy being the heroine of all his stories. I found he owed this day's excursion entirely to her begging papa to let him come; nurse was strongly against it – "cross old nurse!" he called her once, and then said, "No, not cross; kind nurse; Sophy tells Walter not to say cross nurse." I never saw so young a child so brave. The horse shied at a log of wood. Walter looked very red, and grasped the mane, but sat upright like a little man, and never spoke all the time the horse was dancing. When it was over he looked at me, and smiled:

'"You would not let me be hurt, Mr. Harrison, would you?" He was the most winning little fellow I ever saw.

'There were frequent cries to me from the cart, "Oh, Mr. Harrison! do get us that branch of blackberries; you can reach it with your whip handle." "Oh, Mr. Harrison! there were such splendid nuts on the other side of that hedge; would you just turn back for them?" Miss Caroline Tomkinson was once or twice rather faint with the motion of the cart, and asked me for my smelling-bottle, as she had forgotten hers. I was amused at the idea of my carrying such articles about with me. Then she thought she should like to walk, and got out, and came on my side of the road; but I found little Walter the pleasanter companion, and soon set the horse off into a trot, with which pace her tender constitution could not keep up.

'The road to the old hall was along a sandy lane, with high hedge-banks; the wych-elms almost met overhead. "Shocking farming!" Mr. Bullock called out; and so it might be, but it was very pleasant and picturesque-looking. The trees were gorgeous, in their orange and crimson hues, varied by great dark green holly-bushes, glistening in the autumn sun. I should have thought the colours too vivid, if I had seen them in a picture, especially when we wound up the brow, after crossing the little bridge over the brook – (what laughing and screaming there was as the cart splashed through the sparkling water!) – and I caught the purple hills beyond. We could see the old hall, too, from that point, with its warm rich woods billowing up behind, and the blue waters of the moat lying still under the sunlight.

'Laughing and talking is very hungry work, and there was a universal petition for dinner when we arrived at the lawn before the hall, where it had been arranged that we were to dine. I saw Miss Carry take Miss Tomkinson aside, and whisper to her; and presently the elder sister came up to me, where I was busy, rather apart, making a seat of hay, which I had fetched from the farmer's loft for my little friend Walter, who, I had noticed, was rather hoarse, and for whom I was afraid of a seat on the grass, dry as it appeared to be.

"'Mr. Harrison, Caroline tells me she has been feeling very faint, and she is afraid of a return of one of her attacks. She says she has more confidence in your medical powers than in Mr. Morgan's. I should not be sincere if I did not say that I differ from her; but, as it is so, may I beg you to keep an eye upon her? I tell her she had better not have come if she did not feel well; but, poor girl, she had set her heart upon this day's pleasure. I have offered to go home with her; but she says, if she can only feel sure you are at hand, she would rather stay."

'Of course I bowed, and promised all due attendance on Miss Caroline; and in the meantime, until she did require my services, I thought I might as well go and help the Vicar's daughter, who looked so fresh and pretty in her white muslin dress, here, there, and everywhere, now in the sunshine, now in the green shade, helping every one to be comfortable, and thinking of every one but herself.

'Presently Mr. Morgan came up.

"'Miss Caroline does not feel quite well. I have promised your services to her sister."

"'So have I, sir. But Miss Sophy cannot carry this heavy basket."

'I did not mean her to have heard this excuse; but she caught it up and said:

"'Oh, yes, I can! I can take the things out one by one. Go to poor Miss Caroline, pray, Mr. Harrison."

'I went; but very unwillingly, I must say. When I had once seated myself by her, I think she must have felt better. It was, probably, only a nervous fear, which was relieved when she knew she had assistance near at hand; for she made a capital dinner. I thought she would never end her modest requests for "just a little more pigeon-pie, or a merry-thought of chicken." Such a hearty meal would, I hope, effectually revive her; and so it did; for she told me she thought she could manage to walk round the garden, and see the old peacock yews, if I would kindly give her my arm. It was very provoking; I had so set my heart upon being with the Vicar's children. I advised Miss Caroline strongly to lie down a little, and rest before tea, on the sofa in the farmer's kitchen; you cannot think how persuasively I begged her to take care of herself. At last she consented, thanking me for my tender interest; she should never forget my kind attention to her. She little knew what was in my mind at the time. However, she was safely consigned to the farmer's wife, and I was rushing out in search of a white gown and a waving figure, when I encountered Mrs. Bullock at the door of the hall. She was a fine, fierce-looking woman. I thought she had appeared a little displeased at my (unwilling) attentions to Miss Caroline at dinner-time; but now, seeing me alone, she was all smiles.

'"Oh, Mr. Harrison, all alone! How is that? What are the young ladies about to allow such churlishness? And, by the way, I have left a young lady who will be very glad of your assistance, I am sure – my daughter, Jemima (her step-daughter, she meant). Mr. Bullock is so particular, and so tender a father, that he would be frightened to death at the idea of her going into the boat on the moat unless she was with some one who could swim. He is gone to discuss the new wheel-plough with the farmer (you know agriculture is his hobby, although law, horrid law, is his business). But the poor girl is pining on the bank, longing for my permission to join the others, which I dare not give unless you will kindly accompany her, and promise, if any accident happens, to preserve her safe."

'Oh, Sophy, why was no one anxious about you?

CHAPTER VI

'Miss Bullock was standing by the water-side, looking wistfully, as I thought, at the water party; the sound of whose merry laughter came pleasantly enough from the boat, which lay off (for, indeed, no one knew how to row, and she was of a clumsy flat-bottomed build) about a hundred yards, "weather-bound," as they shouted out, among the long stalks of the water-lilies.

'Miss Bullock did not look up till I came close to her; and then, when I told her my errand, she lifted up her great, heavy, sad eyes, and looked at me for a moment. It struck me, at the time, that she expected to find some expression on my face which was not there, and that its absence was a relief to her. She was a very pale, unhappy looking girl, but very quiet, and, if not agreeable in manner, at any rate not forward or offensive. I called to the party in the boat, and they came slowly enough through the large, cool, green lily-leaves towards us. When they got near, we saw there was no room for us, and Miss Bullock said she would rather stay in the meadow and saunter about, if I would go into the boat; and I am certain from the look on her countenance that she spoke the truth; but Miss Horsman called out, in a sharp voice, while she smiled in a very disagreeable knowing way:

'"Oh, mamma will be displeased if you don't come in, Miss Bullock, after all her trouble in making such a nice arrangement."

'At this speech the poor girl hesitated, and at last, in an undecided way, as if she was not sure whether she was doing right, she took Sophy's place in the boat. Helen and Lizzie landed with their sister, so that there was plenty of room for Miss Tomkinson, Miss Horsman, and all the little Bullocks; and the three vicarage girls went off strolling along the meadow side, and playing with Walter, who was in a high state of excitement. The sun was getting low, but the declining light was beautiful upon the water; and, to add to the charm of the time, Sophy and her sisters, standing on the green lawn in front of the hall, struck up the little German canon, which I had never heard before:

'"Oh wie wohl ist mir am Abend." etc.

'At last we were summoned to tug the boat to the landing-steps on the lawn, tea and a blazing wood fire being ready for us in the hall. I was offering my arm to Miss Horsman, as she was a little lame, when she said again, in her peculiar disagreeable way, "had you not better take Miss Bullock, Mr. Harrison? It will be more satisfactory."

'I helped Miss Horsman up the steps, however, and then she repeated her advice; so, remembering that Miss Bullock was in fact the daughter of my entertainers, I went to her; but, though she accepted my arm, I could perceive that she was sorry that I had offered it.

'The hall was lighted by the glorious wood fire in the wide old grate; the daylight was dying away in the west; and the large windows admitted but little of what was left, through their small leaded frames, with coats of arms emblazoned upon them. The farmer's wife had set out a great long table, which was piled with good things; and a huge black kettle sang on the glowing fire, which sent a cheerful warmth through the room as it crackled and blazed. Mr. Morgan (who I found had been taking a little round in the neigbourhood among his patients) was there, smiling and rubbing his hands as usual. Mr. Bullock was holding a conversation with the farmer at the garden-door on the nature of different manures, in which it struck me that, if Mr. Bullock had the fine names and the theories on his side, the farmer had all the practical knowledge and the experience, and I know which I would have trusted. I think Mr. Bullock rather liked to talk about Liebig in my hearing; it sounded well, and was knowing. Mrs. Bullock was not particularly placid in her mood. In the first place, I wanted to sit by the Vicar's daughter, and Miss Caroline as decidedly wanted to sit on my other side, being afraid of her fainting fits, I imagine. But Mrs. Bullock called me to a place near her daughter. Now, I thought I had done enough civility to a girl who was evidently annoyed rather than pleased by my attentions, and I pretended to be busy stooping under the table for Miss Caroline's gloves, which were missing; but it was of no avail; Mrs. Bullock's fine severe eyes were awaiting my reappearance, and she summoned me again.

'"I am keeping this place on my right hand for you, Mr. Harrison. Jemima, sit still!"

'I went up to the post of honour and tried to busy myself with pouring out coffee to hide my chagrin; but, on my forgetting to empty the water put in ("to warm the cups,"' Mrs. Bullock said), and omitting to add any sugar, the lady told me she would dispense with my services, and turn me over to my neighbour on the other side.

'"Talking to the younger lady was, no doubt, more Mr. Harrison's vocation than assisting the elder one." I dare say it was only the manner that made the words seem offensive. Miss Horsman sat opposite to me, smiling away, Miss

Bullock did not speak, but seemed more depressed than ever. At length, Miss Horsman and Mrs. Bullock got to a war of inuendoes, which were completely unintelligible to me, and I was very much displeased with my situation; while, at the bottom of the table, Mr. Morgan and Mr. Bullock were making the young ones laugh most heartily. Part of the joke was Mr. Morgan insisting upon making tea at the end; and Sophy and Helen were busy contriving every possible mistake for him. I thought honour was a very good thing, but merriment a better. Here was I in the place of distinction, hearing nothing but cross words. At last the time came for us to go home. As the evening was damp, the seats in the chaises were the best and most to be desired. And now Sophy offered to go in the cart; only she seemed anxious, and so was I, that Walter should be secured from the effects of the white wreaths of fog rolling up from the valley; but the little violent, affectionate fellow would not be separated from Sophy. She made a nest for him on her knee in one corner of the cart, and covered him with her own shawl; and I hoped that he would take no harm. Miss Tomkinson, Mr. Bullock, and some of the young ones walked; but I seemed chained to the windows of the chaise, for Miss Caroline begged me not to leave her, as she was dreadfully afraid of robbers; and Mrs. Bullock implored me to see that the man did not overturn them in the bad roads, as he had certainly had too much to drink.

'I became so irritable before I reached home, that I thought it was the most disagreeable day of pleasure I had ever had, and could hardly bear to answer Mrs. Rose's never-ending questions. She told me, however, that from my account the day was so charming that she thought she should relax in the rigour of her seclusion, and mingle a little more in the society of which I gave so tempting a description. She really thought her dear Mr. Rose would have wished it; and his will should be law to her after his death, as it had ever been during his life. In compliance, therefore, with his wishes, she would even do a little violence to her own feelings.

'She was very good and kind; not merely attentive to everything which she thought could conduce to my comfort, but willing to take any trouble in providing the broths and nourishing food which I often found it convenient to order, under the name of kitchen-physic, for my poorer patients; and I really did not see the use of her shutting herself up, in mere compliance with an etiquette, when she began to wish to mix in the little quiet society of Duncombe. Accordingly I urged her to begin to visit, and, even when applied to as to what I imagined the late Mr. Rose's wishes on that subject would have been, answered for that worthy gentleman, and assured his widow that I was convinced he would have regretted deeply her giving way to immoderate grief, and would have been rather grateful than otherwise at seeing her endeavour to divert her thoughts by a few quiet visits. She cheered up, and said, "As I really thought so, she would sacrifice her own inclinations, and accept the very next invitation that came."

CHAPTER VII

'I was roused from my sleep in the middle of the night by a messenger from the vicarage. Little Walter had got the croup, and Mr. Morgan had been sent for into the country. I dressed myself hastily, and went through the quiet little street. There was a light burning upstairs at the vicarage. It was in the nursery. The servant, who opened the door the instant I knocked, was crying sadly, and could hardly answer my inquiries as I went upstairs, two steps at a time, to see my little favourite.

'The nursery was a great large room. At the farther end it was lighted by a common candle, which left the other end, where the door was, in shade; so I suppose the nurse did not see me come in, for she was speaking very crossly.

'"Miss Sophy!" said she, "I told you over and over again it was not fit for him to go, with the hoarseness that he had; and you would take him. It will break your papa's heart, I know; but it's none of my doing."

'Whatever Sophy felt, she did not speak in answer to this. She was on her knees by the warm bath, in which the little fellow was struggling to get his breath, with a look of terror on his face that I have often noticed in young children when smitten by a sudden and violent illness. It seems as if they recognised something infinite and invisible, at whose bidding the pain and the anguish come, from which no love can shield them. It is a very heart-rending look to observe, because it comes on the faces of those who are too young to receive comfort from the words of faith, or the promises of religion. Walter had his arms tight round Sophy's neck, as if she, hitherto his paradise-angel, could save him from the grave shadow of Death. Yes! of Death! I knelt down by him on the other side, and examined him. The very robustness of his little frame gave violence to the disease, which is always one of the most fearful by which children of his age can be attacked.

'"Don't tremble, Watty," said Sophy, in a soothing tone; "it's Mr. Harrison, darling, who let you ride on his horse." I could detect the quivering in the voice, which she tried to make so calm and soft to quiet the little fellow's fears. We took him out of the bath, and I went for leeches. While I was away, Mr. Morgan came. He loved the vicarage children as if he were their uncle; but he stood still and aghast at the sight of Walter – so lately bright and strong – and now hurrying along to the awful change – to the silent mysterious land, where, tended and cared for as he had been on earth, he must go – alone. The little fellow! the darling!

'We applied the leeches to his throat. He resisted at first; but Sophy, God bless her! put the agony of her grief on one side, and thought only of him, and began to sing the little songs he loved. We were all still. The gardener had gone to fetch the Vicar; but he was twelve miles off and we doubted if he would come in time. I don't know if they had any hope; but, the first moment Mr. Morgan's eyes met mine, I saw that he, like me, had none. The ticking of the house clock sounded through the dark quiet house. Walter was sleeping now, with the black leeches yet hanging to his fair, white throat. Still Sophy went on singing little lullabies, which she had sung under far different and happier circumstances. I remember one verse, because it struck me at the time as strangely applicable.

"'Sleep, baby, sleep!
Thy rest shall angels keep;
While on the grass the lamb shall feed,
And never suffer want or need,
Sleep, baby sleep."

The tears were in Mr. Morgan's eyes. I do not think either he
or I could have spoken in our natural tones; but the brave girl
went on clear though low. She stopped at last, and looked
up.

"'He is better, is he not, Mr. Morgan?"

"'No, my dear. He is – ahem" – he could not speak all at
once. Then he said – "My dear! he will be better soon. Think
of your mamma, my dear Miss Sophy. She will be very
thankful to have one of her darlings safe with her, where she
is."

'Still she did not cry. But she bent her head down on the
little face, and kissed it long and tenderly.

"'I will go for Helen and Lizzie. They will be sorry not to
see him again." She rose up and went for them. Poor girls,
they came in, in their dressing-gowns, with eyes dilated with
sudden emotion, pale with terror, stealing softly along, as if
sound could disturb him. Sophy comforted them by gentle
caresses. It was over soon.

'Mr. Morgan was fairly crying like a child. But he thought
it necessary to apologise to me, for what I honoured him for.
"I am a little overdone by yesterday's work, sir. I have had one
or two bad nights, and they rather upset me. When I was your
age I was as strong and manly as any one, and would have
scorned to shed tears."

'Sophy came up to where we stood.

"'Mr. Morgan! I am so sorry for papa. How shall I tell
him?" She was struggling against her own grief for her father's
sake. Mr. Morgan offered to await his coming home; and she
seemed thankful for the proposal. I, new friend, almost a
stranger, might stay no longer. The street was as quiet as ever;
not a shadow was changed; for it was not yet four o'clock. But
during the night a soul had departed.

'From all I could see, and all I could learn, the Vicar and his
daughter strove which should comfort the other the most.

Each thought of the other's grief – each prayed for the other rather than for themselves. We saw them walking out, countrywards; and we heard of them in the cottages of the poor. But it was some time before I happened to meet either of them again. And then I felt, from something indescribable in their manner towards me, that I was one of the

> "Peculiar people, whom Death had made dear."

That one day at the old hall had done this. I was, perhaps, the last person who had given the poor little fellow any unusual pleasure. Poor Walter! I wish I could have done more to make his short life happy!

CHAPTER VIII

'There was a little lull, out of respect to the Vicar's grief, in the visiting. It gave time to Mrs. Rose to soften down the anguish of her weeds.

'At Christmas, Miss Tomkinson sent out invitations for a party. Miss Caroline had once or twice apologised to me because such an event had not taken place before; but, as she said, "the avocations of their daily life prevented their having such little *réunions* except in the vacations." And, sure enough, as soon as the holidays began, came the civil little note:

'"The Misses Tomkinson request the pleasure of Mrs. Rose's and Mr. Harrison's company at tea, on the evening of Monday, the 23rd inst. Tea at five o'clock."

'Mrs. Rose's spirit roused, like a war-horse at the sound of the trumpet, at this. She was not of a repining disposition, but I do think she believed the party-giving population of Duncombe had given up inviting her, as soon as she had determined to relent, and accept the invitations, in compliance with the late Mr. Rose's wishes.

'Such snippings of white love-ribbon as I found everywhere, making the carpet untidy! One day, too

unluckily, a small box was brought to me by mistake. I did
not look at the direction, for I never doubted it was some
hyoscyamus which I was expecting from London; so I tore it
open, and saw inside a piece of paper, with "No more grey
hair," in large letters, upon it. I folded it up in a hurry,
and sealed it afresh, and gave it to Mrs. Rose; but I could
not refrain from asking her, soon after, if she could recommend me anything to keep my hair from turning grey, adding
that I thought prevention was better than cure. I think she
made out the impression of my seal on the paper after that;
for I learned that she had been crying, and that she talked
about there being no sympathy left in the world for her since
Mr. Rose's death; and that she counted the days until she
could rejoin him in the better world. I think she counted the
days to Miss Tomkinson's party, too; she talked so much
about it.

'The covers were taken off Miss Tomkinson's chairs, and
curtains, and sofas; and a great jar full of artificial flowers was
placed in the centre of the table, which, as Miss Caroline told
me, was all her doing, as she doted on the beautiful and artistic
in life. Miss Tomkinson stood, erect as a grenadier, close to
the door, receiving her friends, and heartily shaking them by
the hands as they entered; she said she was truly glad to see
them. And so she really was.

'We had just finished tea, and Miss Caroline had brought
out a little pack of conversation cards – sheaves of slips of
cardboard, with intellectual or sentimental questions on one
set, and equally intellectual and sentimental answers on the
other; and, as the answers were fit to any and all the questions,
you may think they were a characterless and "wersh" set of
things. I had just been asked by Miss Caroline:

'"*Can you tell what those dearest to you think of you at this
present time?*" and had answered:

'"*How can you expect me to reveal such a secret to the present
company!*" when the servant announced that a gentleman, a
friend of mine, wished to speak to me downstairs.

'"Oh, show him up, Martha; show him up!" said Miss
Tomkinson, in her hospitality.

'"Any friend of our friend is welcome," said Miss Caroline,
in an insinuating tone.

'I jumped up, however, thinking it might be some one on business; but I was so penned in by the spider-legged tables, stuck out on every side, that I could not make the haste I wished; and, before I could prevent it, Martha had shown up Jack Marshland, who was on his road home for a day or two at Christmas.

'He came up in a hearty way, bowing to Miss Tomkinson, and explaining that he had found himself in my neighbourhood, and had come over to pass a night with me, and that my servant had directed him where I was.

'His voice, loud at all times, sounded like Stentor's in that little room, where we all spoke in a kind of purring way. He had no swell in his tones; they were *forte* from the beginning. At first it seemed like the days of my youth come back again, to hear full manly speaking; I felt proud of my friend, as he thanked Miss Tomkinson for her kindness in asking him to stay the evening. By-and-by he came up to me, and I dare say he thought he had lowered his voice, for he looked as if speaking confidentially, while in fact the whole room might have heard him.

'"Frank, my boy, when shall we have dinner at this good old lady's? I'm deuced hungry."

'"Dinner! Why, we had had tea an hour ago." While he yet spoke, Martha came in with a little tray on which was a single cup of coffee and three slices of wafer bread-and-butter. His dismay, and his evident submission to the decrees of Fate, tickled me so much, that I thought he should have a further taste of the life I led from month's end to month's end, and I gave up my plan of taking him home at once, and enjoyed the anticipation of the hearty laugh we should have together at the end of the evening. I was famously punished for my determination.

'"Shall we continue our game?" asked Miss Caroline, who had never relinquished her sheaf of questions.

'We went on questioning and answering, with little gain of information to either party.

'"No such thing as heavy betting in this game, eh, Frank?" asked Jack, who had been watching us. "You don't lose ten pounds at a sitting, I guess, as you used to do at Short's. Playing for love, I suppose you call it?"

'Miss Caroline simpered, and looked down. Jack was not thinking of her. He was thinking of the days we had had "at the Mermaid." Suddenly he said, "Where were you this day last year, Frank?"

'"I don't remember!" said I.

'"Then I'll tell you. It's the 23rd – the day you were taken up for knocking down the fellow in Long Acre, and that I had to bail you out ready for Christmas Day. You are in more agreeable quarters tonight."

'He did not intend this reminiscence to be heard, but was not in the least put out when Miss Tomkinson, with a face of dire surprise, asked:

'"Mr. Harrison taken up, sir?"

'"Oh, yes, ma'am; and you see it was so common an affair with him to be locked up that he can't remember the dates of his different imprisonments."

'He laughed heartily; and so should I have done, but that I saw the impression it made. The thing was, in fact, simple enough, and capable of easy explanation. I had been made angry by seeing a great hulking fellow, out of mere wantonness, break the crutch from under a cripple; and I struck the man more violently than I intended, and down he went, yelling out for the police, and I had to go before the magistrate to be released. I disdained giving this explanation at the time. It was no business of theirs what I had been doing a year ago; but still Jack might have held his tongue. However, that unruly member of his was set a-going, and he told me afterwards he was resolved to let the old ladies into a little of life; and accordingly he remembered every practical joke we had ever had, and talked and laughed, and roared again. I tried to converse with Miss Caroline – Mrs. Munton – any one; but Jack was the hero of the evening, and everyone was listening to him.

'"Then he has never sent any hoaxing letters since he came here, has he? Good boy! He has turned over a new leaf. He was the deepest dog at that I ever met with. Such anonymous letters as he used to send! Do you remember that to Mrs. Walbrook, eh, Frank? That was too bad!" (the wretch was laughing all the time). "No; I won't tell about it – don't be afraid. Such a shameful hoax!" (laughing again).

'"Pray do tell," I called out; for it made it seem far worse than it was.

'"Oh no, no; you've established a better character – I would not for the world nip your budding efforts. We'll bury the past in oblivion."

'I tried to tell my neighbours the story to which he alluded; and they were attracted by the merriment of Jack's manner, and did not care to hear the plain matter of fact.

'Then came a pause; Jack was talking almost quietly to Miss Horsman. Suddenly he called across the room – "How many times have you been out with the hounds? The hedges were blind very late this year, but you have had some good mild days since."

'"I have never been out," said I shortly.

'"Never! – whew! – Why, I thought that was the great attraction to Duncombe."

'Now was not he provoking! He would condole with me, and fix the subject in the minds of every one present.

'The supper trays were brought in, and there was a shuffling of situations. He and I were close together again.

'"I say, Frank, what will you lay me that I don't clear that tray before people are ready for their second helping? I'm as hungry as a hound."

'"You shall have a round of beef and a raw leg of mutton when you get home. Only do behave yourself here."

'"Well, for your sake; but keep me away from those trays, or I'll not answer for myself. 'Hould me, or I'll fight', as the Irishman said. I'll go and talk to that little old lady in blue, and sit with my back to those ghosts of eatables."

'He sat down by Miss Caroline, who would not have liked his description of her; and began an earnest, tolerably quiet conversation. I tried to be as agreeable as I could, to do away with the impression he had given of me; but I found that every one drew up a little stiffly at my approach, and did not encourage me to make any remarks.

'In the middle of my attempts, I heard Miss Caroline beg Jack to take a glass of wine, and I saw him help himself to what appeared to be port; but in an instant he set it down from his lips, exclaiming, "Vinegar, by Jove!" He made the most

horribly wry face: and Miss Tomkinson came up in a severe
hurry to investigate the affair. It turned out it was some black-
currant wine, on which she particularly piqued herself; I drank
two glasses of it to ingratiate myself with her, and can testify to
its sourness. I don't think she noticed my exertions, she was so
much engrossed in listening to Jack's excuses for his *mal-àpropos*
observation. He told her, with the gravest face, that he had been
a teetotaller so long that he had but a confused recollection of
the distinction between wine and vinegar, particularly
eschewing the latter, because it had been twice fermented; and
that he had imagined Miss Caroline had asked him to take
toast-and-water, or he should never have touched the decanter.

CHAPTER IX

'As we were walking home, Jack said, "Lord, Frank! I've had
such fun with the little lady in blue. I told her you wrote to
me every Saturday, telling me the events of the week. She
took it all in." He stopped to laugh; for he bubbled and
chuckled so that he could not laugh and walk. "And I told her
you were deeply in love" (another laugh); "and that I could
not get you to tell me the name of the lady, but that she had
light brown hair – in short, I drew from life, and gave her an
exact description of herself; and that I was most anxious to
see her, and implore her to be merciful to you, for that you
were a most timid, faint-hearted fellow with women." He
laughed till I thought he would have fallen down. "I begged
her, if she could guess who it was from my decription – I'll
answer for it she did – I took care of that; for I said you
described a mole on the left cheek, in the most poetical way,
saying Venus had pinched it out of envy at seeing any one
more lovely – oh, hold me up, or I shall fall – laughing and
hunger make me so weak; – well, I say, I begged her, if she
knew who your fair one could be, to implore her to save you.
I said I knew one of your lungs had gone after a former
love-affair, and that I could not answer for the other if the

lady here were cruel. She spoke of a respirator; but I told her that might do very well for the odd lung; but would it minister to a heart diseased? I really did talk fine. I have found out the secret of eloquence – it's believing what you've got to say; and I worked myself well up with fancying you married to the little lady in blue."

'I got to laughing at last, angry as I had been; his impudence was irrisistible. Mrs. Rose had come home in the sedan, and gone to bed; and he and I sat up over the round of beef and brandy-and-water till two o'clock in the morning.

'He told me I had got quite into the professional way of mousing about a room, and mewing and purring according as my patients were ill or well. He mimicked me, and made me laugh at myself. He left early the next morning.

'Mr. Morgan came at his usual hour; he and Marshland would never have agreed, and I should have been uncomfortable to see two friends of mine disliking and despising each other.

'Mr. Morgan was ruffled; but with his deferential manner to women, he smoothed himself down before Mrs. Rose – regretted that he had not been able to come to Miss Tomkinson's the evening before, and consequently had not seen her in the society she was so well calculated to adorn. But when we were by ourselves, he said:

'"I was sent for to Mrs. Munton's this morning – the old spasms. May I ask what is this story she tells me about – about prison, in fact? I trust, sir, she has made some little mistake, and that you never were – that it is an unfounded report." He could not get it out – "that you were in Newgate for three months!" I burst out laughing; the story had grown like a mushroom indeed. Mr. Morgan looked grave. I told him the truth. Still he looked grave. "I've no doubt, sir, that you acted rightly; but it has an awkward sound. I imagined from your hilarity just now that there was no foundation whatever for the story. Unfortunately, there is."

'"I was only a night at the police-station. I would go there again for the same cause, sir."

'"Very fine spirit, sir – quite like Don Quixote, but don't you see you might as well have been to the hulks at once?"

'"No, sir; I don't."

'"Take my word, before long, the story will have grown to that. However, we won't anticipate evil. *Mens conscia recti,* you remember, is the great thing. The part I regret is, that it may require some short time to overcome a little prejudice which the story may excite against you. However, we won't dwell on it. *Mens conscia recti!* Don't think about it, sir."

'It was clear he was thinking a good deal about it.

CHAPTER X

'Two or three days before this time, I had had an invitation from the Bullocks to dine with them on Christmas Day. Mrs. Rose was going to spend the week with friends in the town where she formerly lived; and I had been pleased at the notion of being received into a family, and of being a little with Mr. Bullock, who struck me as a bluff, good-hearted fellow.

'But this Tuesday before Christmas Day, there came an invitation from the Vicar to dine there; there were to be only their own family and Mr. Morgan. "Only their own family." It was getting to be all the world to me. I was in a passion with myself for having been so ready to accept Mr. Bullock's invitation – coarse and ungentlemanly as he was; with his wife's airs of pretension and Miss Bullock's stupidity. I turned it over in my mind. No! I could not have a bad headache, which should prevent me going to the place I did not care for, and yet leave me at liberty to go where I wished. All I could do was to join the vicarage girls after church, and walk by their side in a long country ramble. They were quiet; not sad, exactly; but it was evident that the thought of Walter was in their minds on this day. We went through a copse where there were a good number of evergreens planted as covers for game. The snow was on the ground; but the sun was clear and bright, and the sun glittered on the smooth holly-leaves. Lizzie asked me to gather her some of the very bright red berries, and she was beginning a sentence with:

"'Do you remember" – when Helen said, *"Hush,"* and looked towards Sophy, who was walking a little apart, and crying softly to herself. There was evidently some connection between Walter and the holly-berries, for Lizzie threw them away at once when she saw Sophy's tears. Soon we came to a stile which led to an open breezy common, half covered with gorse. I helped the little girls over it, and set them to run down the slope; but took Sophy's arm in mine, and, though I could not speak, I think she knew how I was feeling for her. I could hardly bear to bid her good-bye at the vicarage gate; it seemed as if I ought to go in and spend the day with her.

CHAPTER XI

'I vented my ill-humour in being late for the Bullock's dinner. There were one or two clerks, towards whom Mr. Bullock was patronising and pressing. Mrs. Bullock was decked out in extraordinary finery. Miss Bullock looked plainer than ever; but she had on some old gown or other, I think, for I heard Mrs. Bullock tell her she was always making a figure of herself. I began today to suspect that the mother would not be sorry if I took a fancy to the step-daughter. I was again placed near her at dinner, and, when the little ones came in to dessert, I was made to notice how fond of children she was – and, indeed, when one of them nestled to her, her face did brighten; but, the moment she caught this loud-whispered remark, the gloom came back again, with something even of anger in her look; and she was quite sullen and obstinate when urged to sing in the drawing-room. Mrs. Bullock turned to me:

"'Some young ladies won't sing unless they are asked by gentlemen." She spoke very crossly. "If you ask Jemima, she will probably sing. To oblige me, it is evident she will not."

'I thought the singing, when we got it, would probably be

a great bore; however, I did as I was bid, and went with my request to the young lady, who was sitting a little apart. She looked up at me with eyes full of tears, and said, in a decided tone (which, if I had not seen her eyes, I should have said was as cross as her mamma's), "No, sir, I will not." She got up, and left the room. I expected to hear Mrs. Bullock abuse her for her obstinacy. Instead of that, she began to tell me of the money that had been spent on her education; of what each separate accomplishment had cost. "She was timid," she said, "but very musical. Wherever her future home might be, there would be no want of music." She went on praising her till I hated her. If they thought I was going to marry that great lubberly girl, they were mistaken. Mr. Bullock and the clerks came up. He brought out Liebig, and called me to him.

"'I can understand a good deal of this agricultural chemistry," said he, "and have put it in practice – without much success, hitherto, I confess. But these unconnected letters puzzle me a little. I suppose they have some meaning, or else I should say it was mere book-making to put them in."

"'I think they give the page a very ragged appearance," said Mrs. Bullock, who had joined us. "I inherit a little of my late father's taste for books, and must say I like to see a good type, a broad margin, and an elegant binding. My father despised variety; how he could have held up his hands aghast at the cheap literature of these times! He did not require many books, but he would have twenty editions of those that he had; and he paid more for binding than he did for the books themselves. But elegance was everything with him. He would not have admitted your Liebig, Mr. Bullock; neither the nature of the subject, nor the common type, nor the common way in which your book is got up, would have suited him."

"'Go and make tea, my dear and leave Mr. Harrison and me to talk over a few of these manures."

'We settled to it; I explained the meaning of the symbols, and the doctrine of chemical equivalents. At last he said, "Doctor! you're giving me too strong a dose of it at one time. Let's have a small quantity taken 'hodie'; that's professional, as Mr. Morgan would call it. Come in and call, when you have leisure, and give me a lesson in my alphabet. Of all you've been telling me I can only remember that C means carbon and O oxygen; and I see one must know the meaning of all these confounded letters before one can do much good with Liebig."

'"We dine at three," said Mrs. Bullock. "There will always be a knife and fork for Mr. Harrison. Bullock! don't confine your invitation to the evening."

'"Why, you see, I've a nap always after dinner; so I could not be learning chemistry then."

'"Don't be selfish, Mr. B. Think of the pleasure Jemima and I shall have in Mr. Harrison's society."

'I put a stop to the discussion by saying I would come in in the evenings occasionally, and give Mr. Bullock a lesson, but that my professional duties occupied me invariably until that time.

'I liked Mr. Bullock. He was simple and shrewd; and to be with a man was a relief, after all the feminine society I went through every day.

CHAPTER XII

'The next morning I met Miss Horsman.

'"So you dined at Mr. Bullock's yesterday, Mr. Harrison? Quite a family party, I hear. They are quite charmed with you, and your knowledge of chemistry. Mr. Bullock told me so, in Hodgson's shop, just now. Miss Bullock is a nice girl, eh, Mr. Harrison?" She looked sharply at me. Of course, whatever I thought, I could do nothing but assent. "A nice little fortune, too – three thousand pounds, Consols, from her own mother."

'What did I care? She might have three millions for me. I had begun to think a good deal about money, though, but not in connection with her. I had been doing up our books ready to send out our Christmas bills, and had been wondering how far the Vicar would consider three hundred a

year, with a prospect of increase, would justify me in
thinking of Sophy. Think of her I could not help; and, the
more I thought of how good, and sweet, and pretty she was,
the more I felt that she ought to have far more than I could
offer. Besides, my father was a shop-keeper, and I saw the
Vicar had a sort of respect for family. I determined to try and
be very attentive to my profession. I was as civil as could be
to every one; and wore the nap off the brim of my hat by
taking it off so often.

'I had my eyes open to every glimpse of Sophy. I am
overstocked with gloves now that I bought at that time, by
way of making errands into the shops where I saw her black
gown. I bought pounds upon pounds of arrowroot, till I was
tired of the eternal arrowroot puddings Mrs. Rose gave me. I
asked her if she could not make bread of it, but she seemed to
think that would be expensive; so I took to soap as a safe
purchase. I believe soap improves by keeping.

CHAPTER XIII

'The more I knew of Mrs. Rose, the better I liked her. She
was sweet, and kind, and motherly, and we never had any
rubs. I hurt her once or twice, I think, by cutting her short in
her long stories about Mr. Rose. But I found out that when
she had plenty to do she did not think of him quite so much;
so I expressed a wish for Corazza shirts, and, in the puzzle of
devising how they were to be cut out, she forgot Mr. Rose
for some time. I was still more pleased by her way about
some legacy her elder brother left her. I don't know the
amount, but it was something handsome, and she might
have set up housekeeping for herself; but, instead, she told
Mr. Morgan (who repeated it to me), that she should
continue with me, as she had quite an elder sister's interest in
me.

'The "county young lady," Miss Tyrrell, returned to Miss
Tomkinson's after the holidays. She had an enlargement of

the tonsils, which required to be frequently touched with caustic, so I often called to see her. Miss Caroline always received me, and kept me talking in her washed-out style, after I had seen my patient. One day she told me she thought she had a weakness about the heart, and would be glad if I would bring my stethoscope the next time, which I accordingly did! and, while I was on my knees listening to the pulsations, one of the young ladies came in. She said:

'"Oh dear! I never! I beg your pardon, ma'am," and scuttled out. There was not much the matter with Miss Caroline's heart: a little feeble in action or so, a mere matter of weakness and general languor. When I went down I saw two or three of the girls peeping out of the half-closed schoolroom door, but they shut it immediately, and I heard them laughing. The next time I called, Miss Tomkinson was sitting in state to receive me.

'"Miss Tyrrell's throat does not seem to make much progress. Do you understand the case, Mr. Harrison, or should we have further advice. I think Mr. Morgan would probably know more about it."

'I assured her that it was the simplest thing in the world; that it always implied a little torpor in the constitution, and that we preferred working through the system, which of course was a slow process; and that the medicine the young lady was taking (iodide of iron) was sure to be successful, although the progress would not be rapid. She bent her head, and said, "It might be so; but she confessed she had more confidence in medicines which had some effect."

'She seemed to expect me to tell her something; but I had nothing to say, and accordingly I bade goodbye. Somehow, Miss Tomkinson always managed to make me feel very small, by a succession of snubbings; and, whenever I left her I had always to comfort myself under her contradictions by saying to myself, "Her saying it is so does not make it so." Or I invented good retorts which I might have made to her brusque speeches, if I had but thought of them at the right time. But it was provoking that I had not had the presence of mind to recollect them just when they were wanted.

CHAPTER XIV

'On the whole, things went on smoothly. Mr. Holden's legacy came in just about this time; and I felt quite rich. Five hundred pounds would furnish the house, I thought, when Mrs. Rose left and Sophy came. I was delighted, too, to imagine that Sophy perceived the difference of my manner to her from what it was to any one else, and that she was embarrassed and shy in consequence, but not displeased with me for it. All was so flourishing that I went about on wings instead of feet. We were very busy, without having anxious cares. My legacy was paid into Mr. Bullock's hands, who united a little banking business to his profession of law. In return for his advice about investments (which I never meant to take, having a more charming, if less profitable, mode in my head), I went pretty frequently to teach him his agricultural chemistry. I was so happy in Sophy's blushes that I was universally benevolent, and desirous of giving pleasure to every one. I went, at Mrs. Bullock's general invitation, to dinner there one day unexpectedly: but there was such a fuss of ill-concealed preparation consequent upon my coming, that I never went again. Her little boy came in, with an audibly given message from cook, to ask:

'"If this was the gentleman as she was to send in the best dinner-service and dessert for?"

'I looked deaf, but determined never to go again.

'Miss Bullock and I, meanwhile, became rather friendly. We found out that we mutually disliked each other, and were contented with the discovery. If people are worth anything, this sort of non-liking is a very good beginning of friendship. Every good quality is revealed naturally and slowly, and is a pleasant surprise. I found out that Miss Bullock was sensible, and even sweet-tempered, when not irritated by her step-mother's endeavours to show her off. But she would sulk for hours after Mrs. Bullock's offensive praise of her good points. And I never saw such a black passion as she went into, when she suddenly came into the room when Mrs. Bullock was telling me of all the offers she had had.

'My legacy made me feel up to extravagance. I scoured the country for a glorious nosegay of camellias, which I sent to Sophy on Valentine's Day. I durst not add a line; but I wished the flowers could speak, and tell her how I loved her.

'I called on Miss Tyrrell that day. Miss Caroline was more simpering and affected than ever, and full of allusions to the day.

'"Do you affix much sincerity of meaning to the little gallantries of this day, Mr. Harrison?" asked she, in a languishing tone. I thought of my camellias, and how my heart had gone with them into Sophy's keeping; and I told her I thought one might often take advantage of such a time to hint at feelings one dared not fully express.

'I remembered afterwards the forced display she made, after Miss Tyrrell left the room, of a valentine. But I took no notice at the time; my head was full of Sophy.

'It was on that very day that John Brouncker, the gardener to all of us who had small gardens to keep in order, fell down and injured his wrist severely (I don't give you the details of the case, because they would not interest you, being too technical; if you've any curiosity, you will find them in the *Lancet* of August in that year). We all liked John, and this accident was felt like a town's misfortune. The gardens, too, just wanted doing up. Both Mr. Morgan and I went directly to him. It was a very awkward case, and his wife and children were crying sadly. He himself was in great distess at being thrown out of work. He begged us to do something that would cure him speedily, as he could not afford to be laid up, with six children depending on him for bread. We did not say much before him; but we both thought the arm would have to come off, and it was his right arm. We talked it over when we came out of the cottage. Mr. Morgan had no doubt of the necessity. I went back at dinner-time to see the poor fellow. He was feverish and anxious. He had caught up some expression of Mr. Morgan's in the morning, and had guessed the measure we had in contemplation. He bade his wife leave the room, and spoke to me by myself.

'"If you please, sir, I'd rather be done for at once than have my arm taken off, and be a burden to my family. I'm not afraid of dying; but I could not stand being a cripple for life, eating bread, and not able to earn it."

'The tears were in his eyes with earnestness. I had all along been more doubtful about the necessity of the amputation than Mr. Morgan. I knew the improved treatment in such cases. In his days there was much more of the rough and ready in surgical practice; so I gave the poor fellow some hope.

'In the afternoon I met Mr. Bullock.

'"So you're to try your hand at an amputation, tomorrow, I hear. Poor John Brouncker! I used to tell him he was not careful enough about his ladders. Mr. Morgan is quite excited about it. He asked me to be present, and see how well a man from Guy's can operate; he says he is sure you'll do it beautifully. Pah! no such sights for me, thank you."

'Ruddy Mr. Bullock went a shade or two paler at the thought.

'"Curious, how professionally a man views these things! Here's Mr. Morgan, who had been all along as proud of you as if you were his own son, absolutely rubbing his hands at the idea of this crowning glory, this feather in your cap! He told me just now he knew he had always been too nervous to be a good operator, and had therefore preferred sending for White from Chesterton. But now any one might have a serious accident who liked, for you would be always at hand."

'I told Mr. Bullock, I really thought we might avoid the amputation; but his mind was preoccupied with the idea of it, and he did not care to listen to me. The whole town was full of it. That is a charm in a little town, everybody is so sympathetically full of the same events. Even Miss Horsman stopped me to ask after John Brouncker with interest; but she threw cold water upon my intention of saving the arm.

'"As for the wife and family, we'll take care of them. Think what a fine opportunity you have of showing off, Mr. Harrison!"

'That was just like her. Always ready with her suggestions of ill-natured or interested motives.

'Mr. Morgan heard my proposal of a mode of treatment by which I thought it possible that the arm might be saved.

'"I differ from you, Mr. Harrison," said he. "I regret it; but I differ *in toto* from you. Your kind heart deceives you in this instance. There is no doubt that amputation must take place – not later than tomorrow morning, I should say. I have made myself at liberty to attend upon you, sir; I shall be happy to officiate as your assistant. Time was when I should have been proud to be principal; but a little trembling in my arm incapacitates me."

'I urged my reasons upon him again; but he was obstinate. He had, in fact, boasted so much of my acquirements as an operator that he was unwilling I should lose this opportunity of displaying my skill. He could not see that there would be greater skill evinced in saving the arm; nor did I think of this at the time. I grew angry at his old-fashioned narrow-mindedness, as I thought it; and I became dogged in my resolution to adhere to my own course. We parted very coolly; and I went straight off to John Brouncker to tell him I believed that I could save the arm, if he would refuse to have it amputated. When I calmed myself a little, before going in and speaking to him, I could not help acknowledging that we should run some risk of lock-jaw; but, on the whole, and after giving some earnest conscientious thought to the case, I was sure that my mode of treatment would be best.

'He was a sensible man. I told him the difference of opinion that existed between Mr. Morgan and myself. I said that there might be some little risk attending the non-amputation, but that I should guard against it; and I trusted that I should be able to preserve his arm.

'"Under God's blessing," said he reverently. I bowed my head. I don't like to talk too frequently of the dependence which I always felt on that holy blessing, as to the result of my efforts; but I was glad to hear that speech of John's, because it showed a calm and faithful heart; and I had almost certain hopes of him from that time.

'We agreed that he should tell Mr. Morgan the reason of his objections to the amputation, and his reliance on my opinion. I determined to recur to every book I had relating to such cases, and to convince Mr. Morgan, if I could, of my wisdom. Unluckily, I found out afterwards that he had met Miss Horsman in the time that intervened before I saw him again at his own house that evening; and she had more than hinted that I shrunk from performing the operation, "for very good reasons no doubt. She had heard that the medical students in London were a bad set, and were not remarkable for regular attendance in the hospitals. She might be mistaken; but she thought it was, perhaps, quite as well poor John Brouncker had not his arm cut off by —. Was there not such a thing as mortification coming on after a clumsy operation? It was, perhaps, only a choice of deaths!"

'Mr. Morgan had been stung at all this. Perhaps I did not speak quite respectfully enough: I was a good deal excited. We only got more and more angry with each other; though he, to do him justice, was as civil as could be all the time, thinking that thereby he concealed his vexation and disappointment. He did not try to conceal his anxiety about poor John. I went home weary and dispirited. I made up and took the necessary applications to John; and, promising to return with the dawn of day (I would fain have stayed, but I did not wish him to be alarmed about himself), I went home, and resolved to sit up and study the treatment of similar cases.

'Mrs. Rose knocked at the door.

'"Come in!" said I sharply.

'"She said she had seen I had something on my mind all day, and she could not go to bed without asking if there was nothing she could do. She was good and kind; and I could not help telling her a little of the truth. She listened pleasantly; and I shook her warmly by the hand, thinking that though she might not be very wise, her good heart made her worth a dozen keen, sharp hard people, like Miss Horsman.

'When I went at daybreak, I saw John's wife for a few minutes outside the door. She seemed to wish her husband had been in Mr. Morgan's hands rather than mine; but she gave me as good an account as I dared to hope for of the manner in which her husband had passed the night. This was confirmed by my own examination.

'When Mr. Morgan and I visited him together later on in the day, John said what we had agreed upon the day before; and I told Mr. Morgan openly that it was by my advice that amputation was declined. He did not speak to me till we had left the house. Then he said – "Now, sir, from this time, I consider this case entirely in your hands. Only remember the poor fellow has a wife and six children. In case you come round to my opinion, remember that Mr. White could come over, as he has done before, for the operation."

'So Mr. Morgan believed I declined operating because I felt myself incapable! Very well! I was much mortified.

'An hour after we parted, I received a note to this effect:

'"DEAR SIR, – I will take the long round today, to leave you at liberty to attend to Brouncker's case, which I feel to be a very responsible one.

'"J. MORGAN"

'This was kindly done. I went back, as soon as I could, to John's cottage. While I was in the inner room with him, I heard the Miss Tomkinsons' voices outside. They had called to inquire. Miss Tomkinson came in, and evidently was poking and snuffing about. (Mrs. Brouncker told her that I was within; and within I resolved to be till they had gone.)

'"What is this close smell?" asked she. "I am afraid you are not cleanly. Cheese! – cheese in this cupboard! No wonder there is an unpleasant smell. Don't you know how particular you should be about being clean when there is illness about?"

'Mrs. Brouncker was exquisitely clean in general, and was piqued at these remarks.

'"If you please, ma'am, I could not leave John yesterday to do any housework, and Jenny put the dinner things away. She is but eight years old."

'But this did not satisfy Miss Tomkinson, who was evidently pursuing the course of her observations.

'"Fresh butter, I declare! Well now, Mrs. Brouncker, do you know I don't allow myself fresh butter at this time of the year? How can you save, indeed, with such extravagance!"

'"Please, ma'am," answered Mrs. Brouncker, "you'd think it strange, if I was to take such liberties in your house as you're taking here."

'I expected to hear a sharp answer. No! Miss Tomkinson liked plain-speaking. The only person in whom she would tolerate round-about ways of talking was her sister.

'"Well, that's true," she said. "Still, you must not be above taking advice. Fresh butter is extravagant at this time of the year. However, you're a good kind of woman, and I've a great respect for John. Send Jenny for some broth as soon as he can take it. Come, Caroline, we have got to go on to Williams's."

'But Miss Caroline said that she was tired, and would rest where she was till Miss Tomkinson came back. I was a prisoner for some time, I found. When she was alone with Mrs. Brouncker, she said:

'"You must not be hurt by my sister's abrupt manner. She means well. She has not much imagination or sympathy, and cannot understand the distraction of mind produced by the illness of a worshipped husband." I could hear the loud sigh of commiseration which followed this speech. Mrs. Brouncker said:

'"Please, ma'am, I don't worship my husband. I would not be so wicked."

'"Goodness! You don't think it wicked, do you? For my part, if . . . I should worship, I should adore him." I thought she need not imagine such improbable cases. But sturdy Mrs. Brouncker said again:

'"I hope I know my duty better. I've not learned my Commandments for nothing. I know Whom I ought to worship."

'Just then the children came in, dirty and unwashed, I have no doubt. And now Miss Caroline's real nature peeped out. She spoke sharply to them, and asked them if they had no manners, little pigs as they were, to come brushing against her silk gown in that way? She sweetened herself again, and was as sugary as love when Miss Tomkinson returned to her, accompanied by one whose voice, "like winds in summer sighing," I knew to be my dear Sophy's.

'She did not say much; but what she did say, and the manner in which she spoke, was tender and compassionate in the highest degree; and she came to take the four little ones back with her to the vicarage, in order that they might be out of their mother's way; the older two might help at home. She offered to wash their hands and faces; and when I emerged from my inner chamber, after the Miss Tomkinsons had left, I found her with a chubby child on her knees, bubbling and spluttering against her white wet hand, with a face bright, rosy, and merry under the operation. Just as I came in, she said to him, "There, Jemmy, now I can kiss you with this nice clean face."

'She coloured when she saw me. I liked her speaking, and I liked her silence. She was silent now, and I "lo'ed her a' the better." I gave my directions to Mrs. Brouncker, and hastened to overtake Sophy and the children; but they had gone round by the lanes, I suppose, for I saw nothing of them.

'I was very anxious about the case. At night I went again. Miss Horsman had been there; I believe she was really kind among the poor, but she could not help leaving a sting behind her everywhere. She had been frightening Mrs. Brouncker about her husband, and been, I have no doubt, expressing her doubts of my skill; for Mrs. Brouncker began:

'"Oh, please, sir, if you'll only let Mr. Morgan take off his arm, I will never think the worse of you for not being able to do it."

'I told her it was from no doubt of my own competency to perform the operation tha I wished to save the arm; but that he himself was anxious to have it spared.

'"Ay, bless him! he frets about not earning enough to keep us, if he's crippled; but, sir, I don't care about that. I would work my fingers to the bone, and so would the children; I'm sure we'd be proud to do for him, and keep him; God bless him! it would be far better to have him only with one arm, than to have him in the churchyard, Miss Horsman says —"

'"Confound Miss Horsman!" said I.

'"Thank you, Mr. Harrison," said her well-known voice behind me. She had come out, dark as it was, to bring some old linen to Mrs. Brouncker; for, as I said before, she was very kind to all the poor people of Duncombe.

'"I beg your pardon"; for I really was sorry for my speech – or rather that she had heard it.

"'There is no occasion for any apology," she replied, drawing herself up, and pinching her lips into a very venemous shape.

'John was doing pretty well; but of course the danger of lock-jaw was not over. Before I left, his wife entreated me to take off the arm; she wrung her hands in her passionate entreaty. "Spare him to me, Mr. Harrison," she implored. Miss Horsman stood by. It was mortifying enough; but I thought of the power which was in my hands, as I firmly believed, of saving the limb; and I was inflexible.

'You cannot think how pleasantly Mrs. Rose's sympathy came in on my return. To be sure she did not understand one word of the case, which I detailed to her; but she listened with interest, and, as long as she held her tongue, I thought she was really taking it in; but her first remark was as *mal-àpropos* as could be.

"'You are anxious to save the tibia – I see completely how difficult that will be. My late husband had a case exactly similar, and I remember his anxiety; but you must not distress yourself too much, my dear Mr. Harrison; I have no doubt it will end well,"

'I knew she had no grounds for this assurance, and yet it comforted me.

'However, as it happened, John did fully as well as I could have hoped for; of course, he was long in rallying his strength; and, indeed, sea-air was evidently so necessary for his complete restoration, that I accepted with gratitude Mrs. Rose's proposal of sending him to Highport for a fortnight or three weeks. Her kind generosity in this matter made me more desirous than ever of paying her every mark of respect and attention.

CHAPTER XV

'About this time there was a sale at Ashmeadow, a pretty house in the neighbourhood of Duncombe. It was likewise an easy walk, and the spring days tempted many people thither, who had no intention of buying anything, but who liked the idea of rambling through the woods, gay with early primroses and wild daffodils, and of seeing the gardens and house, which till now had been shut up from the ingress of the townspeople. Mrs. Rose had planned to go, but an unlucky cold prevented her. She begged me to bring her a very particular account, saying she delighted in details, and always questioned Mr. Rose as to the side-dishes of the dinners to which he went. The late Mr. Rose's conduct was always held up as a model to me, by the way. I walked to Ashmeadow, pausing or loitering with different parties of townspeople, all bound in the same direction. At last I found the Vicar and Sophy, and with them I stayed. I sat by Sophy and talked and listened. A sale is a very pleasant gathering after all. The auctioneer, in a country place, is privileged to joke from his rostrum, and, having a personal knowledge of most of the people, can sometimes make a very keen hit at their circumstances, and turn the laugh against them. For instance, on the present occasion, there was a farmer present, with his wife, who was notoriously the grey mare. The auctioneer was selling some horse-cloths, and called out to recommend the article to her, telling her, with a knowing look at the company, that they would make her a dashing pair of trousers, if she was in want of such an article. She drew herself up with dignity, and said, "Come, John, we've had enough of this." Whereupon there was a burst of laughter, and in the midst of it John meekly followed his wife out of the place. The furniture in the sitting-rooms was, I believe, very beautiful, but I did not notice it much. Suddenly I heard the auctioneer speaking to me, "Mr. Harrison, won't you give me a bid for this table?"

'It was a very pretty little table of walnut-wood. I thought it would go into my study very well, so I gave him a bid. I saw Miss Horsman bidding against me, so I went off with a full force, and at last it was knocked down to me. The auctioneer smiled, and congratulated me.

'"A most useful present for Mrs. Harrison, when that lady comes."

'Everybody laughed. They like a joke about marriage; it is so easy to comprehend. But the table which I had thought was for writing, turned out to be a work-table, scissors and thimble complete. No wonder I looked foolish. Sophy was not looking at me, that was one comfort. She was busy arranging a nosegay of wood-anemone and wild sorrel.

'Miss Horsman came up, with her curious eyes.

'"I had no idea things were far enough advanced for you to be purchasing a work-table, Mr. Harrison."

'I laughed off my awkwardness.

'"Did not you, Miss Horsman? You are very much behindhand. You have not heard of my piano, then?"

'"No, indeed," she said, half uncertain whether I was serious or not. "Then it seems there is nothing wanting but the lady."

'"Perhaps she may not be wanting either," said I; for I wished to perplex her keen curiosity.

CHAPTER XVI

'When I got home from my round, I found Mrs. Rose in some sorrow.

'"Miss Horsman called after you left," said she. "Have you heard how John Brouncker is at Highport?"

'"Very well," replied I. "I called on his wife just now, and she had just got a letter from him. She had been anxious about him, for she had not heard for a week. However, all's right now; and she has pretty well enough of work, at Mrs. Munton's, as her servant is ill. Oh, they'll do, never fear."

'"At Mrs. Munton's? Oh, that accounts for it, then. She is so deaf, and makes such blunders."

'"Accounts for what?" said I.

'"Oh, perhaps I had better not tell you," hesitated Mrs. Rose.

'"Yes, tell me at once. I beg your pardon, but I hate mysteries."

'"You are so like my poor dear Mr. Rose. He used to speak to me just in that sharp, cross way. It is only that Miss

Horsman called. She had been making a collection for John Brouncker's widow and —"

"'But the man's alive!" said I.

"'So it seems. But Mrs. Munton had told her that he was dead. And she has got Mr. Morgan's name down at the head of the list, and Mr. Bullock's."

'Mr. Morgan and I had got into a short, cool way of speaking to each other ever since we had differed so much about the treatment of Brouncker's arm; and I had heard once or twice of his shakes of the head over John's case. He would not have spoken against my method for the world, and fancied that he concealed his fears.

"'Miss Horsman is very ill-natured, I think," sighed forth Mrs. Rose.

'I saw that something had been said of which I had not heard, for the mere fact of collecting money for the widow was good-natured, whoever did it; so I asked, quietly, what she had said.

"'Oh, I don't know if I should tell you. I only know she made me cry; for I'm not well, and I can't bear to hear any one that I live with abused."

'Come! this was pretty plain.

"'What did Miss Horsman say of me?" asked I, half laughing, for I knew there was no love lost between us.

"'Oh, she only said she wondered you could go to sales, and spend your money there, when your ignorance had made Jane Brouncker a widow, and her children fatherless."

"'Pooh! pooh! John's alive, and likely to live as long as you or I, thanks to you, Mrs. Rose."

'When my work-table came home, Mrs. Rose was so struck with its beauty and completeness, and I was so much obliged to her for her identification of my interests with hers, and the kindness of her whole conduct about John, that I begged her to accept of it. She seemed very much pleased; and, after a few apologies, she consented to take it, and placed it in the most conspicuous part of the front parlour, where she usually sat. There was a good deal of morning calling in Duncombe after the sale, and during this time the fact of John being alive was established to the conviction of all except Miss Horsman, who, I believe, still doubted. I myself told Mr. Morgan, who immediately went to reclaim his money; saying to me that he was thankful for the information; he was truly glad to hear it; and he shook me warmly by the hand for the first time for a month.

CHAPTER XVII

'A few days after the sale, I was in the consulting-room. The servant must have left the folding-doors a little ajar, I think. Mrs. Munton came to call on Mrs. Rose; and the former being deaf, I heard all the speeches of the latter lady, as she was obliged to speak very loud in order to be heard. She began:

"'This is a great pleasure, Mrs. Munton, so seldom as you are well enough to go out."

'Mumble, mumble, mumble, through the door.

"'Oh, very well, thank you. Take this seat, and then you can admire my new work-table, ma'am; a present from Mr. Harrison."

'Mumble mumble.

"'Who could have told you, ma'am? Miss Horsman? Oh, yes, I showed it Miss Horsman."

'Mumble, mumble.

"'I don't quite understand you, ma'am."

'Mumble, mumble.

"'I'm not blushing, I believe. I really am quite in the dark as to what you mean."

'Mumble, mumble.

"'Oh, yes, Mr. Harrison and I are most comfortable together. He reminds me so of my dear Mr. Rose – just as fidgety and anxious in his profession."

'Mumble, mumble.

"'I'm sure you are joking now, ma'am" Then I heard a pretty loud:

"'Oh, no;" mumble, mumble, mumble, for a long time.

"'Did he really? Well, I'm sure I don't know. I should be sorry to think he was doomed to be unfortunate in so serious an affair; but you know my undying regard for the late Mr. Rose."

'Another long mumble.

"'You're very kind, I'm sure. Mr. Rose always thought more of my happiness than his own" – a little crying – "but the turtle-dove has always been my ideal, ma'am"

'Mumble, mumble.

"'No one could have been happier than I. As you say, it is a compliment to matrimony."

'Mumble.

"'Oh, but you must not repeat such a thing! Mr. Harrison would not like it. He can't bear to have his affairs spoken about."

'Then there was a change of subject; an inquiry after some poor person, I imagine. I heard Mrs. Rose say:

"'She has got a mucous membrane, I'm afraid, ma'am."

'A commiserating mumble.

"'Not always fatal. I believe Mr. Rose knew some cases that lived for years after it was discovered that they had a mucous membrane." A pause. Then Mrs. Rose spoke in a different tone.

"'Are you sure, ma'am, there is no mistake about what he said?"

'Mumble.

"'Pray don't be so observant, Mrs. Munton; you find out too much. One can have no little secrets."

'The call broke up; and I heard Mrs. Munton say in the passage, "I wish you joy, ma'am, with all my heart. There's no use denying it; for I've seen all along what would happen."

'When I went in to dinner, I said to Mrs. Rose:

"'You've had Mrs. Munton here, I think. Did she bring any news?" To my surprise, she bridled and simpered, and replied, "Oh, you must not ask, Mr. Harrison; such foolish reports."

'I did not ask, as she seemed to wish me not, and I knew there were silly reports always about. Then I think she was vexed that I did not ask. Altogether she went on so strangely that I could not help looking at her; and then she took up a hand-screen, and held it between me and her. I really felt rather anxious.

"'Are you not feeling well?" said I innocently.

"'Oh, thank you, I believe I'm quite well; only the room is rather warm, is it not?"

"'Let me put the blinds down for you? the sun begins to have a good deal of power." I drew down the blinds.

"'You are so attentive, Mr. Harrison. Mr. Rose himself never did more for my little wishes than you do."

"'I wish I could do more – I wish I could show you how much I feel" – her kindness to John Brouncker, I was going on to say; but I was just then called out to a patient. Before I went I turned back, and said:

"'Take care of yourself, my dear Mrs. Rose; you had better rest a little."

"'For your sake, I will," said she tenderly.

'I did not care for whose sake she did it. Only I really thought she was not quite well, and required rest. I thought she was more affected than usual at tea-time; and could have been angry with her nonsensical ways once or twice, but that I knew the real goodness of her heart. She said she wished she had the power to sweeten my life as she could my tea. I told her what a comfort she had been during my late time of anxiety; and then I stole out to try if I could hear the evening singing at the vicarage, by standing close to the garden-wall.

CHAPTER XVIII

'The next morning I met Mr. Bullock by appointment to talk a little about the legacy which was paid into his hands. As I was leaving his office, feeling full of my riches, I met Miss Horsman. She smiled rather grimly, and said:

"'Oh, Mr. Harrison, I must congratulate you, I believe. I don't know whether I ought to have known, but as I do, I must wish you joy. A very nice little sum, too. I always said you would have money."

'So she had found out my legacy, had she? Well, it was no secret, and one likes the reputation of being a person of property. Accordingly I smiled, and said I was much obliged to her; and, if I could alter the figures to my liking, she might congratulate me still more.

'She said, "Oh, Mr. Harrison, you can't have everything. It would be better the other way, certainly. Money is the great thing, as you've found out. The relation died most opportunely, I must say."

'"He was no relative," said I; "only an intimate friend."

'"Dear-ah-me! I thought it had been a brother! Well, at any rate, the legacy is safe."

'I wished her good morning, and passed on. Before long I was sent for to Miss Tomkinson's.

'Miss Tomkinson sat in severe state to receive me. I went in with an air of ease, because I always felt so uncomfortable.

'"Is this true that I hear?" asked she, in an inquisitorial manner.

'I thought she alluded to my five hundred pounds; so I smiled, and said that I believed it was.

'"Can money be so great an object with you, Mr. Harrison?" she asked again.

'"I said I had never cared much for money, except as an assistance to any plan of settling in life; and then, as I did not like her severe way of treating the subject, I said that I hoped every one was well; though of course I expected some one was ill, or I should not have been sent for.

'Miss Tomkinson looked very grave and sad. Then she answered: "Caroline is very poorly – the old palpitations at the heart; but of course that is nothing to you."

' I said I was sorry. She had a weakness there, I knew. Could I see her? I might be able to order something for her.

'I thought I heard Miss Tomkinson say something in a low voice about my being a heartless deceiver. Then she spoke up. "I was always distrustful of you, Mr. Harrison. I never liked your looks. I begged Caroline again and again not to confide in you. I foresaw how it would end. And now I fear her precious life will be a sacrifice."

'I begged her not to distress herself, for in all probability there was very little the matter with her sister. Might I see her?

'"No!" she said shortly, standing up as if to dismiss me. "There has been too much of this seeing and calling. By my consent, you shall never see her again."

'I bowed. I was annoyed, of course. Such a dismissal might injure my practice just when I was most anxious to increase it.

"'Have you no apology, no excuse to offer?"

'I said I had done my best; I did not feel that there was any reason to offer an apology. I wished her good morning. Suddenly she came forwards.

"'Oh, Mr. Harrison," said she, "if you have really loved Caroline, do not let a little paltry money make you desert her for another."

'I was struck dumb. Loved Miss Caroline! I loved Miss Tomkinson a great deal better, and yet I disliked her. She went on:

"'I have saved nearly three thousand pounds. If you think you are too poor to marry without money, I will give it all to Caroline. I am strong, and can go on working; but she is weak, and this disappointment will kill her." She sat down suddenly, and covered her face with her hands. Then she looked up.

"'You are unwilling, I see. Don't suppose I would have urged you if it had been for myself; but she has had so much sorrow." And now she fairly cried aloud. I tried to explain; but she would not listen, but kept saying, "Leave the house, sir! leave the house!" But I would be heard.

"'I have never had any feeling warmer than respect for Miss Caroline, and I have never shown any different feeling. I never for an instant thought of making her my wife, and she has had no cause in my behaviour to imagine I entertained any such intention."

"'This is adding insult to injury," said she. "Leave the house, sir, this instant!"

CHAPTER XIX

'I went, and sadly enough. In a small town such an occurrence is sure to be talked about, and to make a great deal of mischief. When I went home to dinner I was so full of it, and foresaw so clearly that I should need some advocate soon to set the case in its right light, that I determined on making a confidante of good Mrs. Rose. I could not eat. She watched me tenderly, and sighed when she saw my want of appetite.

"'I am sure you have something on your mind, Mr. Harrison. Would it be – would it not be – a relief to impart it to some sympathising friend?"

'It was just what I wanted to do.

"'My dear, kind Mrs. Rose", said I, "I must tell you, if you will listen."

'She took up the fire-screen, and held it, as yesterday, between me and her.

"'The most unfortunate misunderstanding has taken place. Miss Tomkinson thinks that I have been paying attentions to Miss Caroline; when, in fact – may I tell you, Mrs. Rose? – my affections are placed elsewhere. Perhaps you have found it out already?" for indeed I thought I had been too much in love to conceal my attachment to Sophy from any one who knew my movements as well as Mrs. Rose.

'She hung down her head, and said she believed she had found out my secret.

"'Then only think how miserably I am situated. If I have any hope – oh, Mrs. Rose, do you think I have any hope —"

'She put the hand-screen still more before her face, and after some hesitation she said she thought, "If I persevered – in time – I might have hope." And then she suddenly got up, and left the room.

CHAPTER XX

'That afternoon I met Mr. Bullock in the street. My mind was so full of the affair with Miss Tomkinson that I should have passed him without notice, if he had not stopped me short, and said that he must speak to me; about my wonderful five hundred pounds, I supposed. But I did not care for that now.

"'What is this I hear," said he severely, "about your engagement with Mrs. Rose?"

"'With Mrs. Rose!' said I, almost laughing, although my heart was heavy enough.

"'Yes! with Mrs. Rose!' said he sternly.

"'I'm not engaged to Mrs. Rose,' I replied. 'There is some mistake.'

"'I'm glad to hear it, sir,' he answered, 'very glad. It requires some explanation, however. Mrs. Rose has been congratulated, and has acknowledged the truth of the report. It is confirmed by many facts. The work-table you bought, confessing your intention of giving it to your future wife, is given to her. How do you account for these things, sir?'

'I said I did not pretend to account for them. At present a good deal was inexplicable; and, when I could give an explanation, I did not think that I should feel myself called upon to give it to him.

"'Very well, sir; very well,' replied he, growing very red. 'I shall take care and let Mr. Morgan know the opinion I entertain of you. What do you think that man deserves to be called who enters a family under the plea of friendship, and takes advantage of his intimacy to win the affections of the daughter, and then engages himself to another woman?'

'I thought he referred to Miss Caroline. I simply said I could only say that I was not engaged; and that Miss Tomkinson had been quite mistaken in supposing I had been paying any attentions to her sister beyond those dictated by mere civility.

"'Miss Tomkinson! Miss Caroline! I don't understand to what you refer. Is there another victim to your perfidy? What I allude to are the attentions you have paid to my daughter, Miss Bullock.'

'Another! I could but disclaim, as I had done in the case of Miss Caroline; but I began to be in despair. Would Miss Horsman, too, come forward as a victim to my tender affections? It was all Mr. Morgan's doing, who had lectured me into this tenderly deferential manner. But, on the score of Miss Bullock, I was brave in my innocence. I had positively disliked her; and so I told her father, though in more civil and measured terms, adding that I was sure the feeling was reciprocal.

'He looked as if he would like to horsewhip me. I longed to call him out.

"'I hope my daughter has had sense enough to despise you; I

hope she has, that's all, I trust my wife may be mistaken as to her feelings."

'So, he had heard all through the medium of his wife. That explained something, and rather calmed me. I begged he would ask Miss Bullock if she had ever thought I had any ulterior object in my intercourse with her, beyond mere friendliness (and not so much of that, I might have added). I would refer it to her.

'"Girls," said Mr. Bullock, a little more quietly, "do not like to acknowledge that they have been deceived and disappointed. I consider my wife's testimony as likely to be nearer the truth than my daughter's, for that reason. And she tells me she never doubted but that, if not absolutely engaged, you understood each other perfectly. She is sure Jemima is deeply wounded by your engagement to Mrs. Rose."

'"Once for all, I am not engaged to anybody. Till you have seen your daughter, and learnt the truth from her, I will wish you farewell."

'I bowed in a stiff, haughty manner, and walked off homewards. But when I got to my own door, I remembered Mrs. Rose, and all that Mr. Bullock had said about her acknowledging the truth of the report of my engagemeent to her. Where could I go to be safe? Mrs. Rose, Miss Bullock, Miss Caroline – they lived as it were at the three points of an equilateral triangle; here was I in the centre. I would go to Mr. Morgan's, and drink tea with him. There, at any rate, I was secure from any one wanting to marry me; and I might be as professionally bland as I liked, without being misunderstood. But there, too, a *contretemps* awaited me.

CHAPTER XXI

'Mr. Morgan was looking grave. After a minute or two of humming and hawing, he said:

'"I have been sent for to Miss Caroline Tomkinson, Mr.

Harrison. I am sorry to hear of this. I am grieved to find that there seems to have been some trifling with the affections of a very worthy lady. Miss Tomkinson, who is in sad distress, tells me that they had every reason to believe that you were attached to her sister. May I ask if you do not intend to marry her?"

'I said, nothing was farther from my thoughts.

'"My dear sir," said Mr. Morgan, rather agitated, "do not express yourself so strongly and vehemently. It is derogatory to the sex to speak so. It is more respectful to say, in these cases, that you do not venture to entertain a hope; such a manner is generally understood, and does not sound like such positive objection."

'"I cannot help it, sir; I must talk in my own natural manner. I would not speak disrespectfully to any woman; but nothing should induce me to marry Miss Caroline Tomkinson; not if she were Venus herself, and Queen of England into the bargain. I cannot understand what has given rise to the idea."

'"Indeed, sir; I think that is very plain. You have a trifling case to attend to in the house, and you invariably make it a pretext for seeing and conversing with the lady."

'"That was her doing, not mine!" said I vehemently.

'"Allow me to go on. You are discovered on your knees before her – a positive injury to the establishment as Miss Tomkinson observes; a most passionate valentine is sent; and, when questioned, you acknowledge the sincerity of meaning which you affix to such things." He stopped; for in his earnestness he had been talking more than usual, and was out of breath. I burst in with my explanations:

'"The valentine I know nothing about."

'"It is in your handwriting," said he coldly. "I should be most deeply grieved to – in fact, I will not think it possible of your father's son. But I must say, it is in your hand-writing."

'I tried again, and at last succeeded in convincing him that I had been only unfortunate, not intentionally guilty of winning Miss Caroline's affections. I said that I had been endeavouring, it was true, to practise the manner he had recommended, of universal sympathy, and recalled to his mind some of the advice he had given me. He was a good deal hurried.

"'But, my dear sir, I had no idea that you would carry it out to such consequences. 'Philandering,' Miss Tomkinson called it. That is a hard word, sir. My manner has been always tender and sympathetic; but I am not aware that I ever excited any hopes; there never was any report about me. I believe no lady was ever attached to me. You must strive after this happy medium, sir."

'I was still distressed. Mr. Morgan had only heard of one, but there were three ladies (including Miss Bullock) hoping to marry me. He saw my annoyance.

"'Don't be too much distressed about it, my dear sir; I was sure you were too honourable a man, from the first. With a conscience like yours, I would defy the world."

'He became anxious to console me, and I was hesitating whether I would not tell him all my three dilemmas, when a note was brought in to him. It was from Mrs. Munton. He threw it to me, with a face of dismay.

"'MY DEAR MR. MORGAN, — I most sincerely congratulate you on the happy matrimonial engagement I hear you have formed with Miss Tomkinson. All previous circumstances, as I have just been remarking to Miss Horsman, combine to promise you felicity. And I wish that every blessing may attend your married life. — Most sincerely yours,
                                        "'JANE MUNTON."

'I could not help laughing, he had been so lately congratulating himself that no report of the kind had ever been circulated about himself. He said:

"'Sir! this is no laughing matter; I assure you it is not."

'I could not resist asking, if I was to conclude that there was no truth in the report.

"'Truth, sir! it's a lie from beginning to end. I don't like to speak too decidedly about any lady; and I've a great respect for Miss Tomkinson; but I do assure you, sir, I'd as soon marry one of Her Majesty's Life Guards. I would rather; it would be more suitable. Miss Tomkinson is a very worthy lady; but she's a perfect grenadier."

'He grew very nervous. He was evidently insecure. He thought it not impossible that Miss Tomkinson might come and marry him, *vi et armis*. I am sure he had some dim idea of abduction in his mind. Still, he was better off than I was; for he was in his own house, and report had only engaged him to one lady; while I stood, like Paris, among three contending beauties. Truly, an apple of discord had been thrown into our little town. I suspected at the time, what I know now, that it was Miss Horsman's doing; not intentionally, I will do her the justice to say. But she had shouted out the story of my behaviour to Miss Caroline up Mrs. Munton's trumpet; and that lady, possessed with the idea that I was engaged to Mrs. Rose, had imagined the masculine pronoun to relate to Mr. Morgan, whom she had seen only that afternoon *tête-à-tête* with Miss Tomkinson, condoling with her in some tender deferential manner, I'll be bound.

CHAPTER XXII

'I was very cowardly. I positively dared not go home; but at length I was obliged to. I had done all I could to console Mr. Morgan, but he refused to he comforted. I went at last. I rang at the bell. I don't know who opened the door, but I think it was Mrs. Rose. I kept a handkerchief to my face, and, muttering something about having a dreadful toothache, I flew up to my room and bolted the door. I had no candle; but what did that signify. I was safe. I could not sleep; and when I did fall into a sort of doze, it was ten times worse wakening up. I could not remember whether I was engaged or not. If I was engaged, who was the lady? I had alway considered myself as rather plain than otherwise; but surely I had made a mistakee. Fascinating I certainly must be; but perhaps I was handsome. As soon as day dawned, I got up to ascertain the fact at the looking–glass. Even with the best disposition to be convinced, I could not see any striking beauty in my round face, with an unshaven beard and a nightcap like a fool's cap at the top. No! I must be content to be plain, but agreeable. All this I tell you in confidence. I would not have my little bit of vanity known for the world. I fell asleep towards morning. I was awakened by a tap at my door. It was Peggy: she put in a hand with a note. I took it.

"'It is not from Miss Horsman?" said I, half in joke, half in very earnest fright.

"'No, sir; Mr. Morgan's man brought it."

'I opened it. It ran thus:

"'MY DEAR SIR, – It is now nearly twenty years since I have had a little relaxation, and I find that my health requires it. I have also the utmost confidence in you, and I am sure this feeling is shared by our patients. I have, therefore, no scruple in putting in execution a hastily-formed plan, and going to Chesterton to catch the early train on my way to Paris. If your accounts are good, I shall remain away probably a fortnight. Direct to Meurice's. – Yours most truly.

J. MORGAN.

"P.S. – Perhaps it may be as well not to name where I am gone, especially to Miss Tomkinson."

'He had deserted me. He – with only one report – had left me to stand my ground with three.

"'Mrs. Rose's kind regards, sir, and it's nearly nine o'clock. Breakfast has been ready this hour, sir."

"'Tell Mrs. Rose I don't want any breakfast. Or stay" (for I was very hungry), "I will take a cup of tea and some toast up here."

'Peggy brought the tray to the door.

"'I hope you're not ill, sir?" said she kindly.

"'Not very, I shall be better when I get into the air."

"'Mrs. Rose seems sadly put about," said she; "she seems so grieved like."

'I watched my opportunity, and went out by the side-door in the garden.

CHAPTER XXIII

'I had intended to ask Mr. Morgan to call at the vicarage, and give his parting explanation before they could hear the report. Now I thought that, if I could see Sophy, I would speak to her myself; but I did not wish to encounter the Vicar. I went along the lane at the back of the vicarage, and came suddenly upon Miss Bullock. She coloured, and asked me if I would allow her to speak to me. I could only be resigned; but I thought I could probably set one report at rest by this conversation.

'She was almost crying.

'"I must tell you, Mr. Harrison, I have watched you here in order to speak to you. I heard with the greatest regret of papa's conversation with you yesterday." She was fairly crying. "I believe Mrs. Bullock finds me in her way, and wants to have me married. It is the only way in which I can account for such a complete misrepresentation as she had told papa. I don't care for you, in the least, sir. You never paid me any attentions. You've been almost rude to me; and I have liked you the better. That's to say, I never have liked you."

'"I am truly glad to hear what you say," answered I. "Don't distress yourself. I was sure there was some mistake."

'But she cried bitterly.

'"It is so hard to feel that my marriage – my absence – is desired so earnestly at home. I dread every new acquaintance we form with any gentleman. It is sure to be the beginning of a series of attacks on him, of which everybody must be aware, and to which they may think I am a willing party. But I should not much mind if it were not for the conviction that she wishes me so earnestly away. Oh, my own dear mamma, you would never —"

'She cried more than ever. I was truly sorry for her, and had just taken her hand, and began – "My dear Miss Bullock" – when the door in the wall of the vicarage garden opened. It

271

was the Vicar letting out Miss Tomkinson, whose face was all swelled with crying. He saw me; but he did not bow, or make any sign. On the contrary, he looked down as from a severe eminence, and shut the door hastily. I turned to Miss Bullock.

"'I am afraid the Vicar has been hearing something to my disadvantage from Miss Tomkinson, and it is very awkward" – she finished my sentence – "To have found us here together. Yes; but, as long as we understand that we do not care for each other, it does not signify what people say."

"'Oh, but to me it does," said I. "I may, perhaps, tell you – but do not mention it to a creature – I am attached to Miss Hutton."

"'To Sophy! Oh, Mr. Harrison, I am so glad; she is such a sweet creature. Oh, I wish you joy."

"'Not yet; I have never spoken about it."

"'Oh, but it is certain to happen." She jumped with a woman's rapidity to a conclusion. And then she began to praise Sophy. Never was a man yet who did not like to hear the praises of his mistress. I walked by her side; we came past the front of the vicarage together. I looked up, and saw Sophy there, and she saw me.

'That afternoon she was sent away – sent to visit her aunt ostensibly; in reality, because of the reports of my conduct, which were showered down upon the Vicar, and one of which he saw confirmed by his own eyes.

CHAPTER XXIV

'I heard of Sophy's departure as one heard of everything, soon after it had taken place. I did not care for the awkwardness of my situation, which had so perplexed and amused me in the morning. I felt that something was wrong; that Sophy was taken away from me. I sank into despair. If anybody liked to marry me, they might. I was willing to be sacrificed. I did not speak to Mrs. Rose. She wondered at me, and grieved over my coldness, I saw; but I had left off feeling anything. Miss

Tomkinson cut me in the street; and it did not break my heart. Sophy was gone away; that was all I cared for. Where had they sent her to? Who was her aunt that she should go and visit her? One day I met Lizzie, who looked as though she had been told not to speak to me; but I could not help doing so.

'"Have your heard from your sister?" said I.

'"Yes."

'"Where is she? I hope she is well."

'"She is at the Leoms" – I was not much wiser. "Oh, yes, she is very well. Fanny says she was at the Assembly last Wednesday, and danced all night with the officers."

'I thought I would enter myself a member of the Peace Society at once. She was a little flirt, and a hard-hearted creature. I don't think I wished Lizzie goodbye.

CHAPTER XXV

'What most people would have considered a more serious evil than Sophy's absence, befell me. I found that my practice was falling off. The prejudice of the town ran strongly against me. Mrs. Munton told me all that was said. She heard it through Miss Horsman. It was said – cruel little town – that my negligence or ignorance had been the cause of Walter's death; that Miss Tyrrell had become worse under my treatment; and that John Brouncker was all but dead, if he was not quite, from my mismanagement. All Jack Marshland's jokes and revelations, which had, I thought, gone to oblivion, were raked up to my discredit. He himself, formerly, to my astonishment, rather a favourite with the good people of Duncombe, was spoken of as one of my disreputable friends.

'In short, so prejudiced were the good people of Duncombe that I believe a very little would have made them suspect me of a brutal highway robbery, which took place in the neighbourhood about this time. Mrs. Munton told me, *à propos* of the robbery, that she had never understood the cause of my year's imprisonment in Newgate; she had no doubt, from what Mr. Morgan had told her, there was some good reason for it; but if I would tell her the particulars, she should like to know them.

'Miss Tomkinson sent for Mr. White, from Chesterton, to see Miss Caroline; and, as he was coming over, all our old patients seemed to take advantage of it, and send for him too.

'But the worst of all was the Vicar's manner to me. If he had cut me, I could have asked him why he did so. But the freezing change in his behaviour was indescribable, though bitterly felt. I heard of Sophy's gaiety from Lizzie. I thought of writing to her. Just then Mr. Morgan's fortnight of absence expired. I was wearied out by Mrs. Rose's tender vagaries, and took no comfort from her sympathy, which indeed I rather avoided. Her tears irritated, instead of grieving me. I wished I could tell her at once that I had no intention of marrying her.

CHAPTER XXVI

'Mr. Morgan had not been at home above two hours before he was sent for to the vicarage. Sophy had come back, and I had never heard of it. She had come home ill and weary, and longing for rest: and the *rest* seemed approaching with awful strides. Mr. Morgan forgot all his Parisian adventures, and all his terror of Miss Tomkinson, when he was sent for to see her. She was ill of a fever, which made fearful progress. When he told me, I wished to force the vicarage door, if I might but see her. But I controlled myself; and only cursed my weak indecision, which had prevented my writing to her. It was well I had no patients: they would have had but a poor chance of attention. I hung about Mr. Morgan, who might see her, and did see her. But, from what he told me, I perceived that the measures he was adopting were powerless to check so sudden and violent an illness. Oh! if they would but let me see her! But that was out of the question. It was not merely that the Vicar had heard of my character as a gay Lothario, but that doubts had been thrown out of my medical skill. The accounts grew worse. Suddenly my resolution was taken. Mr. Morgan's very regard for Sophy made him more than usually timid in his practice. I had my horse saddled, and galloped to Chesterton. I took the express train to town. I went to Dr. —. I told him every particular of the case. He listened; but shook his head. He wrote down a presciption, and recommended a new preparation, not yet in full use – a preparation of a poison, in fact.

'"It may save her," said he. "It is a chance, in such a state of things as you describe. It must be given on the fifth day, if the pulse will bear it. Crabbe makes up the preparation most skilfully. Let me hear from you, I beg."

'I went to Crabbe's; I begged to make it up myself; but my hands trembled, so that I could not weigh the quantities. I asked the young man to do it for me. I went, without touching food, to the station, with my medicine and my prescription in my pocket. Back we flew through the country. I sprang on Bay Maldon, which my groom had in waiting, and galloped across the country to Duncombe.

'But I drew bridle when I came to the top of the hill – the hill above the old hall, from which we catch the first glimpse of the town, for I thought within myself that she might be dead; and I dreaded to come near certainty. The hawthorns were out in the woods, the young lambs were in the meadows, the song of the thrushes filled the air; but it only made the thought the more terrible.

'"What if, in this world of hope and life, she lies dead!" I heard the church bells soft and clear. I sickened to listen. Was it the passing bell? No! it was ringing eight o'clock. I put spurs to my horse, down hill as it was. We dashed into the town. I turned him, saddle and bridle, into the stable-yard, and went off to Mr. Morgan's.

'"Is she —" said I. "How is she?"

'"Very ill. My poor fellow, I see how it is with you. She may live – but I fear. My dear sir, I am very much afraid."

'I told him of my journey and consultation with Dr.—, and showed him the prescription. His hands trembled as he put on his spectacles to read it.

'"This is a very dangerous medicine, sir," said he, with his finger under the name of the poison.

'"It is a new preparation," said I. "Dr.— relies much upon it."

'"I dare not administer it," he replied. "I have never tried it. It must be very powerful. I dare not play tricks in this case."

'I believe I stamped with impatience; but it was all of no use. My journey had been in vain. The more I urged the imminent danger of the case requiring some powerful remedy, the more nervous he became.

'I told him I would throw up the partnership. I threatened him with that, though, in fact, it was only what I felt I ought to do, and had resolved upon before Sophy's illness, as I had lost the confidence of his patients. He only said:

'"I cannot help it, sir. I shall regret it for your father's sake; but I must do my duty. I dare not run the risk of giving Miss Sophy this violent medicine – a preparation of a deadly poison."

'I left him without a word. He was quite right in adhering to his own views, as I can see now; but at the time I thought him brutal and obstinate.

CHAPTER XXVII

'I went home. I spoke rudely to Mrs. Rose, who awaited my return at the door. I rushed past, and locked myself in my room. I could not go to bed.

'The morning sun came pouring in, and enraged me, as everything did since Mr. Morgan refused. I pulled the blind down so violently that the string broke. What did it signify? The light might come in. What was the sun to me? And then I remembered that that sun might be shining on her – dead.

'I sat down and covered my face. Mrs. Rose knocked at the door. I opened it. She had never been in bed, and had been crying too.

'"Mr. Morgan wants to speak to you, sir."

'I rushed back for my medicine, and went to him. He stood at the door, pale and anxious.

'"She's alive, sir," said he, "but that's all. We have sent for Dr. Hamilton. I'm afraid he will not come in time. Do you know, sir, I think we should venture – with Dr.—'s sanction – to give her that medicine. It is but a chance; but it is the only one, I'm afraid." He fairly cried before he had ended.

"'I've got it here," said I, setting off to walk; but he could not go so fast.

"'I beg your pardon, sir" said he, "for my abrupt refusal last night."

"'Indeed, sir," said I; "I ought much rather to beg your pardon. I was very violent."

"'Oh! never mind! never mind! Will you repeat what Dr. — said?"

'I did so; and then I asked, with a meekness that astonished myself, if I might not go in and administer it.

"'No, sir," said he, "I'm afraid not. I am sure your good heart would not wish to give pain. Besides, it might agitate her, if she has any consciousness before death. In her delirium she has often mentioned your name; and, sir, I'm sure you won't name it again, as it may, in fact, be considered a professional secret; but I did hear our good Vicar speak a little strongly about you; in fact, sir, I did hear him curse you. You see the mischief it might make in the parish, I'm sure, if this were known.

'I gave him the medicine, and watched him in, and saw the door shut. I hung about the place all day. Poor and rich all came to inquire. The county people drove up in their carriages – the halt and the lame came on their crutches. Their anxiety did my heart good. Mr. Morgan told me that she slept, and I watched Dr. Hamilton into the house. The night came on. She slept. I watched round the house. I saw the light high up, burning still and steady. Then I saw it moved. It was the crisis, in one way or other.

CHAPTER XXVIII

'Mr. Morgan came out. Good old man! The tears were running down his cheeks: he could not speak: but kept shaking my hands. I did not want words. I understood that she was better.

'"Dr. Hamilton says, it was the only medicine that could have saved her. I was an old fool, sir. I beg your pardon. The Vicar shall know all. I beg your pardon, sir, if I was abrupt."

'Everything went on brilliantly from this time.

'Mr. Bullock called to apologise for his mistake, and consequent upbraiding. John Brouncker came home, brave and well.

'There was still Miss Tomkinson in the ranks of the enemy; and Mrs. Rose too much, I feared, in the ranks of the friends.

CHAPTER XXIX

'One night she had gone to bed, and I was thinking of going. I had been studying in the back room, where I went for refuge from her in the present position of affairs – (I read a good number of surgical books about this time, and also *Vanity Fair*) – when I heard a loud, long-continued knocking at the door, enough to waken the whole street. Before I could get it open, I heard that well-known bass of Jack Marshland's – once heard, never to be forgotten – pipe up the negro song –

'"Who's dat knocking at de door?"

'Though it was raining hard at the time, and I stood waiting to let him in, he would finish his melody in the open air; loud and clear along the street it sounded. I saw Miss Tomkinson's night-capped head emerge from a window. She called out "Police! police!"

'Now there were no police, only a rheumatic constable, in the town; but it was the custom of the ladies, when alarmed at night, to call an imaginary police, which had, they thought, an intimidating effect; but, as everyone knew the real state of the unwatched town, we did not much mind it in general. Just now, however, I wanted to regain my character. So I pulled Jack in, quavering as he entered.

"'You've spoilt a good shake," said he, "that's what you have. I'm nearly up to Jenny Lind; and you see I'm a nightingale, like her."

'We sat up late; and I don't know how it was, but I told him all my matrimonial misadventures.

"'I thought I could imitate your hand pretty well," said he. "My word! it was a flaming valentine! No wonder she thought you loved her!"

"'So that was your doing, was it? Now I'll tell you what you shall do to make up for it. You shall write me a letter confessing your hoax – a letter that I can show."

"'Give me pen and paper, my boy! you shall dictate. 'With a deeply penitent heart' – Will that do for a beginning?"

'I told him what to write; a simple, straightforward confession of his practical joke. I enclosed it in a few lines of regret that, unknown to me, any of my friends should have so acted.

CHAPTER XXX

'All this time I knew that Sophy was slowly recovering. One day I met Miss Bullock, who had seen her.

"'We have been talking about you," said she, with a bright smile; for, since she knew I disliked her, she felt quite at her ease, and could smile very pleasantly. I understood that she had been explaining the misunderstanding about herself to Sophy; so that, when Jack Marshlands's note had been sent to Miss Tomkinson's, I thought myself in a fair way to have my character established in two quarters. But the third was my dilemma. Mrs. Rose had really so much of my true regard for her good qualities, that I disliked the idea of a formal explanation, in which a good deal must be said on my side to wound her. We had become very much estranged ever since I had heard of this report of my engagement to her. I saw that she grieved over it. While Jack Marshland stayed with us, I felt at my ease in the presence of a third person. But he told me confidentially he durst not stay long, for fear some of the ladies should snap him up, and marry him. Indeed I myself did not think it unlikely that he would snap one of them up if he could. For when we met Miss Bullock one day, and heard her hopeful, joyous account of Sophy's progress (to whom she was a daily visitor) he asked me who that bright-looking girl was? And when I told him she was the Miss Bullock of whom I had spoken to him, he was pleased to observe that he thought I had been a great fool, and asked me if Sophy had anything like such spendid eyes. He made me repeat about Miss Bullock's unhappy circumstances at home, and then became very thoughtful – a most unusual and morbid symptom in his case.

'Soon after he went, by Mr. Morgan's kind offices and explanations, I was permitted to see Sophy. I might not speak much; it was prohibited, for fear of agitating her. We talked of the weather and the flowers; and we were silent. But her little white thin hand lay in mine; and we understood each other without words. I had a long interview with the Vicar afterwards, and came away glad and satisfied.

'Mr. Morgan called in the afternoon, evidently anxious, though he made no direct inquiries (he was too polite for that) to hear the result of my visit at the vicarage. I told him to give me joy. He shook me warmly by the hand, and then rubbed his own together. I thought I would consult him about my dilemma with Mrs. Rose, who, I was afraid, would be deeply affected by my engagement.

'"There is only one awkward circumstance," said I – "about Mrs. Rose." I hesitated how to word the fact of her having received congratulations on her supposed engagement with me, and her manifest attachment; but, before I could speak, he broke in:

'"My dear sir, you need not trouble yourself about that; she will have a home. In fact, sir," said he, reddening a little, "I thought it would, perhaps, put a stop to those reports connecting my name with Miss Tomkinson's, if I married some one else. I hoped it might prove an efficacious contradiction. And I was struck with admiration for Mrs. Rose's undying memory of her late husband. Not to be prolix, I have this morning obtained Mrs. Rose's consent to – to marry her, in fact, sir!" said he, jerking out the climax.

'Here was an event! Then Mr. Morgan had never heard the report about Mrs. Rose and me. (To this day, I think she would have taken me, if I had proposed.) So much the better.

'Marriages were in the fashion that year. Mr. Bullock met me one morning , as I was going to ride with Sophy. He and I had quite got over our misunderstanding, thanks to Jemima, and were as friendly as ever. This morning he was chuckling aloud as he walked.

'"Stop, Mr. Harrison!" he said, as I went quickly past. "Have you heard the news? Miss Horsman has just told me Miss Caroline has eloped with young Hoggins! She is ten years older than he is! How can her gentility like being married to a tallow-chandler? It is a very good thing for her, though", he added, in a more serious manner; "old Hoggins is very rich, and, though he's angry just now, he will soon be reconciled."

'Any vanity I might have entertained on the score of the three ladies who were, at one time, said to be captivated by my charms, was being rapidly dispersed. Soon after Mr. Hoggin's marriage, I met Miss Tomkinson face to face, for the first time since our memorable conversation. She stopped me, and said:

'"Don't refuse to receive my congratulations, Mr. Harrison, on your most happy engagement to Miss Hutton. I owe you an apology, too, for my behaviour when I last saw you at our house. I really did think Caroline was attached to you then; and it irritated me, I confess, in a very wrong and unjustifiable way. But I heard her telling Mr. Hoggins only yesterday that she had been attached to him for years; ever since he was in pinafores, she dated it from; and when I asked her afterwards how she could say so, after her distress on hearing that false report about you and Mrs. Rose, she cried, and said I never had understood her; and that the hysterics which alarmed me so much were simply caused by eating pickled cucumber. I am very sorry for my stupidity and imroper way of speaking; but I hope we are friends now, Mr. Harrison, for I should wish to be liked by Sophy's husband."

'Good Miss Tomkinson, to believe the substitution of indigestion for disappointed affection! I shook her warmly by the hand; and we have been all right ever since. I think I told you she is baby's godmother.

CHAPTER XXXI

'I had some difficulty in persuading Jack Marshland to be groomsman; but, when he heard all the arrangements, he came. Miss Bullock was bridesmaid. He liked us all so well, that he came again at Christmas, and was far better behaved than he had been the year before. He won golden opinions indeed. Miss Tomkinson said he was a reformed young man. We dined all together at Mr. Morgan's (the Vicar wanted us to go there; but, from what Sophy told me, Helen was not confident of the mincemeat, and rather dreaded so large a party). We had a jolly day of it. Mrs. Morgan was as kind and motherly as ever. Miss Horsman certainly did set out a story that the Vicar was thinking of Miss Tomkinson for his second; or else, I think, we had no other report circulated in consequence of our happy, merry Christmas Day; and it is a wonder, considering how Jack Marshland went on with Jemima.'

Here Sophy came back from putting baby to bed; and Charles wakened up.

63 MWſf she